UPHILL
Both Ways

Neta Jackson

CASTLE
ROCK
CREATIVE

Evanston, Illinois 60202

Published in Evanston, Illinois. Castle Rock Creative.

Scripture quotations are taken from the following:

> The Holy Bible, New International Version®. NIV®. Copyright © 1973, 1978, 1984, 2011 by International Bible Society. Used by permission of Zondervan Publishing House. All rights reserved.

> *"It's okay to look behind you ..."* —an African saying from *Don't Look Behind You,* by Peter Allison, (Guilford, CT:. The Lyons Press, 2009).

This novel is a work of fiction. Names, characters, places, and incidents are either products of the author's imaginations or used fictitiously. All characters are fictional, and any resemblance to people living or dead is entirely coincidental.

ISBN: 978-0-9982107-7-3

Cover Design: Dave Jackson

Printed in the United States of America

For a complete list of
books by Dave and Neta Jackson visit
www.daveneta.com
www.riskinggrace.com
www.trailblazerbooks.com

"It's okay to look behind you. Sometimes it's the best way to get yourself home."

—an African saying

Prologue

As the motorcycle engine roared to life, shaking the walls of the small one-car garage, the black-and-tan mutt sitting in the sidecar gave a startled yelp, leaped out, and started barking. Sitting astride the reconditioned metallic-blue BMW, James "Coop" Cooper laughed aloud as he revved the engine a few times.

"What's the matter, Rocky? This is what it's all about! Now get back in here." Idling the motor to a dull rumble, the silver-haired retiree patted the seatback of the sidecar. After a few prancing steps this way and that, the dog hopped back into the sidecar as the man pulled down the visor of his big black helmet. "Gonna have to get you a pair of goggles if you're gonna ride with me, ol' boy."

After working most of the day checking and rechecking that the classic 1981 bike was finally road-worthy after months of restoration, Coop was tired. He really should call it a day—but it was just too tempting to take it for a spin. Just a short ride. He had enough juice left for that.

Slowly pulling out of the open garage door into the alley, Coop paused the bike a moment as he hit the button for the garage door to close, then grinned at the dog as he stowed the remote in the pocket of his leather jacket. "All set, boy? Here we go."

At the end of the alley, Coop turned right onto the sleepy side street of his Oak Park neighborhood. A right here, a left there . . . he rode in zig-zags around the neighborhood streets, glancing now and then at Rocky to make sure the dog wasn't about to jump out. But Rocky was leaning around the sidecar windshield, mouth open in a doggy-smile, tongue and ears flopping in the breeze. Yep, he definitely needed to get Rocky some goggles.

Pleased at how the bike was handling, Coop was tempted to take it onto the 290 expressway that headed west out of Chicago, past Oak Park and into the western 'burbs. But, better not. Not the first time out. Not until Rocky was a sure bet to stay in the sidecar. Besides, Maggie would be home soon. And he'd left the motorcycle catalog somewhere in the house when he'd placed that order, and he better find it before she did, or his surprise would be ruined.

It had rained recently—typical April weather—and there were large puddles in some of the side streets he couldn't avoid. *Rats.* He'd need to clean the bike again when they got back. Didn't want Maggie to see it all muddy when he announced the bike was ready to go now.

Maggie . . . His heart warmed as he thought of his wife. Her retirement was just a few weeks away, end of May. Now they'd be free to do some of the things they'd dreamed about in recent years. Travel. Explore. Visit old friends and places. He knew she wasn't keen on him fixing up this old bike after his heart attack a couple years ago, but he was practically good as new. And it'd been a soothing balm for his soul. Maggie was a good sport. She'd come around to taking a trip on the bike. After all, *déjà vu,* right?

Their kids would have a conniption, of course. Mike and Stacy anyway. *Ha.* Far as the two oldest were concerned, he and Maggie should sell the house and go vegetate quietly in an old folks' home. Not going to happen. Not yet, anyway. As for Chris, he'd be all over this bike if he saw it now. If only he hadn't blown a gasket when the kid—

Coop winced inside the helmet. The estrangement with Chris was painful. He still struggled, wondering if the whole thing was his fault. Had he been that kind of dad? Too busy, too distant, too blind to see what was happening with his son? It didn't compute. He'd spent a lot of time with all three kids!

But the estrangement—he took the blame for that. But maybe . . . maybe there was still hope for some kind of reconciliation. The kid was his son, after all. But he'd have to make the first move. Hard to do when their youngest lived in California. Didn't even know where for sure. But Coop had an idea. A crazy idea, but sometimes God used crazy ideas.

Turning into their alley, Coop sent the garage door up, pulled the bike into the garage, and turned off the motor. Dismounting, he took off his helmet and shrugged off the jacket, tossing them on top of a stack of boxes in the corner. Rocky panted happily, reluctant to get out of the sidecar.

"Okay, fine. Stay there. I'll be back in a minute." After he got his wind, that is. Coop steadied himself with a hand on the bike and took several long, slow breaths. Glad Maggie wasn't home yet. She'd fuss at him if she saw him short of breath and make him go lie down. But he'd be fine in a minute. And he did need to get into the house before she got home and hide that catalog. He wanted to shine up the BMW again, too.

All he needed was another minute or two.

* * * *

Oh, please. Not another 'exit bomb'!

Hearing her name, Maggie Cooper paused at the double glass doors of the medical clinic and slowly turned around, juggling her computer case, briefcase, and extra file folders. "What is it, Karen?" Why did this always happen as she was trying to leave for the night?

Maggie's secretary hustled down the hall toward her, sassy sisterlocks bouncing, waving a small piece of paper. "I'm sorry, Sister Maggie, I know you're trying to get home. But Dr. Emery just called, wants you to give him a call ASAP."

Maggie tried not to roll her eyes. "About?"

"Uh, didn't say exactly. Something about a board meeting tomorrow." The young woman shrugged. "Could be just details about your retirement."

Her retirement. She'd already tried to retire twice from her job as Chief Operating Officer of the Good Neighbor Medical Clinic. To no avail. "Haven't found the right person for the job," Jeff Emery had said. The clinic's Executive Director and head physician had tried to sweeten it by adding, "You're a hard act to follow, Maggie."

She did know. After seventeen years as the glorified office manager at the nonprofit clinic, Maggie held everything together, like a teamster gripping the reins of a twenty-mule wagon team—though sometimes it felt more like a balancing act with twelve spinning plates.

3

But finally, Good Neighbor's board had found a viable candidate, and Maggie had turned in her resignation, effective the end of May. *Hallelujah!* Only five weeks to go.

"About time," Coop had groused. Her husband had retired four years earlier at sixty-five, and he'd fussed that she should retire, too, so they could take spontaneous trips, go camping, visit the grandkids, take a second honeymoon. Financially, it hadn't made sense for her to retire when he did—she was four years younger than Coop—but she'd promised him she'd retire when she hit sixty-five, come hell or high water or even Dr. E begging on his knees. Now her sixty-fifth birthday was coming up the end of next month, the deadline she'd given the board and—

Wait a minute.

"Board meeting?" Her gray eyes narrowed at Karen. "What board meeting? The board already had its April meeting."

The secretary shrugged. "Guess Dr. E called a special meeting." She eyed Maggie's armload, and then stuck the sticky note on the computer case. "There. Message delivered. In case he asks. Up to you if you go." The young black woman wrinkled her nose sympathetically. "Hope your replacement hasn't backed out."

Now Maggie did roll her eyes as she pushed open the double front doors of the medical clinic and headed for the parking lot. *Whatever.* She was retiring at the end of May, even if the last trumpet sounded and the entire staff of the faith-based clinic went to heaven, and there was no one left to hold the fort.

She snorted at the thought. Okay, so that wasn't funny. But some of the members at the small urban church she and Coop attended made such a big deal of "end times" timelines and prophecies. Not something she worried about too much. She'd just keep busy, retirement or no retirement. Let God figure it out.

Balancing her computer and briefcase—the files and folders she was creating for her replacement to ensure a smooth transition—Maggie found her car keys and unlocked her ancient Subaru Outback.

The most direct route from the clinic in Austin—one of Chicago's most impoverished neighborhoods—to her home in nearby Oak Park took her past Julian Percy Middle School where all three of their kids had attended—in the last century, ha. But it was already three-thirty—she'd missed her golden window a half hour ago when she could sail down Madison Avenue into Oak Park, turn at the school, and get home in fifteen minutes flat. Now traffic was already backed up with parents and buses picking up the flood of preteens pouring out of the school.

She didn't really miss those days when she was one of the parents picking up Mike or Stacy or Chris from school. But she did miss having her kids around. Especially Chris. Yes, especially Chris, because it'd been so long . . .

Don't go there, Maggie, she told herself. Not when she was going to see Coop in a few minutes. Coop didn't talk about Chris much anymore.

After inching her way through traffic and stair-stepping a few side streets, she finally pulled the Subaru to the curb on their block of South Ridgeland. No rusty yellow Civic parked out front, which meant their boarder, Jiang Liu, wasn't home yet. No surprise there. Like most exchange students the seminary kept sending them even after Coop retired, Jiang often had evening classes or worked late. The bedrooms her kids had abandoned after college usually housed at least one, sometimes two, and occasionally even three students who needed off-campus housing. It helped the students, their rent for room and board helped the Coopers, and it gave Maggie and Coop an excuse to hang onto this big, old house.

She couldn't help smiling as she climbed the steps to the wide, front porch of their two-story frame. She loved this old house. She loved this old neighborhood. She loved Oak Park. She loved being close—but not too close—to all the urban treats of the Windy City and Lake Michigan. Oak Park was like a village in the pocket of Chicago's urban overcoat.

Maggie unlocked the front door and stepped into the foyer. "Coop? I'm home!"

No answer. No wild barking and tail wagging either. Which meant both Coop and Rocky were probably out in the garage working on that motorcycle he'd been restoring. She dumped her things on the foyer bench at the foot of the polished wood staircase leading to the second floor and made her way to the sunroom at

the back of the house. Talk about *déjà vu*. When she first met James Cooper at one of those Jesus People
concerts on the West Coast, he'd had a second-hand Harley, and she'd ridden on the seat behind, gripping him tightly around the waist, even to their honeymoon cabin in the Washington mountains a couple years later. It'd been fun in their early years, but once the babies came, well, the Harley just sat in a corner of the garage and Coop had finally sold the thing. She'd barely noticed.

But what did he do the minute he retired from his job as chair of the Urban Studies department at Chicago Biblical Seminary? Bought an old 1981 BMW—with a sidecar, no less! She'd certainly had mixed feelings about him getting another bike. Honestly! In his sixties! He'd talked about fixing it up and taking a big cross-country trip back to the West Coast where they'd both grown up—but then he'd had a triple by-pass, and all talk about a big trip got shelved.

Recovery took a while, and she still felt badly about going to work those long months and leaving him alone most of the day. Thank God he was a lot better now. He'd even started working on the bike again a few months ago. She wasn't so sure it was a good idea, but at least it kept him busy. Sometimes too busy. It was like he had ants in his pants. What was the hurry? She wasn't that eager to climb into that sidecar.

Stepping out the back door of the sunroom, she called again. "Coop! I'm home!"

A split-second later their black-and-tan shorthair came bounding out the side door of the one-car garage, barking excitedly and leaping up the back steps to where she was standing on the tiny deck. "I see you, you silly mutt—and no, it's not time for supper yet." She gave Rocky a good scratch behind his floppy ears, and then headed for the garage as the dog danced around her feet.

Her husband looked up as she stepped inside the door. "Oh, hey, Maggie." He was sitting on an upended bucket, dressed in a pair of old coveralls, grease streaking his face. His silvery-gray hair stuck out in odd places under a baseball cap. He looked tired to her. But he pointed a wrench at the machine he'd been working on. "What d'you think?"

She nodded. The old BMW had been classy in its heyday—and she had to admit he'd brought it a long way back to its regal self. "Looking good. You get it running yet?"

He grinned. Gosh, she loved that grin. Made him look ten years younger. "Yep!" The grin got bigger. "Took Rocky for a ride around the neighborhood a while ago. He loved it." Coop's chuckle was deep.

"What? You took the dog? In the sidecar? Weren't you scared he'd jump out?"

"Nah. I've been letting him sit in the sidecar while I've been working on the bike. He owns it." Coop looked up at her with a twinkle in his eyes. "You want a ride?"

Maggie sputtered a laugh. "Uhhh, not right this minute. Connie down the street is supposed to come by for a haircut." She snatched the baseball cap from his head and ruffled his shock of silvery gray hair. "About time *you* had a haircut, too, you old hippie you. Getting a little long over the ears, don't you think?"

Coop dismissed her with a wave of the wrench and went back to tinkering on the bike.

* * * *

The neighbor from two houses down had just gone home after a thirty-minute hair trim—and thirty minutes of nonstop neighborhood chitchat—when Maggie's cell phone rang.

"Mom! She did it. She did it even after I told her not to!"

Maggie sighed and cradled the cell phone between ear and shoulder as she pulled a package of frozen fish fillets out of the freezer and popped them in the microwave to thaw. "What is it now, Stacy?" Stacy was their middle child who lived in one of the northern 'burbs. Took an hour to get there from Oak Park. Stacy and Chad Young were so busy with work and running their girls around to all kinds of activities that Maggie and Coop were lucky to see them once a month, if that.

"It's Reagan. She got a nose ring *and* two rings pierced in her lip." Stacy's voice turned to a wail. "Why does she do this to me, Mom? How can I take her anyplace now? She looks even more like those punk kids you see on TV."

7

Maggie punched in the weight of the fish on low power and hit "Start." Reagan was sixteen and driving her mother nuts. First, a big tattoo of a fish on her upper arm. Then the heavy black eyeliner and mascara. Then streaking her gorgeous chestnut hair three different colors and cutting it short-short on one side and letting it fall over her face on the other—as well as telling her mother she was dropping out of cheer squad at Deerfield High School, even if it wasn't the end of the season.

"It's just a phase, Stacy. She's trying her wings. It's what teenagers do when they're sixteen." Maggie shook her head as she hauled out a frying pan. Her own declaration of independence from her parents' middle-class culture had happened during her college years at the height of the late sixties, which was when she'd met Coop—at a tie-dyed and bell-bottomed Jesus People concert. And Stacy, wouldn't you know it, had "rebelled" the other way by rushing a posh sorority at university and marrying a fast-track corporate tax lawyer.

"But, Mom! She signed up for auto mechanics next year. *Auto mechanics!* It'll be her senior year! And all she does after school is hang out at the skateboard park or hide in her room listening to that horrible punk rock stuff—I can't even call it music."

"So, she really likes the skateboard her grandfather bought her?"

"Hmph. Yeah, thanks a lot."

Maggie could almost hear Stacy rolling her eyes.

"Oh—sorry, Mom. Gotta go. I've got a house showing in half an hour. But I wish you'd talk to her. Or Dad. She listens to you guys."

Maggie's cell phone went dead in her ear. Putting the phone down, she gathered the rest of the stuff for their supper—potatoes, fresh broccoli, salad stuff. Well, she didn't care for the tattoos and black makeup or body piercings either. But she liked her oldest granddaughter. A lot. Reagan had a spark to her that was like . . . like Rocky, all coiled and ready to spring. Just not sure where to spring *to*. But even at almost seventeen, Reagan still gave big hugs to her and Coop when her parents weren't around.

A whine and a scratch at the back door caught her attention. Speaking of Rocky . . .

Maggie opened the door of the sunroom. "Still not time for your supper, you beggar. But come on in. I'll—"

The dog gave a sharp bark, whirled and scrambled back down the steps to the yard, then stopped at the bottom and looked up at her.

"Hey, you. I don't have time to play games. Get your buddy out there to play with you. I'm making supper." She started to close the door, but Rocky leaped back up the steps and pushed his nose into the doorway before she got it shut. When she opened the door wider, he backed up and barked again.

"Oh, all right. Where's your ball?" Maggie found one of Rocky's old tennis balls on the deck and threw it into the yard. "Go get it, boy!"

Rocky didn't budge. Just barked at her.

That's when she noticed his tail wasn't wagging. This wasn't a game.

A sudden panic rose in her throat. "Oh, God." Rushing down the back steps, Maggie half-ran toward the garage, Rocky streaking in front of her, still barking. "Coop? Coop!" she yelled. Stepping inside the open side door, Maggie paused for half a second for her eyes to adjust to the dimmer light. Where—?

And then she saw him.

James Cooper lay on the concrete floor beside the BMW bike, the bucket he'd been sitting on toppled over on its side, the wrench still clutched in his hand.

Chapter 1

MAGGIE COOPER THREW HER ARM OVER THE LUMP beside her in the bed—*uhhh*. Even in her half-asleep state, something didn't seem right. She forced her eyelids open a crack. The light sifting through the window blinds was still muted, not bright. She turned her head a couple inches. The dark lump beside her was on top of the covers, not under the sheet. The lump shifted and sighed, then *wuffled* through its mouth, as though having a dream.

Maggie's eyes focused in the dim light.

The dog. Not Coop.

That's what was wrong.

Sensing she was awake, Rocky lifted his head and whined softly. "It's okay, boy," she murmured. She stroked the dog's floppy ears. They'd never let Rocky sleep on the bed before. He had his own dog bed on the floor on Coop's side where he'd slept the past four years since he was a pup.

But ever since Coop died, Maggie felt lost in their queen bed. Too empty. Too alone. The night after the funeral, she'd invited the black-and-tan mutt up onto the bed. His warmth and steady breathing were somewhat comforting as she fell asleep—a process that sometimes took hours.

But mornings . . . mornings she always felt confused for a few moments. A heavy sensation sat on her chest. Tears lurked somewhere behind her eyes. Until she remembered . . .

Coop was gone.

Maggie lay still for several long minutes . . . then finally pushed back the comforter and swung her feet over the side of the bed. What time was it? She squinted at her alarm clock. Ten after five. Might as well get up. Her alarm usually rang at 5:30 to give her time to get ready for work and leave the house before traffic—

Her shoulders slumped. *Stupid.* What was she thinking? Her last day at work had been Wednesday. Three days ago. Jeff Emery had insisted she take two weeks off after Coop died to make necessary arrangements, plan the funeral, and just give her some space. But then he'd asked if she could come in for a week or so to train her replacement. Nice lady. African American. Mid-forties. Had been director of two faith-based social service agencies in the city. Chicago born and raised. Asked all the right questions. Maggie had liked her from the start.

Just, couldn't remember her name right now.

Rocky crawled off the bed and came around to her side, pushing his nose into her lap. She absently scratched his noggin. What was she going to do now with Coop gone and her job gone, too? The last two days—Thursday and Friday—had been miserable. She'd walked around the house in a stupor, wandering from room to room, starting one thing, then another, finishing nothing.

She never should have retired. It'd be better to have a schedule. Go to work. Work overtime. Keep busy.

Maggie flopped back onto the bed. Why get up? She couldn't un-retire now. Dr. Emery had already hired Mrs. Wilson—oh, right, that was her name. Denise Wilson. It wouldn't be fair to ask for her job back.

An alarm clock rang somewhere in the distance. Jiang must've forgotten to turn his off last night. Their boarder usually slept in on Saturday. He held down two part-time jobs with different hours during the week between classes. Then worked a third job on Saturday, sometimes Sunday. She never could keep it straight. The jobs were pretty mundane for a young man as bright as Jiang Liu, but he never complained.

That was another worry. What was she going to do about Jiang now that Coop was gone?

Struggling upright again, she decided to get up anyway. Too many questions, too many unknowns swirling around in her brain. Pulling Coop's terrycloth bathrobe around her, she followed Rocky as he scrambled down the stairs, let the dog out into the backyard, then trudged back up the stairs with her daughter Stacy's voice in her ears: *"Use the railing, Mom! Last thing we need is for you to have a fall!"*

11

Huh. As if a fall would hurt her kids more than it'd hurt her.

Bypassing the second-floor bathroom Jiang used, Maggie headed for the "master bath" Coop had put in when Mike and Stacy were teenagers, even though it had meant giving up one of their closets. Coop had said smugly, "Let the kids duke it out"—over whose turn to use the common bathroom, he meant. The new master bath had been strictly off limits to their progeny.

Locking the door to her bedroom and then to her bathroom— something she never did when Coop was alive—she turned on the hot water in the shower, shampooed her hair, then let the steamy water run over her head. How long she let it run, she didn't know, but suddenly the water turned cold.

Aii-yii, that was a wake up.

It took her a good half hour to get her clothes on and her still-wavy gray hair to behave, even with a bit of gel and the hair dryer. Why did everything take twice as long the past few weeks? Rocky would be whining at the back door, if he weren't barking already. Huh. The neighbors would love that.

But as Maggie made her way down the stairs again, she smelled coffee. And Rocky met her in the foyer, tail wagging, doggy smile on his face. Maggie suddenly felt light-headed and grabbed onto the post at the bottom of the stairs. *Coop?* He had always gotten up and made the coffee, even after he'd retired.

The slender form of Jiang Liu materialized from the dining room into the foyer, presenting a mug of steaming coffee. "*Ni hao*, Mrs. Cooper. Happy birthday!"

"What? Oh—thank you, Jiang." Maggie took the mug. *Her birthday.* She'd totally forgotten—this morning anyway. Of course, she had a birthday this week—that was her retirement goal, after all. But that brought up something else she'd momentarily forgotten. Her oldest son and middle daughter *and* their spouses *and* the grandkids were all coming today to celebrate her birthday.

Maggie's knees suddenly felt weak, and she sank down onto the foyer bench. Jiang reached for the mug of coffee, gently taking it back before it spilled. "Are you all right, Mrs. Cooper? I am making special Chinese breakfast for you. To give your birthday a happy start. But I can stop if you don't feel well."

She looked up at his face, so concerned. How could she tell him she wasn't hungry—hadn't eaten much for breakfast *or* lunch *or* dinner since Coop died?

"I'm . . . I'm fine. Really. I just need some time to wake up. It's still early."

Jiang's smile returned. "*Shi*, I know. I did not expect you to get up with the sun. I need another hour or so. Can you wait that long?"

Maggie managed a smile and nodded. "That is very sweet of you, Jiang. Yes, I can wait."

Wait forever, if need be.

* * * *

It was nearly eight o'clock by the time Jiang announced that Maggie's birthday breakfast was ready. She'd been sitting on the small deck outside the sunroom, wrapped in an old favorite sweater as the cool morning temperature slowly gave way to what promised to be an 80-degree day. *April showers bring May flowers—* except this year she hadn't planted any of her usual flowers along the backyard fence. Only the clematis was starting to climb up the trellis alongside the small garage.

Jiang had set the small table in the sunroom with several serving dishes, which he proudly pointed to. "Congee rice porridge, dumplings stuffed with much vegetables—a favorite *dim sum* dish—and Guilin rice noodles with shrimp and mushrooms. And green tea."

Maggie made an effort to eat and had to admit the food was delicious. She let Jiang do most of the talking, chattering about his boyhood in Tianjin, which was unusual for the normally reserved young man. *He has something on his mind*, she figured. And sure enough, it came out.

"You will stay in this house next year?" He seemed embarrassed to ask. "Or go to live with your children now that Mr. Cooper has, um, has—"

13

She laid a hand on his arm. "It's all right, Jiang. I know you have another year of seminary and need a place to stay. But, I don't know. I honestly don't know."

Jiang nodded, eyes down on his plate. "Of course. I understand."

Glancing at his watch, he suddenly jumped up. "I must go. I have to be at work by nine but . . ." He looked in anguish at the table. "I do not mean to leave these dirty dishes for you to clean up."

"Nonsense. It's no trouble. Go, go. The breakfast was wonderful."

Given the complexity of the various foods he'd served, however, Maggie expected the kitchen to be a mess—but the counters were clear, and the dishwasher was already running with whatever he'd used in preparation. All she had to do was put away the leftovers and wash the dishes from the sunroom table by hand. A task that felt doable, even good. Hands in hot sudsy water.

But Jiang's question hung over her head like a comic-strip speech balloon. Indeed. Was she going to stay in this big house? Or go to live with one of her children?

Anger suddenly surged up from her gut, like a bitter reflux. She didn't want to stay in this big house alone *or* go to live with one of her children! Move to Indianapolis and live with Mike and his brood? They didn't have room. Move in with Stacy? Really bad idea. They'd drive each other nuts!

Maggie gripped the edge of the sink, staring at the dish suds winking and popping slowly. Suddenly she grabbed a plastic bowl waiting to be washed and threw it across the kitchen where it bounced off the refrigerator and spun out over the floor. "You had to go and die, James Cooper!" she yelled. "It's not fair! You left me! You promised you'd never leave me!" Maggie slid to the floor and buried her face in her hands as painful sobs rose to the surface. ". . . and I don't know what to do!"

Chapter 2

T HE DOORBELL RANG AT LEAST THREE TIMES in succession. Setting down her watering can, Maggie headed for the front door. Had to be Jacob. Her eight-year-old grandson always announced his arrival this way, providing cover for big brother Alex to run around to the back and sneak in the sunroom door. But they'd tried it so often she was on to them, and sometimes locked the back door just to derail the inevitable jump out at her from behind some corner.

"Hey, Grandma!" Jacob gave her a quick hug around her middle and glanced behind her. "Reese here yet?" Reese was his cousin, same age, Stacy's youngest.

"Not yet, honey. Soon, I'm sure." Wasn't that the way it always was? The ones who lived closest were always last to arrive.

"Happy birthday, Mom." Mike came in, dressed in good jeans and a pullover shirt, and planted a kiss on her forehead. "Hope we aren't too early. Oh, here's your mail."

Maggie took the batch of mail he handed her and laid it on the telephone table. She'd look at it later. "No, no, not too early. You're fine." She glanced at the schoolhouse clock ticking on the wall at the bottom of the stairway. Almost two. What had she been doing the last four or five hours since Jiang's breakfast? She'd walked Rocky, unloaded the dishwasher, got half her houseplants watered. That was about it.

That and the brief birthday call from Chris. He'd remembered. It was so good to hear his voice. Her youngest sounded good. He'd asked about Rocky—his birthday gift to her four years ago. He had one of Rocky's litter-mates, a girl-pup he'd named Bella. She and Chris were soulmates when it came to dogs, but they hadn't talked about why he hadn't come to Coop's memorial service, and it was still a sore point.

15

She looked out the open door. "Where're Susan and Shannon?"

"Oh. Gotta go back out and help them bring in stuff. Be right back." A second later Mike poked his head back inside. "Uh, don't look. Your birthday, you know."

Maggie hadn't wanted a big fuss for her birthday. But—here they were. She obediently walked into the living room—and jumped as someone grabbed her just beyond the living room archway. "Boo!" Fourteen-year-old Alex grinned, revealing new braces. "Hi, Grandma! Happy birthday."

"Look at you! You got braces. How do they feel?"

They sat on the piano bench and talked braces as footsteps scurried behind her through the foyer, into the dining room, and into the kitchen. "Don't peek, Grandma!" a girlish voice called out on one trip back and forth, but a few minutes later, twelve-year-old Shannon flew into the living room and gave her a big hug. "Happy birthday, Grandma! How are you doing? Are you okay?"

Maggie gave Mike and Susan's middle child a little smile. "I'm fine, honey. Thanks for asking." Shannon was a sweetheart. Blonde hair in a ponytail, blue eyes, denim jumper. Sensitive.

"Happy birthday, Mother Cooper." Maggie's daughter-in-law appeared in a matching denim jumper, bent down and gave her a warm hug. "Mom" or even "Maggie" would've been just fine with Maggie, but Susan homeschooled the three children and seemed enamored with old-fashioned manners.

"Hellooo!" called a new male voice from the open front door. Stacy's husband, Chad. The Youngs had arrived. Maggie stood up. More "Happy birthdays" would be forthcoming. It was sweet of everyone to come to celebrate her sixty-fifth milestone, but she was already looking forward to the end of all this "happy birthday" stuff.

Or maybe not. Bedtime just meant crawling into that big bed—alone.

Get a grip, Maggie Cooper, she chided herself. *This is your family. They love you. Stop feeling so sorry for yourself.*

Chad Young, crisp and pressed even on a Saturday, gave her a nod as he passed through the foyer lugging a cooler. Stacy was still standing on the front porch hissing tense words at her oldest daughter, who stood with shoulders hunched, arms crossed, and head turned. But when Maggie caught her daughter's eye, Stacy put on a smile, came inside, and pecked her mother on the cheek. She held out a bouquet of pink roses and alyssum. "Happy birthday, Mom. Where would you like these?"

"Oh, uh, vases are in the sunroom cupboard. Usual place." Maggie smelled one of the roses. "Mmm, beautiful. Thank you, Stacy—oh, there are my two R's!" Maggie stepped out onto the porch and beamed at Stacy's two daughters, Reagan and Reese. It had taken a while to get used to her granddaughters bearing "boy names," but the names were popular these days for girls.

Reese, eight, brown-eyed and brunette like her mother, gave her grandmother a quick squeeze, then ran off looking for her cousins. Reagan, at sixteen a good two inches taller than Maggie, sullenly waited until her mother had disappeared with the flowers, then she dropped into one of the Adirondack chairs on the porch.

"You okay?" Maggie gently touched Reagan's shoulder.

Reagan rolled her eyes. "I am *not* going to that dumb summer camp while Mom and Dad go on that . . . that stupid cruise this summer. Four weeks with those stuck-up snobs? I'd rather *die*."

Cruise . . . Maggie vaguely remembered Stacy mentioning a Mediterranean cruise. Was that this summer? Whatever. She didn't want to get in the middle of that fight.

"Sorry, hon. I'm sure something will work out." Maggie turned to go. "Wouldn't mind sitting out here with you, but guess I better go join my birthday party."

Reagan sighed, dragged herself out of the chair and draped a tattooed arm over her grandmother's shoulder. "Bet you don't feel much like having a party with Gramps gone, huh, Grams?"

Surprised, Maggie tipped her head to the side and studied her oldest grandchild. She was still a bit startled by the small nose ring and the two tiny rings piercing the girl's lower lip she'd first seen after Coop died. But Reagan's eyes were sympathetic—in spite of the heavy black eyeliner, thick mascara, and shock of multi-colored hair falling over one side of her face.

Maggie's mouth tipped in a wry smile. "It's okay, honey. Bet you don't feel much like partying, either. You miss him, don't you?"

She kissed the girl on the cheek, then locked arms with Reagan and started for the back of the house where everyone else seemed to be gathering. "We'll get through it, you and I. Say, I hear you're dropping out of cheer squad? And taking auto mechanics?"

Reagan snickered. "Yeah, somethin' like that."

"Well, good. Maybe I can call *you* when I have a flat tire."

* * * *

Both families had brought food—lots of food—for the early dinner. Susan had made homemade chili with grated cheese, sour cream, and chopped green onion toppings, plus cornbread and a huge tossed salad. Stacy had picked up two roasted chickens at the grocery store, along with chips and hummus and guacamole and a large sampler of cut-up fruit in a plastic tray. The day was warm enough that they opened the windows on all three sides of the sunroom, which allowed for a nice breeze coming through. Maggie and the two youngest grandkids sat at the small table bedecked with the bouquet of roses, while the others balanced plates on their laps or used assorted TV trays. Rocky had been banished to the yard after snitching some chicken off Reese's plate.

Maggie nibbled a bit of everything, knowing she'd better save room for the inevitable birthday cake, which came in the form of large gourmet cupcakes of all different flavors from a specialty shop—Stacy's contribution—with a red velvet one for her with a "6" and a "5" candle on top. She blew out the two candles while her family clapped and cheered and even managed to eat a quarter of the red velvet cupcake before setting it aside.

"You don't want the rest?" Alex started to reach for it.

She gave his hand a playful slap. "Hands off, buddy. I'm saving it to enjoy later." Which was sort of true.

There were gifts. A framed family photo, a hand-and-body-lotion set, and homemade fudge from the Coopers, plus handmade cards from each of the three kids. Besides the bouquet of roses, Stacy and Chad gave her a pearl necklace-and-earring set in a velvet case and a humidifier for the master bedroom—Maggie didn't know she needed one, certainly not heading into a Chicago summer—and a Hallmark card all four of the Youngs had signed. When no one was looking, Reagan slipped a small package into her grandmother's hand. "Not now," the girl whispered. "Later."

The kids scattered while the adults cleaned up. The younger set disappeared into the family room in the basement. No one let Maggie help in the kitchen, so she wandered into the living room, feeling useless. She'd asked Mike if they'd like to stay the night— it was a three-hour drive back to Indianapolis—but no, they had church in the morning. Mike was an elder and Susan taught Sunday school, so they couldn't miss.

Alex poked his head into the living room. "Hey, Grandma. Can I take Rocky for a walk? Over to that park so he can run?"

"Of course, dear. His leash is hanging in the sunroom next to his food dishes. Just be sure to take some plastic bags in case he poops." She sighed. She was already weary from the day's hoopla. Just thinking about taking Rocky for his bedtime walk this evening made her even more tired.

Maggie heard her two children and their spouses talking in low voices in the kitchen. What were they up to? A short while later, the four adults joined her in the living room. "Uh, Mom, we'd like to talk," Mike said gravely as they all found seats.

Now they wanted to talk? She'd tried to mention Coop a few times during the birthday supper, but Stacy had brushed her off. "Oh, Mom. We don't want to feel sad today. Just enjoy your birthday. Besides, it's been a whole month now." Maggie had pressed her lips together. After forty-five years of marriage to the love of her life, she was supposed to bounce back after one month and be "all okay"?

Mike leaned forward, elbows on his knees, hands clasped. Her son had obviously been appointed spokesperson. "Mom, we know it's only been a few weeks since Dad died—"

Twenty-nine days. Four weeks and one day exactly.

"—but we need to talk about your future. What you're going to do now that, uh, Dad is gone, and you're retired."

Maggie's eyes wandered to the brass urn on the mantle. Coop's ashes. She hadn't even buried him yet. Wasn't sure what he'd want. They hadn't talked about it much. Just that neither one of them wanted tons of money spent on a funeral and burial. "If I go first, Maggie girl, just keep it simple," was all he'd said. Well, she'd tried to keep it simple, but a lot of people had turned out for his memorial service anyway. Standing room only at Grace and Mercy Community Church. Professors and staff from the seminary. Out of town relatives. Friends, neighbors, staff at the medical clinic. People she didn't even know. Stacy had rolled her eyes that the "repast" had been potluck instead of catered, but that's the way Grace and Mercy did it. Just ask Mother Jones, Kitchen Chair and head of any event that involved food.

". . . welcome to stay with us, of course," Mike was saying. "Right, Susan?"

Susan nodded, her voice kind. "Of course, Mother Cooper."

"Oh, don't be silly, Mike." Maggie flitted her hand in their direction. "You know good and well you don't have room. Whenever we visit you, Shannon gives up her bedroom and sleeps on that futon in the family room! Fine for a weekend, but no way am I going to kick that girl out of her room. She's almost a teenager. She needs her own room. Especially with two brothers."

Mike and Susan looked at each other. Maggie almost smiled. They knew she was right. Maybe even hoped she'd say that.

Stacy cleared her throat. "Well, of course, staying with one of us isn't the only option. There's that retirement village where you and Dad are on the list."

Maggie stared at her daughter. "What retirement village?"

"Oh, Mom. You remember! When Dad had his heart surgery. We talked about getting you guys on the list at Covenant Village. Dad agreed it was a good idea just in case, you know, he didn't make it."

"But he did make it," Maggie said tersely. "That was almost three years ago."

"True, but you're still on the list," Mike said gently. "It might be a good idea to follow up on it, now that your, uh, situation has changed."

Maggie sucked in a big breath and blew it out slowly. This had to stop. "Look. I don't want to move into a retirement village—fancy name for old folks' home in my opinion. I'm only sixty-five. And I've got a house. And a boarder. And a dog."

"But—"

"I just don't want to talk about it now, Stacy. I'm fine."

"But, Mom!" Stacy frowned and tossed the silky brown hair she wore shoulder length. "This house is too big for you! You can't manage all the upkeep. It would make sense to put it on the market sooner rather than later—after all, the housing market is slow right now. But we could list it with my agency, and I would give it my personal attention—we'd have almost five weeks before Chad and I go on our cruise."

Maggie noticed Stacy hadn't actually invited her to come live with *them*. Thank goodness. She and her daughter were like the opposite ends of a magnet. Push. Pull. Besides, Maggie just couldn't see herself fitting into a lily-white North Shore suburb and shopping at Neiman Marcus.

"Mom? I said—"

"I *know* what you said, Stacy." Maggie stood up. "But I'm tired. It's been a big day. The birthday party was great, and I know you all are concerned about me since your dad died. But, I don't want to talk about this right now. Another time, all right?"

With reluctant sighs and glances, the little confab in the living room broke up, and soon parents were packing dishes and rounding up children. "Is Alex back from walking the dog?" "Kids! Put away that game and get up here!" "Where's Reagan?" "Haven't seen her." "Chad! Help me carry this stuff out to the car!"

Maggie slipped out the back door into the small yard. She'd go in and say goodbye to everyone when they were actually ready to leave, but she needed some fresh air and a few moments of peace and quiet. Not to think. She was tired of thinking.

Studying her unkempt flower garden, she smiled to the smattering of white lilies-of-the-valley that popped up every spring no matter what she did. A few other brave perennials from previous years poked their noses up through the dirt. And the clematis on the trellis by the garage was already sending out—

Wait. Why was the side door to the garage open? It shouldn't be open. She hadn't been in the garage since Coop had died, and she was sure she'd left it locked.

Walking to the side of the garage, Maggie slowly pushed the door further open. Reagan was standing beside the abandoned motorcycle with her back to the door. She was holding something, looked like a map. But Maggie didn't care what it was.

"Reagan!"

The girl whirled around, eyes wide.

"What are you doing? Why are you in here?"

"Uh, hi, Grams. I just, um, wanted to see Gramps's motorcycle he'd been working on. It really looks great. But look what I found! A map in the saddlebag! And he must've been planning a big trip, because it's—"

"Put that back!" Maggie snapped. "And come out of there. I don't want anyone in here."

"But, Grams! I—"

"*Now*, Reagan!" Maggie stood aside and pointed back to the house, her hand shaking.

Reagan glared at her grandmother from beneath the shock of streaked hair. "Fine!" The girl stuffed the map back in the hard-shell saddlebag and flounced out of the garage.

Maggie pulled the door shut with a bang as her granddaughter ran up the walk to the house. Maggie followed, lips pressed together. She needed to catch Mike before he left, get him to move the bike into the corner and cover it with a tarp so she wouldn't have to look at it.

Chapter 3

MAGGIE PUT ON THE TEAKETTLE. She needed a cup of chamomile, something to calm her nerves. She still felt rattled, even though the last carload had finally pulled away half an hour ago. The Youngs had left first while Mike was taking care of the motorcycle—in fact, she didn't get to say goodbye to Reagan, because the girl had holed up in the car right after Maggie had chased her out of the garage. She felt bad about that— but what was the girl thinking?! Her granddaughter should've known better. How did she get in there anyway? Must've taken the key that still hung by the back door. Maggie hadn't been in the garage herself since the paramedics had come and removed Coop's body. The memory of that day, seeing Coop on the garage floor—it was just too painful.

The teakettle whistled. While her tea steeped, Maggie briefly scanned through the stack of mail her son had brought in earlier. Junk mail, bills, more sympathy cards. She laid the stack down again. Later.

Taking her tea out onto the front porch, Maggie settled into one of the Adirondack chairs. The sun had already disappeared behind the house, and twilight would soon creep over the neighborhood. Felt a little cooler already. She always loved this time of day. Porch sitting. A lost art in many neighborhoods. Too many houses with not even a hint of a porch, just front doors for going in and out. Apartment buildings were even worse. But here in Oak Park, a lot of the older homes had porches, even wrap-around verandas. One of the things she and Coop had loved about this house. They had often sat out here in the seasonal march from the sweet early days of spring through sultry summer evenings and into the musky smell of fall—sometimes to watch the brief Midwest thunderstorms roll through. It would be hard to give up the house for that reason alone.

She snorted. *Retirement village, my foot.*

At least she'd stood up to them and they'd backed off. For now, anyway. She wasn't ready to talk about the big What's Next? Except, what *was* she going to do tomorrow? And next week? The days ahead stretched like yawning caverns, dark and unknown, swallowing life as she knew it.

If only she hadn't retired! She would love to go to work on Monday. Go early. Stay late. Redo the clinic's filing system. Organize a Saturday crew to repaint the three examination rooms, which had been showing signs of fatigue the past couple of years. Out with the beige! In with warm, bright colors. Maybe Perfect Peach. Sea Green. Sunny Yellow. She could say cheerfully, "Dr. Emery will see you in the Green Room" to old Mr. Washington who came in every six months for a cortisone shot in both knees.

The house phone was ringing. She was tempted to let it go to voicemail, but her tea could use a warm-up. Might as well answer.

"Mom!" Stacy launched into her best "new crisis" tone. "Reagan locked herself in her room when we got home and won't talk to any of us. All I got out of her was a snarl, 'Ask Grams.' *I* didn't have a fight with her—not since this morning anyway. What did she do now?"

Maggie sighed. "She's probably upset at me. She got into the garage, and I found her there. Chased her out. I didn't want anyone in there where your father died."

"The garage! What in the world was she doing in the garage?"

"Checking out the motorcycle her grandpa had been fixing up, I think."

"Oh, *that* thing. Mom, get rid of it! It was just a nutty idea Dad had anyway. Put an ad in the paper. Or list it on Craigslist or E-bay. Something."

"I . . . well, of course. One of these days. I'm just not up to it right now."

"Well, let me do it then. You should give his clothes away, too. They aren't doing anyone any good just hanging in his closet. We have a great consignment shop up here in Wilmette. I could come down and help you sort and pack stuff next week if I don't have a house showing."

Full-fledged irritation flickered dangerously behind Maggie's eyes. "Stacy, stop! I'm not ready to wipe out all signs that your dad lived here, too. Please. Just back off and give me some time. I'll do it when I'm ready."

A big sigh filtered through the phone. "If that's what you want. But let me know when you're ready, and I'll help, okay? And call Reagan and talk to her, will you? I can't stand her moping around here like it's the end of the world."

Maggie's irritation morphed into a twinge of guilt. "All right. I'll call tomorrow afternoon, after church. She's probably not ready to talk to me right now anyway."

Ending the call, Maggie turned the teakettle on again. Was she going to church tomorrow? She wasn't in the habit of skipping—she loved Grace and Mercy Community Church. But she'd had enough of the sympathetic murmurs, the gushy hugs and predictable comments. "He's in a better place." *Yeah, well, he would've been fine here with me for a while longer.* "Oh honey. It'll get better, you'll see." *But what about right now? It hurts now.* "God must've needed another angel." *Oh, please.* If one more person said that, she might let loose with some real cuss words.

But if she didn't go to church, it would be just another long day with too much time on her hands to think. To feel.

Rocky nudged her leg and whined. "You need to go out again, boy? All right, one more short walk." Daylight was rapidly fading. She got his leash and headed for the front door. They'd just walk up and down their own block. And tomorrow she would go to church—but she'd arrive a few minutes late and sit in the back and slip out during the last song. That would work.

She and Rocky were already to the end of the block before Maggie realized she'd forgotten to turn off the teakettle on the stove.

* * * *

Maggie was glad she'd decided to go to church. It felt good to be on a schedule the next morning. She woke to the alarm, got decent enough to go downstairs and let Rocky out into the backyard, and then back upstairs to take her shower and get dressed. As she came downstairs, she met Jiang in the foyer just as he was going out.

"Nǐ hǎo ma, Mrs. Cooper? How are you this morning?"

"Good, thank you, Jiang."

He seemed breathless. "Excuse me. I must go. I cannot be late."

She waved her hand at him and smiled. "Of course. Go, go."

Jiang tipped his head in a tiny bow and then hurried out to his car. She watched him go. He was certainly a dedicated young man. She and Coop had once visited the Chinese church where Jiang was doing his pastoral internship—a strange experience since the whole service was conducted in Mandarin. But Jiang had invited them to come the first Sunday he gave the sermon as an intern and seemed so appreciative that they had come. If he thanked them once, he thanked them a dozen times. He even made the effort to translate his entire sermon into English for them to read afterward. Straight up Gospel—the story of Nicodemus—with an invitation to be "born again" at the end. No one had gone forward, but after the service, numerous people had pumped his hand, beaming at him and chattering in Mandarin, which Maggie had presumed were congratulations to the new young preacher.

She watched as the little yellow Civic disappeared from sight. What would happen to Jiang if she moved to that retirement home?

No, no, she didn't want to think about that. Maggie let the dog in, poured herself a bowl of granola and took it out to the sunroom. All her birthday gifts were still piled on the little breakfast table— the vase of roses, the family photo of Mike and his family, the handmade cards, the jewelry from Stacy—and one little package still wrapped.

Oh crud. She'd totally forgotten about Reagan's little gift and her whisper: *"Not now. Later."*

Well, later it was.

Maggie opened the little package, no ribbon, just clear tape. A little braided band of different colored string fell out. What was this? She held it up. About six inches long, with long strings at both ends. Looked like one of those friendship bracelets that were popular with some of the kids. It also seemed vaguely familiar . . .

Suddenly her eyes filled. Reagan had been wearing one just like it yesterday.

Had her granddaughter made it? For her? Even if she'd bought it, it was obviously something she'd given her grandmother that linked them together. Twin friendship bracelets. And Maggie had yelled at her to "get out."

Oh Lord, what have I done?

She had to call her granddaughter. But a quick glance at the clock told her if she was going to go to church this morning—even late—she'd better finish her breakfast and get going. Besides, the Youngs had probably already left for that big megachurch they attended on the North Shore—the one with three services and big screens on both sides of the stage and enough stage lights to put on a production of *Les Miserables.*

She'd call Reagan this afternoon. Drive up to Wilmette if she had to.

* * * * *

Grace and Mercy Community Church met in a one-story brick building that used to be an auto-body paint shop that had sat empty for several years. The congregation was a remnant who'd decided to stay in the city when their evangelical church had moved out to the suburbs. Maggie and Coop were among those who'd chosen to stay—had vigorously campaigned for the whole church to stay in fact—even though the group of about thirty diehards had struggled for several years to keep the little congregation going. But over the past ten years attendance had slowly grown to fifty, then seventy-five, then one hundred, and now hovered around one-fifty. They'd had to be intentional about becoming more multi-cultural, which wasn't easy since the original remnant was mostly white. But slowly more people came because it was a "neighborhood church" plonked right in the middle of a community that reflected the diversity of Oak Park—a Chex Mix of Caucasian and African American and Hispanic, with a growing number of Eastern European and Middle Eastern immigrants.

Maggie pulled into the parking lot, made her way unnoticed into the building, and slipped into the back row of folding chairs. Good. The "praise team" was well into their first set. At least the youthful musicians, brought up on contemporary Christian music, had gradually been helped to understand that upbeat "praise" songs should come first and gradually meld into the more thoughtful, soulful "worship" songs. And today the music even included a good ol' hymn, "Come Thou Fount of Every Blessing."

Her plan was working. Well, almost. Just before Pastor Eric got up to preach, Regina Harris, a few rows up and to the side, craned her neck and caught Maggie's eye. Quicker than a blink, the black woman who worked third shift as a nurse at Stroger Hospital was out of her seat and heading Maggie's way.

"There you are!" Regina stage-whispered, plopping down into the chair beside Maggie. "I know what you're doin', Maggie Cooper. Hidin' back here so you can slide in an' out without the rest of us knowin' you were even here. Well, all right. But when you leave today, you will know *I* knew you were here. An' that you're still grievin' that beautiful man of yours. An' we're grievin' with you." Without waiting for Maggie to say anything, Regina put a plump arm around Maggie's shoulders, pulled her close into a sideways embrace, and kept her arm there during Pastor Eric's thirty-minute sermon in his series on the Gospel of John.

At first Maggie appreciated the gesture—after all, Sister Regina had been one of the movers and shakers who'd helped Mother Jones pull off an eye-popping repast after Coop's memorial service. But as the minutes dragged on she felt imprisoned in the woman's well-meaning embrace. Not wanting to be rude, she stayed put . . . and gradually relaxed, leaning against Regina's side, absorbing the comfort of another person's body bulk next to hers after weeks of deep loneliness.

She blinked back tears. *O God, I miss Coop's touch.* Skin on skin.

But as Pastor Eric gave the benediction and the praise team gathered at the front for one last song, Maggie wiggled out of the embrace and slipped out of the row. But from behind the chairs, she bent close to the woman's ear. "Thanks, Sister Regina. Love you for that."

Once in the car, she let the pent-up tears flow and used up a whole travel pack of tissues, feeling as if conflicting emotions had been dumped into a blender and turned on high. *Don't want to talk to anyone. Need to talk. Don't want people's sympathy. Need people to know, to understand how hard it is.*

A few teenagers burst out of the front door of the church. The service was over. Maggie gave her face one last wipe with a wadded-up tissue, turned on the ignition, and headed out of the parking lot. Should she go home? Or—

She did a quick check in her purse. Reagan's friendship bracelet lay swaddled in its tissue paper wrapping alongside her wallet, reading glasses, and house keys. Turning the car east, she headed toward the closest expressway that would take her to the North Shore suburbs. To Wilmette.

Chapter 4

THE YOUNGS' BLACK MERCEDES SUV STOOD in the driveway of the large brick house. Good. They were home—unless they'd taken Stacy's sporty red Lexus. Maggie knew they often went out to eat after church. Except when Stacy had a house showing on Sunday, in which case she sometimes didn't go to church—and the rest of the family often took that as reason to stay home, too.

Maggie rang the doorbell. Her son-in-law answered the door. "Oh! Hello, Maggie." Chad Young looked puzzled. "Uh, were we expecting you?"

"No. Sorry, Chad. I should have called."

"No, no, it's fine. Come on in." Stacy's husband swung the door open and called over his shoulder. "Stacy! Your mom's here!"

"Uh, actually, I came to see Reagan. Is she here?" Maggie's eyes traveled up the staircase that rose from the foyer.

But before Chad Young could answer, Stacy appeared, wiping her hands on a dishtowel. "Mom! What are you doing here?"

"Came to see Reagan. Take her to lunch if that's all right."

Stacy frowned. "You should've called. I'm already making lunch."

"You're right. I should've called. It was spur of the moment. But, would you mind if I stole Reagan and took her out?"

Stacy rolled her eyes. "Fine with me. If she'll go. She's still in a big pout."

"I'll get her," Chad said, and took the stairs two at a time.

"Hmph." Stacy tossed her hair and headed back to the kitchen.

From the bottom of the stairs, Maggie heard Chad knocking on a door, then indistinct voices back and forth. After a few minutes he came down, gave Maggie a hopeful shrug, and disappeared. More waiting . . . but finally, Reagan appeared at the top of the stairs, arms folded across her chest. "What?"

"I came to apologize, honey. But, could you come down here? I'm getting tired of standing and craning my neck."

Reagan slowly sashayed down the stairs and took up her arms-folded-across-chest stance again.

Maggie sucked in a breath. "I want to apologize for getting upset at you yesterday, sweetie. That wasn't fair. And I'd really like to take you to lunch so we can talk a little more—" She lowered her voice and eyed the passageway toward the kitchen. "—privately. You know."

After what seemed like a long minute, the corner of Reagan's mouth tilted in a slight smirk. "Okay." Without another word she marched out the front door and made for Maggie's car. Then she turned back. "Coming?"

Teenagers. Her granddaughter was dressed in a tight tee shirt, scruffy ripped jeans, and gym shoes with no socks, but Maggie decided not to suggest she change. "Stacy!" she called out toward the kitchen. "We're going! I'll bring her back in an hour or so." And she hustled out the door without waiting for a response.

"Where to? Anything good around here?" Dangerous question. This was Wilmette. Could be expensive.

Reagan grinned. "Walker Brothers. My fave place. You'll love it, Grams."

Funny, in all the years they'd lived in Chicago, Maggie had never been to the popular pancake house, a local chain on the North Shore, and she wasn't too happy when she saw the line that wound out the door. But the line moved fairly quickly, and once they were seated she looked around and said, "Wow." The bustling restaurant featured an enormous collection of stained-glass windows and Tiffany-style ceiling lamps hanging over every table and booth.

"Cool, huh?" Reagan said.

The girl ordered an apple cinnamon pancake while Maggie went for the banana crepes. And coffee. So glad for that bottomless cup of coffee.

While they waited for their food, Maggie reached into her purse and pulled out Reagan's birthday gift. "I opened this last night." She shook out the friendship bracelet. "But I can't tie it on one-handed. Would you . . .?"

31

Reagan stared at the bracelet in Maggie's outstretched hand for a moment, then slowly took the bracelet and tied it around her grandmother's right wrist. "That okay?"

"Yes." Maggie smiled. "I love it. Especially because you have one just like it. That's really special to me, Reagan. Thank you."

Reagan nodded slightly, though she didn't look her grandmother in the eye. "I wanted to get one for Gramps, too, but I didn't know, you know, didn't know he'd . . ." Her voice wobbled, and she grabbed a napkin to blow her nose.

"I know, honey. None of us were ready to lose Grandpa."

They were both silent for several minutes. Their waiter came by and topped off Maggie's coffee. Then Maggie reached for her granddaughter's hand. "Like I said when I came to the house, honey, I wanted to apologize for getting upset at you in the garage yesterday. I wanted to explain—"

"Yeah, yeah, I know, Grams." Reagan pulled her hand away. "I get it."

"Still, I—"

"I wasn't gonna hurt anything. The bike is just somethin' that belonged to Gramps an' I was missing him, ya know?"

Maggie studied her granddaughter. Exactly. The motorcycle had James "Coop" Cooper all over it, which made it so painful to see it standing there in the middle of the garage, framing the memory of her husband lying beside it on the concrete floor.

Dead. Gone.

And yet, that wasn't the memory Reagan had. She wasn't there when her grandfather died. So, the restored motorcycle was just a part of him, something that reminded her of somebody she loved. And she was missing him, too.

Maggie sighed. "I know. We're both missing him. It's just hard, knowing he was working on that motorcycle when he died. But, I over-reacted. Forgive me?"

The girl shrugged. "Yeah, sure, Grams. Sorry. I shoulda asked first. Didn't think it'd matter if I took a peek in the garage—oh, yum." Reagan's eyes brightened as the waiter unloaded a plate with the gooey apple cinnamon pancake in front of her. "Ya gotta taste this, Grams. It's totally awesome."

Maggie decided not to give her opinion that "awesome" should be reserved for Niagara Falls or the Rocky Mountains, and just said, "Thank you," to the waiter as he laid the banana crepes in front of her. But after a bite or two of the light-as-air crepes stuffed with sliced bananas and sour cream and topped with apricot puree, she was tempted to declare them "awesome" as well.

"So, whatcha gonna do with Gramps' bike?" Reagan dug into her gooey pancake.

Maggie sighed. "Your mom offered to sell it for me—"

"Oh, Grams." Reagan's eyes went wide. "Don't let my mom get her hands on Gramps' bike! You can't *sell* it! I mean, it was Gramps' pride and joy! And it's really cool with that sidecar an' everything. I think he was planning some big trip—you know, that map I found in the saddlebag. You oughta—"

"Reagan." Maggie cleared her throat. "Uh, honey, maybe we could talk about this another time, okay? I'm not going to do anything right away. Like I told your mom, I need some time before I make those decisions."

Reagan slumped. "Okay. Just don't let my mom get her hands on his bike. Promise me that, at least."

Maggie managed a smile. "Okay. I promise."

* * * *

Her phone alarm went off at 6:00 A.M.

Maggie groaned and groped for the phone, but finally had to sit up and turn on the bedside lamp in order to actually turn it off. *Crud.* Her alarm was still set to go off at six on weekdays. She absolutely needed to cancel the alarm today, at least until she called the clinic and asked about coming in as a volunteer.

Rocky stretched on top of the covers beside her and then hopped off the bed. Ugh. The dog's body clock was still on her work schedule, too, and wanted to go out. Might as well get up and get on with her day. Pulling on a pair of jeans, tee shirt, and a soft zipper sweatshirt, she decided to make a good breakfast for Jiang before he left for school, and then . . . well, she'd figure that out after breakfast.

She had oatmeal and toast on the table by seven o'clock, but Jiang hadn't appeared yet. Maggie stood at the bottom of the stairs but didn't hear anything from the second floor. Her knees had been bothering her a bit lately, so she wasn't too happy about an extra trip up the stairs, but up she went. No noise from his bedroom either. Strange.

She tapped lightly and waited. Then tapped again.

Shì shéi ya . . . who is it?" a groggy voice called from inside. A few seconds later Jiang opened the door a few inches and peeked out. "Oh! Mrs. Cooper. Uh, is everything all right?"

"I made breakfast for you. It's seven o'clock. Don't you have to be at school by eight?"

Jiang's face broke into a sleepy grin. "Oh, no, no! It is holiday today. Your Memorial Day? No school."

"Oh! Jiang, I am so sorry." *Duh.* How did she forget that this was Memorial Day? "You go back to bed."

"No, no. You made nice breakfast for me. I will come."

"Absolutely not. Go back to bed. I can save your breakfast for later. I mean it. You deserve to sleep in."

Maggie waved her boarder back into his room and went back downstairs. How stupid of her. She sighed as she scooped out one bowl of oatmeal and put a cover on the pot to keep the rest warm. Why didn't any of her kids or grandkids mention that Monday was Memorial Day? Usually her birthday was almost a week before this May holiday. But a quick glance at the kitchen calendar showed the problem: the last day of May was a Sunday this year, bumping "the last Monday" to her birthday weekend.

Rocky lay patiently in the sunroom as she finished her oatmeal, but the moment she got up to rinse her dishes, he got up, too, and stood by the sunroom door, making little "woofs."

Maggie shrugged. Still no sign of Jiang. Might as well walk the dog. Lifting the leash from its hook, she opened the back door—but before she could snap the leash onto Rocky's collar, the dog scurried down the steps of the little deck and shot toward the garage, where he sat down, his nose pointed at the side door.

"Rocky! Get back here." She didn't want to have to chase the dog all over the yard. But the dog didn't move, just sat by the

34

garage door under the wooden trellis. Her heart did a little tug. Rocky was missing Coop, too. Maybe she should let him in, help the dog realize that Coop wasn't in there, wasn't coming back.

Lifting the garage door key from the key hooks Coop had hung there to be handy, Maggie went outside and approached the garage. Rocky stood up, tail wagging, and gave a couple woofs, still facing the door. "Okay, okay, Rocky. But he's not in there. You'll see."

She unlocked the door and pushed it open. It took a moment for her eyes to adjust to the dim light. The floor space was empty—Mike had moved the cycle into a corner and covered it with a tarp, just as she'd asked him to on Saturday. Rocky sniffed the floor where the bike had stood while Coop worked on it, whimpered a little, and then followed his nose to the corner. He seemed agitated.

"Come on, Rocky. Let's go. He's not here."

The dog ignored her. More sniffing, and then Rocky took hold of the edge of the tarp and pulled. A few tugs and the tarp slid off. There stood the bike backed into the corner, the sidecar on the side facing them.

Rocky gave a few happy barks, hopped into the sidecar, turned awkwardly a few times, then sat down facing Maggie, panting, a doggy smile on his face.

Chapter 5

Maggie spoke sharply. "Rocky! Come on. Get out of there!" The dog didn't move. Just panted happily, his left ear flopping in that comical way of his.

Maggie marched back to the open door. "Fine. Sit in the stupid sidecar." If she went back to the house and left the door open, Rocky would eventually get out of the sidecar and come in. But for some reason she hesitated. Even in the dim light of the garage with its two small windows, the motorcycle seemed to gleam. No rusty spots. No mud or dirt on the fenders. The metallic blue paint looked polished. Every inch of the bike and sidecar showed Coop's loving care.

Slowly walking back to the corner where the bike was parked, Maggie reached out and touched the closest handlebar. Coop had been happy working on this bike. But what in the world did he think he was going to do with it? He'd talked about taking a trip, but she'd never actually sat down with him to discuss it. The whole idea had seemed such a fantasy, she hadn't wanted to encourage him.

But right now, she'd give anything to listen to his voice, watch his eyes light up, let him dream a little. Now she'd never know.

Except . . .

When she'd found Reagan in the garage, the girl said she'd found a map. What had she done with it? Maggie hooked a finger in Rocky's collar and dragged the dog out of the sidecar, then peered into the interior. Nothing there she could see. Where had Reagan found it? She'd been excited, said she'd found it in . . .

The saddlebag?

Maggie squeezed her eyes shut and tried to remember. The motorcycle had been standing in the middle of the floor last Saturday, facing the back wall as if it'd been driven in, with the sidecar on the right side, the far side. Which meant Reagan had probably found the map in the saddlebag that was fastened on the left side of the bike—the side that was now stuck furthest in the corner away from Maggie, with the sidecar sticking out on the near side. Huh. No way could she reach that far.

Forget it.

"Come on, Rocky. Let's go for that walk." Maggie snapped the leash onto Rocky's collar, pulled the reluctant dog out of the garage, and shut the door.

* * * *

By the time Maggie and Rocky got back to the house from their walk, Jiang was up, had eaten his oatmeal, and was putting dishes into the dishwasher. "Did you get enough to eat, Jiang?" she asked. "I was going to make you some toast, too. And orange juice. And don't worry about the dishes. I can finish that."

"*Xièxie,* Mrs. Cooper. I am fine." Another dish in the dishwasher.

Maggie recognized enough simple Chinese phrases to know that *xièxie,* which sounded something like *shia-shia,* meant *thank you.* "So, what are you going to do with your holiday?"

"Ah. Very good question. I still have final exams to study for and a paper to write. I wish I could use the seminary library, but—"

"—it's closed today. Yes. That used to frustrate my husband, too."

"Yes, frustrating." Jiang shrugged. "So, today I have to be content with Google and the Internet for research. If you will excuse me, please?"

"Of course." She shooed him out of the kitchen and finished wiping down the counters. Huh. The question really was, what was *she* going to do with the day?

First on her list: call the medical clinic and ask Dr. Emery about volunteering. Cradling the house phone between her shoulder and left ear as it rang, she wandered into the living room rehearsing what she'd say. Surely her former boss could understand that Coop's death had definitely not been part of her retirement plan.

She needed something to do. She'd promise not to interfere with her replacement, that Mrs. Wilson. She was already familiar with the workings of the clinic, so he wouldn't have to—

"You have reached the Good Neighbor Medical Clinic. Our offices are closed for Memorial Day weekend. If this is an emergency, please hang up and dial 9-1-1. For our regular office hours—"

Maggie hung up. Of course. Memorial Day. Now what?

Her eye caught the urn on the fireplace mantel. Coop's ashes. A flash of anger caught her off guard. "Why'd you have to go and leave me, Coop?!" she cried out. "If you hadn't been working so many hours on that damn bike, maybe you'd still be here!"

Snatching the urn off the mantel, she tucked it under her arm and marched to the sunroom, grabbing the garage key on the way out the back door. Rocky was right at her heels as she headed for the garage, unlocked the side door, and strode over to the motorcycle. "There!" She plunked the urn down in the seat of the sidecar. "You wanted to take a trip in this road warrior of yours. Go ahead. Just go—wherever it was you wanted to go!"

Rocky stuck his nose into the sidecar, sniffed the urn, then turned his head and looked up at her, forehead wrinkled, the black marks over his big brown eyes twitching as if thoroughly puzzled. *What's got into you, lady?*

"Silly dog." Maggie felt the anger sliding away as quickly as it had come, replaced with a sudden urge to laugh. An urge that soon had her giggling, and then laughing so hard she had to sit down on the cement floor. Rocky came over and licked her face—which set her off even more. Grabbing the dog around the neck, she pulled him half into her lap, and they rocked back and forth together between bouts of laughing, crying, and licks to the face.

Finally, Rocky wiggled out of her embrace and just sat back on his haunches, looking at her. Maggie heaved a long shuddering sigh. She felt spent. "Oh, dear Jesus, I'm a mess." She fished for a tissue in the pocket of her jeans and mopped her face. Good thing she hadn't put on any eye makeup that morning or she'd look like Mad Max. "Could use some help here, Lord. Don't know what to do with myself." It was the best prayer she could muster under the circumstances.

The map.

It was as if someone had spoken the words inside her head. For some reason, whatever Reagan had found in the saddlebag suddenly seemed important. Or maybe not. Maybe it was just a map of Chicago or Illinois, which would make sense if Coop had planned to ride the thing around town or take some day trips. "Won't know one way or the other unless I find the thing, will I, Rocky?"

She got awkwardly to her feet, grabbing onto the sidecar for leverage, then brushed grit and dirt off the seat of her jeans. After carefully removing the urn from the sidecar, Maggie studied the bike. Okay, if she stepped *into* the sidecar and then kneeled on the bike seat, she could reach back and open the top cover of the saddlebag on the other side.

Several teetering moments later, Maggie felt folded paper beneath her fingers as she fished in the far saddlebag and pulled it out. Yep, definitely a map. Actually, two maps, one stuck inside the other. "But," she muttered to Rocky as she gingerly backed out of the sidecar, "no way am I sitting down on that floor again. We're taking this into the house and making some fresh coffee."

* * * *

Steaming mug in hand, Maggie stared at the two maps spread out on the dining room table. One was a map of the Midwestern states, the other the West Coast states. A yellow highlighter marked a route running from Chicago, through Wisconsin and Minnesota, into South Dakota, then off the left side. She pushed that map aside and pulled the second map close. The yellow line picked up at the Wyoming border, through Idaho, along the Columbia River, over to Portland, Oregon, and then halfway down the Pacific Coast.

What in the world? Had Coop really been hoping to make a trip all the way to the West Coast on that bike? With the sidecar? Meaning . . .

She sat the coffee mug down with a thump. Meaning he'd been planning—assuming—they'd do this trip together.

The man was nuts! Why hadn't he talked to her about this? Well, maybe he *had* tried to bring it up, and she'd always put him off. Probably because he knew she'd tell him it was a crazy idea.

For several long moments, she stared at the two maps spread out on the table.

Wait a minute.

Several places along the way were circled in pen. Pulling the first map close to her, she again followed the yellow line with her finger. The first circle was Minneapolis. But nothing else on the first map, just the yellow line going on. She pulled the second map to her and traced the yellow line again. Second circle was in Wyoming, then a circle along the Columbia River, then Portland, and a couple other places in Oregon. The yellow line and last circle ended in San Francisco.

Taking a deep breath, Maggie blew it out slowly. For a moment, the map blurred, and she blinked rapidly to refocus. All those circles represented places and people framing their forty-three-year marriage, plus places where they'd each grown up.

What was this? A trip down memory lane? Didn't sound like Coop. Had to be some other reason. But what? And why?

Chapter 6

MAGGIE CALLED THE GOOD NEIGHBOR MEDICAL CLINIC as soon as it opened the next day and asked for Jeff Emery. But Karen, her former secretary, said Dr. Emery was in a meeting. "Sorry, Sister Maggie. Do you want to talk to Ms. Wilson instead?—oh, forget it. That's who he's having the meeting with. I'll have him call you, okay?"

Maggie fought a pang of jealousy. Dr. E was meeting with Denise Wilson, her replacement. No doubt working out the week's schedule: patient appointments and cancellations, agenda for staff meeting, dealing with patient or staff complaints, how to best use volunteers, maybe brainstorming new initiatives. All the things she used to handle with the efficiency of a good blender.

Rocky whined at the back door. Maggie let him out and followed him down the steps. While waiting for the dog to do his business in the yard, she unlocked the garage and leaned against the doorjamb, eyeing Coop's motorcycle in the far corner, no longer covered by the tarp. A moment later, Rocky snuck past her, hopped into the sidecar, and cocked his head expectantly.

"Don't look at me," she snorted. "I'm not taking you for a ride."

But her granddaughter was right. The bike *was* part of Coop, the work of his hands. And his heart. Unlike a few days ago, when it brought back such painful memories, today she found a smidgen of comfort looking at the machine. She could almost imagine him working on it in his baggy coveralls, spotted with paint and grease, an impish grin peeking out from under the baseball cap he always wore.

Her cell phone rang. "Dr. Emery! Thank you so much for calling back." Breathlessly rushing on, she laid out her idea of coming back to the clinic. "As a volunteer," she stressed. "With Coop gone,

I need something to keep my mind occupied. To keep busy. I'm sure you can understand."

"I do understand, Maggie. We already miss you around here. But—"

"What better place for me to volunteer than the clinic? You wouldn't have to train me. I know the clinic inside and out. Just point me toward something you want me to do, and I'll do it. I mean, just say the word, and I'll come up with a plan to blitz the neighborhood about well-baby checkups and vaccinations. Contact churches for more volunteers. Clean out that old broom closet. Play monopoly with kids while their moms see the doctor. Whatever."

"That would be great, Maggie. But—"

"But what, Jeff? You've always said the clinic needs more help but can't afford any more staff positions. I'm offering my services free of charge!"

"I know, I know, Maggie. But Denise Wilson hasn't even been on the job a whole week. I'm afraid she'd feel intimidated if you're around. She needs to find her own pace without her predecessor looking over her shoulder."

"Oh, but I wouldn't—"

"I know you wouldn't mean to, Maggie. Look, why don't we wait a couple of weeks while Denise gets settled into the job, and then you can come in, and we'll talk about ways we could use you. You would be a great asset. But, it's just too soon. I hope you can understand."

"All right. I understand." Is what she said. But what she thought was, *I might go crazy if I have to wait that long to make myself useful!*

As she and Rocky returned to the house, her phone rang again. No caller ID. "What?" she snapped.

"Uh, Mother Cooper? Are you all right?"

Maggie winced. Her daughter-in-law. "I'm so sorry, Susan. I didn't recognize the number. Thought you were some kind of spam."

"Sorry. I'm using the church phone. Is everything okay?"

"I—never mind. I was upset about something. Nothing really. How are things with the family?"

"Everybody's fine. But that's why I'm calling. We haven't gotten your RSVP to Alex's eighth grade graduation, so I'm wondering if you'll be able to come."

Maggie's mind scrambled. Alex's graduation? Had they said something about it? She came up blank. "I'm sorry. Did we talk about this? I can't seem to remember."

"Well, we sent you an invitation. You should have gotten it last week. I guess we didn't mention it on Saturday because we were celebrating your birthday. It's not too late or anything—but we'd love to have you come. I'm sure it would mean a lot to Alex."

An invitation? Probably in the stack of mail that had been piling up on the hall table. "Of course, I want to come, Susan. Uh, let me find the invitation to get the details, and I'll call you back."

"Oh, good," Susan chirped. "It's next Saturday afternoon. Now, if it feels too much to drive, maybe you could take the train, or get a ride with Stacy's family. I haven't heard from them either, but hopefully they can come, too."

"No worries. I'll find a way. 'Bye! Love to the kids."

Maggie headed for the front hall and sorted through the stack of unopened mail. Ah, this must be it—no return address, but an Indianapolis postmark. She'd thought it was just another sympathy card. Hmm. Beautiful calligraphy on the envelope—another one of her daughter-in-law's talents, no doubt.

She curled up in a living room chair and opened the envelope.

You are invited to celebrate
The Eighth Grade Graduation of
Alex Cooper
Mustard Seed Academy
Eagle Creek Community Church
3:00 p.m. Saturday, May 30
Please RSVP

Well, that was nice. She'd never really thought about how they graduated homeschool kids. Reagan's eighth grade graduation from public school had been, well, tedious to put it mildly—especially the middle school band performance that came first. She wondered what this would be like. Held at their church no less! Was it just for Alex? A group of homeschool kids? Or was the local Christian school letting homeschool kids join their graduation?

Guess she'd find out.

* * * *

Maggie was glad she had something to look forward to, because the rest of the week crawled by like watching paint dry. No phone call from Jeff Emery. Well, he'd said a couple of weeks, so she'd try again when she got home from Indy. She checked out the Amtrak schedule, but the only direct route was a late evening train. Otherwise she'd have to take a train to Champaign, then a bus over to Indianapolis.

She'd rather drive. Faster, too.

Maggie didn't even consider calling Stacy. Couldn't imagine being stuck in a car with her opinionated daughter for three or four hours. And her granddaughters were usually plugged into their iPods or iPads for the duration.

Nope. She'd drive down on Saturday morning, come home Sunday afternoon. She'd call back and let Mike and Susan know the plan.

Trying to keep herself busy, Maggie planted some impatiens in the front porch boxes, tried to sort through Coop's clothes, setting aside two still-wearable suits to take to the local resale shop, shopped for groceries, ran the vacuum, and spent too much time watching cute cat videos on the Internet.

But anytime she let Rocky out into the backyard, the dog headed for the side garage door and whined. Against her better judgment at first, she let him in. He trotted straight to the motorcycle, hopped into the sidecar, and just sat there. Maggie shrugged and left him there, letting the dog decide when it was time to come out. Except for the times she went in, too, and sat on one of the overturned buckets Coop used, letting the memories of their years together creep out of their protected niches to play with her heart.

Definitely needed more boxes of tissues the next time she went shopping.

* * * *

Jiang found her in the garage on Friday when he got home from school. "Mrs. Cooper? You are uncomfortable sitting on that bucket, yes? Should I get a chair for you?"

"No, no." Maggie hastily arose and brushed off the seat of her pants. "I'm not staying."

Jiang wandered over to the motorcycle, patted Rocky on the head, then ran his hand admiringly over the handlebars, gas tank, and leather seat. "Very nice bike. Very nice." He glanced shyly at Maggie. "I had motorcycle, too, in China."

"You did? Like this?"

Jiang shook his head. "No, no. Not so nice. But everyone rides motorcycle in China—or bicycle. But many, many motorcycles in Shanghai."

"What about cars?"

"Yes, more cars now. But—" He shook his head and snorted. "Drivers crazy. Here, there, everywhere. Red light means nothing. Bicycles, pedestrians, watch out!"

Maggie chuckled, coaxed Rocky out of the sidecar, and locked the garage behind them. "Oh, Jiang, I meant to tell you, I'll be gone this weekend. I'm driving to Indianapolis tomorrow to attend my grandson's graduation from eighth grade. I'll be home Sunday night. Just wanted you to know."

She smiled at him, ready to ask if he'd mind taking care of the dog for the weekend, when he said, "Ah. Very good. I have much studying to do for exams and a paper to write for Old Testament class besides work. Spending much time at school library. I will not even know you are gone."

Maggie's smile now felt pasted on. Looked like she'd have to take Rocky with her.

* * * *

The drive to Indianapolis was uneventful, in spite of a light rain that wet the highway from time to time. She pulled into the driveway of Mike and Susan's house just before noon and snapped Rocky's leash onto his collar before getting out. The wide front porch with wicker chairs and flowered cushions looked inviting, but she pushed the doorbell.

"Grandma's here!" Jacob yelled, flinging the front door open. "Hey, you brought Rocky! Cool." The eight-year-old gave the black-and-tan mutt a big hug and got a slobbery dog-kiss in return.

Mike appeared at the door. "Hi, Mom. Uh, you brought the dog?"

"I know. I'm sorry, Mike. I should've called and asked. I didn't plan on bringing him, but as it turned out, Jiang couldn't take care of him and, uh, I didn't have time to find someone else."

Mike glanced back over his shoulder. "Well, it's just that we're going to have quite a few people over here later. But, hey, don't worry. We'll work something out. Come on in. Just in time for a quick bite before we head over to the church. Oh, Susan's parents are here already."

The "quick bite" was an array of cold cuts, cheese slices, bagels and buns, a veggie tray, a bowl of grapes, and chips laid out buffet style. Jack and Joan Miller, Susan's parents, greeted her pleasantly, though Joan drew back, alarmed, when she saw Rocky.

"Oh! Mother Cooper!" Susan's eyes went wide. "I didn't know you were bringing the dog. My mom, uh, doesn't like dogs—I mean, they frighten her, especially big ones. Do you, um, mind putting Rocky out in the yard?"

"Of course. I'm so sorry." Maggie felt stupid as she dragged Rocky out the back door to the yard—which was unfenced—and tried to think of a way to tie him up. The sky didn't look too happy either—the clouds were darkening in the west. Storm coming. *Great, just great.* She should've asked Jiang to look after Rocky anyway, exams or no exams. She finally asked Mike to unlock the detached garage and put Rocky inside, trying to ignore the pitiful whine as she hurried back into the house to join the family.

A loud crack of thunder just before they got ready to leave for the graduation sealed Rocky's fate. He'd have to stay in the garage till they got back. *And then what?* Maggie put his food dish and water bowl in the garage, then hurried to Mike's SUV idling in the driveway. Maybe she'd have to go home tonight after all.

The Fellowship Hall of Eagle Creek Community Church was decorated with purple and black and gold balloons, as well as tables decorated in the same colors. Each table had a sign with the name of a graduate in beautiful calligraphy, eleven in all. Maggie found Alex's table, which displayed an album of photos, several folders with papers he'd written in different subjects—Literature, History, Science—plus awards he'd won, a robot he'd built that had won second place in a citywide competition, and several other mementoes from his homeschool studies.

Maggie's throat caught. *Coop would be so proud of his grandson. Look at that—second place in a robotics competition.* The boy was smart, no doubt about that.

Alex looked slightly uncomfortable wearing a sport coat, white dress shirt, and tie, but several other young teen guys in similar garb, plus a few girls in pretty spring dresses, clustered around him when they arrived. *Must be the other graduates from the homeschool group.*

The clock was creeping toward three o'clock, and people had started to gather in the folding chairs facing the low platform at one end of the room when Maggie saw Stacy blow in, followed by Reagan and Reese, hair plastered by rain. No Chad. Either parking the car or he'd stayed home.

"Heaven help us, it's a mess out there! You wouldn't believe the traffic!" Stacy's voice carried across the room. "But we made it! Where's my nephew? Alex, come here and give Aunt Stacy a hug. So sorry Uncle Chad couldn't make it. Don't you look all grown up!"

Reagan scurried away from her mother and slid into a chair beside Maggie. "Good grief," she muttered. "They better start quick before she embarrasses Alex to death."

Chapter 7

EVEN WITH ONLY ELEVEN GRADUATES, the ceremony took almost two hours. After the welcome and a short history of the homeschool academy, the graduates each presented some kind of talent. One of the boys played Chopin's Nocturne in B-flat, a girl sang "Ave Maria," followed by a recitation of The Gettysburg Address, a violin solo, a liturgical dance to a contemporary praise song, and a trombone trio. Maggie was surprised but tickled that Alex and a girl named Ava did a fun number *a capella* from the Broadway show, "Annie Get Your Gun."

"Anything you can do, I can do better!" Ava sang with an impish grin.

"No, you can't!" Alex challenged, hands on hips.

"Yes, I can!"

"No, you can't!"

"Yes, I ca-a-a-an!"

And on it went through a slew of verses as they tried to out-boast each other, complete with theatrical poses. The audience broke up laughing and gave them a round of enthusiastic applause.

Maggie felt like busting her buttons. *What a kid.*

Each of the parent-teachers then invited their graduate to the "stage," shared several highlights from their homeschool journey, followed by the presentation of their eighth grade diploma and a personal blessing. The students then gave a short speech thanking their parents, God, and . . .

Maggie felt herself nodding off, except for when it was Mike and Susan and Alex's turn. She was a little surprised to hear that Alex had chosen to attend a public high school next year and had passed the Selective Enrollment Admissions Exam with flying colors, which meant he got to choose the high school he wanted to attend—a college prep with an emphasis on science and math.

"He shoulda chosen a high school with a good theater department," Reagan hissed in Maggie's ear. "He oughta go into acting!"

Mike's blessing on Alex made Maggie catch her breath. "Alex, there's one person who couldn't be with us today, and that's your grandfather, James Cooper—or Coop as most people called him. Grandpa Coop to you." Faces around the room smiled and nodded. "But I know he would be so proud of you, just as I know the three grandparents who are here today are. And I know what he would say to you, son. He'd say, 'Alex, we have only one life and it will soon be past. Only what's done for Christ will last.'"

By this time, Maggie's eyes had blurred.

"Think of it this way, Alex. Your talents and skills and ability to learn are God's gifts to you. What you do with them are your gifts back to God."

Oh. My. Maggie fished for a tissue and cast a sideways glance at Reagan. Was her oldest grandchild listening?

Maggie barely heard the final congregational hymn or the closing prayer by the pastor of Eagle Creek Community Church. She was so glad to be here, to celebrate this milestone in the life of one of her grandchildren. But Coop's absence loomed large in her heart. And what about Chris? He'd always been a favorite uncle for Alex and the other cousins. Had Mike and Susan even sent Uncle Chris an invitation? Was he *persona non grata* or just out of sight, out of mind?

Afterward, everyone was invited to stay for cake and punch and coffee, but a lot of the parents and guests took advantage of a break in the stormy weather to hustle to their cars and get home to more personal celebrations. Even Mike rounded up all the Coopers, Millers, and Youngs and suggested they head back to the house.

Good thing, because they barely made it before another downpour rolled through the city. Mike looked crestfallen. "So much for grilling steaks in the yard. Guess we'll have to have our BBQ in the house."

So much for letting Rocky out of the garage, too. Maggie felt stuck. She couldn't bring the dog into the house but hated leaving him alone in the garage all night. She didn't want to drive home in this weather either, especially when it was dark. Best she could do was slip out to the garage with a newspaper over her head to give the dog a little comfort. Scrounging around inside the two-car garage, she found a small step stool to sit on and an old car blanket for Rocky to lie on. "Wonder how long it'll take them to miss us, eh, boy?"

The side door to the garage swung open with a gust of wind and rain. "Grams?" Reagan pushed the door shut behind her. "What are you doing out here—oh! You brought Rocky! Hey, there, fella." The girl crouched down, her tricolored hair swinging over one side of her face, and scratched behind the dog's floppy ears.

"Could ask you the same thing. What are *you* doing out here?"

Reagan rolled her eyes. "Oh, you know. Mom's on the warpath again. Trying to get Uncle Mike and Aunt Susan on her side about me dropping off the cheer squad and signing up for auto mechanics."

"I see." Maggie wasn't going to get in the middle of that one either. "As you can tell, it was a dumb idea to bring Rocky. Didn't know Grandma Joan was afraid of dogs. Didn't know the weather was going to rival Noah's flood, either."

Her granddaughter snickered. "I'll stay out here with him if you want, keep him company for a while."

"Sweet of you, honey." But Maggie didn't move. It was rather peaceful in the garage with the rain pelting on the roof.

Reagan—still dressed in the tights, short skirt, tank top and over-shirt she'd worn to the graduation—started massaging the dog's back from head to rump. Stacy would have a fit if she saw her daughter down on that musty old blanket. But Maggie mentally shrugged. The girl's clothes all looked washable.

How long they listened to the distant thunder—getting further away now—she wasn't sure. Then Reagan broke the silence. "Rocky seems really relaxed out here in the garage," she mused. "Maybe it's because he spent so much time in your garage with Gramps while he was working on the motorcycle."

"Mmm. Or maybe because he's got us for company right now, and you're giving him a doggy massage." *Although . . .* should she tell Reagan? Maggie cleared her throat. "Uh, Rocky still likes to go out to the garage and sit in the sidecar."

"Really?" Reagan's face lit up with a grin. "That's so cool."

More silence. More doggy massage. Then Reagan said casually, "Have you decided what to do with Gramps' bike?"

"Not yet."

"Know what I think?"

"I think you're going to tell me what you think."

"I think you oughta keep it and learn to ride."

Maggie snorted. "Ha. Not likely."

"Why not, Grams?"

"Because I'm sixty-five, that's why."

"So?"

The side door burst open again, and Jacob stuck his head in. "Hey, you guys! Everybody's asking where you are. We're having a picnic inside—come an' get it!" The little boy made a mad dash back to the house as fast as he'd come.

"Guess we've been found out." Maggie got up from the stool, feeling a bit stiff. She gave Reagan a wink. "Tell you what. If you want to sneak some steak out here for Rocky, I'll pretend I don't know you if you get caught."

* * * *

The family table was lively, in spite of being crowded. After banana splits and opening graduation cards, which yielded a nifty little stack of gift cards for Alex, the Miller grandparents excused themselves to go to a nearby Holiday Inn Express for the night, with plans to head home to Columbus in the morning. Stacy and the girls had planned to head home that night, in spite of the three-hour drive, but the weather report said thunderstorms continuing until at least ten o'clock, and Mike persuaded both his sister and mother to stay. Once the Millers had left, Rocky was permitted back in the house and slept in Shannon's bedroom with Maggie, while Stacy took the living room couch and the girl cousins had a sleepover in sleeping bags in the basement family room.

Maggie was up early, wanting to get on the road. Susan handed her a cup of coffee when she came downstairs. "Oh, Mother Cooper, you're welcome to go to church with us this morning. Then you could drive home this afternoon. You, too, Stacy," she added, as her sister-in-law came into the kitchen, looking a bit worse for wear after a night on the couch.

"Can't," Stacy mumbled, pouring herself a cup of coffee. "Got a house showing at two this afternoon. Is there a shower free?" And she headed for the lower level to wake up Reagan and Reese.

With Mike's family scurrying around getting ready for church, nine people juggling bagels and bowls of cold cereal for the do-it-yourself breakfast Susan had set out, and Reagan and Reese grumbling about getting dragged out of bed after a late night, Maggie was more than ready to get in the car. But Alex had offered to take Rocky for a short walk, so she was still waiting for them to come back when Stacy cornered her.

"Mom, I've got Wednesday free this week. How about if I come over and we can start sorting things. Have you thought about where you want to donate Dad's clothes?"

"I *said* I'd let you know when I'm ready, Stacy."

"Mom." Stacy's voice took on exaggerated patience, as if she was talking to a child. "It's been over a month since Dad died. I know it's hard—but that's why I'm offering to help you. That's what a daughter's for, right? And Chad and I will be gone several weeks this summer on that Mediterranean cruise. So, Wednesday?"

Maggie shook her head. "I don't know, Stacy. I have to check my calendar back home. I haven't turned the calendar to June yet—isn't it the first tomorrow? I might have something scheduled for Wednesday."

Stacy shot her an amused look. "Oh, Mom. You're retired, remember? What have you got to do next week?" She gave Maggie a peck on the cheek. "Look, I'll call you Monday or Tuesday, and we can plan a day to get together, maybe go out for lunch. Wouldn't that be fun?"

Jiggling her car keys, Stacy yelled over her shoulder, "Reagan! Reese! Leaving now!"

Mike came up beside her as Stacy pulled out of the driveway. "Down to a dull roar, Mom. Sure you don't want to stay for church?"

Maggie shook her head. "Thanks, honey. But given the uncertain weather, I'd like to get home. Sorry for bringing Rocky. I think it's best if I took him home—soon as Alex brings him back." She hesitated a moment, then blurted, "Mike, did you invite your brother to Alex's graduation?"

Mike gave his mother a dry look. "Mom. Chris lives in California. He didn't make it for Dad's funeral. You think he's gonna come all this way for an eighth-grade graduation?"

"Maybe not. But, wouldn't have hurt to invite him anyway, just to let him know about it and that he'd be welcome."

Mike sighed. "Okay, you're right. That would've been good. Although, unless you know something we don't know, he hasn't let anyone know his address."

The sticking point. "No—though I do have a phone number for him. Not sure if it's a cell phone, or if he buys a phone card."

"Well, let me know what you have, and I'll try to get in touch with him, okay?"

Maggie stood on tiptoes and gave Mike a peck on the cheek. "Thanks, honey."

* * * *

Maggie's mind bounced around like Tigger on steroids as she drove back to Chicago, but kept coming back to Chris. If only he didn't live so far away! She felt like a mother hen, wanting to gather all her kids and grandkids under her wings. But unlike the older two, who'd settled here in the Midwest after graduating from the University of Illinois, Chris had seemed determined to go to college out west, ending up at the University of Arizona, which offered a degree in veterinary medicine.

No surprise to Maggie about *that*. Her youngest had always been crazy about animals, owning a succession of gerbils, parakeets, hamsters, lizards, and white mice until he was old enough to adopt a dog from the humane society in seventh grade.

In fact, Chris seemed more interested in animals than in girls as a teenager—a relief to Maggie after Stacy's boy-crazy years. Unfortunately, his dog, a beagle mix that loved to run off anytime it could sneak out the door, got hit by a car his junior year. Chris had been inconsolable for weeks—after which he'd announced his intention to become a vet.

But his grades at UA didn't add up to getting into veterinary school, and he'd floundered for a few years, ending up with a general Bachelor of Science degree. Maggie had been hoping he'd come back to the Midwest after graduation, praying he'd find some direction. But Chris had found a job as a vet assistant somewhere in southern California and decided he'd work on the necessary requirements to become a "vet tech."

Why couldn't he do that back here? She missed her youngest son. Sister Regina at church had said, "Honey, of course you miss him. He'll *always* be your baby. Just the way it is." But her "baby" said he liked it out in California. "Don't worry, Mom. I promise I'll come and visit."

Which he did for a while. Chris had still been in high school when his older brother and sister got married. He'd been a thirteen-year-old candle lighter at Mike's wedding, a sixteen-year-old usher at Stacy's. But he was crazy about his nieces and nephews when they came along, and he always made it home for Christmas, sometimes Thanksgiving, and usually a week or two in the summer, all through his twenties. And he had come home for his dad's retirement party, the same weekend he'd brought Rocky the Pup as a birthday present for his mom.

The same weekend it all fell apart.

Chris hadn't been home since.

* * * *

Rocky trotted eagerly into the house when she unlocked the front door and let him in. The schoolhouse clock said almost noon—not bad timewise. "Jiang?" she called out. No answer, even when she lugged her overnight bag up to the second floor. Well, of course not. It was Sunday, and the Chinese church Jiang attended often went until two o'clock. Even Grace and Mercy would still be going for another hour. Hmm. Some rousing praise and worship might be a good thing to rout out the "what ifs" that had been plucking at her heartstrings during the drive home. Should she go to church late?

No. Given the number of people lined up to use the two bathrooms at Mike's house that morning, she could use a hot shower and a change of clothes now, and a fresh cup of coffee. Maybe take some personal "quiet time" as her "church" today. Jesus did that, didn't he? Go off sometimes to pray by himself?

Half an hour later Maggie came back downstairs feeling squeaky clean and hungry. But as she passed through the foyer, she noticed a large package sitting on the bench in the hallway with a UPS label on it. What was this? She hadn't ordered anything lately. She squinted at the label—it was addressed to James Cooper.

Tiny goose bumps prickled her neck. Who had sent something to Coop—after he'd been gone for over a month? No return address—just a company name and logo in the left corner of the label, something called CycleGear. Hmm. More likely Coop had ordered something weeks ago, and it was just now getting here.

Getting a small kitchen knife, she slit open the packing tape and peeked inside. The packing slip inside said "BACKORDER" in large type. So, that was it. Coop had ordered something, but it'd been backordered.

Too late now. Whatever it was, she'd just have to send it back.

But since the box was already opened, she lifted out the bubble wrap and dug beneath the tissue paper. What was this? She held up the black, soft leather garment.

A fitted leather jacket. Would never fit Coop. A woman's size.

A woman's motorcycle jacket.

She saw another box inside the first—this one square and a little heavy. She lifted it out but didn't have to open it because its contents were blazoned all over the box: *Women's Modular Motorcycle Helmet—Medium.* A full face helmet complete with chin guard and protective visor that slid open and shut.

An envelope fluttered to the floor. She picked it up and pulled out a card—a printed card with a personal message you can include when you order a gift:

HAPPY BIRTHDAY, SWEETHEART!
LET'S GO ON THAT ADVENTURE!
LOVE, COOP

Chapter 8

THE LEATHER RIDING JACKET AND BOXED HELMET lay on the bench in the foyer all day Monday. Maggie felt a strange ambivalence every time she passed them. She should just wrap them up and send them back, shouldn't she? But Coop's note lay on the jacket. His last communication. His last gift to her. His last wish . . .

Only when Jiang noticed them that evening and raised a delighted fuss about the contents of the mysterious package that had been delivered while she was away did she gather up the packing box, jacket, and helmet, and take them up to her bedroom.

Which made her wonder, where was Coop's jacket and helmet? Not hanging in the closet. She hadn't seen his old leather jacket for years—wouldn't have fit him now anyway. But he'd said he'd taken the dog for a ride around the neighborhood. Surely, he'd worn a helmet at least. Coop was nothing if not safety conscious.

Maggie marched out to the garage, Rocky at her heels. She'd rarely paid attention to the miscellaneous boxes stacked in various corners, tools hanging from nails on the rough wall or scattered on Coop's "shop table," or the old buckets of paint, screens that needed repair, and mysterious bits of metal wire lining the walls. Mostly Coop's stuff. Things that mattered to Maggie—seasonal clothes, boxes of mementoes—were stored in the basement.

Rocky immediately scrambled into the sidecar and sat on the seat panting as Maggie poked around. And there it sat—Coop's big old helmet atop a stack of boxes in the far corner behind the bike and what looked like his old leather jacket tossed beside it. But on closer inspection, she remembered his old one had been brown. This one was black, though obviously worn. Maybe he'd picked it up at a resale shop.

Maggie sank down onto an overturned bucket staring at the bike, while Rocky sat patiently in the sidecar. How long she sat there, she wasn't sure. But her thoughts floated about like feathers on the breeze. As far as Coop had been concerned, everything was all set. He'd spent hours—days, weeks, months—restoring the bike. He'd attached a sidecar for her to ride in, which Rocky seemed to have taken over. He'd carefully plotted a route on a couple of maps. He'd dug out his old helmet, found a used jacket that supposedly fit him, and ordered a new leather jacket and bike helmet for her.

"Let's go on that adventure!" his note said.

Only one thing was missing.

Coop.

* * * *

Stacy called on Tuesday. Three times. *Thank God for caller ID.* Maggie let the calls go to voicemail. She knew what Stacy wanted. A Mother-Daughter Day on Wednesday to bundle up Coop's clothes. She still wasn't ready. But when would she be ready?

Finally decided she'd better call back, or her daughter might just show up anyway. She'd agree to lunch. They could meet somewhere, less time for Stacy to get all busy-body around the house. Come to think of it, she could donate that box of winter stuff Coop hadn't worn for a couple of years to the consignment shop. Maggie couldn't even remember offhand what was in it. Probably wouldn't miss those old clothes.

Lunch was a good idea. At least the part about getting away from the house. They met at a nice little place in Oak Park called Mama Thai that offered standard popular fare. Maggie ordered Tom Yum Hot and Sour Soup, her favorite. Stacy got the sampler plate but spent most of the lunchtime picking at her food and moaning about Reagan.

"I just don't know what we're going to do with that girl this summer! She's refusing to go to summer camp—even though she's all signed up for a girls' sports camp the four weeks we'll be in Europe on that Mediterranean cruise and tour. She went last year—

we thought she liked it. *Now* says she'd rather stay home and get a job—but where? Does anybody hire teenagers these days?"

Maggie cautiously sipped her hot-and-sour soup from the porcelain spoon. "What about babysitting? Or a mother's helper? With so many moms working these days, surely one of the moms in your neighborhood would be glad for help with childcare once kids are out of school."

Stacy snorted. "Mom. In *my* neighborhood, everybody either has a nanny or they send the kids to summer camp in northern Wisconsin for six weeks. Which is exactly what we plan to do while we're on our Mediterranean cruise. Reese, thankfully, is all excited about a drama camp we found. She's signed up for four weeks. Leading up to a production of *The Wizard of Oz*—or maybe it's *The Wiz*. Something like that. But not Reagan, oh no." An exaggerated eye roll. "Her latest idea—get this—last night she asked her dad about buying a junker and letting her tinker with it, get it running again. A grease monkey! My daughter!"

"Sounds rather clever, if you ask me."

Stacy sputtered. "Oh, right. Can you imagine some old wreck sitting in our driveway with spare parts strewn all over the place? We'd have the neighborhood association knocking on our door with a signed petition to cease and desist." She jabbed a fork into an egg roll and waved it in the air. "Besides, Reagan can't stay home while we're gone. She needs to go to camp and that's it."

Maggie patiently listened to Stacy's complaints, then insisted on paying for lunch. Stacy shrugged. "Okay, fine. But next time lunch is on me. We probably won't get everything of Dad's packed up today anyway, so maybe I can come another day next week, too."

"Oh, speaking of that." Maggie cleared her throat. "I've already got a box of your dad's clothes ready to go. It's on our front porch. Jiang carried it out there for me. All you have to do is swing by and pick it up."

Stacy frowned. "You already—? I thought we were going to do this together. That's why I came down today."

"I know, dear. But, I started with things he hasn't worn for a while. Easiest to part with. So, I went ahead and bagged them up."

She gave Stacy a sweet smile. "All you have to do is pick them up. You want to follow me to the house?"

* * * *

The box and Stacy were gone. Maggie had begged off a longer visit, saying she needed to lie down and rest. She did lie down for a short time on the living room couch to justify her excuse. Visits with Stacy *were* exhausting. But fishing in her pocket for the note from Coop that came with her birthday gift, Maggie read it again another dozen times . . .

Happy Birthday, Sweetheart! Let's go on that adventure! Love, Coop.

Swinging her legs off the couch, Maggie headed into the kitchen to make herself a mug of tea, Coop's note still echoing in her head like a song that wouldn't go away.

Happy Birthday, Sweetheart! Let's go on that adventure!

Taking her mug, Maggie wandered out to the garage and sat on the overturned bucket again, sipping her tea as Rocky hopped into the sidecar. Almost felt like sitting *Shiva* with the motorcycle. Just sitting, remembering. Remembering the feel of Coop's slim waist as she hung on tight, riding away on the back of his old motorcycle after their outdoor wedding. Tossing the bridal bouquet over her shoulder, the squeals of her attendants drowned out by the roar of the motor . . .

Let's go on that adventure!

Huh. Their life had already been an adventure. Those early years in the Jesus People commune on the West Coast, trying to live simply, wearing peasant dresses and bellbottoms and bandanas, sharing everything—much to her parents' consternation. Coop getting restless, then whispering in her ear one night as he held her in his arms that he felt God calling him to bring Good News to the city, so what did she think about him going to seminary? The warmth and welcome of the little inner-city church in Minneapolis where Coop had been assigned after getting his M-Div, co-pastoring with Pastor Vic—he of the shaved head and big belly laugh—while she taught at the local high school, trying to keep her students from dropping out. And then the move to Chicago. Raising kids. Coop teaching urban studies at Chicago

Biblical Seminary. Maggie finding her niche at the Good Neighbor Medical Center. Making Grace and Mercy Community Church their spiritual home—that odd congregation of PhDs and blue-collar folks, grandmothers raising grandkids, black and white and brown and everything in between, not to mention old-school Pentecostals rubbing shoulders with Baptists and Presbyterians and even a few Episcopalians thrown in.

But what did it all mean at the end of the day without Coop?

Let's go on that adventure!

Yeah, right. All she had now was a sidecar-motorcycle and a map.

Maggie got up from the bucket and ran her hand over the cool metal of the gas tank. Could she sit on the thing? Would it tip over? Probably not. With the sidecar attached, the cycle stood straight up. Didn't even need the kickstand. She squeezed behind the cycle on the side away from the sidecar and hefted her right leg over the seat, hopping and scooting until she was sitting in the driver's seat, hands on the handlebars. Where Coop would sit if he were still alive.

She closed her eyes and tried to imagine Coop sitting on this seat, she behind him, her arms holding tight around his waist—

Beside her in the sidecar, Rocky gave a short bark.

Maggie sighed. "Sorry, buddy. We're not going anywhere. Except inside." She slid off the cycle and picked her way toward the door. "C'mon."

The maps Reagan had found were still laid out on the dining room table. Maggie paused, her eyes tracing the route once more. Chicago . . . Minneapolis . . . Wyoming . . . Portland . . . San Francisco. Why did Coop make those maps? Why did he want to go back? He must've had a reason.

Oh, Coop. I miss you so much. If you were here, I'd say, "Yes, let's go on that adventure!"

If only she could. She'd do it for Coop. But she didn't know how to ride a motorcycle, much less take such a trip by herself.

* * * *

"Let's go on that adventure, Sweetheart!"

Maggie sat straight up in bed. "Coop?" she called out. The bedroom was just beginning to lighten with morning's first light. But Coop's voice had awakened her, hadn't it? She listened. Just the faint hum of early morning traffic on the Eisenhower Expressway in the far distance.

Of course. Just a dream.

Rocky raised his head on the bed and looked at her, and then grunted before laying his head down again as if to say, "It's not time to get up yet, lady. Go back to sleep."

But Maggie slid out of bed, found her slippers, and tiptoed quietly into the upstairs hall. She was awake now. The dream, the refrain in her head, and a nudge from somewhere in her spirit prodded her down the stairs. Making her way to the fireplace mantle in the dim light, she picked up the brass urn with Coop's ashes and hugged it to her nightshirt. Taking it with her into the dining room, she gently set it down on top of the second map and murmured, "Where do you want to be buried, Coop?" Buried or scattered—they'd never talked about that. But just in case, she'd asked for an urn with a lid that screwed on and could be opened.

Let's go on that adventure, Sweetheart!

What if . . .

Would that give her the answer? But how? Was it even possible now that Coop was gone?

She glanced at the small oak table that served as her computer desk nestled beneath the tall bay windows. Pulling over one of the dining room chairs, Maggie opened the lid of her laptop. A tap to the "On" button, and the screen glowed.

Hunched over the computer, Maggie did a search. *Ah ha.* There were such places! She clicked on "Locations," and when the list came up, she typed in her own address to find the closest one to where she lived.

There! She copied down the address and phone number, shut down the laptop, and trundled quietly back up the stairs. She'd call in the morning after nine. Surely a place like that would be open by nine.

Chapter 9

Jiang was already gone by the time Maggie woke again. Eight-fifteen. Still too early to call. But by the time she'd showered, dressed, and chewed her way through a bowl of granola, her watch said 9:03.

Taking the piece of paper on which she'd written the phone number into the front hall, Maggie dialed from the home phone. But when it started ringing, she hung up. What in the world was she doing! This was silly. She was sixty-five, for Pete's sake!

Still, she argued with herself, it wouldn't hurt to call and get information. Then she could decide whether the idea tumbling around in her head was worth pursuing, or whether she was out-and-out crazy.

Maggie giggled. Mike and Stacy would definitely go with crazy. But Coop would love it.

She dialed again and forced herself to wait through one . . . two . . . three rings . . . four—

"Motorcycle Safety Foundation."

Maggie nearly dropped the receiver but managed to hang on. "Uh, yes. I'm wondering, uh, I'd like to know if there's a basic rider course near where I live." *There. I said it!*

"Which is . . .?"

"Uh, Oak Park, Illinois, Chicago area."

"Zip code?"

Maggie gave it.

"One moment." Silence on the other end for several moments. Then: "Ma'am, there are several facilities that offer our basic rider course in the Chicago area. I could send you the link with the various locations by email if you'd like."

"Oh, sure. Great." She spelled out her email address.

Five minutes later, Maggie squinted at a map on her computer screen that had little motorcycle icons sprinkled around the Chicago area. Clicking on the closest one to Oak Park, she got the phone number from its home page, sucked in a deep breath, and dialed.

The answer to her query was short and to the point. "I'm sorry. All our classes are filled for June and July. But we have a few spaces in August. Would you like to sign up for one of those?"

Maggie politely declined and hung up. Maybe that was a sign. This was a stupid idea, and she should give it up right now. Wandering into the kitchen she refilled her coffee, leaned against the counter, and stared into the dark liquid. *What? You're going to give up after one phone call? That's not like the Maggie I know!* She could almost hear Coop's voice in her head.

Okaaaay. Back at her laptop, phone in hand, she tried the next one. And the next one. Same answer. Classes full. Would she be interested in August? Or September?

She finally clicked on a Harley-Davidson facility in Glenview, a suburb just west of Wilmette where Stacy's family lived. "I'm sorry," the woman on the other end said. "Most of our classes are already full this summer—oh wait." Maggie heard little clicks as if the woman was navigating her computer. "Actually, we had a cancellation yesterday for our class next week. Would you be interested?"

Interested? I have no idea! I don't really know what I'm doing calling you! But she heard herself say, "Well, tell me what's involved. And how much is it?"

The woman's voice warmed up to her topic. "We offer a four-day course that meets Thursday and Friday evenings for the classroom part of the course. Then on Saturday and Sunday it's hands on all day, actually practicing with the bike." Ms. Harley-Davidson sounded relaxed, unhurried, as if chatting over coffee at a sidewalk café. No, Maggie didn't need to have a bike, they provided basic Harleys and helmets for each student. No, they didn't ride in the street, they practiced in a large parking lot. Maggie would need to wear long pants, long sleeves, and boots that covered the ankles. The cost was $350. "Oh, and you need to get a motorcycle learner's permit in order to take the class. Can you do that by next week?"

Maggie swallowed. "Uh, do you have an age limit? I've never ridden a motorcycle before except as a passenger. And I'm, uh, sixty-five."

The laughter on the other end was friendly, not derisive. "Oh, honey, good for you. Why, my oldest student was in his seventies! You'll do fine."

* * * *

Learner's permit. I need a motorcycle learner's permit.

Maggie's cheeks were flaming as the last person in front of her at the driver's license facility stepped away from the counter, and it was her turn. *Don't mumble,* she told herself. *Act like it's the most normal thing in the world.* "I'd like to apply for, uh, um, a motorcycle learner's permit." *Drat!* She still stumbled over the words.

The middle-aged woman in the half-moon glasses behind the counter didn't bat an eye. "Here's the form." She pushed a paper toward Maggie. "You'll need documentation of your birthdate, legal status, and social security number. Do you have an Illinois driver's license?"

Maggie nodded and started to fish in her fanny pack for her wallet.

The clerk held up her hand. "Not now. We'll check your documentation after you fill out the form. Would you like to take the written test now? Or—" She handed Maggie a booklet titled *Illinois Motorcycle Operator Manual.* "—you can take this home and study it if you'd prefer." Her voice implied, *That would be a good idea.*

"Uh, sure, I'll study it and come back." Maggie stuffed the booklet and application into her carryall and scuttled back out to the parking lot.

She blew out a long breath. *Whew.* Okay, this was good. She could study the manual over the weekend and go back on Monday to take the written exam. Hopefully she'd have her learner's permit when the basic rider course started next Thursday.

If she decided to go through with it, that is.

The light was flashing on her answering machine when she got back to the house. She pushed the button. "Hi, Maggie. This is Dr. Emery. Do you still want to talk about some volunteer hours at the clinic? We could set up an appointment next week. Give me a call when you're ready." *Click.*

Hmph. 'Dr. Emery' indeed. When did Jeff Emery get so formal? At least he'd gotten back to her. Well, she'd call next week. Right now, she had to study for that written exam. When was the last time she'd had to take the written exam just to renew her driver's license? Ages. Probably a good thing to review all the rules of the road and stuff like that.

But the manual wasn't "stuff like that." As she paged through the booklet, Maggie realized it was all "motorcycle stuff." Getting familiar with the controls. Shifting gears. (What? Using your feet?) Protective clothing. Riding at night. Swerving around obstacles. Stuck throttle. Riding with passengers.

O dear Lord. What am I doing? This IS crazy.

Well. She could toss the manual *and* the idea, and nobody would be the wiser.

Feeling a sense of relief, Maggie shook her head to clear her mind and busied herself cooking supper for herself and Jiang, who should be home by six or six-thirty. Friday night—she and Coop had gotten into the habit of having fish on Friday nights, even though they weren't Catholic. He'd studied up on why the first Christians ate fish on Friday as part of the weekly "fasts," which consisted of abstaining from rich foods—and fish was considered a poor person's food. Whatever. It felt good to continue some of their traditions and habits.

She heard Jiang come through the front door. "*Ni hao*, Mrs. Cooper!" he called. "Something smells very good!" The young Chinese student wandered into the kitchen, still wearing his bulging backpack. "Ah! Fish. Excellent. We are feasting tonight, I see."

Maggie gave him a warm smile. "Ready in five minutes—oh." She saw him pick up the motorcycle manual from the kitchen counter. Oh dear. She didn't mean to leave it out. Should've thrown it in the recycle bin!

"Mrs. Cooper!" Jiang's mouth widened in a happy smile. "You are going to learn to ride Mr. Cooper's motorcycle?"

"Oh, that." She flitted a hand in front of her face as if brushing away a fly. "I was just curious. Nothing really."

"Oh, but Mrs. Cooper. The mister would be so happy for you to learn about his bike! Come! Come! I can show you."

Still holding the manual, Jiang headed for the back door, lifting the garage key from its hook on his way out. "Jiang! Wait!" Maggie cried, just as the timer for the fish went off, but he was gone. With a sigh, Maggie pulled the fish out of the oven, covered it with a lid, turned off the other pots on the stove, and followed.

Jiang was already looking over the bike, glancing back and forth from it to the manual. When Maggie came into the garage, he handed the manual to her, which was turned to the page showing various parts of the motorcycle. "See? It is not exactly the same, but the book will help. Here—" He started to point to various parts of the bike. "This is the gas tank . . . speedometer . . ."

Good grief. She knew where the gas tank and speedometer were, even back when she was a passenger on Coop's old Harley.

". . . over here, the throttle and front brake lever." Jiang laid his hand on the handgrip of the right handlebar and squeezed the lever. "And on the left side of the handlebar, the clutch."

Okay, now he was into unfamiliar territory. She tried to focus.

"Rear brake—this foot pedal on the right side. And on the left side, the gear change foot lever . . ."

Now her head was swimming. Front brake—a lever on the handle bar. But rear brake, a foot pedal? Clutch on the handlebar, but you used your foot to change gears? *O God, help. I'll never be able to do this!*

"Of course, you will," Jiang encouraged. "You learned to drive a car, didn't you?"

Wait—had she said that out loud?

The young man held up an ignition key. "Do you want to start it?"

Maggie swallowed and forced a smile. "Not now, Jiang. I appreciate what you have shown me. But, uh, supper is ready— let's eat before the fish gets cold. Maybe you can show me more this weekend." *Or not. Hmph.* Learning to ride Coop's rehabbed bike and getting a motorcycle permit was ludicrous.

* * * *

Saturday was destined to be sunny and mild, a perfect early June day, but Maggie hadn't done a darn thing yet except make the coffee and munch a piece of toast. She stood at the bank of windows in the sunroom with a mid-morning cup of coffee, staring at the garage. What was she so afraid of? What would Coop think of her if she backed down now, before even trying?

She fingered his note in her pocket. She didn't need to read it, had it memorized backwards and forwards. *Happy Birthday, Sweetheart! Let's go on that adventure! Love, Coop.* His last words to her.

Get a grip Maggie, she told herself. *You practically have a tutor living in your own house. It's just a written test, for goodness sake. Read the manual, let Jiang question you, take the test on Monday, get your permit. It's only ten dollars. Not a big loss if you don't actually get your license.* "Right, Rocky?" She gave the dog a good scratch behind his ears.

Jiang was studying in his room, but when she knocked and asked if he'd help her study for the learner's permit, he practically knocked his books off the desk in his hurry to pick up where they'd left off last evening.

"Whoa!" Maggie laughed, waving him back to his seat. "Not right now. I have to study the book first. Maybe after lunch?"

Chapter 10

MAGGIE CLIMBED BACK IN HER CAR Monday morning in the DMV parking lot and just sat for several minutes, windows down. Both the temperature and the humidity had climbed over the weekend. But she wasn't thinking about the weather. She stared at the card-stock piece of paper in her hand. "Punch out the card, keep it in your wallet," the woman at the counter had advised.

The card in the corner said: "Class M Motorcycle Learner's Permit. Margaret Ruth Cooper." And her birthdate: "May 23, 1950." The rest of the page had other information. *Good for 12 months. May operate a motorcycle only during daylight hours. Under direct supervision of a licensed motorcycle driver.*

Maggie giggled. She couldn't help it. She'd passed the written test with a 92 percent! Only got two wrong. "Good job," the instructor had said. *Thank you, Jiang.* Passed her vision test, too—with her contacts. "But you'll need goggles or a full-face helmet," the instructor had advised. A motorcycle helmet was optional in Illinois. *Really?* Every time Maggie had passed a motorcyclist—or more usually, been passed *by* a motorcyclist—without a helmet, she'd thought, *"How stupid is that!"*

The helmet Coop had bought for her was full face.

Maggie punched out the card and slid it into her wallet in front of her driver's license. Then she turned the key in the ignition of the Subaru and headed for home.

Now what? She'd signed up for the basic rider course later in the week but hadn't paid any money yet. The woman had said just bring a check Thursday night. She still had a few days to decide if she was going to do it.

Next on her "To Do List" was call Dr. Emery and set up an appointment to talk about volunteering at the clinic—but why not just drop in? It was on her way home. But it felt strange pulling into the clinic parking lot a short while later. She'd parked in this lot for seventeen years in the spaces marked "Staff." Now she parked in a space marked "Visitor." Maggie sighed. Would she ever get used to being retired?

"Sister Maggie!" Karen Watson beamed at her from behind the receptionist's desk as she came through the double glass doors. "What brings you back to Good Neighbor?" The young woman bounced up from her chair and came around the desk to give Maggie a big hug. Three women in the reception area looked up from the magazines they were flipping through, two of whom looked familiar.

"What are you doing out here in reception?" Maggie felt a sudden surge of protectiveness. She'd assumed her former secretary would retain her same job when the new COO took over Maggie's position. Had Karen been demoted? If she had, Jeff Emery was going to get an earful—

"Oh, just filling in today. Celia's out sick." Karen looked her up and down with a practiced eye from years of working together. "You doing okay since that wonderful man of yours passed?"

Maggie managed a nod as her internal temperature returned to normal. "Not easy, but yes, okay. Is, uh, Dr. Emery in? I don't have an appointment. Was supposed to call, but dropped in instead."

"Think so. I'll give him a ring." Karen returned to her phone, punched in an extension, talked to whoever picked up, then nodded at Maggie. "He says come on back."

A few moments later Maggie walked into Jeff Emery's office. She apologized for dropping in instead of calling before she even said hello. "I was just, uh, in the neighborhood so—"

"No, no, it's fine. Good to see you, Maggie. Have a seat."

Jeff Emery was still a nice-looking man at fifty-seven, a full shock of dark hair that was turning silver at the temples. Maggie patiently went through the "how are you doing" and "so sorry about Coop" chit-chat for a few minutes, then abruptly said, "Do you have a volunteer position for me, Jeff?"

Her former boss folded his hands on the desk. "Not a position per se, no. But we could use a sub—someone like you who knows the whole operation of the clinic and could fill in anywhere. Not for the RNs, of course, but the nurse techs, as well as various administration or support services." He gestured toward the front of the building. "As you noticed, we had to pull Karen off her job as Mrs. Wilson's assistant to cover reception this morning."

"Sub for the janitor, too?" Maggie kept a straight face.

"Ha ha. No. The agency usually sends someone to cover for Herb if he gets sick." Dr. Emery eyed Maggie across the desk. "What do you think? You'd have to be flexible—we don't usually know when someone's going to get sick! But vacations, days off, hospital stays—we should know that ahead of time. Oh—Saturdays. You know how busy we can get Saturdays. Even when we have full staff, we can always use an extra hand to fill in."

Maggie pursed her lips thoughtfully. This wasn't exactly what she had in mind. She was more project-minded—like brainstorming new ways to promote the clinic, or upgrade one of the examining rooms, or convert the old filing system to a digital program—where she could let her creative juices flow. Not answering the phone.

Still . . .

"In fact, we could really use you this Saturday. One of our nurse techs will be out of town at a family wedding." Jeff Emery's full eyebrows lifted questioningly. "You game?"

Saturday. Nurse tech. Mostly patient care, taking vitals, recording patient history, all the pre-exam stuff she'd done many times over the years when they needed an extra hand. She opened her mouth to say yes—when she suddenly remembered. The basic rider course. The hands-on-actually-riding-a-motorcycle was all day *this* Saturday and Sunday.

"I—I'm sorry, Jeff. I'm not available this Saturday."

Wait—did I really say that?

The doctor looked surprised. "Ah. Already busy in your retirement?"

Maggie almost said, *"I'm taking a class."* But then he'd ask politely, what class? Yeah, right. No way was she going to say, *"Learning to ride a motorcycle."* So, she just nodded her head and said, "Sorry."

She stood up. "And I need some time to think about being a sub. Had been hoping for something a little more regular—you know, ten to fifteen hours a week, three days a week or something. But I really appreciate the offer. Just need to think about the flexibility needed, how that would work with my new schedule."

Jeff also stood up and extended his hand. "Of course. Just let me know. And if you change your mind about Saturday, we could really use you."

* * * *

Maggie really needed a cup of tea. Her hand shook as she took a mug from the cupboard and turned the heat on under the teakettle. Turning down Jeff Emery's offer to come in Saturday was tantamount to making a definite decision to take the basic rider course this weekend. But saying yes to the offer would be tantamount to giving up the whole idea of learning to ride. The fact that the Harley-Davidson place had an opening this week was serendipity. All the other facilities she'd called had been full for the next two or three months.

Rocky whined, sitting on his haunches beside the kitchen counter and looking up at her as she poured hot water over her Earl Grey tea bag. "Yeah, me too, Rocky." Rocky would love to ride in the sidecar. But speaking of the sidecar, would learning to ride a two-wheeler equip her to drive a cycle-sidecar combination? It had to be different, more stable, three wheels on the ground. Would she be wasting her money on the basic rider course?

She should call that lady back at the Harley-Davidson place and ask.

* * * *

The next day, Maggie's insides still felt like a taffy machine, pulled in all different directions. Should she sub at the Good Neighbor clinic? Could she limit the subbing to just certain days or so many hours? Should she go to the class on Thursday night? When she called, the Harley-Davidson woman said the course would be valuable even for those who wanted to ride a three-wheeler—like learning to drive a car with manual transmission, even if later you'd drive an automatic. That way you were good to go on either—though, the woman admitted, there were some differences for sidecar drivers that Maggie would need to learn. But how would she learn those differences?

Maggie's internal gymnastics were interrupted by a call from Stacy. "So. Mom. Shall we do lunch again this week and then go through more of Dad's stuff? I don't have any houses to show on Thursday this week. Good day for you?"

"Uh, Stace, can you hold on a minute?" Maggie put the phone on mute, took a deep breath, and counted to twenty. She needed a moment to think. Just then Rocky whined at the back door. "Good timing, Rocky," she murmured and let him out. Now she didn't have to make up an excuse for making her daughter wait. She released the mute button. "Sorry, hon. Had to let the dog out. Uh, what were you saying?"

"Thursday. I'm free that day. Let's have lunch and pack up some more of Dad's things."

"I'm not sure I'll be free. Just talked to Dr. Emery yesterday, they want me to sub at the clinic."

"Sub? At the clinic? You're kidding. They're going to pay you, right?"

"Well, no. I'd told them I wanted to volunteer."

"Mom! That's like being a substitute teacher! Especially since you'll probably get calls at six a.m. asking if you can come in that day. They definitely should pay you! What kind of retirement is that? You won't be able to plan anything!"

Maggie nodded at the phone. Definite downsides to being a sub.

"So, they've already asked you to come in Thursday?"

"Well, no. But they might. If I take this, uh, job, I don't want to say no the very first week." Besides, Maggie thought, the class started Thursday night. That was enough stress for one day.

"But Mom! Chad and I will be gone the whole month of July. You don't want to wait clear till August to take care of some of these things. Like, what about that relic out in the garage? It's no good to you. It only brings heartache, since Dad was working on it when he died. Like I said, you don't have to deal with it. I'm sure I can sell it on e-bay or Craig's List or something."

Maggie felt her back stiffen. Stacy needed to get her nose out of where it didn't belong. She was tired of pussyfooting around. "That 'relic,' as you called it, is my business, Stacy. Mine and Coop's. There are things you don't know anything about. So, please. Like I've said before, I'll take care of the motorcycle when I'm good and ready."

"What do you mean, there're things I don't know anything about? Mom—"

"I'm sorry, Stacy. I can't do lunch this week. I've got several things I need to think about and make decisions about. I need time to think. And pray." Yeah, she needed to pray. Hadn't been doing too much of that lately. "But I know you're just trying to help. How about next week? Let's look for a day next week to get together, okay?"

"Mom—"

"Thanks for calling, honey. Love you. 'Bye."

Maggie hung up the phone, surprised at herself. It wasn't easy standing up to Stacy. No wonder her daughter was the top-selling agent at her real estate firm.

She heard scratching at the back door and let Rocky in. "What d'ya think, Rocky? I just hung up on Stacy. Now Reagan and I will both be in the doghouse—oops, sorry, buddy." But she giggled. Couldn't help it.

The dog looked up at her, the little black "eyebrows" above his big brown eyes twitching like question marks. She bent down and took his face in her hands. "Hey, buddy. How about you and me going shopping? Gotta get you some goggles if you're going to ride in that sidecar."

Chapter 11

WELL, THAT WAS PREMATURE. PetSmart didn't have any goggles for dogs. Neither did the closest PetCo. But the manager there recommended "Doggles," told Maggie she could find them online, which she did once they got home. But just before clicking on a pair of red medium-size dog goggles, Maggie shut down the site. Good grief. She was acting as if she'd actually decided to keep the bike and sidecar—

The house phone rang. ID said Good Neighbor Medical Center. "Hello?"

"Maggie." It was Jeff Emery. "Don't mean to bother you so soon after we talked yesterday. I know you need time to consider, but—"

"But you want me to sub for somebody tomorrow."

Her former boss sounded embarrassed. "If you could. Celia is still out sick, and Karen has covered the front desk for two days, but needs to get back to her regular work."

Maggie hesitated. She felt torn. It felt good to be needed. It'd feel good to get back into the hustle and bustle of the clinic. Might help fill that big empty place inside that ached day and night since Coop died. But she didn't want to feel pressured to take a job "subbing." Like Stacy said, it would be hard to plan anything—always on call, whether they called or not.

"Maggie? You still there?"

"I'm sorry, Jeff. Trying to think. Tell you what. I'll sub for Celia tomorrow. *Only* tomorrow. I've got a lot going on the rest of the week. And I need more time to consider what subbing might mean. It's not what I had in mind when I said I'd like to volunteer."

"I know, Maggie. But we're in a bit of a crunch here."

"The clinic's always in a bit of a crunch, Jeff."

"I know. But, well, thanks for tomorrow. See you at seven?"

* * * *

By the end of the next day, Maggie was clear about one thing: the receptionist for a medical clinic serving a population that didn't have anywhere else to turn for medical care—many of whom didn't have any medical insurance *or* childcare if mommy needed to see the doctor—was underappreciated and certainly underpaid. In the few weeks she'd been away from the clinic, she'd almost forgotten the crunch times when walk-ins with a nasty glass cut or a broken arm or a kid with a 105 fever jammed the already full schedule of people with appointments. On top of fielding anxious questions about meds and symptoms, fetching water for a woman with a hacking cough, and answering the phone that seemed to ring constantly, she ended up entertaining a bevy of kids when their moms went in to see the doctor or nurse. And the clinic's AC had a hard time keeping up with the ninety-degree temperature outside that Wednesday.

Maybe she was older than she thought.

She was making a list of things the reception area could use— more kids books, coloring books and crayons, a few stuffed animals, a set of matchbox cars, some puzzles, donated copies of *Reader's Digest*—when Jeff Emery stopped by at the end of the day to thank her for filling in. But she held up her hand when he opened his mouth. "If you're going to say Celia is still sick and will I come in tomorrow, the answer is no. I already have several things scheduled for the rest of the week."

Dr. Emery grinned ruefully. "Okay. Got it. But thanks for today, Maggie. We do miss you around here."

Maggie just nodded and waved goodbye as she hustled out to her car, squelching the temptation to ask how Mrs. Wilson was doing taking over her old job. None of her business really. And scratch puzzles off the list. Too many pieces to get lost.

* * * *

Maggie left a note on the kitchen counter for Jiang the next afternoon with a few supper options and left the house at 4:30. The basic rider class was scheduled for 5:30 p.m., and she wasn't sure how long it would take her to drive to Glenview, especially if there was rush hour traffic or construction on the way.

But traffic wasn't too bad on the I-294 tollway north, and the phone call she'd gotten from Sister Regina Harris at Grace and Mercy last night nudged its way back into her thoughts. "Sister Maggie! Girl, this is the sixth or seventh prayer meetin' you've missed since Brother Coop passed."

You're counting? Maggie had thought, a little annoyed.

"Honey, I know what you're goin' through 'cause I've buried two of my sisters and a brother in the past ten years. But this is no time to hide yourself away from your spiritual family. Two is better'n one, and three even better—the Holy Book says that somewhere."

"I'm sorry, Sister Regina—"

"Maggie, honey, you don't have to 'pologize to *me*! It's you I'm thinkin' about."

"I meant I'm sorry for your loss—your brother and sisters. That's rough."

"Well, thanks, sweetie. They're in a better place now, no more sufferin'."

Maggie's back had stiffened. *Don't go there with Coop, Sister Regina.* Well-meaning comments like that were one of the reasons she'd been avoiding weeknight meetings at Grace and Mercy Community Church. Navigating Sunday morning was enough right now—though she'd actually considered going last night, missing the good Bible study discussions led by Pastor Eric and the warmth of her church friends. But the grueling day at the clinic yesterday plus the rising heat and humidity had drained the last bit of energy out of her system by the time she got home. Still, she'd thanked her friend and told her she'd try and make it next week.

"Well, all right, honey. You call me if you need anything, y'hear?"

Sister Regina's words echoed in her head as Maggie saw the sign for the exit to Willow Road. The Harley-Davidson place should be just a mile or two now. She wondered what her friend would say if she called and said, "Sister Regina, I need prayer about this cross-country motorcycle trip Coop wanted us to do. He bought me a leather jacket and helmet, and I'm taking a class to learn how to ride . . ." Ha! The no-nonsense ER nurse would probably blister her ear. As a trauma nurse, Regina Harris had no doubt seen her share of motorcycle injuries where she worked at Stroger Hospital—or "County" as everyone still called it.

The Harley-Davidson sign on a big industrial-size building came into view. Maggie pulled into the parking lot near the front entrance and walked through the glass doors. *Oh. My.* The huge showroom was wall-to-wall motorcycles. A burly guy in a black Harley-Davidson T-shirt called out, "Can I help you, ma'am?"

"I'm, uh, here for the class?"

"Right. Go through those double doors back there and turn right. The classroom is right there—you'll see it."

Feeling self-conscious, Maggie threaded her way through more bikes than she'd ever seen in her life and pushed through the double doors into what looked like the service area.

A young man with blonde whiskers on his chin looked up from a bike he was working on. "Class meets in there," jerking a thumb to her right.

The classroom was brightly lit, and already several other people sat around the tables pushed into a U-shape. A gleaming black Harley with strange orange parts sticking out here and there stood off to one side. A woman in her forties with a long, blonde ponytail strode over to Maggie and stuck out her hand. "Hi! I'm Katie Sharp. You are . . .?"

"Uh, Maggie Cooper. I called last week. You had a last-minute opening for this class."

"Right! Glad you could make it. Here, fill out this application." The woman picked out a sheet of paper from a stacker and handed it to Maggie. "You can turn it in at the end of the class with your check. Or credit card. We can do either."

Maggie took a seat along the near side of the U. A few more people filed into the classroom. Maggie counted noses—six men of varying ages, a pert young woman with a pixie haircut who couldn't be a day over twenty-five, and herself. Eight students. She thought the class would be bigger. Wouldn't be easy to hide in the back row here.

The teacher, Katie, got down to business. "I think we're all here. If you haven't done it yet, fill out those name tags, and then let's introduce ourselves. We're going to spend the next four days together, and we're all going to need some encouragement from our classmates. Dan?" She pointed to a man opposite Maggie. "Why don't you start?"

Dan—dark-haired, clean-shaven—was an accountant who had a couple friends who were encouraging him to get a bike and join their motorcycle club. "I don't have a bike yet. Thought I'd take the class first, see if it's what I want to do."

"Smart move." Ms. Sharp nodded her approval. "Next—Dessi, is it?"

Dessi was the cute twenty-something. Her dad rode a cycle, she said, and wanted her to learn so they could ride together. Maggie was impressed. Dad and daughter. How cool was that?

Jack had salt-and-pepper hair, thinning on top, nearing retirement, and said learning to ride a motorcycle was at the top of his bucket list.

Tony—in his late twenties or early thirties—had already bought himself a big Harley Road King. "Are you sure I can't bring it in and learn to ride on it?" He nodded at the model sitting in the classroom. "I mean, it's twice as big as that thing."

Maggie pegged him as a braggart. But Katie Sharp said mildly, "Sorry. Best if everyone learns on the same model." She looked at her clipboard. "Carlos?"

Carlos said he'd had a motorcycle briefly in his late teens, crashed it, and hadn't ridden in the past thirty years. "Thought I'd do it right this time." Laughter circled the room.

Mick and Trey were friends who'd signed up together. Mick's wife wouldn't let him get a motorcycle unless they both took a safety class first. Katie Sharp grinned. "Smart woman." She nodded at Maggie. "Last but not least, our newest signup."

Maggie cleared her throat. "My, uh, late husband was restoring a vintage BMW with a sidecar, hoping we could take a cross-country road trip when I retired. Now I have a motorcycle but no husband." Whoa! Way too much information. "Anyway, I decided to learn to ride as a way to honor his wishes. Not sure about the road trip though."

She heard a few sympathetic murmurs, even a few nervous chuckles. *Ouch.* She needed to work on her elevator pitch. But Tony—he of the big Harley Road King—crowed, "Oh, lady! You definitely oughta do the road trip!" A few others nodded.

Thankfully, Katie Sharp intervened. "Thanks, everyone. Dan, would you help me pass out these handbooks? We'll cover as much information as we can the next two evenings before you actually get on the bikes Saturday, but you'll also need to study on your own . . ."

A few of the guys seemed a bit impatient with some of the initial information—preparing to ride, wearing protective gear, inspecting the machine, risk awareness, mental attitude—but Maggie soaked up everything like a sponge. If she'd learned anything over the course of her life, it was that attitude and confidence and being prepared made a huge difference in applying acquired skills in the best way.

But Ms. Sharp was a good instructor, using the model motorcycle as a visual as they talked about the various controls and their different functions. The orange metal parts screwed strategically here and there were protectors to keep the bike from getting damaged if a student tipped it over or let it drop. Maggie took a picture of the bike with her cell phone to study later along with the handbook. They covered starting and stopping the engine, using the clutch and finding the "friction zone," shifting, turning, braking—all of which the instructor reviewed the second night before moving on to street strategies for staying alive while riding among whizzing cars and huge trucks that could make you feel like a pencil in a lumberyard.

The confidence Maggie felt at the end of the first class was shaken by the discussion the second night on emergency stops, skidding on ice or gravel, and swerving to avoid debris in the road or cars backing out of driveways. "But it's basically the same as preparing yourself for the unknown when learning to ride a bicycle or drive a car," Katie said. "Thinking ahead to possible problem situations and practicing what to do can save your life."

The instructor eyed the clock. "Okay, that's it, everybody. See you bright and early tomorrow morning." Handbooks slapped shut. "Be here before eight o'clock wearing long pants, long sleeves, boots that cover the ankle, and gloves—not too bulky, not too tight. If you have your own helmet, fine. But we'll provide helmets *and* motorcycles."

Nervous laughter as they all filed out.

Maggie's mind was swimming as she drove home that evening. She could probably take a written motorcycle test and get most of the answers right. So far it was all "book learnin'"—like when she took Spanish in college. She could learn vocabulary, read simple sentences, and say a number of phrases helpful to the average tourist. But to actually *speak* Spanish? Or carry on a conversation with someone who spoke Spanish fluently? Like night and day.

But tomorrow was the real deal—getting on a motorcycle and making it move without crashing into anything or falling over. Should she quit now while she was ahead? A good "book learnin'" student? An armchair motorcyclist?

It was tempting.

But her own unrehearsed "elevator speech" the first night about why she was taking the basic rider class pushed itself into the front of her thoughts. *"I decided to learn to ride as a way to honor his wishes."*

There it was.

Maggie turned on her blinker as her exit for Oak Park came into view. "Okay, Coop," she breathed. "This is for you."

And just before she crawled into bed a while later, she set her alarm for 5:30.

Chapter 12

MAGGIE WAS TOO NERVOUS TO EAT BREAKFAST on Saturday, but she tucked an extra nut bar for a pick-me-up if needed into the bag lunch she was supposed to bring today. She checked the way she was dressed: jeans, ankle boots, long-sleeve shirt, jean jacket. Hopefully that would do. She'd bring the new leather jacket along just in case, but the day promised to be hot. The only sturdy gloves she had were gardening gloves. Maybe she should buy a pair of actual riding gloves today at the Harley-Davidson place. At least she had a helmet.

She glanced at her watch—only 6:30 a.m. Still had a few minutes before she had to leave. Time to calm herself and enjoy the fresh mug of coffee she'd just poured.

Letting Rocky out into the backyard, Maggie curled up in the wicker rocker on the sun porch and stared out the large windows toward the garage where Coop's restored BMW sat, waiting. Would she be able to ride it after learning on a Harley?

Sipping her coffee, she noticed her Bible and prayer journal sitting on the small side table next to the rocker. Mostly untouched this past week. *Good grief*. Had she even *prayed* about learning to ride Coop's bike? Or about taking this riding course? About whether she should even take this cross-country trip Coop had mapped out for them? What was God's opinion about all this?

After all, the point of it all wasn't to learn how to ride a motorcycle. The point was . . .

Huh. What *was* the point?

Maggie set down her coffee cup and sighed. Better get going. She let the dog in, left a note for Jiang, stuffed her lunch, wallet, and keys in her tote bag, and started toward the front door. But in the dining room she paused at the two maps still laid out on the table. Her eye followed the yellow line highlighting the route from Chicago to Portland, and then down the coast. But the roads Coop had highlighted weren't the important thing. It was the places he'd circled—the places they'd grown up, and places they'd spent time trying to serve God in their life together. Those places were the point—except she wasn't sure why.

But she *was* sure of one thing: She wouldn't know why unless—until—she went.

* * * *

Sweat trickled down Maggie's face under the full-face helmet Coop had bought for her. She'd expected Ms. Sharp to be the instructor, but instead the students were met by two beefy guys named Pete and Bob who looked like typical bikers. Pete wore faded jeans belted under a sagging beer belly, and a red bandana covered most of his head except for a long skinny ponytail that hung halfway down his back. Bob had a scruffy salt-and-pepper beard and was dressed in leathers—leather jacket, leather chaps, boots with silver chains.

The bikes were lined up waiting for them in the large parking lot behind the Harley-Davidson showroom when Maggie and the other students arrived. Each bike had a white nameplate on the front with their first names written in black erasable marker. Maggie stood nervously beside the bike with her name as Pete and Bob introduced themselves and gave them an overview of the day. In spite of their tough-guy looks, the instructors' steady, even voices had a calming effect on the group.

"Even if you've ridden a bike before," Pete said, eyeing the group, "forget everything you think you know because we're going to start at the beginning, nice and slow." He backed up a few paces. "Stand beside your bike, grab the handlebars, and put up the kickstand. Now, ignition on, start the bike!"

Maggie swallowed and strained to follow each instruction. *Slowly release the clutch* (left hand!) *making sure gear is in neutral. Rev the throttle* (right hand!), *but keep your hand off the brake lever! Now push the bike.* Maggie huffed a little pushing the machine, hoping it would not take off on its own without a rider.

When they'd regrouped, Bob got on his own demo bike as Pete talked about "finding the friction zone," that magic catch between clutch and first gear. She watched closely as Bob rocked the bike back and forth, then used his left foot to move the gearshift lever down a notch to first gear and his right hand to gently twist the throttle. "Bob's gonna walk the bike while he's on it," Pete said, "but he's letting the motorcycle do the work. It's called 'power walking.'" The students watched as Bob power-walked his bike to the end of the lot and back again.

"Okay," Pete hollered. "Mount up."

The moment of truth. She was actually going to get on the motorcycle. Awkwardly, Maggie got her right leg over the bike and slid onto the seat, feeling an unexpected thrill to actually be sitting on the Harley.

If only Coop could see me now.

Bob rode his bike to the end of the lot and waited there as Pete told the group to "power walk" their bikes to the far end of the parking lot, and back again. Then: "Do it again! Get used to how it feels when the clutch engages!"

Maggie tried not to giggle. Felt like riding a kiddie kart when she was three, pushing it along with her feet—except she didn't push. She let the engine move the bike as she engaged the clutch.

The third time Pete called out, "This time, feet up! When you need to stop, remember to use *both* the hand and foot brakes."

Like the others, Maggie started the bike by power-walking a few steps, and then lifted her boots onto the foot pegs. Her heart pounded as the bike kept moving forward. She was actually riding the thing! But in her excitement, she must've twisted the throttle because the bike suddenly leaped forward. Brakes! Brakes! Where were the brakes! She squeezed the right brake lever and lurched to a stop, almost sending her body over the handlebars.

Bob came running toward her. "You okay, darlin'?"

Maggie nodded shakily, ignoring the "darlin'." "What'd I do?"

Bob grinned through his beard. "Probably gave the throttle a good twist. Don't worry, you'll get the hang of it. Just gotta coordinate the clutch, gearshift, and the throttle as you increase your speed."

Uh huh. "Just . . ."

After a few more practice runs, Pete called a break, handing out icy bottles of water from a cooler. Several of the students chatted or laughed nervously, but Maggie and the others sank onto the grass at the edge of the parking lot, removed their helmets, and drank thirstily. Learning to ride was hard work.

* * * *

Maggie was so tired when she got home that evening, she fell asleep on the couch. She woke to Rocky's whine near her ear and a semi-darkened house. *Uhhh,* what time was it? Struggling to sit up, she realized someone—Jiang, obviously—had covered her with an afghan. The ticking schoolhouse clock said almost ten o'clock. What? She hadn't eaten any supper, hadn't taken Rocky for a walk, hadn't taken off her riding clothes—and now it was bedtime.

"Sorry, boy," she murmured to the dog as she shuffled her way to the kitchen and flipped on the light. "You'll just have to do your business in the yard tonight." She intended to grab a banana to tide her over till morning and just go upstairs to bed. But a plate of food covered with aluminum foil sat on the counter with "For Mrs. Cooper" written on a scrap of paper next to it. She lifted the foil. *Mmm.* Fried rice tossed with bits of egg, vegetables, and chicken. Looked homemade.

Maggie was suddenly very hungry, and it only took two minutes to warm the food in the microwave.

But once in bed a half hour later, Maggie couldn't fall asleep. Over and over her mind replayed that day's riding lessons. Pairing up—her partner was Carlos, the one who'd crashed a bike in his late teens—they'd practiced starting and stopping, starting and stopping, again and again around the parking lot. Then shifting from first to second, second to third. Carlos was super cautious, which made Maggie feel a bit superior as she finally began to get the hang of shifting smoothly and rumbling around the parking lot at thirty miles per hour.

Until the next lesson—swerving. Dividing the students into two groups, Pete and Bob had placed staggered plastic cones up and down each side of the parking lot, and showed them how to ride in and out of the cones, swerving to avoid the cones. Maggie knocked over her share of cones on her first few tries, forgot to shift down, forgot to use both the hand and foot brake simultaneously, making her ride as jerky as her first childhood attempts at riding a two-wheeler—except with a quarter-ton machine between her legs.

But at the end of the day, she'd warmed to Pete's "Good job, Maggie. You're getting there." Well, yeah. At least she hadn't dropped the bike or crashed into anything or anybody. That counted for something, right?

She finally fell asleep with, *"Good job, Maggie. You're getting there"* whispering in her mind. Except it sounded like Coop's voice. *"Good job, Maggie."*

* * * *

"Congratulations, Maggie." Pete's face widened in a grin beneath the red bandana as he handed her a signed certificate. "You passed the course. Ready to get that license?"

It was the end of the second, long day on the riding course. While the congregation at Grace and Mercy Community Church had been swaying and clapping to praise and worship songs that Sunday, she'd been astraddle her basic Harley reviewing all the lessons from the day before, plus mini-lectures and demonstrations on pre-ride checks, using proper signals, picking up a bike that's fallen over.

"You've got the basics. Now you just need to practice till it's second nature," Bob and Pete had drilled into them, making them do just that: starting, stopping, shifting up, shifting down, turning wide, turning tight, swerving. And doing it again.

It had rained during the night, and even though the temperature didn't break eighty-nine, the humidity was a hundred percent and she'd sweated right through her clothes till she was sure she'd have to peel them off.

All the students had passed—even hot-dog Tony, who'd kept bragging about the big Harley Road King he'd bought, until Bob told him to shut up and learn to ride the basic cruiser they used for the course. Maggie had felt a bit smug when Tony knocked over more plastic cones than she had.

But, she too joined the giddy laughter and high fives as the students gathered up their gear and headed for their cars, certificates in hand. Completion of an IDOT-approved motorcycle education course would waive both the riding and written parts of the exam needed to get an actual license.

Throwing her tote bag and helmet into the backseat of the Subaru, Maggie turned her cell phone back on. Good grief! Why did she have so many messages? Two voicemails—one from her pharmacy, another from Jiang Liu. A "missed call" from an unlisted number. Three text messages from Stacy. Well, they could all wait until she got home—on second thought, she should listen to Jiang's voicemail in case something was wrong at home.

Nope. Her boarder just wanted to let her know he wouldn't be home for supper tonight, as he'd been invited to a birthday party for another seminary student. *Huh.* If only her kids had been that responsible when they lived at home, letting her know where they were going, when they'd be home. But she was a little disappointed. It'd be nice if she could tell someone about her big accomplishment this weekend. Jiang would be excited for her. And besides, she had something important to ask him.

Should she tell the kids? Mike or Stacy? Um, no. Not yet. Reagan? Her granddaughter would probably do a Snoopy happy dance and show up wanting a ride. Too risky. Maggie wasn't ready for her family to know what she was thinking. They'd try to talk her out of it, and she felt shaky enough, she might give in.

But once home she did text Stacy. *Sorry, my phone was turned off. Everything okay?* A few minutes later her phone rang as she opened a can of tomato soup to go with the toasted cheese sandwich she was making. Stacy . . .

"Mom! You can't turn your phone off. What if something happened to you? Or we need to get hold of you?"

Maggie turned the flame on under the pan of tomato soup. "Nice to hear from you, too, Stacy. What's up?"

"Oh, it's *Reagan*, of course. She's still making a fuss about going to summer camp. Refusing to go. Says she could stay with you while we're gone. Of course, I told her that's not an option—though, uh, I thought I might run that idea by you, just in case. I didn't tell *her* that I'm asking you—well, not really asking you, Mom. Just, you know, wondering what you think, just in case she pulls one of her stubborn stunts and actually refuses to go. We can't leave her home *alone*."

Maggie was speechless for at least twenty seconds. She suddenly felt caught, like a sixteen-year-old sneaking out of the house at midnight. That's what grandparents were supposed to do, right? Take care of their grandkids when the folks were out of town? But Stacy and Chad were going to be gone the whole month of July! If she was going to do this trip, she couldn't wait till August. It was now or never, before she lost her nerve. Before she went bonkers just hanging around the house running into Coop's ghost, lost in her own vacuous space.

"Mom, now don't be upset. I'm just putting it out there. You don't have to answer right this minute but—"

"Sorry, sorry." Dang it, she sounded like a squeaky mouse toy. "I'm in the middle of making supper, had to turn the heat down under my soup." Which she hastily did, but as she did so her eye caught sight of the signed certificate sitting on the counter. Wait. She—Margaret Ann Cooper, age 65—had just passed the Motorcycle Safety Basic Rider Course. Passed! A surge of confidence found her normal voice. "But no, that won't work. I've, um, decided to do some traveling this summer myself—you know, with all the transitions, I need to get away. Would like to do it while you and Chad are off on your cruise and the girls are at camp."

"Travel? Like where, Mom? And what if Reagan won't go to camp? What am I supposed to *do*?" Now Stacy was whining.

"Stacy, I'm sure it'll be fine. Don't let it faze you. She's just being sixteen. Once Reagan gets to camp, she'll have the time of her life. You and Chad will have a great time. I'll have a great time. It's all going to work out, you'll see—oh! My grilled sandwich is done. Don't want it to burn. Thanks for calling, honey, but I better go. Love you!"

Maggie hung up. Well. Put the lid on *that* idea. Four weeks with Reagan underfoot? She loved her granddaughter, but in smaller doses.

Now if only Jiang didn't get home too late. What happened next really depended on him.

Chapter 13

MAGGIE WAS UP EARLY ON MONDAY, eager to catch Jiang before he left for school. She already had the coffee on and a box of granola and bananas set out when she heard him tripping quickly down the stairs. A moment later he breezed into the kitchen, backpack slung over one shoulder.

"*Zǎoshang hǎo*, Mrs. C." He opened the refrigerator door and pulled out a small paper bag—his lunch, Maggie assumed.

"Good morning to you, too, Jiang. Um, do you have a few minutes?" She gestured toward the bowl and granola on the counter.

He shook his head. "So sorry. My last exams before term is over." He took a banana from the bunch and waved it. "But I will eat this on the way—brain food!" His grin teased her, but he must have seen the disappointment on her face, because he quickly added, "But I will be home for supper tonight. Do you need me to do something?"

"Well, yes. A big favor, actually."

"I will be honored." He stuffed the lunch and banana in his book bag. "What is this favor?"

Maggie kept a straight face, hiding a smile. "I want you to teach me how to ride Coop's motorcycle with the sidecar." She proudly pushed her Motorcycle Safety Foundation certificate across the counter. "I still need to get my license, but I will do that this week now that I have passed the safety course. The road test and written test are both waived with this." She tapped the course certificate.

"That is wonderful, Mrs. C!" Jiang's eyes danced with delight. "Yes, yes, I will be glad to teach you what I can." Then his face clouded. "If my Chinese license is still good. I will have to check."

She followed him to the door. "When—?"

"Only two more days exams, then I am done!" Hustling down the steps, he headed for his yellow Civic, then turned and called back, "Wednesday! We will drive your bike on Wednesday!"

Maggie watched until the little yellow car disappeared around a corner. Two more days. She was hoping to begin today, before she forgot everything she'd learned on the Harley. In fact . . .

A few minutes later she was in the garage, sitting on the BMW, her hands sweating. Wouldn't hurt to just turn it on. Sticking the key in the ignition, she squeezed the clutch lever while she turned the key. The motor purred to life. Keeping a firm grip on the clutch, Maggie revved the motor slightly with the throttle, feeling goose bumps crawl up her neck.

Okay, okay, she needed to wait for Jiang. There were a ton of things she *had* to do before she could start on this foolhardy trip. She turned off the bike and slid off. Might as well get started.

Back in the house, between spoonsful of granola and milk, Maggie started a list.

Get bike license
Make Dr appt for physical
Go to bank—transfer $$ into checking account
Order goggles for Rocky
Tell kids—yikes, how?!

She stared at the list. For a trip like this, the list should be longer. Lots longer. She added, "Buy riding gloves," and stared at the list again. Well, as the time got closer, she'd add more things to the list.

Wait. As the time gets closer? What time was that?! That's what she needed to do—plan an itinerary! When to leave. How many miles to ride each day and where to stop. Contact people where she planned to stay (those circles on Coop's map). Figure out how long such a trip would take. Her kids would want to know.

Her kids—they'd surely try to put a stop to this. Well, she'd get further along in her planning before she told them.

Refilling her coffee, Maggie stopped by the kitchen calendar. Only two more weeks in June. Then Stacy and Chad would be gone the month of July and the girls would be at camp. So, that gave her roughly a month for the trip—except she didn't know the actual dates the Youngs would be gone.

First things first. She needed to call Stacy.

Her daughter answered on the first ring. "Yes? Mom? Can I call you later? I'm just about to go out the door."

"Just a quickie question, hon." She didn't want to wait all day for Stacy to call back. "When are you and Chad leaving for your Mediterranean cruise? And when do the girls leave for camp?"

"What? Oh, hang on. Have to check." Silence. Then, "We fly to Barcelona on the 27th, cruise leaves on the 29th. Didn't I send you our itinerary?"

Maggie stared at the calendar. That was the last Saturday in June—earlier than she'd thought. "And the girls?" she asked sweetly.

"Both girls leave Friday the 26th—so we'll see them off before we go. We'll all be back around the fourth weekend in July. I'll send you the schedule, but really, Mom, I gotta run. Got stuff I need to do before the girls wake up. See you Wednesday?" The phone went dead.

Wednesday? What was Wednesday? Did Stacy want to get together *again* to go through her dad's stuff? Her daughter was nothing if not persistent! Well, Maggie was busy this Wednesday. She and Jiang had a date.

And why were the girls still in bed? It was Monday! She looked at the calendar again. Already mid-June. School must be out—not that she'd remembered. She'd been too busy learning how to ride a Harley.

* * * *

By the time Wednesday rolled around, Maggie had checked off quite a few things from her list. She'd gone to the IDOT facility, proudly showed her MSF certificate, and filled out all the forms she needed to get her Class M motorcycle license. Unlike the first clerk when she'd gotten her permit, this one eyed her over the top of her reading glasses for a long five seconds—before giving her a wink and murmuring, "You go, sister. Just be safe."

She'd managed to get a doctor's appointment for Friday—not time for her yearly physical, but she wanted to update all her meds and, yes, be honest with her doctor about her plans. He'd probably have a fit, too—but she wasn't going to be totally stupid and not get checked out.

Good thing she'd decided long ago not to be a patient at the Good Neighbor Clinic. Too much like family treating family.

She'd ordered "Doggles" for Rocky, plus riding gloves and rain gear for herself—didn't think to buy them when she was up at the Harley-Davidson place.

But the thing that took the most time was plotting her itinerary. How many miles should she try to do each day? Madison, Wisconsin, was a three-hour trip by car from Chicago—but it would take her longer, especially if she avoided the interstate, so maybe Madison would be enough to shoot for the first day.

She'd poured over the maps and made a tentative itinerary to the first destination Coop had circled: Minneapolis. If she left on Saturday the 27th, after Stacy and Chad and the girls were gone, and made it to Madison on Day One, that was about 150 miles. Madison to Eau Claire, Wisconsin, about 200 miles—that could be Day Two. Another hundred miles would take her to Minneapolis on Day Three. Which meant she'd miss being there over a Sunday, the most logical time to visit New Hope Friendship Church. But . . .

Did she still know anybody in Minneapolis? New Hope Friendship Christian Church—a little storefront church in the inner city—had been their first assignment after Coop graduated from seminary. Poor. Almost 100 percent black. Lots of kids. Coop had been the assistant pastor to a middle-aged African American preacher whose enveloping hugs had felt like a gentle mama bear. Several years ago, they'd gotten word that Pastor Vic—Reverend Victor Washington—had passed away, then his wife a few years later. But what about their kids who'd been teenagers back then? Could she find them? Were they still in Minneapolis, or had they moved away? And what about the church itself? Was it still going?

Guess she'd find out.

* * * *

Jiang's Chinese motorcycle license was still valid—at least in China. They decided they'd presume it was valid in Illinois, since she'd found some online info about foreign licenses being valid in California and other states. Besides, they were only going to drive Coop's motorcycle through neighborhood streets to the parking lot at one of the middle schools, since school was out for the summer. Not worth the hassle of checking it out with IDOT.

Maggie settled the full-face helmet Coop had bought for her on her head, feeling a bit claustrophobic behind the chin guard and visor. She'd handed Coop's helmet and leather jacket to Jiang to wear—a bit loose on him, but better than nothing. Stepping into the sidecar, she was actually surprised how much room she had for her legs and feet. With just Rocky for a passenger, there would be room to store stuff in the leg area.

But she gripped the sides of the sidecar nervously as Jiang revved up the BMW and moved slowly out of the garage, paused till the garage door closed, then headed down the alley. They only had to travel a mile or so to the school parking lot, but Maggie felt exposed and awfully close to the ground. Shouldn't there be a seat belt in this thing?

Once in the parking lot, however, she clambered out of the sidecar and paid close attention as Jiang went over the various controls and instruments. Then it was Maggie's turn to sit on the bike and get it started. Jiang fit himself into the sidecar as she drove slowly around the parking lot, finding that magic "friction zone" between the clutch and first gear as she slowly rolled the throttle. Back and forth, around and around in a big circle. The main thing that felt different to Maggie was that the sidecar added a third wheel, keeping the bike upright even when stopped.

"I like it," she told Jiang. "Feels more stable to me. Like riding a big trike instead of a two-wheeler."

He nodded. "*Shì*, more stable. But turns will be different. You don't notice it much going slowly around parking lot. But turning corners with a sidecar will feel different. With a two-wheel bike, you lean the bike *into* the turn. But with a sidecar, you need to turn the handlebars in the direction of the turn because the bike doesn't lean. To turn right, open the throttle to give it some gas and lean toward the sidecar. To turn left, let off the gas a bit, which allows the rear wheel to spin slower than the sidecar's, which is traveling in a wider circle."

Maggie frowned. "I don't get it. Show me."

"Okay, get in." As they switched places, he added, "Don't ride with an empty sidecar. Put some weight in it—fifty, maybe a hundred pounds. Otherwise it can lift off the ground going around turns, especially at a faster speed, which some show-offs do for fun."

Maggie swallowed. Yikes. This wouldn't be so easy after all.

Jiang drove clockwise around the parking lot, then stepped up his speed. Maggie noticed he did turn the handlebars as he went around corners and leaned slightly toward her, as though adding extra weight to the sidecar. Then he reversed and drove counter-clockwise, slowing down slightly on the corners.

He pulled to a stop. "You try, Mrs. C."

Once again, they changed places, Jiang in the sidecar. Maggie did clockwise circles, then counter-clockwise. Then figure eights. She could hardly believe the time when she looked at her watch. One-thirty! Had they really been practicing for three hours? She was suddenly very hungry.

She started to get off the bike, but Jiang said, "You drive home, Mrs. C. No problem. Just go slowly."

Maggie started to protest, then set her lips tight. She had to ride on the streets sometime—and soon. Might as well start with neighborhood streets with Jiang for moral support. And even traveling under the speed limit, she pulled up to the garage in less than ten minutes.

"You did it, Mrs. C!" Jiang crowed happily as the garage door went up and she pulled in. "If you keep practicing, you will soon be Number-One-Motorcycle-Woman!"

Grinning, Maggie turned off the machine and dismounted. Well, maybe not Number-One-Motorcycle-Woman yet—but she wished Coop were here to give her a shout-out. He'd be so proud of her! Still grinning, she pulled off her helmet and headed out the side door—and ran smack into Stacy, who looked madder than a wet cat.

Chapter 14

*M*OTHER*! D*ID YOU JUST RIDE IN THAT BUCKET OF BOLTS Dad threw together?"

Maggie was so startled at Stacy's appearance that her mind went blank. Which gave Stacy room to turn on Jiang. "And you! What are you doing encouraging my mother to do something so crazy? Unless—" Stacy eyed the young man shrewdly. "Unless you want to buy that bike. Is that it? If so, we can talk a price right now."

Jiang glanced at Maggie, the corners of his mouth tipping up slightly. But he merely gave a polite nod and murmured, "If you ladies will excuse me . . ." as he headed toward the house.

Maggie's momentary muteness evaporated. "Stacy Marie Young! How dare you think you have permission to negotiate a price for your father's bike—*if* it was for sale, which it *isn't*." She tucked her helmet under one arm and tried to follow Jiang, but Stacy stood in her way, arms folded.

"Then why is he driving that bike? And taking you for a ride in that tin can attached to it? And what's with this silly getup?" She flicked a hand at Maggie's helmet and leather jacket.

Maggie tilted her chin up. "Who said he was driving?"

It was Stacy's turn to be speechless, long enough for Maggie to march around her and head for the back door. Well, the cat was out of the bag now. Behind her she heard Stacy finally sputter, "*What?*" But she ignored her daughter and went inside.

Maggie had her jacket off and the teakettle on by the time Stacy appeared in the doorway between the sunroom and kitchen. "Mom." Stacy cleared her throat. "What do you mean? Are you saying *you* were driving the motorcycle?"

Maggie flipped through a stack of papers on the kitchen counter, pulled out the certificate from the Motorcycle Safety Foundation, and then laid her new Class M license beside it. "There." She tapped them with her forefinger. "All safe. All legal."

In shock, Stacy picked up the certificate, then the license, studying each. "But, Mom! Why?"

Maggie pulled sandwich makings out of the refrigerator, then turned and faced her daughter. "Because. That's what your father wanted."

"That's nuts!" Stacy threw up her hands. "Okay, so he fixed up that bike. Gave him something to do while he was recovering from heart surgery. And, okay, he probably wanted to take you riding with him in that sidecar thing—his little fantasy. But I'm sure he never intended for you to get a license and *drive* it."

Maggie opened her mouth to say, *"Why not?"* but shut it again, reaching for the teakettle as it whistled. After all, even she was shocked at herself. And if Stacy was appalled at the idea of Maggie getting her motorcycle license, her daughter would throw a conniption fit if she knew her mother was considering a cross-country trip—

Maggie's hand froze.

The maps.

Coop's maps were laid out on the dining room table, the cross-country highways marked in yellow highlighter. She wasn't ready to explain *that* to Stacy just yet.

Her hand came to life. Shutting off the flame under the kettle, Maggie put on a smile. "Uh, honey, you came for lunch, right? Here—" She shoved bread, a package of sliced ham, another of Swiss cheese, and a squeeze jar of mayo across the bar counter in Stacy's direction. "Would you mind starting these sandwiches? I need to run upstairs a moment. Be back in a jiff—oh!" She cast a sweet smile over her shoulder as she headed for the dining room. "Would you make one for Jiang, too? Thanks, sweetheart."

Out of sight from the kitchen, Maggie snagged the two open maps without stopping and hurried through the foyer and up the stairs, trying to keep the paper from flapping noisily. Once in her bedroom, she quickly folded the maps and stuck them in a dresser drawer. Then she sank onto the bed, shoulders shaking, not knowing whether to laugh or cry.

* * * *

Somehow Maggie managed to get through lunch with Stacy, which they ate on the sun porch, windows and back door open to catch a breeze. She did explain about the birthday package from Coop, the jacket and helmet, which told her just how much his heart had been set on them riding the bike together.

"But now he's gone, Mom!" Stacy had protested. "You can't ride together now. So, what's the point of doing all this craziness? It *is* crazy, you know."

"Maybe." *Well, yes, it was.* But she'd looked Stacy straight in the eye. "It's my way of honoring your father. This was his joy, his dream." She'd smiled, drifting back in her memories. "You didn't know him back in the day, when we first met. He had a motorcycle back then, too, you know. We even did our getaway from our wedding on the bike." She couldn't help chuckling.

"Yes, I know, Mom. I've seen your wedding pictures." But Stacy had sighed and seemed to drop it. Maggie had even tried to smooth things over by agreeing to go upstairs and select some of Coop's suits and dress shirts for Stacy to take to the fancy consignment shop in Wilmette.

But she knew this wasn't the last of it. Not when she told the kids about the bigger plan, to follow the route Coop had laid out. And she wasn't too surprised when she got a call from Mike that evening.

"Mom! What's this about you getting a motorcycle driver's license? Stacy called, said you'd even taken a riding course."

Of course, Stacy had called her brother. "Yes, it's all true. Guilty as charged," she said lightly—then added, "A *safety* riding course."

"Mom, are you sure that's wise? I mean, you're sixty-five."

"I know how old I am, son. And I don't know if it's wise or not. But I did it. And I think your dad would be very proud of me."

She heard a masculine chuckle from Mike's end. "Yes, I think he would." Oh, goodness. He sounded like Coop. "But still, Mom, this worries me. I mean, it would be one thing if Dad was still alive and you two wanted to take some day trips or something. But riding by yourself . . ."

"I won't go by myself, son. I'll take Rocky."

"Rocky!"

"Yes. In the sidecar. He loves it—your dad trained him to sit in it. And besides, the sidecar needs weight in it, so it's perfect."

"Yeah, well . . ." Maggie heard Mike chuckle again and could just imagine him shaking his head. "Mom, please, please be careful."

They'd barely hung up when the phone rang again. Stacy's home number on the Caller ID, not her cell. She almost didn't answer—except Stacy always called from her cell. "Hello?"

"Grams? For real? You got your motorcycle license?!" The voice was excited but also low and conspiratorial.

"Reagan? Why are you whispering?"

"Mom doesn't know I know. But I overheard her telling Dad. She was pretty upset. But I think it's totally *awesome*."

"Well, don't get too excited." She had to calm the girl down. "Just something I needed to do—to honor your grandpa, you know." Maggie realized she was repeating what she'd said to Stacy, because it had seemed to help make sense. But she didn't want it to become a crutch, something flip and casual. Because it was true. And precious.

"He would be so freakin' geeked over you doin' that, Grams." Reagan giggled. "Hey, you gotta take me for a ride. For real. Promise?"

"Not promising anything, young lady. Maybe when you're twenty-one."

"Grams! No, no, soon! I wanna ride in the—uh oh. Gotta go. I hear Mom. Love you." The phone went dead.

* * * *

Maggie was hoping to have another riding lesson with Jiang the next day, but heavy rain and a loud thunderstorm during breakfast wiped out that idea. It also gave Maggie pause. What in the world was she going to do if she ran into rain or a thunderstorm on the road?

She definitely needed a weather app on her cell phone.

The storm settled down to a light drizzle by mid-morning and had stopped altogether by noon. By then she had done a couple loads of laundry and gone food shopping to restock her staples. When had the fridge and cupboards gotten so empty? Jiang had gone to work, but said he'd be home early enough to go for a ride that evening if she wanted.

She definitely wanted.

Already the BMW was starting to feel more comfortable as she circled the school parking lot that evening and practiced starting, stopping, and more figure eights. In fact, the lot was beginning to feel too small. "I'd like to ride around Oak Park, maybe try one of the bigger streets?" she told Jiang.

"You are the boss!" he grinned.

Madison Street, one of Oak Park's primary east-west streets, was a little scary with cars and stoplights and pedestrians wanting to cross. But by the time she pulled into the garage forty-five minutes later, she was feeling exhilarated.

"Good job, Mrs. C," Jiang said, unfolding his leg from the sidecar and taking off his helmet. "I am sorry, I have to work both my jobs tomorrow. But we could go riding again Saturday. Yes?"

Maggie nodded. She had a doctor's appointment tomorrow morning anyway. But if the weather was decent on Saturday, maybe they could take a ride out into the country—not an easy feat since Chicago and its suburbs sprawled north, south, and west of Lake Michigan, like a river overflowing its banks. But she'd like to try some of the "lesser highways"—two lane roads, or even four-lane, since she had no intention of riding on the toll roads or interstates.

And then there was Rocky. She needed to practice riding with him in the sidecar. Hadn't Coop said he loved to ride in it? Didn't he jump into the sidecar every time she let him into the garage? But she had to admit she felt anxious about riding with the dog. What if he jumped out?

Her doctor's appointment the next morning felt a bit like going to confession—not that she'd ever gone to confession in a Catholic church, but she'd seen plenty of movies. People who went to confession got honest about a whole lot of stuff in order to be "absolved" or forgiven. Dr. Stevens knew about Coop's death and had already expressed his heartfelt sympathy. The fifty-something physician, prematurely gray, seemed most interested in how she was coping. Was she feeling anxious or depressed? Was she sleeping all right? Getting some exercise? Taking her meds and eating small, frequent meals? Staying in touch with friends and family?

His questions pulled her up short. A few weeks ago, Maggie would've had to admit that she wasn't coping very well. Depressed? Probably. Lethargic. Forgetful. Feeling lost. But ever since she'd found Coop's maps—or was it after she got his belated present of the leather jacket and helmet? Or signed up for the motorcycle course?—she had felt . . . what? More energized. Motivated. Even excited. And yes, scared.

She had to get honest with her primary doc. "I'm learning to ride my husband's motorcycle," she admitted. "And, uh, I'm planning a road trip. A long trip. And I want to make sure my health is up to it."

The doctor's eyebrows went up, but all he said was, "Mmm-hmm. Well, let's check you out." He listened to her heart, lungs, took her blood pressure, tapped her knees, probed her stomach, and peered into her eyes, ears, and mouth, nodding genially from time to time. He finally pushed his stool-on-wheels back from the exam table and crossed his arms. "I still want you to get a blood test—need to check your thyroid levels. Your iron was on the low side last time. Would've ordered a blood test before seeing you, if this had been your regular physical. But," he shrugged, "other than that, physically I think you're doing pretty great for a woman your age."

She started to grin—but he peered at her sternly over the top of his glasses. "It's not your health I'm concerned about. It's going on this motorcycle 'road trip' you described. I've seen more than my share of motorcycle accidents in the ER, and I don't want you to be one of them."

* * * *

Standing in front of the fireplace mantle a few hours later, Maggie touched the urn holding her husband's ashes. "I don't want to be one of them either, Coop," she murmured. "What d'ya think? Should I call the whole thing off?" Her eyes wandered over the high school portraits of her three children, still holding a place of honor on the mantle. Mike, his serious hazel eyes and determined expression hinting at the talented architect and steady family man he would become. Stacy, beautiful brunette, brown eyes like her dad, her nose a little in the air as if to say, "Watch out, world, here I come!" And Chris . . .

She lingered, studying the face of her youngest. His gray eyes and saucy grin laughed at her from the frame. Her heart tugged. She missed Chris so much—missed his robust hugs, his sensitive spirit, his compassion toward people and animals. She missed the dog-lover bond they'd always shared. How well she remembered his mischievous grin when he'd brought her Rocky as a pup when he came for his dad's retirement four years ago. He knew she'd fall in love the moment he put the dog in her arms.

But he'd also been excited to see the old classic bike his dad had bought to fix up now that he had some time. They'd chatted about replacing the carburetor and re-chroming the pipes. She'd been glad to see Coop and Chris finding something in common, hoped it might bring Chris home more often.

But that was before the fallout . . .

* * * *

It had all started so innocently—they thought. They'd thrown a retirement party for Coop in the backyard that weekend, inviting folks from church, faculty friends from Chicago Biblical Seminary, as well as several students from his classes. Chris was twenty-nine, the only one of their kids not married yet, so Coop had slyly made a special effort to include a few "eligible young ladies" in the group, and hadn't been exactly subtle when he'd called out, "Hey Chris! C'mere and take over the grill for me. Jennifer, why don't you help him—just don't get distracted and let those ribs burn, you two!" Coop had laughed, winked at Jennifer, then grabbed a

LaCroix from the cooler and joined his faculty co-workers, who were ogling the classic motorcycle in the garage.

But later, Maggie had come into the house to put the new puppy in his cage and caught Chris angrily confronting his father. "Dad! Just *stop*! Stop trying to hook me up with a girlfriend. If you haven't figured it out by now, guess I'll spell it out for you. I'm *gay*. Period." And he'd stomped out of the room.

Coop had looked like he'd just been slapped. "What did he say, Maggie? Did Chris just say he's *gay*?"

Maggie had been as stunned as her husband. The rest of the retirement party had passed in a blur. But when everyone had finally cleared out, Chris apologized to his parents. "Didn't mean to spring it on you like that, Dad. I meant to talk to you guys this weekend, let you know what I've been figuring out about myself. Just didn't mean to do it that way. But can we talk now? I—"

"Don't need to talk," Coop had said stiffly. "I've got nothing to say to you." And he'd walked out of the room.

Chris had left the next morning. Maggie had pled with her husband to talk with his son, but he didn't even appear when it was time to say goodbye. Before Chris left, she had given him a tearful hug. "Honey, I don't understand this at all. But give your father some time. It's just been a shock. We do need to talk, okay?" He'd hugged her back, said he'd be in touch. And he'd kept his promise with the occasional phone call to her—remembering her birthday, asking how Rocky was doing. But they'd never really talked about . . . about *that*. And Coop had put her off whenever she said *she* wanted to talk about Chris. It had been the cause of some of the few fights she and Coop had had in the past four years.

It had really hurt that Chris hadn't come home for his dad's funeral. "Mom," he'd said on the phone, "I'm really sorry not to be there for you. But I can't. He hasn't talked to me or written to me in four years. He wouldn't want me there!" She'd heard the quiver in his voice. "Look at it this way. I'm respecting his wishes by not coming. Can you understand?"

* * * *

103

Looking at those laughing eyes in the high school photo again, Maggie sighed. She should call Chris, tell him about getting her motorcycle license and that she was thinking seriously about going on this trip. She could almost hear her youngest saying, "Do it, Mom. Don't let the naysayers hold you back. Be true to yourself. Be *alive*. It's worth the risk."

Coop. Chris. Her estranged men. But this was something they'd agree on. They'd both say, *"Go for it."*

Chapter 15

Maggie rolled out of bed Saturday morning excited to get further out of the city on the bike and take Rocky along. But as she put on the coffee and scrambled some eggs for herself and Jiang, she started chuckling to herself. God really did have a sense of humor. Her primary support group for this adventure so far was her dead husband, her teenage granddaughter, her Chinese houseguest, and her estranged son—or he would be, she was sure, once she told him about it. But she was most surprised by her own determination, which grew more confident each day. There was a purpose to this whole thing she wouldn't ever know if she didn't go.

The weather was perfect for a ride. Cool in the morning, heading up into the 70s by noon, and overcast. The dog goggles and riding gloves had arrived by FedEx the day before, and Rocky was beyond excited to be invited to hop into the sidecar. Maggie wasn't sure it was going to work to take the dog along with Jiang, too, but somehow Jiang managed to fit himself onto the seat of the sidecar behind Rocky, though the dog was practically in the young man's lap.

Maggie grinned as she strapped on her helmet. "Jiang, I owe you one."

It took an hour to get beyond Chicago's sprawling suburbs, but she and Jiang had plotted their route carefully, following Route 64 and then 20 out toward Elgin. Not exactly back roads—both had four lanes—but not the interstate, either. She'd decided to stay in the right lane, so sometimes got stuck behind a truck, but didn't feel confident enough to pass. In fact, because she kept her speed just under the posted limit, she was the one who often got passed, earning her a couple rude "fingers" from impatient drivers.

They stopped for gas and a break in Elgin, a river town northwest of Chicago. Maggie walked Rocky on the leash in a grassy area behind the station, glad for a chance to stretch her own legs. Her knees were complaining. She was tempted to let Jiang drive the rest of the way, but they'd only been on the road an hour and a half. She needed to be able to put in a few more hours each day—and the projected day for the start of her trip was only a week away. The day Stacy and Chad flew out of O'Hare for the Mediterranean.

Out beyond Elgin, they found some two-lane roads without much traffic, giving her a chance at a stop sign to slide back the face shield on her helmet. "Can you smell that?" she said, grinning at Jiang as they passed newly planted fields and horse pastures, rich with the smell of dirt, cut grass, and newly-leafed trees. A smell that suddenly brought back a flood of memories of her first rides on the back of Coop's motorcycle when they first met. The smell of nature neglected by fast-moving cars, all shut up with either the heater or the air conditioner or the radio blasting away.

Maggie was both elated and exhausted when they finally got back to the house around 1:30. She'd driven the bike for three hours, not counting the half-hour break for gas and a bite to eat. They'd gotten some strange looks and a few snickers when she'd walked into McDonald's with her helmet under her arm. Well, so what? She'd just have to get used to it.

Rocky hadn't seemed to mind the crowded conditions in the sidecar, merely panted in delight as he stuck his head around the windshield. In fact, Maggie had felt a little more secure that he'd stay put with his hind end on the floor of the sidecar rather than on the seat. But she'd have to make a few more trial runs before next Saturday with just Rocky in the sidecar to see how that went.

She'd still planned to go to the bank and do some other errands after a "quickie nap" on the living room couch—but she awoke with a start at four o'clock and realized the bank would be closed now. And tomorrow was Sunday! Now she'd have to wait until Monday to transfer some money out of their retirement funds. How much would a trip like this cost, anyway? She'd have to stay in a motel between destinations, plus gas for the bike and food for her and Rocky. She should buy some motorcycle insurance, too, and figure out how to pack for a cross-country trip with only a couple of saddlebags to carry luggage. Yikes! What if a week wasn't enough time?

She pushed herself off the couch. Okay, time to make another "To Do List."

* * * *

Maggie made a point to be on time for the morning service at Grace and Mercy Community Church the next morning, realizing this was the last time she'd be at worship here for a while. Pastor Hickman gave her a big hug as she came in. "Sister Cooper, how are you? We sure do miss that big man of yours around here. Haven't seen you too much since his 'going home' service. Are you all right?"

Maggie nodded. Eric Hickman, in his sixties himself, had been the mover and shaker who spearheaded Grace and Mercy's commitment to stay close to the city rather than move further out to the "safer" suburbs. A good man. "I did come a few times, kind of slipped in and out," she said, feeling her face flush. "But I'm fine. Oh, yes, one weekend I was gone to my grandson's eighth grade graduation in Indiana." And one Sunday she'd been learning to ride a motorcycle. "But I do want to let you know I won't be here for the next several weeks. I'm, uh, taking a trip. Out of state."

"A trip? Well. Sounds like a good idea to get away for a while. But we'll miss you. We'll keep you in our prayers."

"Thank you. I need them." Pastor had no idea how much she needed those prayers.

She again sat in the back and soaked in the gospel music, trying not to think about all she had to do before leaving next Saturday. She was struck by the text of Pastor Hickman's sermon—a familiar verse from Proverbs chapter five: "'Trust in the Lord with all your heart, and don't lean on your own understanding. In all your ways'"—"*ALL* your ways, people," the pastor re-emphasized—"'acknowledge Him and He *will* direct your paths.'" Then he preached about Abraham, who up and went when God said, "Go," even though he didn't know exactly where he was going or why. He just depended on God to show him the next step along the way.

Whew. Was Pastor preaching to her? She didn't understand why she was feeling she needed to "go," to do the craziest thing she'd ever done in her life. *"God,"* she breathed silently, *"I'm going to keep rolling unless you tell me to stop, because I know I can't do this without your help and protection."* She would have to rely on guidance from the Holy Spirit—big time.

* * * *

Maggie spent Sunday afternoon trying to figure out what clothes to take—layers? windbreaker? rain poncho? It was summer, but who knew what kind of weather she'd run into—but was interrupted by a call from Stacy.

"Mom? Wanted to let you know we, uh, have a slight change in plans—"

Uh-oh.

"If we leave a couple days early, we'll be able to meet up with some old college friends in Barcelona and spend a couple days there seeing the sights! So, Chad is trying to get our tickets changed to Thursday."

"What about the girls? Don't they leave for camp on Friday?"

"Well, that's, uh, why I'm calling. Wondering if you'd be able to come up here Thursday and stay with them until Reese's ride picks her up on Friday. And Reagan will need a ride to the bus station."

Maggie didn't trust herself to say anything for a moment. No! She didn't have time to babysit her granddaughters—this week of all weeks. She had too much to do.

Stacy picked up on her silence. "Of course," she said hastily, "if it's too much to ask, I can probably find someone else. Though I know the girls would love to see you before they're gone for a month."

Stick the dagger in.

Maggie sucked in a long breath and silently let it out. "I don't know, Stacy. Let me call you back, okay?"

She felt a little guilty hanging up so fast, but Maggie headed straight to the kitchen calendar. She'd been planning on leaving Saturday, once Stacy and Chad and the girls were gone, to avoid any drama about her taking this trip. The first stop on Coop's map was Minneapolis, where they'd spent their early years at New Hope Friendship Church after he graduated from seminary. By car, she could make Minneapolis in a day. But on the bike? Realistically it would take her two, even three days at the rate she was able to travel, which would put her there Sunday night at the earliest, and probably Monday. Which was a problem. Because, frankly, she didn't have a clue if she'd be able to track down people from New Hope Friendship on a weekday.

But if *she* could leave earlier on Thursday as well, she'd surely be able to get to Minneapolis in three easy days, which meant she'd be there in time to show up at New Hope Friendship Sunday morning—her best chance to meet up with people who might still be at their old church after all these years!

Suddenly Stacy's change of plans seemed like a gift on a golden platter for her, too. She bucked up some courage and picked up the phone. Surely Stacy could find someone else to cover for the girls. And *she* would just have to get everything done that still needed doing in the next three days.

And after this, there were still a couple of phone calls she needed to make.

* * * *

Maggie tried Chris first, but the call went to voicemail. So, she just left a message: "Call me when you get a chance, okay? Love you!"

Mike was next. "Mom," her oldest said, "really? I mean, you just barely got your motorcycle license! To take a trip all the way to the west coast seems a little bit—"

"Crazy?" she finished. "I know how it sounds. But, Mike, this is something I need to do. Something your dad really wanted us to do. I can't think of a better way to honor his memory than to take this trip." There. She'd said it again. But it was true. The only thing she really understood about the force driving her from within.

Her son was silent for a moment. Then: "Have you told Stacy?"

"Uh, no. I know that's not fair, but I can't deal with Stacy right now." She laughed a little. "Didn't you once tell me when you were a teenager, after we caught you doing something or other, that you'd decided it was better to ask forgiveness than permission?"

"Ha!" Mike chuckled. "Can't believe you're using *that* as your excuse. But, okay, I understand about Stacy."

"I promise I'll tell her once they've landed on the other side of the ocean."

Now Mike really laughed. "Mom, you are so bad!" But his laughter quickly sobered. "Okay, can't say I'm happy about this trip, but I kind of understand. Look, promise me one thing—load the Find Friends app on your phone and add my name so I can find where you are if I need to. I'd really like you to check in with me every day—just so I know you're safe. Even a quick text saying, 'I arrived' or 'Everything's good.' Can you promise me that much?"

Huh. Talk about role reversals. But it was the least she could do. "Okay, promise. Thanks, Mike. Love you."

Well. That went better than she'd expected.

What she didn't expect was a call later that evening from Reagan. "Grams! Mom is still making me go to that dumb summer camp next weekend. Please, *please*, can I come stay with you while they're off on this totally bunk cruise?"

"Reagan—"

"Please, Grams! I *promise* I won't be any trouble. In fact, I'll be a real help. I'll walk Rocky, I'll do the dishes. I'll do anything you want me to do. Just please let me stay with you. It's the only way Mom would even consider letting me stay home."

"Reagan, slow down, honey." Maggie felt for the girl. Another time, she'd consider it. But she had to put a stop to this fantasy. "Honey, if I were going to be home, I'd consider it. But, I'm not going to be here. Since you all are going to be gone, I decided to take a, uh, vacation myself. You know, get away for a while. Take my mind off your granddad being gone. You can understand, can't you?"

"A vacation? Where are you going? How long will you be gone?"

Maggie hesitated. The girl asked too many questions. "Just, you know, visit some friends here and there."

There was a long pause—then a sudden screech on the other end. "*Grams!* You're going to take that trip Gramps planned on those maps! Aren't you! On the bike!"

"Reagan—"

"I knew it! I knew it! That's why you got your motorcycle license. Oh, Grams, let me go with you! Please, please, let me go with you."

"Reagan! *Hush.* Please lower your voice. I, uh, haven't told your mother yet. And coming with me is impossible. Your parents would never give you permission. And I'd be foolish to take you."

"Oh-h-h, Grams!" she wailed. Then a whisper: "Does anyone else know?"

"I told your Uncle Mike. He's not happy about it, but he's being a grownup. Made me get an app on my phone so he'd know where I am."

"Oh. Yeah, I know that app. I use it with some of my friends." Silence stretched long on the other end. Then Maggie heard a long sigh. "Wish I could go with you, but, guess I understand. But, Grams, would you add me to your Find Friends app so I can at least see where you are? I won't show my folks, promise. It'll be our secret."

Maggie squirmed. "Don't want to put you in that position, honey. You shouldn't be keeping secrets from your parents. Look, I plan to tell your mom. I just want to pick the right time. So, let me do it. And, okay, I'll add you to the app, so you can follow my trip." A simple enough concession. "Pray for me, okay? I'll pray for you, too. And let me know how camp turns out. I'm sure it can be a lot of fun if you give it a chance. We'll both have a lot of stories to share when we get back, right?"

"Yeah. Guess so." Another sigh. "Guess I'll see you when you get back."

Maggie told herself not to let Reagan's disappointment get to her. She'd survive. Dealing with disappointment was part of growing up. But coming with her? Impossible!

Chapter 16

A LOUD THUNDERCLAP SENT MAGGIE straight up in bed. What? Rain? No, no, not good! She didn't want to set out on her trip in the rain. She glanced at her glowing digital clock. Just 2:16.

Crawling out of bed, she padded downstairs in the dark with Rocky at her heels, clicked on the stove nightlight, and made herself a cup of valerian herbal tea to calm her nerves. She'd been so keyed up Wednesday night, she wasn't sure she'd be able to sleep. But obviously she'd been out for the count for a few hours at least—until God's bowling party in the heavenlies had cut loose.

Sweetening the tea with honey to make it palatable, Maggie squinted at her "To Do List" on the kitchen counter. Didn't have her contacts in, but she could still make it out. Everything so far had been checked off: *transfer funds into checking account . . . buy motorcycle insurance . . . practice with Rocky in sidecar . . . buy rain gear and shock cords . . . take bike for trip checkup . . . load Find Friends app onto phone . . . groceries for Jiang?* For that one, she'd decided to waive Jiang's rent for the next several weeks if he'd buy his own groceries.

And then there was the packing list: *Rocky's duffle—dry food, water bowl, brush, leash, long rope, goggles . . . snacks—trail mix, nuts, dried fruit . . . fit clothes into saddlebags and duffle . . . backpack—meds, vitamins, toilet kit, sunglasses, contacts, goggles, ID, cash, credit cards, phone, charger, journal, New Testament . . .*

She was as ready as she could be. As for the weather—nothing she could do about it. Like a whisper in her spirit, a voice seemed to say, *"Just roll with it, Maggie. You don't* have *to be anywhere at a certain time. Wait for the weather to clear. Listen to your body. Stop when you're tired. Take it day by day. That's it."*

Roll with it, Maggie. Guess that should be her new travel mantra. "Good reminder, Lord," she murmured. That was the first "takeaway" from this trip. Hold her plans lightly. Like that verse from Proverbs Pastor Hickman had preached on: "'Trust in the Lord with all your heart, don't lean on your own understanding.'"

With a last swig of the tea, she climbed up the stairs and crawled back into bed.

* * * *

The smell of bacon and coffee woke her. And the rain had stopped. "Hey, Rocky." Maggie pushed the dog off the bed. "Jiang is making breakfast for us. Time to go, buddy."

She was downstairs in another twenty minutes, showered and dressed, her bulging duffle bags and backpack in hand. Everything else had already been packed on the bike. Jiang beamed at her from the stove where he slid a cheese omelet onto a plate. "*Zǎoshang hǎo*, Mrs. C! Good morning! I made American breakfast for your trip!"

While she ate, they went over last-minute details about the house and what to do with the mail. He had her general itinerary and a few emergency contact numbers—Mike, her doctor, the pastor. She'd added Jiang to her Find Friends app, grateful to have someone she trusted to stay in the house and take care of things while she was gone.

Jiang followed her out to the garage and waited while she stuffed one duffle into the toe of the sidecar along with Rocky's duffle, tied down the backpack behind her seat with the shock cords, and let Rocky hop into the sidecar. The duffle bags she stuffed into the hard-shell saddlebags were a snug fit, but all in all she was proud of how tightly she'd packed.

"May I pray for you, Mrs. C?" Jiang said shyly as she settled onto the bike seat.

"Yes, yes, please do, Jiang." She clutched her helmet, feeling humbled when the young man let loose with a passionate prayer in Mandarin as he laid hands on the bike, laid hands on Rocky, then gently touched her shoulder. His hand still on her shoulder, he said, "Amen," then added in English, "God has a purpose for this trip, Mrs. C. Do not worry. God will show you when it is time!"

His confidence touched her. But he had no sooner finished than Maggie suddenly slid off the bike. "Forgot something!" She was back in two minutes with the sealed urn that held Coop's ashes. "We're taking this trip together, one way or another, James Cooper," she said as she dragged a reluctant dog out of his seat and stowed the urn in the nose of the sidecar, wedged tightly between the two duffle bags. And then she laughed.

* * * *

Maggie was glad she and Jiang had taken a trial run out to Elgin last weekend, because she followed the same route now on her first leg toward Madison, Wisconsin. She'd gone riding several times in the past few days with just Rocky in the sidecar, and he'd stayed put with no inclination to get out unless she stopped and got off herself. *Good dog.* The rain had stopped, the sun was peeking out, but the roads were still wet, and spray from passing vehicles kept misting her visor. Between her anxiety about Rocky's ability to stay in the sidecar all day, constantly wiping off her misty visor, and trying to stay clear of traffic, it took a while for her to relax and begin to enjoy the ride.

She made it to Rockford before stopping at a Wendy's for lunch, a bit damp, but otherwise none the worse for wear. If the rain started again, she should probably get out her rain gear. But as she tackled a grilled chicken wrap, she felt a little giddy. She was actually on her way! And so far, so good. She'd filled Rocky's water bowl and tied him to a bike rack where she could keep an eye on him from a window. Should she fill up before going on? But the gas gage still showed over a half tank left. Even if she didn't ride the interstate, she should be able to make it into Wisconsin, or even close to Madison, before filling up.

But avoiding the interstate meant pulling off the road every hour or so to plot her next route, pouring over the paper maps she'd brought along. She knew this route was taking her longer. Should she try . . . nope. She was still a newbie and couldn't imagine going 70 miles an hour with monster trucks crowding her on both sides.

When she came out of Wendy's, she saw three other motorcycles—big Harleys— had pulled into the parking lot, and the drivers were hovering around her elderly BMW like ants at a picnic. She untied Rocky's leash from the bike rack, dumped the water from his water bowl, and headed for her bike, feeling nervous. The three burly guys were encased in black leather, but no helmets that she could see. Just bandanas tied around their heads, eyes covered by wraparound sunglasses.

Rocky gave a sharp *woof* as they came up to the little group, and the threesome parted slightly, looking her up and down. "Hey, Granny," one said, sporting a scraggly ponytail. "This your rig?"

"You got it." Maggie said, putting on a smile. "In you go, buddy." She unsnapped Rocky's leash before he hopped into the sidecar, then stowed the plastic water bowl.

The three guys exchanged glances. "You traveling alone?" ponytail said.

"Nope. Got my dog here." That got a chuckle.

"Nice classic you got," a second guy said. This one sported a shaved head under his yellow bandana. "You fix this up yourself?"

They were just being friendly, right? She shook her head warily. "No, that was my husband—before he died."

"Oh. Sorry for your loss, lady." Yellow bandana did some throat clearing.

The third one finally spoke. "Your man did a nice job. Running okay for you?"

She nodded this time. "So far, so good." Number three wore an American flag bandana, red, white, and blue.

"So, where you headed?" he said.

"Madison." Uh oh, how stupid. Too much information. She settled the helmet on her head. Should she lower the visor and put an end to this conversation?

The three guys looked at each other, then ponytail said, "Which way you goin'? We could ride with you, give you some company on the highway. Safer in a group. Easier to see four bikes than just one—even with that sidecar."

Maggie hesitated. Were they just being friendly and helpful? Or was she getting herself into something she'd regret. "That's kind of you to offer. But, uh, I'm not riding the interstate. Taking a roundabout way. Thanks anyway."

"You sure? Don't like to see a lady your age riding alone."

She shrugged, settled on the bike, and turned on the ignition. "Thanks. I appreciate it. But I'll be fine." Snapping her visor shut, she took the bike out of gear and walked it back as they parted and got out of her way. Starting up the bike, she gave a wave and drove carefully out of the parking lot, this time following the GPS on her phone that would take her across the Illinois-Wisconsin border heading north toward Madison on Route 104. She hadn't figured on other bikers, but of course she should have known. Bikers begat bikers, a community of sorts. But she knew bikers were like any other group—good ones and bad ones. Weekenders and full-timers. Biker clubs and biker gangs. How was she going to navigate this?

"Guess this is where you come in, Lord," she gulped. Well, God and Rocky. The dog was a good judge of character, too.

* * * *

Maggie made it to the outskirts of Madison by mid-afternoon, but it took her another forty-five minutes on her phone to find a motel that was "pet-friendly"—for a non-refundable deposit of thirty bucks. But the motel also had a free hot breakfast, an indoor pool, and a hot tub.

The hot tub was the clincher.

After soaking her sore muscles in the hot tub for a good half hour, she wasn't about to get back on the bike and go out looking for a restaurant, so she ordered Asian takeout to be delivered to the front desk while her damp clothes were drying in a motel laundry room. Dutifully, she sent a text to Mike while she waited: "*Arrived safely in Madison. Uneventful trip. Heading for Eau Claire tomorrow. Looks like Route 12 will take me all the way—no interstate!*" And in a burst of gratitude for an encouraging first day, she copied the text and sent it to Jiang and her granddaughter as well. The least she could do to keep faith with her "crew."

After letting Rocky slurp up the last of her Pad Thai, Maggie took the dog for a walk around the premises, then stopped in the parking lot to make sure the bike was locked and the sidecar cover zipped. Not very secure—she ought to take the duffle bags and the urn inside for the night. By the time she returned the luggage cart to the foyer, it was eight o'clock, and she was ready to turn in. Why not? Then she'd be able to get an early start.

As she crawled beneath the fluffy comforter, Rocky rested his nose over the side of the bed and whined. "Whatcha want, buddy? Don't think they want you sleeping up here on the bed." Except, thirty non-refundable bucks ought to cover any dog hair he left on this fancy bedcover. "Okay, boy, c'mon up here."

And for the first time in weeks, Maggie slept clear through the night.

* * * *

After the hotel's complimentary hot breakfast of coffee, bacon and eggs, and a side of biscuits and gravy—passing up the do-it-yourself waffles—Maggie and Rocky were on the road again by eight o'clock. A brand-new sunny day, no hint of rain. With a start this early, she mused, maybe she could go all the way to Minneapolis. But another look at her map pulled her back to reality. By car, sure, she could make it to the Twin Cities in four or five hours on the interstate. But on the bike, going at her new-driver speed along Route 12, that'd be a much longer day. Might as well stick to her plan.

What she hadn't realized was that Route 12 paralleled Interstate 94 almost all the way. Cars and trucks and yes, motorcycles, zoomed along the highway nearby, making good time. Traffic didn't seem too bad. Was she being overly cautious to avoid the main road? It'd be faster.

But, she wasn't in any rush. Still had plenty of time. Her muscles were still not used to sitting astride this machine for long periods.

Watching Rocky out of the corner of her eye, Maggie couldn't help grinning as the dog leaned around the windshield, ears flopping backward in the wind, eyes protected by his doggie goggles. They got lots of friendly honks and waves from passing cars—it was the dog, she decided. People couldn't help but smile.

But she was plenty glad when she saw signs for Eau Claire city limits. It'd taken her a good five hours, including the layover for lunch, and she was ready to stop. A Super 8 on the outskirts of the town allowed pets for an extra ten dollars this time. "Ha. That's more like it, Rocky." After settling into their room, Maggie took a long, hot shower and then flopped on one of the two queen-size beds for thirty minutes before admitting she was really hungry. And tired of fast food. Tonight, she'd find a nice restaurant and get a good meal.

Did she dare leave Rocky alone in the room? At home, he stayed in the house when they were out without barking. But this was a strange place. She could at least try. Telling the dog sternly to "Stay!" Maggie went out into the hallway. She heard snuffling and then a whine on the other side of the door. Well, duh. Of course, Rocky could sense she was still there. She called out, "Bye, Rocky!" and walked down the hall. She listened again. Silence. *Good dog.*

She should tell Chris what a good traveler he was. She and Chris had played phone tag for a couple of days, still hadn't connected. She hadn't sent a message to Stacy yet either. But not tonight. She was too hungry. Maybe when she got to Minneapolis.

The front desk gave her a couple of suggestions for nearby restaurants and Maggie headed for her bike. Pulling her helmet on, she turned the ignition.

Nothing.

What? Maggie turned the key again. Again nothing.

No, no, no. She tried again. Nothing.

Sliding off the bike, Maggie hustled back inside the Super 8. "Do you have a phone directory? My motorcycle won't start, and I need a mechanic."

The woman at the desk handed her a local phone book with Yellow Pages—did Chicago even have Yellow Pages anymore?—and Maggie started calling numbers under Motorcycle Dealers. But it was after five o'clock by now and all she got were messages giving the hours they were open. The one person who answered the phone at a Harley dealer turned out to be on the other side of town. How could she get the bike there if it wouldn't start?

This was unbelievable!

Hunger finally drove her back to her room, and she ordered a pizza. Her stomach rumbled while she waited, flicking through TV channels to keep her mind from spinning on worst-case scenarios. How long would it take to get the bike fixed? Would she be able to continue her trip? *O God, if only Coop was here.* He'd know what to do.

Finally, there was a knock on the door. The pizza. She'd expected a call from the front desk, but they must've just sent it up.

"Coming!" she called, and opened the door—and stared, her jaw dropping.

Chapter 17

Reagan!" Maggie blinked twice, thinking surely this apparition would disappear. "*What* are you doing here?"

With a backpack slung over one shoulder and a flat cardboard box in the other hand, Maggie's granddaughter stood there with a forelock of tri-colored hair flopping over one eye. "Here's your pizza, Grams. They delivered it just as I got here. Told them who I was and that I'd bring it up. They let me sign—hey there, Rocky!"

The dog had barreled over to the door and was having a tail-wagging, face-licking reunion with the girl. In a daze, Maggie stepped aside so they could all get inside and then she shut the door. She had to be dreaming. This was impossible.

"They let you *sign*?" What kind of delivery let a teenager sign a credit slip instead of an adult? Wait—she couldn't get distracted. "Never mind. *What* are you doing here, young lady?"

Reagan flipped open the box, ignoring the last question. "Told 'em I was your granddaughter and if I signed, it would save you a trip downstairs—you know, being a senior citizen and all that." She loosened a wedge of gooey pizza and lifted it out. "Can I have a piece? I'm starving!"

Maggie rolled her eyes. "Yes, yes, eat. But you've got a lot of explaining to do, young lady. How did you find me?"

"Easy. Got your text saying you were heading for Eau Claire today, so I got a Megabus ticket to Minneapolis—it's frickin' cheap! —and they had a rest stop in Eau Claire." Reagan stuffed her mouth with another bite. "The Find Friends app showed you were at this motel, Grams. So, I just got off, got a taxi—and here I am!" Reagan grinned, pleased with herself.

"But—but you're supposed to be on your way to camp today! The camp will be frantic when you don't arrive."

Reagan shrugged, her mouth full of pizza. "Nah. I called 'em last night, said I wasn't comin' after all."

"Then your parents will be frantic when they find out you didn't go to camp."

Another shrug. "Just tell 'em I'm with you."

"You can't—" *O Lord, give me patience.* "Reagan. You can't go with me. They don't even know I'm—" Maggie stopped. She felt caught. She was sixty-five, for goodness sake, and behaving like a teenager herself, keeping her own daughter in the dark about what she was doing. "I—I was planning to call your folks tonight. But I got all distracted, because the bike won't start."

"What?" Reagan stopped in mid-chew. "What's wrong with the bike?"

"I don't *know.* It just won't start. I'll have to find someone to come look at it tomorrow morning. And who knows how long *that* will take." Frustration licked up Maggie's gullet like a bitter taste. The bike on the fritz—and now Reagan. It felt like the end of her dream—or the beginning of a nightmare!

Reagan frowned, then handed her the box. "Here, Grams. Better eat some pizza."

* * * *

By ten o'clock, Reagan was sound asleep on one of the queen beds, Rocky curled up beside her on a couple of the motel towels. But Maggie lay wide-awake, staring at the green pinpoint of light on the smoke detector on the ceiling. What in the world was she going to do? She'd told Reagan she was putting her right back on the bus to go home tomorrow, until her granddaughter reminded her that no one was home and wouldn't be home for the next four weeks.

Maggie had summoned up some resolve and sent a text to Stacy's cell phone, but got an iPhone message saying, *"Undeliverable."* What? Stacy had told her she would get international phone service for their trip, to be used in case of an emergency. Well, this was an emergency. Even though she hadn't really wanted to talk directly to Stacy, she'd next tried calling the number. This time she got a recorded message saying the number was temporarily not in service. Now what? Were they out of range or something? Email was her next option—until she realized she didn't have Stacy's email address stored in her phone, and Reagan didn't have it either. "Huh. Mom only uses email for real estate stuff," she'd scoffed. "Probably won't look at it anyway."

Maggie stared into the darkness. Should she call Mike, see if she could send Reagan by bus to Indianapolis? Would they be willing to keep her for the next few weeks? Well, actually a month. Not really fair to spring that on Mike and Susan, but what else could she do?

Disappointment ate at Maggie's spirit as she lay in the dark. Maybe she'd have to turn around and go home. *No!* This was her trip. Hers and Coop's. At least that's what she'd thought. She'd told God she was going to keep moving forward unless He shut the door.

Was God shutting the door?

She really didn't know what to do. But there wasn't a thing she could do about it tonight. Punching a pillow into a comfy position, Maggie slid down beneath the covers and closed her eyes. Familiar words from Pastor Hickman drifted through her mind and became her last thought. *Trust in the Lord with all your heart . . . don't lean on your own understanding . . . and He will direct your paths . . .*

* * * *

Maggie was awake early, but nothing would be open before eight anyway. She had time to get a shower, take Rocky out, and grab a cup of coffee before jumping on a call to the closest motorcycle dealer. She wanted to get someone out here as soon as possible to look at the bike.

Then she'd deal with Reagan.

When she came back to the room after taking Rocky out to do his business, Reagan had just gotten out of the shower. "Good, you're up," Maggie said, trying to ignore the piercings and tattoos that decorated her granddaughter's body here and there. "I've got some calls to make about the bike, but if you're hungry, they have a complimentary breakfast here."

"Why don't you try starting the bike again?" Reagan said, pulling on her jeans, which sported "designer rips" in numerous places. "Maybe it just got overheated or something yesterday."

Maggie didn't think so, but—why not. It wouldn't hurt. Reagan was right on her heels as they went outside to the parking lot with Rocky on the leash. As soon as the cover was off the sidecar, the dog jumped in, panting happily. "Sorry, buddy, not going anywhere right now." Maggie slid her leg over the seat, stuck the key in the ignition, and turned.

Nothing.

She sighed. "Well, it was worth a try." Maggie looked at her watch. Two minutes till eight. She slid off the bike. "I'm going inside to use the phone directory. Can you take care of Rocky?"

"Okay. But hey! You don't need a directory. Just tell Siri to 'Find the closest motorcycle dealer.' It's easy!"

Easy. Huh. Maybe for her. Maggie hustled into the lobby and borrowed the phone directory again anyway. The third place she called had a service department and said they could get her in Monday. "Monday! I need service today! I'm on a road trip, and my bike won't start. I can't come to you. Can you send someone out here?" She was beginning to feel desperate. So much for making it to New Hope Friendship Church in Minneapolis in time for church tomorrow morning. She couldn't go anywhere if the bike wouldn't start.

"Please hold," said the voice in her ear. Great. Now she was in la-la land.

"Grams?" Reagan poked her head inside the sliding doors into the lobby. "Come outside. Got somethin' to show ya."

Maggie shook her head and pointed at the phone she was holding to her ear.   Her granddaughter beckoned furiously. "It's important!"

Whatever. Canned music played in Maggie's ear. No telling how long she'd be on hold. Still keeping the phone to her ear, she reluctantly followed Reagan out the door and over to where the BMW was parked. Rocky still sat in the sidecar and gave a *woof* as she approached. "So, what did you want to show me?"

Reagan slid a long slim leg over the bike and settled into the driver's seat. The girl reached for Maggie's keys that were still in the ignition. *Oh, good grief.* Was that what Reagan wanted to show her? That she'd left the keys in the ignition? Okay, that was stupid.

But the next moment the engine purred to life.

Maggie nearly dropped the phone. "Reagan! How—? What—?" That's when she noticed Coop's tool kit on the ground beside the sidecar, a screwdriver and a pair of needle-nose pliers sitting on the hood of the sidecar.

Her granddaughter grinned. "I was just checking out the wiring when I noticed one of the ignition wires had come loose. So, I tightened it up, tried the key and—ta da!"

Maggie didn't know whether to laugh or cry with relief. Could this situation get any crazier? Shaking her head, she clicked off the phone and leaned over to give Reagan a hug. "You are something else, girl." Had God just opened the door again?

A new thought sprang into her mind and seemed to reach down to her very spirit. Reagan just might make a good partner on this road trip after all.

* * * *

It wasn't like she didn't have some doubts about this absurd option. But after sorting through all the possibilities in her mind of what to do with Reagan—more like one long, unpunctuated prayer—Maggie took a deep breath, called Mike, and told him the situation. "I'm going to let her go with me at least to Minneapolis, then I'll figure out what to do."

She didn't blame her son for spouting, "Good grief, Mom, this is crazy! Are you sure? What will Stacy say?" At the same time, bless him, he added, "Man, when Alex gets wind of this, he's gonna be so jealous." Which caused them both to laugh a little hysterically.

Next, the big question: could Reagan *and* Rocky fit in the sidecar? That seemed the safest. Maggie didn't feel confident having a passenger ride behind her, not yet anyway. And the girl would add more weight to the sidecar, giving it even more stability—if they could fit. Taking out one of the duffle bags that had been traveling in the nose of the sidecar with Coop's ashes, she let Rocky get in the car first, then Reagan settled into the seat with the dog on the floor between her legs.

"Do you have room for your legs?"

"No problem, Grams!" Reagan said gleefully. "We'll be fine!"

Maggie wasn't so sure, but Rocky panted happily, leaning against his new copilot. Reagan had brought just a backpack, so with some creative juggling and a few more shock cords, they managed to get everything to fit in the saddlebags, on the seat behind Maggie, and on the luggage rack on the back of the sidecar.

But they had to unload it all again, because there was one more thing. Leaving the dog and luggage in the motel room, they took a taxi to the closest motorcycle dealer—which Reagan located using Siri's unfathomable cyber knowledge—and outfitted Reagan with a proper helmet and leather jacket. Maggie hadn't figured *that* cost into her so-called budget for this trip. But if Reagan was going to ride with her, there was no way around it.

It was noon when they got back to the motel. Maggie was anxious to get on the road, still hoping to make Minneapolis before nightfall, and Reagan was beyond excited. "We'll stop down the road and get some lunch," Maggie said as they repacked the bike. She hoped. Route 12 looked like it would take them most of the way to the Twin Cities, enabling them to avoid the interstate. But she also knew the local routes didn't exactly feature the usual popular food stops and gas stations found along the main highways.

What she hadn't figured on was the heat. The sky was clear, the westward-moving sun shone brightly in her eyes, and the temperature was climbing into the 80s. Sweat trickled down her neck. The leather jacket had to go! Route 12 wasn't exactly "less-traveled" either. Traffic was limited to two lanes, with only an occasional stretch of four lanes that made passing easier.

Glancing at her new passenger, whose face was almost invisible behind the helmet's face shield, Maggie realized she felt a weight of responsibility in her chest she hadn't felt the first two days. Was Reagan safe riding in the sidecar? Was she hungry? Did she have to go? The girl must be really hot in the leather jacket.

O Lord, what have I done? This will never work!

Less than an hour down the road, Maggie slowed as they came into a tiny town named Elk Mound. On their right, a tan building with a red roof sported a sign that said, "THE JUNCTION—Dine in or Carry Out." She pulled into a shady parking spot and read the fine print: "Pizza, Burgers, Appetizers."

She sent Reagan inside to order while she took Rocky on the leash to do his business. When she got inside, Reagan grinned. "I ordered an 'everything' pizza-for-two—hope that's okay."

Maggie sank into a chair. She had a feeling she was going to end up eating more pizza on this trip than she had for all her sixty-five years so far.

Chapter 18

THE PIZZA WAS ACTUALLY REALLY GOOD. So much for her prejudice about Chicago pizza being the only decent pizza worth eating. But she hurried Reagan along, not wanting to leave the dog outside long in this heat, as well as wanting to get close enough to Minneapolis to figure out how to get to New Hope Friendship tomorrow morning.

But as she paid the bill, the roar of multiple motorcycles rumbled outside. She glanced out the window—and saw three familiar bandanas parking their bikes next to her BMW. Uh oh.

"Uh, Reagan, would you ask the waitress if we could have some water for the dog? Here, use my big paper cup. I'll get out his water bowl."

"Sure, Grams." Reagan was obviously on her best *see-I-can-be-a-big-help* behavior.

Maggie slipped out the door while Reagan went looking for their waitress. Rocky yelped happily as she came toward the Harleys, now parked in a row next to her BMW. She spoke first. "Well, hello. Again. You guys lost?" She meant it to be funny, but it sounded snarky.

But ponytail just grinned. "Nope. The Junction has the best pizza and burgers in Wisconsin. We almost always stop here on our way to the rally."

"Rally?" Maggie dug out the dog's water bowl.

"Yeah. We're heading for the big one in Hollister over the Fourth—" He stopped midsentence as Reagan came out the restaurant door carrying the big paper cup, helmet swinging by its strap from her elbow. "Well now. Who's this?"

"Hi. I'm Reagan." The girl handed the cup of water to Maggie, then stuck out her free hand before Maggie could open her mouth. "Who are you?"

Ponytail shook her hand, still grinning. "Name's Buzz. These two bozos are my cousins, Smoky and Hawk."

"Pleased to meetcha." Reagan shook hands with the other two, and then looked at each one quizzically. "Those your real names?"

The guy with the American flag bandana guffawed. "Yeah. My mama took one look at my beak when I popped into the world and named me Hawk." He slapped Smoky on the shoulder and they both laughed.

"Don't mind those two," Buzz snorted. "Those are our biker handles. Names we go by. You got a handle, kid?"

"This *kid* is my granddaughter," Maggie interrupted. "No, we don't have 'handles.' But we do need to get going if we're going to make the Twin Cities today." She poured the water into Rocky's bowl and motioned for Reagan to put her helmet on.

Buzz frowned. Sending the other two inside to order some pizza slices, he beckoned for Maggie to step away from the bikes and lowered his voice. "Ma'am, I want to apologize. I shouldn't have called you 'Granny' the other day, that was kinda rude. Shoulda shown more respect. Also, didn't know you was ridin' with your granddaughter. Gotta take my hat off to you—well, if I had a hat. You got balls." Realizing what he just said, he looked a little flustered, covered it up by pointing down the road that ran past The Junction. "You said the other day you were takin' a 'roundabout' way. You doin' 12 all the way to the Twins?"

Maggie nodded.

"Been this way before?"

She shook her head and admitted, "Not on the bike."

"Well, like I said, we come this way nearly ever' year, goin' out to Hollister. And I can tell you for a fact that this here 12 runs smack into 94 before you get to St. Paul, and then it's the interstate through town into Minneapolis, if that's where you're goin'."

Maggie had guessed as much, but thought she'd get closer before figuring out what to do, still hoping to take local streets through town.

"Look. I realize you don't know us from a can of beans, but me and my cousins got regular day jobs when we're not bikin'. All three of us hail from the Detroit area. I'm a car mechanic, my cousins are brothers who work in their daddy's family business. Signs. They make signs."

His voice was sober, and he looked at her straight on. Maggie decided to listen.

"I wanna make my offer again to ride with you, especially to help get you through the city on 94 if you ain't done that before." He jerked a thumb down the road again. "We can take 12 far as it goes, then get on the highway, take you through the city. Like I said, it can be safer in a pack. Wherever you wanna go, we'll see you get there."

Maggie frowned, her mind tumbling. She really hadn't planned yet how to get to the Near North neighborhood in Minneapolis where New Hope was located, and now she had Reagan to worry about.

"Look," Buzz said. "If you're worried about your granddaughter, I don't blame you. She's just a kid and too cute for her own good. But I promise you, if either one of those bozo cousins of mine makes a pass at her or shoots off his mouth, I'll kill 'im myself."

Maggie gave him a wry smile. "Huh. If I don't do it first."

Buzz laughed out loud, causing Reagan to look their way.

Trust. A voice in Maggie's head seemed to be saying, *Trust.*

She held out her hand. "All right. Thank you, Buzz. I appreciate it." They shook hands and started back toward the bikes. "As for 'Granny,' don't worry about it." She grinned. "Sounds like a good handle to me."

* * * *

Reagan was wide-eyed when she found out they were going to ride with the three bikers, but Maggie gave her a stern look, so the girl just strapped on her helmet and settled into the sidecar with Rocky to wait till they came back out, "to go" burgers in hand. Maggie asked Buzz to take it easy on the speed, so they started down the road at about forty miles per hour, Buzz leading the way. He motioned to Maggie to drive behind him and slightly to his right, taking up the middle of their lane in the two-lane road, with Smoky and Hawk bringing up the rear. When traffic was light, he took it up to fifty, then fifty-five—and Maggie was surprised when he pulled off the road an hour or so later, waving the others to stop. At the junction already?

Buzz sauntered back to the BMW. "Road merges with the highway just up there. Where you wantin' to go once we cross the river?"

Maggie dug out her paper map, flipped it over to the detailed inset of Minneapolis, and pointed to the Near North section as Reagan crawled out of the sidecar, snapped on Rocky's leash, and took him to pee in the grassy ditch. Maggie had half-thought they'd find a motel this side of the Twin Cities and go the rest of the way into the city in the morning. But since they had an escort . . .

"I need to find a place for us to stay tonight. Mind if I take a few minutes here?" *Like five or ten?*

Buzz shrugged and went back to talk to his cousins, who were idling their bikes and revving the motors now and then impatiently. Pulling out her cell phone, Maggie tried to ask "Siri" to find a pet-friendly motel in the Near North neighborhood of Minneapolis, but the voice-activated smart-phone assistant kept saying, "Here are pet stores I found in Minneapolis."

"Let me, Grams," Reagan said, coming up with the dog. A few minutes later she handed the phone back to her grandmother. "Found a Motel 6—it's this side of the river, but they'll let Rocky stay. Not too far from that Near North area. I put the address in your maps. But they need your credit card."

Buzz had come up alongside and overheard. "That's one smart cookie you got there, Granny." He pulled out his own cellphone. "Give me the address. We'll get you there."

Maggie was nervous as they rode up the ramp onto I-94 ten minutes later. Even though it was a Saturday afternoon, traffic was moderately heavy going into St. Paul. "Don't go too slow," Buzz had cautioned. "That's as dangerous as going too fast." He stayed in the right-hand lane, but her speedometer crept up to sixty-five as she did her best to keep up with him. But he was right. It did feel a lot safer to have him riding in front of her and slightly to her left—an emotional buffer between her and the next lane—and comforting to have Smoky and Hawk covering their rear. But Reagan held tight to Rocky with one arm and clutched the side of the sidecar with the other hand, especially when large trucks roared alongside them in the middle lane like loud, moveable walls.

"Could use a few guardian angels around us, Lord," Maggie murmured.

I sent three of them already, said the voice inside her head.

Maggie laughed out loud, her voice muffled inside the helmet. "So you did, Jesus. So you did."

Forty minutes later Buzz led the little pack into the parking lot of the Motel 6 just north of the Minnesota State Fair grounds and east of the Mississippi River, which flowed through both Minneapolis and St. Paul. Maggie breathed a sigh of relief. They'd made it! She turned off the ignition and slid off the bike, doing her best to ignore the throbbing ache on the inside of her thighs. "Thank you, Buzz." She held out her hand to their "angel." "I really appreciate it. Can I, uh"—she thought fast—"buy you guys supper or something?"

Buzz just revved his motor and grinned. "Nah. We'll be on our way. You and Cookie there take it easy now, Granny."

Reagan had hopped out of the sidecar and was saying goodbye to Smoky and Hawk, but they all heard Buzz. The two brothers laughed. "Yeah, take it easy, Granny. You, too, Cookie," Hawk said. A moment later the three bikers were noisily pulling out of the Motel 6 parking lot, waving over their shoulders.

Chuckling, Maggie turned to her granddaughter. "I think we just got christened with our 'handles.' Guess we're official bikers now."

* * * *

Sunday promised to be another warm day later on, but as Maggie navigated local streets the next morning trying to find a bridge to cross the Mississippi River, the temperature felt mild and pleasant. She was still sore from three days straddling the motorcycle, though a long soak in the motel bathtub last night had helped. According to New Hope's web page they'd found last night on her phone, the church was still located on Broadway in the Near North area, and Sunday service started at ten. *Rev. Odell Smith, Pastor.* Not anyone she knew.

She tried not to think about what she was going to do with Rocky when they got there. They'd left their luggage in the motel room, which she'd reserved for two nights, but the motel had a rule that you couldn't leave pets unattended for more than two hours. And who knew how long the service would last.

Maggie took the first bridge that would take them into the Near North area along Plymouth Avenue. "Notice anything about the cross-street names?" she asked Reagan as she drove slowly down Plymouth, one of the main east-west streets in the area.

Reagan studied the street signs as they passed. "Uh, Knox . . . Logan . . . Morgan . . . Newton . . . Huh. They go alphabetically. Awww," she simpered, "how sweet."

"Don't knock it, young lady. Those alphabetical streets helped me find my way around here big time."

"Is this the street the church is on?" Reagan shouted at her from her open visor.

Maggie shook her head. "No, just wanted to see how much has changed."

"Huh. Not much to see," Reagan huffed. "Just a bunch of row houses and parking lots. Not even a Starbucks."

Still no grocery stores either. "When your grandpa and I moved here in the late seventies, most of this street was just a row of empty lots, left over from the race riots after Dr. King was killed in '67. A lot of businesses burned." At least the empty lots had filled in since then, with what looked like decent "affordable housing," though one liquor store, a barbershop, and the lone funeral chapel along the whole stretch didn't exactly count as the thriving commercial area it had once been. Maggie wondered whether she should mention the uprising that had occurred in this same neighborhood back in 1980 while they were still here—fires, looting, broken windows— but decided against it. Not just before introducing Reagan to their former church here.

There wasn't much traffic on a Sunday morning. Making a U-turn and retracing their route, Maggie finally turned north and went another half mile up to Broadway. This east-west street, too, looked different than when she and Coop had lived in the area almost forty years ago. Spruced up a bit, an apartment building now where a row of small retail stores used to be, the old movie theater gone. But she still recognized a few landmarks—a "Wings and Chicken" place, one of the public schools, a wig salon, a storefront sign that read: "Upper Midwest American Indian Center—Foster Care Program."

"Indians live around here?" Reagan pointed at the sign.

Maggie nodded. "Minnesota has a number of Native American tribes in the state."

They were coming up on the corner where New Hope Friendship used to be. Maggie felt a strange nostalgia. This had been her first church where she'd become a member as an adult. So different than the church she'd grown up in—which had been all white, middle-middle class, very conservative, no women in the pulpit. New Hope, on the other hand, was mostly African American—at least it was back then. Why a young, inexperienced white couple had been assigned to assist Pastor Victor Washington, she never did figure out. But they'd been welcomed at the church with open arms when they'd arrived with two little ones in tow. Her Mike had been five, Stacy still a toddler. Maybe it was the children. New Hope loved kids.

There it was. A neatly painted sign faced Broadway: *New Hope Friendship Baptist Church*. Same brick building, two stories. But the outside brick walls, front and side, were covered in colorful murals. A slew of familiar faces ran along the side: Dr. Martin Luther King Jr., Malcom X, W.E.B DuBois, Frederick Douglass— icons of black history. *That* was new. When she and Coop had lived here, the big room used as a sanctuary and a few side rooms had filled the first floor. A couple of apartments took up the second floor, one of which had housed Pastor Vic's family of six, the other the Coopers. Would it be similar now?

Maggie glanced at her watch. They were half an hour early. Only one car sat in the parking area along the side of the building, so she turned the corner and headed up the side street. Looked both the same—and different. The vacant lot behind the church, which used to be little more than hard-packed dirt and a rusty swing set, now boasted some colorful playground equipment. Beyond the lot ran a modest row of one- or one-and-a-half-story clapboard houses on either side of the street, most neat and tidy, but a few in need of paint with old couches or kitchen chairs on the front porch. Chain link fences surrounded most front yards. "Beware of Dog" signs dotted a fence here, another there.

"I thought you said this church was in the inner city," Reagan said, her head swiveling.

"This *is* the inner city for Minneapolis," Maggie said, driving slowly through the working-class neighborhood. "This area and a few other neighborhoods circling downtown."

"Cheese Louise," Reagan muttered. "Somebody shoulda told the Cabrini Green residents to move here when they were torn down."

Cabrini Green—Chicago's notorious public housing high-rises, both symbol and reality for poverty, crime, drugs, and gangs until they were finally torn down and residents moved to scattered-site, mixed-income neighborhoods. Maggie was surprised Reagan even knew anything about Cabrini Green from her family's protected perch in Chicago's northern 'burbs.

Maggie finally swung around again to the church building and saw several more cars had arrived at the church. Feeling like a blinking neon sign, she self-consciously pulled the motorcycle and sidecar into a parking spot alongside the cars. She'd no sooner turned off the motor and removed her helmet when three young men—two of them teenagers—appeared out of nowhere and sauntered over. The youngest, who looked about fourteen, caught sight of the dog and stepped back, eyes wary. A second boy, slightly older, leered at Reagan, who was holding on to Rocky's collar and hadn't moved from the sidecar.

The third young man, older than the other two—early twenties?—nodded at Maggie with exaggerated politeness. "'Mornin', ladies. You goin' ta church here today?" He jerked a thumb at the building behind him. "Tell ya what. We'll watch the bike for ya, make sure nothin' happens to it. We do it for twenty bucks."

Reagan, still in the sidecar and holding tightly to Rocky's collar, sent an anxious glance in her grandmother's direction.

Maggie tensed. *O Lord, what now?*

Chapter 19

Maggie's mind scrambled. Was this one of those "damned if she did, damned if she didn't" choices?

Just then a black SUV pulled in on the other side of the bike and a passel of kids spilled out of the sliding doors. The children openly gaped at the bike, pointing and whispering, but the driver—a woman—hollered, "You kids get your behinds into the church—*now*." With the aplomb of a drill instructor, she hustled them toward the front door.

Once the kids had disappeared into the church, the driver marched back to the three boys on the sidewalk. "And you, Derek Wilson, whatchu doin'? Are you hasslin' these ladies? Tony and Merle, you two get your tails inside or I'll send the reverend out here to drag you in himself."

The two younger boys pulled sour faces but obediently slouched into the church. The young man named Derek held up his hands and stepped back. "Don't get all uptight, Miz Smith. Just offerin' to keep an eye on this here bike for the lady, make sure nobody bothers it."

The SUV driver shook her finger in his face. "Yeah, I know whatchu up to. You either come inside or take your hustle someplace else."

Derek shrugged, his lips curving in a sneer as he sauntered off.

"And nothin' better happen to this here bike on today, 'cause I know where you live, Derek Wilson!" the woman shouted after him.

Blowing out a relieved breath, Maggie slid off the bike while Reagan and Rocky vacated the sidecar. She felt awkward, unsure what to do next. "Thanks," she said to their most recent "angel." "They probably didn't mean any harm." Her words faltered, and she stared. The middle-aged woman looked so familiar—and she suddenly knew why. The smooth, medium-brown skin with just the right touch of makeup, black hair straightened and worn in a neat semi-bob framing her round face, a well-endowed figure a bit on the plump side, but attractive and well-proportioned . . .

Standing before her was the spitting image of First Lady Danielle Washington, Pastor Vic's wife back in the day.

But—that was almost forty years ago. Danielle Washington had passed several years back, just a year or two after Pastor Vic. But the resemblance was so startling. Could it be—?

"Vicky?" Maggie said tentatively. Victoria Washington, Pastor Vic and First Lady Danielle's oldest daughter, a mere child of eleven when she and Coop had arrived at New Hope, a lively sixteen-year-old and frequent babysitter for Mike and Stacy when they'd left five years later.

The woman's dark eyes widened. "Sister *Maggie*? Is that—oh, help me, Jesus! Maggie Cooper! Is that really you?" And with a whoop, she enveloped Maggie in a big bear hug. And just as suddenly, she held Maggie at arm's length and looked at the motorcycle. Then back at Maggie. "What in the world is that thing? Sister Maggie! Are *you* drivin' this death on wheels?!" And she started to laugh—a big, deep husky laugh.

Reagan cleared her throat. "Uh, hello." The girl stuck her hand between the two women. "I'm Reagan."

Maggie's cheeks flushed. "Oh, I'm sorry. Vicky, this, uh, is my granddaughter, Stacy's oldest girl. And Reagan, this is—" Oh, heavens, what should she call her? Was Vicky married? Single? "—uh, Sister Vicky," she finished.

The woman beamed and grabbed Reagan in a hug, too. "Victoria Washington-Smith. Happy to meet you, young lady. And 'Sister Vicky' is just fine." She motioned toward the front doors. "You two comin' in? You *did* come for service, didn't you? And we have a Pot Blessing after service today, too. Last Sunday of May, you know. In fact, Miz Reagan, you can help me with these casseroles." The woman marched to the back of the SUV and opened the rear door. "Here." And she handed Reagan a large rectangular pan covered with aluminum foil. "That one's cornbread. Sister Maggie, can you take this? Careful, it's hot." And she handed a large soup pot to Maggie, this one wrapped in a thick towel.

"Yes, of course, we want to stay for the service—that's why we came. But, uh—" Maggie nodded at Rocky. "I'm not sure what to do with the dog. Sorry. They wouldn't let us leave him back at the motel."

Frowning, Sister Vicky studied the dog. "Hmm. Is he a good dog? I mean, if he won't howl, we can put him in the office."

"The office?" Maggie felt a surge of relief. She really didn't want to leave Rocky outside. Then doubt crowded in. "Uh, won't the pastor mind? I mean, he doesn't know us, and here we show up with a dog." What was she *thinking*?! "I'm so sorry."

"Hmph. Don't you worry." Sister Vicky grinned slyly. "That's my husband. And if I say I'm puttin' a dog in his office, he don't have much to say about it. C'mon. We'll go in the back door, otherwise some of the kids might get a little scared and cause a ruckus."

Reagan gave her grandmother an amused grin, but they both had to hustle to keep up with the woman as she headed toward the backside of the church facing the playground lot. The office lights were on, but it was deserted, and Maggie realized it was still a multi-purpose room, just like the old days—pastor's desk with a nameplate that said, "Reverend Odell Smith," a second desk with a computer and printer and stackers overflowing with papers and file folders, a four-drawer file cabinet, two large storage cabinets, and a standing clothes rack holding maroon choir robes with white stoles.

Maggie took the leash from Reagan and led Rocky to the corner furthest from the door. "Rocky, stay. Lie down." The dog obeyed, sinking to the floor, his tail wagging slightly but the little black "eyebrows" over his eyes wrinkling as if to say, "What's going on?" She and Reagan both put their helmets on the floor next to the dog where they'd be out of the way—and also safe. Rocky wouldn't let anyone touch those helmets.

"C'mon. I'll introduce you to Pastor," Vicky said, leading the way into the main room. The large room was abuzz with childish chatter, someone playing the piano, and folding chairs being set up. Two little boys hopped up and down as they clung to the hands of a middle-aged man wearing a black suit and a white clerical collar, who was talking to a tall elderly gentleman in a rumpled tan suit. "Deacon Walker," Vicky cooed, "do you mind? We have some guests I want to introduce to Pastor." She also gave a stern eye to the two little boys, who ducked out of sight.

Maggie stared. *Deacon* Walker? Was this the same Edward "Fast Eddie" Walker, neighborhood alcoholic and smooth talker, who'd been on Pastor Vic's prayer list the whole five years the Coopers had been at New Hope? "Uh, Mr. Walker, do you remember me? Maggie Cooper. My husband 'Coop' and I were members of New Hope back in the late '70s. Coop was assistant pastor to Pastor Vic for a few years. We lived upstairs and, uh, we knew your girls." Oh, *what* were their names? "They came to the youth group sometimes."

The black freckles on Deacon Walker's latte-colored face fanned into a big smile. He was missing a few teeth. "Yes, yes! I 'member you and that young husband o' yours. Long time ago." His grey head bobbed up and down. "As you can see, the good Lord and Pastor Odell here saved me 'bout ten years back and—here I am. Suki and Shawna, now, they all grown, got kids. Them two boys over there"—he motioned toward a couple of teenagers slouching in the back—"they's Suki's boys."

Maggie glanced their direction. Oh. The two boys who'd been with Derek What's-His-Name offering to "look after" her bike.

The pastor cut in. "Maggie Cooper? Well now, this is an unexpected treat. Don't think you'd remember me, Mrs. Cooper—" A slight smile flickered across his face. "—I was just a street kid back then. Though I remember your husband. That time he—"

Maggie saw Vicky poking her husband and giving him a look. What was that about?

"Ah, anyway . . ." The pastor did a verbal U-turn. "I take it you remember my wife, Vicky. She was just a teenager back then." The man playfully grabbed his wife's hand and kissed it. "Look at her now—First Lady Victoria. Bet you never thought you'd see the day."

"Oh, hush." Vicky pulled her hand away. "Maggie, this is my husband, Pastor Odell Smith. And—where did they go?" She raised her voice. "Damien! DaShawn! You boys come back here!"

The two little boys who'd been hanging on the pastor, dressed sort-of-alike in plaid shirts and bow ties, came running over. "These are our grandboys, our daughter Dani's babies. Twins. Damien and DaShawn, this is Sister Maggie and her granddaughter Reagan. I knew Sister Maggie when I was just a girl, right here in this church."

The two little boys looked shyly up at their grandmother, then at Maggie and Reagan. They seemed a bit puzzled. Maggie could almost hear the thoughts in their heads: *"But they white!"* But at another stern glance from Vicky, they both said, "Hello, Miz Cooper."

Vicky turned to Maggie. "Please excuse me. The choir is meeting back in the kitchen and I need to get my robe on. Odell, honey, would you . . . ?" And she bustled off. Deacon Walker also excused himself and followed Vicky. He must be in the choir, too.

Maggie was suddenly alone with the pastor. She smiled and held out her hand. "I'm very pleased to meet you, Reverend Smith."

"Just Pastor Odell is fine. That's what everyone else calls me." Vicky's husband returned the smile and handshake. "Pastor Vic mentored me after I married Vicky, helped me become ordained. I was assistant pastor with him for several years, then took over when he passed." The man glanced around curiously. "Your husband, is he—?"

Maggie shook her head. "No, Coop died a couple months ago. He was retired—had been a professor at Chicago Biblical Seminary in urban studies. He'd wanted to take a trip to some of the places that made up our life together, so—here I am. With my granddaughter instead." Hopefully that was enough of the story to make some sense.

"Oh. I'm sorry for your loss. I, uh, would have liked to meet him again—I think he would remember me. We had what I might call an 'unforgettable encounter.' But I guess that will have to wait till we get to glory now."

Again? Maggie couldn't remember meeting anyone named Odell Smith when they were here. An 'unforgettable encounter'? What was he talking about?

"Well, I need to excuse myself. Service is about ready to begin. But we're so glad you're here," Pastor Odell said graciously.

"Please. Make yourself at home." He waved a hand around the room and headed for his office.

Uh oh. She should have said something about the dog. Hopefully Vicky was back there to give him a heads up.

For the first time, Maggie realized that Reagan had wandered away. Searching the room, Maggie saw her granddaughter standing at the back near the double doors in the corner, staring up at a strange collage on the wall. Maggie sucked in a surprised breath. *Oh, Lord. They still have that collage?*

Making her way to the back of the room, returning smiles and nods to various people who greeted her warmly with "Hello" or "Welcome" as she passed, she joined Reagan at the back of the room.

"What is this, Grams? It's kinda weird."

Strange indeed. The collage was faded and more tattered than when it had first been made years ago when the Coopers were there, but the items were still recognizable—a board crowded from top to bottom with junk. A dirty sneaker with the shoelace missing hung next to the bottom of a broken bottle. A bicycle tire with slits in the rubber encircled a crushed cigarette pack, a bubble-gum comic, a Cracker Jack box, a jagged tin can lid, and an ace of spades. Scattered all over were pieces of torn burlap, splashed paint, strips of twisted tin. And in the center was a flattened beer can pierced through the middle with a nail.

Trash picked up by the kids back when this neighborhood had been forgotten.

Maggie pointed to a picture frame hanging next to the collage that contained a note written by the kids who had made the collage.

We are going to explain what this is. We are going to tell how we feel about our neighborhood and how it looks. It is a disgrace to the city. This beer can shows how people try to drink their troubles away. This shoe here shows junk can sometimes travel more than some humans do. This tire in a circle represents the world and shows what litterbugs do who don't care.

—Presented to New Hope Friendship Church
by the Junior High Class

"Wow," Reagan said after reading it. "Guess the neighborhood has changed a lot. Seemed pretty nice to me when we rode around a while ago, not fancy, but . . ."

Maggie nodded. "Yes. It has changed a lot. By people like this congregation who chose to stay here and make a difference instead of fleeing to the suburbs."

Just then the pianist struck a few chords, and there was a momentary flurry as people headed for the rows of folding chairs. Maggie and Reagan chose seats toward the back, but they'd no sooner sat down than they realized everyone else was standing.

Of course, Maggie thought, standing back up. *The choir processional.* And then her breath caught as the line of maroon robes marched out of the door from the back rooms, swaying back and forth—step, sway, step, sway—as the choir launched into their song:

> *We've come this fa-ar by-y faith*
> *Leaning on the Lor-ord!*
> *Trusting in His Holy Wor-or-ord*
> *He's never failed us ye-et*
> *We're singin'*
> *Oh, oh, oh, oh—can't turn arou-ou-ound*
> *We've come this far by fai-aith!*

Tears welled up in Maggie's eyes. *That song!* Were they still using that song as their processional? Or had Vicky remembered— remembered that it was Maggie's favorite song that the old choir had done? And done it for her?

Chapter 20

B Y THE TIME THE YOUNGER KIDS were herded out the front door to go
to their Sunday school classes just before the sermon, Maggie
felt wrung out emotionally. Moments later she heard the thud of
many feet overhead. The second-floor apartments must have been
turned into Sunday school classrooms. Great idea.

But the service had triggered so many memories and feelings.
This church had been the first time she'd been a "minority"—a
young, clueless white woman who'd grown up in 99 percent
white environments, totally ignorant about black culture except
what she'd read in books. She'd felt nervous, anxious. What if she
opened her mouth and said something stupid? And yet, she and
Coop had been welcomed warmly—especially by Pastor Vic and
First Lady Danielle.

She was embarrassed to remember how everyone—especially
the kids—seemed to all "look alike" to her at first. But as she
and Coop immersed themselves in the life of the church, people
soon became individuals. Unique. Special. Like elderly Mother
Thompson who always sat in the front row in her yellowed white
dress and white cap that had "Mother" stitched across the front,
which Maggie learned was a position of honor in the black church.
And Shirley Carter, who'd led the choir, her head always held high,
her voice always strong, even though she had a household full of
grandkids and assorted nieces and nephews she was caring for.

The teenagers, too. Vicky, of course, the preacher's kid, along
with her two younger sisters and two younger brothers, usually
looking all innocent when their parents were watching, but quick
to pick on and boss the other kids when they weren't. But also,
Leroy, a skinny kid with glasses who'd taught himself to play the
piano by ear and played for the choir. And Ebony, about fifteen

when they'd first arrived, was sassy and mouthy, but she acted like a second mother to the little ones, always seemed to have somebody's baby or toddler riding around on her hip.

Where are they all now?

"Grams?" Reagan hissed as Pastor Odell started his sermon. "How long is this service gonna go?" It'd already been over an hour and a half, with an "A and B Selection" from the choir, lots of congregational singing, announcements, a skit about the upcoming Vacation Bible School and the need for volunteers, and testimonies and prayer requests from at least five different people: "I thank God I woke up this morning clothed in my right mind!" and "My nephew needs prayer, got himself picked up again for dealin'," and "Lester got downsized, needs a job."

"Sorry, kiddo," Maggie whispered back. "Hang in there. Pot Blessing coming up. The food will be great!"

Reagan stifled a snicker. "Pot Blessing? Isn't it supposed to be Potluck?"

"Think about it," Maggie whispered back.

She didn't blame her granddaughter. The two-hour services had been hard for her to get used to at first as well. Even today, Pastor Odell's sermon got lost on her as she tried to sort through all the memories and emotions stirred up just by being here. New Hope Friendship Church had been the onset of her journey—hers and Coop's—into a lifelong passion for a multi-cultural life, a major reason they'd hunkered down in Chicago and hung in there with Grace and Mercy Community Church through all its bumps and tensions and divisions.

Huh. Their three kids had certainly chosen different paths, and none had followed in their footsteps—well, not directly anyway. Mike was certainly grounded spiritually, though rather conventional with his architectural firm, a traditional evangelical church, and the kids being homeschooled. Stacy? She'd thrown off all the counter-cultural trappings of her parents and ran straight into the arms of sorority life at college and a suburban, upwardly mobile lifestyle.

Chris? Her mystery. With his love for animals, he should've been brought up on a farm. Though, of her three kids, he was the gentle soul with a compassion for everyone and every living thing. Hopefully the choices she and Coop had made in life had nurtured that part of him. But then—

Her eyes suddenly misted. *Oh, Lord. Why did it go so wrong when Chris told us he was gay?*

Maggie felt a poke in her side. "Grams! C'mon. The pastor just told everybody to move our chairs, so they can set up the tables."

Flustered, Maggie realized the service was over and the hubbub had started once more as chairs were pushed aside and long tables set up for the Pot Blessing. Soon Vicky's cornbread showed up on one of the serving tables alongside a big pot of greens. There were several platters of fried chicken—both homemade and in buckets from KFC. Potato salad, mac 'n cheese, corn on the cob, a pot of beans and ham hocks, Jamaican rice and peas, several cakes, a package of doughnuts, a tray of brownies—Maggie's sagging Styrofoam plate wouldn't hold it all.

Sister Vicky waved her over to come sit with her and the twins and several other women holding youngsters on their laps. Glancing around for Reagan, Maggie saw her granddaughter being dragged to a table with a gaggle of teens and younger kids, some of whom were fingering her tri-colored bangs and giggling. Looked like Reagan was holding her own. Maggie smiled. Good for her.

She noticed that Pastor Odell never did sit down, but spent time going from table to table with his plate in hand, talking to people, or teasing a child, or answering somebody's question. *So much like Pastor Vic*, Maggie thought. Somehow between eating and being interrupted by people coming by to greet her or ask Vicky a question, she and Sister Vicky managed to briefly "catch up" on their kids and grandkids and what they'd been doing for the past several decades. One of Vicky's sisters had diabetes, one brother was in the military, another . . . Maggie wished she could take notes. She'd never remember it all.

But she felt guilty when she shared about her own kids. Vicky wanted to hear about Mike and Stacy. She'd babysat for them when they were little and was interested in tidbits about their grownup lives—marriage, kids, jobs. Chris had been born after the Coopers left Minneapolis, so all Maggie said was that her youngest was still single and worked as a veterinarian technician in southern California. "Oh, that's nice," Vicky said vaguely, probably unsure what a "vet tech" was.

Nothing about him being gay. Maggie sensed that would shock Vicky, and she wasn't there long enough to get into the whole story, the heartbreak, the estrangement.

Her plate empty, Maggie glanced at her watch. Two o'clock already! And she'd totally forgotten about Rocky. Oh dear. And Reagan? She didn't see Reagan either. Excusing herself from the table, she quickly made her way back to the pastor's office, but the door was closed. She knocked. No answer. But it wasn't locked, so she opened the door. The light was off. She flipped the switch. "Hey, Rocky!" she called. "Sorry, buddy."

But the room was empty.

No dog.

Oh no. Had he escaped? Been banished? Or maybe Reagan had taken him out. Feeling hopeful, she headed for the back door where they'd first come in. A gaggle of kids were running around the lot behind the church, screeching and climbing all over the play equipment. But no dog and no Reagan.

Where—?

"You lookin' for that white girl?"

Maggie jumped. A boy about seven years old was looking up at her curiously. She nodded vigorously. "Yes. And a dog."

The little boy pointed. "They 'round there."

The parking spaces along the side of the building! Maggie hurried around the corner—and stopped. A small group of kids, mostly young teens, were clustered around the BMW bike and sidecar, but through the jostling bodies, Maggie could see Reagan and Rocky sitting in the sidecar while her granddaughter was chatting away and pointing out things about the bike.

The knot of kids backed up as Maggie walked over. She kept her voice light. "There you are! I was looking for you."

"Oh, hi, Grams." Reagan squeezed herself out of the sidecar, though Rocky just stayed put, panting. "I took Rocky out to, you know, do his business, and the kids were curious about the bike. So, I was just—"

"It's okay. Yes, I'm sure Rocky needed to go out. Thanks." *Just tell me next time, okay?* She needed to establish some expectations.

"Well, we're ready when you are, aren't we Rocky?" Reagan leaned back against the sidecar.

Maggie went back inside, collected their helmets from the church office, and found Vicky. "What? You leavin' so soon?" Vicky said. "You just got here! We still got lots of catchin' up to do."

"I know. I—" Maggie faltered. "I'm sorry. We've got a long trip ahead of us. I—" The words stuck in Maggie's throat. The visit did feel unfinished, though she couldn't put her finger on it. And Reagan and Rocky were ready to go.

Vicky gave her a long hug. "Wish you could stay longer. A lot has happened here since those days. But thanks for comin'. Means a lot to see you again. Sorry to hear about your husband."

Maggie nodded, fishing for a tissue to blow her nose. "I want to stay in touch. Do you have a phone number? Email? I'll give you mine."

Ten minutes later, Maggie started up the bike and pulled away from New Hope Friendship Church with Reagan and Rocky in the sidecar, a cluster of kids and adults standing on the sidewalk, waving goodbye to them. Pastor Odell stood with Vicky, arm around her waist, watching them go. She couldn't help feeling a tug of guilt as she pulled onto Broadway during a break in the traffic. *This is what we white folks do, isn't it? We zip into the inner city, and a couple hours later we zip out. We come, do our thing, and then we leave.* One more time.

* * * *

The phone call came later that afternoon while Maggie was trying to plot a route to their next destination. "Mom! Were . . . trying to text me? I saw . . . called, too . . . everything okay?" The voice popped in and out, a bad cell phone connection, but she knew who it was. Stacy.

"Yes! Have you left on your cruise yet?"

"What? No, tomorrow . . . leave tomorrow!"

"Well, uh, I've got a bit of news." Somehow Maggie managed to tell her daughter that Reagan wasn't at camp, she was with her—

"What?! Oh! I'm . . . murder that girl!" The voice on the other end faded, as if Stacy had turned to talk to someone else, then came back. "Well! Deal with her . . . come back home. At least . . . with you. Do you mind?"

It was tempting to leave the conversation just like this. Reagan was with her. Stacy knew about it. End of story. Except it wasn't.

"No, no, I don't mind. But, um, we are taking a trip. Thought you ought to know."

"What? A trip? Where?"

"Uh, a rather long one." Reagan was shaking her head vigorously and mouthing, *Don't tell! Don't tell her!* But Maggie swallowed and added, "On the bike."

"*What?!*" Maggie had to hold the phone away from her ear, the screech was so loud. "Mom! Are you crazy! . . . could you do this? . . . ruin our vacation!" The voice on the other end had turned into a wail. ". . . cancel the cruise . . . come home!"

"Stacy! Don't cancel your cruise. We are fine. I repeat, we are fine. Don't cancel your cruise. But I'm having a hard time hearing you. Bad connection. Just check in at your next port, okay? Bye, honey! Love you!"

Maggie clicked Off and looked at Reagan. Her granddaughter's mouth was a big round O. "Grams! That was amazing! I can't believe it! Woo hoo!" The girl leaped on the motel bed and started jumping up and down, laughing hysterically.

Maggie shook her head, but she couldn't help the wry grin that snuck onto her face. "You know we're both going to have to face the music when your folks get home, don't you?"

"Oh, I know! I know! But—" Reagan jumped off the bed and gave her grandmother a bone-crushing hug. "You said we're fine! You're going to let me go on the rest of the trip with you! Woo hoo!"

Maggie's phone rang again. A different ring than the one she'd programmed for Stacy. She glanced at the ID. Just a number, no name. "Shh, shh!" She waved vigorously at Reagan to calm down, then answered the call with a cautious, "Hello?"

"Sister Maggie? It's Sister Vicky—"

"Vicky! Yes, it's Maggie. Sorry, I didn't recognize the number."

"Are you still in town?"

"Yes. At the Motel 6 near the Fairgrounds. Not planning to leave until tomorrow morning. What's up?"

"Oh, good. Sister Maggie, if you don't mind, can Odell and I come over, take you out for pie and coffee? Odell really wants to share something with you. About Coop . . ."

Chapter 21

T HE WAITRESS SET HER SERVING TRAY DOWN on the folding tray stand and began passing out their pie orders: pecan pie for Pastor Odell, banana cream for Sister Vicky, triple berry for Maggie, apple pie *a la mode* for Reagan. Unsure what this was going to be about, Maggie had at first asked Reagan if she'd mind staying with Rocky at the motel while she went out with the Smiths for a while. But when the Smiths arrived, they'd asked, "Isn't Reagan coming?" And Odell had added, "This might be important for your granddaughter to hear."

Maggie wasn't sure about that. Couldn't she just tell Reagan later after she knew what this was all about? But, here they were. Guess they'd know soon enough.

The waitress topped off their coffee and smiled sweetly. "Y'all need anything else, just let me know."

Vicky eyed the waitress as she disappeared. "Hm. You can take a girl out of the South, but you can't take the South out of a girl. I'm guessin' . . . Georgia."

Maggie lifted an eyebrow. "Really? You can tell?" All Southern accents sounded the same to her. "I grew up on the West Coast. No accents there."

Vicky snorted. "Ha. Maybe not. But anyone can tell you're from Chicago now."

Reagan snickered, and Maggie gave her a playful shove. She was sure Vicky had never heard a *real* Chicago accent. Taking a sip of her hot coffee, she glanced at Vicky's husband. Odell Smith had been pretty quiet so far. But she had to admit she was curious. "Pastor? Vicky said you have something you'd like to share with me. About Coop."

"Yes. I—" The man cleared his throat. "I don't know if you've heard this story before, but even if you have, I'm sure you haven't

149

heard my side of it." He exchanged a look with Vicky and then said, "Spring of 1980, May it was. I was just eighteen then, just a little older than Reagan here, a street punk who thought he knew everything . . ."

* * * *

The lanky teenager lurked in the doorway of the building across the street from the church on the corner, smoking a cig and waiting. Church should be over soon, shouldn't it? Huh. It was almost two! He didn't really want the preacher catchin' him hangin' around, or he'd probably be on his case in a hot second 'bout comin' to church and gettin' saved. But that Suki Walker was *fine*, man—had a cute swagger that really turned him on. One of his homies had told him Suki an' her sister sometimes came to church here. At least her old man wouldn't be around to yell at him—probably sleepin' off a drunk from Saturday night. "Fast Eddie" Walker had a rep in that neighborhood for scarin' the heck out of any dude who looked twice at his girls.

Oh yeah. They were propping the doors open now. Just had to wait till the girls came out, then he could make his move. He knew exactly the route the Walker girls took to get home.

Waitaminnit. Somethin' was weird. A couple of the church men came out in their black suits and ties, lookin' this way and that like somethin' was wrong, then they motioned for others to come outside. One of the suits was the preacher—Pastor Victor Washington it said on the little sign. And that white preacher guy, too. Odell had heard about the white family who'd moved into the neighborhood a few years back, hookin' up with that church. He'd seen 'em around. Good-lookin' chick for a wife, two little kids. Lived upstairs over the church. The white dude had even been with the regular pastor a few times when the preacher had tried to talk to him. Huh. Fat chance he was gonna go to church. *Especially* not a church with a white preacher.

"Odell!" A hiss at his elbow made him jump.

"Malik! Whatchu doin' sneaking up on me like that!" Odell shoved his younger brother away. "Get outta here, you punk."

He didn't want Malik around while he was trying to hit on Suki Walker. Malik was two years younger than Odell, closer to Suki Walker's age, might even be in her class at the high school, and he didn't want any competition.

"Ain't you heard, man? Somethin's goin' down. People real upset by what happened down in Miami."

"Whatchu talkin' about?" Odell dropped his cig and ground it out with the toe of his shoe, still keeping an eye on what was going on across the street. Looked like the two preachers were urging the women and children to leave quickly and get on home. What in heck was going on?

"Them four cops what shot that McDuffie guy down in Miami last year? Been all over the news. They just got acquitted yesterday. Place is blowin' up down there. Big riot, fires an' everything. People mad here, too. Pops said the Urban League is organizing a march today here on Broadway. But word goin' around the streets *we* takin' to the streets tonight, too, to support our brothers down in Miami."

Odell glared at Malik. "How you know all this stuff, punk?" Yeah, he'd heard about those cops killing that guy last year. Got charged with manslaughter or something. Shoulda been first-degree murder, far as he was concerned. Hadn't heard about them pigs gettin' acquitted though. *Damn!* He didn't like his kid brother knowing more than he did about any action going on in the neighborhood either.

Grabbing Malik by his jacket, he walked quickly away from the church. Suki Walker could wait. If there was any action going on tonight, he was gonna be part of it.

* * * *

Maggie realized she was hardly breathing. Her mouth felt like cotton, and she reached for her glass of water. Yes, she remembered that Sunday. One of the deacons had slipped a note to Pastor Vic during his sermon, and he'd stopped to briefly inform the congregation what was happening in Miami at that very moment. They'd interrupted the service and began to pray right then.

During the prayers, the phone in the office began to ring. Another deacon went to answer it, and a few minutes later came back and pulled Pastor Vic and Coop aside. That was when it was decided everyone should go home—"and stay home," Pastor Vic had said sternly—just in case there was trouble in the neighborhood. These incidents, he reminded them, had a way of spreading from city to city, as they'd seen back in '67—and almost every year since then.

Coop had found Maggie and urged her to take the children up to their apartment, pull the blinds, and stay there. "What about you?" she'd asked him. "Aren't you coming, too?"

"I'm going to stay with Pastor Vic and some of the other men. Just in case we're needed to help keep things calm."

"But—"

"Maggie, go. Don't worry. It's just a precaution."

Which she did. She did go, but she also worried. Though for several hours nothing seemed to be happening, in fact everything was quiet. Too quiet. When she'd peeked through the window blind looking over Broadway, the street seemed unusually deserted. But it was hard to entertain the kids. Seven-year-old Mike had whined about wanting to go to the park, and four-year-old Stacy refused to take her nap.

That was before cell phones. She had no way to call Coop and tell him to just come home. This was ridiculous.

Maggie was trying to feed supper to her restless children when she first became aware of rising voices outside. She wanted to peek through the blind, but Mike was teasing his little sister by stabbing his fork into the hot dog wheels on her plate and Stacy was screeching. And then—

Pop, poppity, pop, pop, pop, bang, bang, bang! Poppity, pop!

Maggie had grabbed both kids and hit the floor.

* * * *

The string of firecrackers going off was the signal. Odell was excited. All hell was about to break loose. One of the guys from one of the neighborhood gangs still had a string of firecrackers from last year's Fourth of July, and someone said they should set them off as a signal to join the protest.

Odell wasn't sure who all would take to the streets. He saw the Urban League types gathering, many carrying signs: JUSTICE FOR McDUFFIE! . . . JAIL RACIST COPS! . . . PARENTS FOR PEACE . . . NOT ONE MORE . . . FIGHT INJUSTICE . . . SAVE OUR BOYS. But he also recognized some dudes from the big rival gangs, others from the small local gangs, and some like himself who just hung around the edges. He'd told Malik to stay with him, but it wasn't long until the pack of young black men who swarmed onto Broadway swallowed up his brother, and he lost sight of him. Regular folks were also spilling into the main drag from the side streets. Working stiffs, old folks, men he saw hanging out at the barbershop, high school friends of Malik, college types, even moms dragging their kids along. Well, maybe his kid brother would be okay. The crowd was a mixed bag.

Somebody started a chant: "No justice! No peace!" The decibels swelled as the crowd got bigger. So far, the crowd was noisy but peaceful. They passed the Minneapolis Public Schools district office, dark and silent, but suddenly somebody from the crowd ran at the building and threw something heavy at one of the windows, and it shattered with a loud clatter of glass. Like a spark igniting dry tinder, part of the crowd—mostly young, many of them members of gangs—started running and Odell heard more glass shattering as the protest passed a line of storefronts in the next block. Others in the crowd, older voices, began yelling, "No! Stop! Stop!" "Keep it peaceful!"

Suddenly Odell heard sirens in the distance and coming closer. More people began running. Odell had to run, too, to keep from being knocked down. But it crossed his mind, why were they running straight for the cops? At least half a dozen black-and-whites were heading straight for them, lights flashing, sirens screaming.

Anxiety took over his earlier excitement. He looked this way and that. Where was Malik? Out of the corner of his eye, Odell saw a flash of fire sail through the air. A bottle bomb, a Molotov cocktail, actually! The next second, a small store burst into flames even as the cop cars screeched to a stop, half of them sideways, blocking the street. Doors flew open. Police spilled out. A bullhorn boomed, "Disperse now! This is the police! Disperse now!"

Another wail filled the air, punctuated by loud blasts of an air horn—a fire truck was barreling up one of the side streets. But it couldn't get through because of the swarm of people in the intersection. Firemen jumped out of the truck, searching for the closest hydrant.

Odell heard new voices pleading, "Please, people! Go home. We don't want you to get hurt." Glancing over people's heads, he realized the "traffic jam" of protestors, cops, cop cars, and the fire truck had converged at the intersection where he'd been hanging around that morning waiting for Suki Walker to appear. The double doors of the corner church were wide open, and the two pastors were walking into the crowd, hands high in the air, trying to calm things down. "Please, people. Go home. If you need a place to go, come inside." They gestured toward the two-story brick building.

"Humph. Good luck," Odell smirked beneath his breath, though he saw some of the parents with children leaving the crowd and hurrying up the closest side street. Others turned around trying to go back the other way, pushing against the crowd.

The bullhorn kept blaring, "Disperse now! Or you will be arrested for disturbing the peace!" The line of cops moved forward toward the protesters. Some of the young guys began taunting them. Then—another Molotov cocktail sailed through the air and smashed against the side of the little church—and suddenly the police were swinging their nightsticks, throwing some of the taunters to the ground and cuffing them. People began screaming, pushing each other this way and that.

Without warning, a blast of water from a fire hose hit the crowd in the intersection. Odell felt himself lifted right off his feet, then crashing down. An explosion of pain ricocheted through his brain as his head hit the edge of a curb. Light and darkness swirled around him. A warm thick liquid filled his throat. He gagged and tried to spit it out—blood?

Malik! He had to find Malik! He tried to get up, but another blast of water held him there. Other people were falling around him. Somebody stumbled over him and stepped on his groin. Panic surged through his gut. *O God, O God!* He was going to be killed right here on Broadway—and his parents didn't even know he was here.

Odell fought to stay conscious, but the din around him faded in and out. He had the sensation of being lifted, arms around his chest and shoulders. Being carried. And then everything went black.

* * * *

Pastor Odell paused in the telling and reached for his glass of water. His pie sat untouched in front of him. The silence stretched for several long seconds as Maggie toyed with the friendship bracelet Reagan had given her, words failing her. But Reagan spoke up. "You, like, fainted?"

Odell nodded. "Not for long. Came to a few minutes later I think, gradually realized I was inside the church. This white face—your husband, Maggie—was bending over me, wiping blood from my mouth and chin. Must've bit my tongue. The back of my head hurt like a jackhammer was going at it—a bit bloody back there, too, it turned out. I tried to get up, said I had to find my brother, but he said Pastor Vic had already gone out to find him."

Maggie licked her dry lips. "Oh! Yes, what happened to your kid brother?"

Pastor Odell grimaced. "He'd been arrested. Ended up in juvie detention for 'inciting to riot,' though they went pretty easy on him because of his age. Pastor Coop wanted to take me to the hospital because of the blow to my head, but I wouldn't go. I could still hear yelling and screams outside. I thought the police might come into the church and get me, too. But your husband said I was safe, the church was a sanctuary. At the time, I wasn't even sure what that meant. But he bandaged my head and brought me water—and when everything finally quieted down outside, he and Pastor Vic took me home. Said they wanted to make sure I got home safely, and also tell my folks what happened to Malik, so they could go post bail or whatever."

Maggie blew out a long breath, her own thoughts scrambling to remember. When Coop had finally come up to the apartment that evening, he said he'd helped a young man who'd gotten injured and had taken him home. That was all. She'd never asked the boy's name. She was just so relieved that Coop and Pastor Vic and the other men were okay. She'd been more worried about the Molotov cocktail that had crashed against the building, which had flashed up and burned for a while, but hadn't done too much damage before the firemen had put it out because the building was brick. Just the wood framing around some of the windows, small and high, had been charred and had to be replaced.

Pastor Odell picked up his story. "You might think this strange, but I avoided that intersection and the church for several months. I was embarrassed that this preacher—a white one at that—had helped me. After all, we were mad at the whites—all the white folks. Cops, teachers, preachers, politicians. But one day when no one was around, I saw the door was open, so I slipped into the church, and sure enough Pastor Coop was there in the back. Down on his knees fixing a clogged toilet, I think. 'Why'd you do it?' I asked him. 'Why'd you help me?' He just shrugged and said, 'I don't know. Why not? I saw you fall when they blasted the crowd with the fire hose, and I knew you needed help.'"

Reagan, who'd been listening soberly to the pastor's story, blurted out. "That's it? That's all my gramps said?"

A small smile appeared on Pastor Odell's face and slowly grew wider. "No. He also said, 'That's the Jesus way.'"

Odell reached out an arm and pulled his wife Vicky closer to him in the booth, his voice husky. "Four words that changed my life."

Chapter 22

*T*HAT'S THE *JESUS WAY. Four words that changed my life."*
Odell Smith's sober declaration still echoed in Maggie's thoughts as she hunched over her maps the next morning. She hadn't been able to respond. The catch in her throat had made words impossible. Besides, how did she say that this church, these people, had opened her eyes and her heart to a larger vision of "the Jesus way," and had changed the course of *her* life, too?

The lump in the other bed stirred as Maggie sipped her first cup of coffee from the in-room coffee maker. She missed her computer where she could zoom in and get a satellite view of the country they'd be going through on their next leg from Minnesota to Wyoming. But if her "guesstimations" were right, it was going to take them about three days to get to her cousin's ranch at the rate she felt comfortable riding the motorcycle. Not to mention the insides of her thighs and her tailbone that were still complaining from the last three-day ride.

Still . . .

We did it, Coop! First stop. So glad we started here. But the circles on Coop's map and the route ahead went backward in time—her childhood, meeting Coop, the Jesus People commune, their first years together.

But stopping at New Hope first somehow seemed significant. It had been a turning point in their life. An immersion into another culture, another people whose life experience was different, who'd faced challenges she'd never had to face, but whose faith in Jesus ran very deep and real.

How would it affect her perspective on her life *before* New Hope?

"Grams?" Reagan mumbled sleepily. "Is it time to get up? You want me to take Rocky out?"

"Mmm, thanks, but we've already been out." Maggie bent over the map again. They might be able to make Watertown just over the South Dakota border today. Route 212 looked pretty good. Avoided the interstate and was a pretty straight shot. Should be able to do it in four or five hours plus a few stops.

Reagan sat up in the bed. "Oh. Guess what? Mom called me about 2:00 a.m. last night. Yeah, she forgot about the time difference. It was already morning over there. You were asleep, didn't want to wake you."

That got Maggie's attention. "She did? And—?"

The girl threw off the comforter and padded past Maggie toward the bathroom. "Whaddya think? She's mad as a bee with its stinger in backwards. She threatened to ground me for the rest of my life and dock my allowance when she gets home." Reagan started to close the bathroom door, and then poked her head out once more. "But she didn't say anything about flying home, and I heard someone hollering in the background that they needed to leave for the ship *right now*. So, I don't think we have to worry about her showing up in Wyoming with the sheriff in tow—for a few weeks anyway." With a smirk in her grandmother's direction, Reagan shut the bathroom door.

As the shower started running, Maggie shook her head and gave Rocky a scratch on the rump. "Hmm. Whaddya say, Rocky? Think Stacy would ground *me* if she could?" The dog cocked his head and gave a *wuff*. Maggie chuckled. "Yeah, me, too." She got up from the desk and stretched. "But, better get moving and get us some breakfast so we can get on the road, right ol' boy? Got a long way to go today."

* * * *

Their leather jackets actually felt good when they finally loaded their stuff onto the bike around 9:30. The sky was clear and blue, no rain predicted, but the temperature kicked back into the low 60s and wasn't supposed to go higher than 70 all day. "Perfect traveling weather, eh, Reagan?" Maggie grinned at her granddaughter through her open visor as she started the engine and pulled out of the motel parking lot. "I'm going to stop at that gas station over there, top off the tank. Then I want you to get me out of this city and onto Route 212 as soon as you can. No interstates though, got it?"

"Got it."

But as Maggie was filling up the gas tank a few minutes later, Reagan said, "Uh oh, Grams, look." She held up the GPS screen on her phone. "There's a crash icon on 212 just out of the city, and the route is marked with lots of red and orange around there." The girl scrolled around on the mobile map for a while, and then said, "Looks like Route 7 is clear. We can meet up with 212 later on, near a town called, uh—" She squinted at the screen. "—Montevideo. But, uh . . ."

"What?"

"Uh, do you mind if we go past your old church on the way out of town? I wanna take a picture of it—you know, start documenting this trip."

Maggie grimaced. "Should've thought of that yesterday." She sighed. "How far does that take us out of the way?"

"Not much. We gotta go west anyway. We can go across the river like we did yesterday, go by the church, and then drop down till we catch Route 7. Easy peasy. See?" She held out the GPS on her phone and gave Maggie a rundown of the route.

Oh, why not. She was glad visiting New Hope Friendship meant something to the girl. Maggie nodded, stuck her credit card in the slot to pay for the gas, and got back on the bike. "Just get us safely into orbit, Ensign Chekov."

Reagan gave her a weird look. What? Didn't the kid know the navigator from Star Trek?

The church was locked when they got there, but Reagan hopped out of the sidecar, took a picture of the front of the building with her phone, and then said, "I'll take Rocky and let him pee out back. Just be a minute." She snapped the leash on the dog and disappeared around the side of the building. More like three minutes, Maggie thought impatiently, but soon girl and dog were shoehorning themselves back into the sidecar. "Thanks, Grams. Uh, go back to Broadway, and then . . ."

Seemed to Maggie they did a lot of zigging and zagging before they got to Route 7, which had four lanes for a while, but eventually they were out in the country on a two-lane road without much traffic. The road threaded between several small lakes—part of a whole cluster of lakes she'd seen on the map west of the city—but soon became a straightaway across Minnesota, as farm buildings and fields of corn and soybeans flew by.

The speed limit was 60, but Maggie kept her speed to a comfortable 50 or 55, which meant any traffic that came up behind her usually passed them. Sometimes the drivers honked impatiently as they sped around, but some people grinned at her and gave her a thumbs up. Must be the sidecar—or her two passengers. Rocky did look cute wearing his goggles with his tongue and ears flopping in the wind, and Reagan more often than not gave everybody a friendly wave. Sometimes too friendly, Maggie thought.

Their visors were down now to avoid eating bugs, which made talking impossible, and Maggie's mind drifted to the conversation they'd had with the Smiths last night at the pie shop. Did Coop have any idea that New Hope's pastor after Victor Washington died was the same young man he'd rescued from the protest chaos that day? She doubted it, or he certainly would've told her.

Oh Coop. I wish you could've heard Odell's story. I know it would've meant so much to you.

It meant a lot to *her*. What if she had never taken this trip? Had never come back to visit New Hope, had never seen the fruit of his actions that day with her own eyes? Guess she'd been taking Coop for granted in some ways, forgetting how much guts it had taken to accept that first pastoral assignment, a white guy in a primarily black neighborhood, sticking out like a sore thumb. Of course, he'd had a great mentor in Pastor Vic, a seasoned pastor, wise to the tragic history and challenges of his people, a man who modeled what it meant to be a shepherd and a peacemaker.

But for Coop to react as he did in that explosive situation, wading into that chaotic crowd, putting himself in danger, picking up a young man he didn't know who'd been hurt, and sheltering him in the church—that had to come from deep in Coop's own character.

Maggie's heart clenched. Yes, that was the man she'd married. She shouldn't be surprised to hear what happened. Of course, that's what he would've done!

She was glad Reagan had come along to hear Pastor Odell's story. They hadn't talked about it yet. She guessed they both needed time to just let it sink in. But it was a reminder—in this case a wonderful, awesome reminder—that everything we say to another person, every act of love or kindness, is a seed planted. And something amazing just might grow from it, whether we ever see it or not.

A farm truck behind them blasted its horn, pulled out, and rattled past them, causing the whole bike and sidecar to shudder. Gripping the handlebars, Maggie shuddered, too, as one more thought crept into her brain: *The opposite is true as well.* Careless words, thoughtless actions—those were seeds, too. With consequences. And sometimes even the best of us, even her usually compassionate husband, sowed those other seeds, hurting those we love.

She winced as one word pushed its way to the front of her thoughts:

Chris.

* * * *

They stopped at a Subway in Montevideo for a lunch break, where Reagan searched online for a pet-friendly hotel in Watertown between bites of her chicken-and-bacon-ranch-melt. "The Super 8 looks pretty decent, not too expensive." She grinned slyly at her grandmother. "It also has a pool."

Good. Keep Reagan happy. "Well, call ahead and make a reservation." Maggie handed over her credit card. She had a feeling that three days in the sidecar was going to get old for her granddaughter sooner rather than later. Even though they only had a few more hours to go till they could stop for the night, the thought of two more days before reaching their next destination made Maggie feel tired. And after that? The long stretch over the mountains to the West Coast?

Her knees felt weak. Nope. Nope. Couldn't go there yet. *One day at a time, Maggie Cooper,* she told herself.

But watching Reagan playing frisbee with Rocky a short while later in a nearby park, giving him some good exercise before packing them into the sidecar again, Maggie murmured a prayer of thanks that her granddaughter had shown up. No way could she run with the dog like that.

A swim in the hotel pool that evening, some tasty Chinese food, and a good night's rest gave Maggie the boost she needed for another day on the road. She'd called her cousin Charly—the one closest to her in age of the three Baker cousins in Wyoming—just to make sure he and his wife Kitty were expecting her. He gave her some directions out to the ranch once they crossed into Wyoming, but they sounded so complicated Maggie knew he'd have to repeat them again.

"Hey," Reagan said, tracing the route Maggie had marked on the map, "you said we're heading for Eagle Butte today? Looks like it's on the Cheyenne River Reservation!" She tapped it into her phone. "Google says it's the tribal headquarters of the Cheyenne River Sioux Tribe. Cool. Wonder what it's like?"

Maggie shrugged and smiled. "Guess we'll see." Her GPS said it was about 225 miles to Eagle Butte—a decent ride, she figured, five hours or so, not too long. The weather was about ten degrees warmer today, still not too bad. But after a couple of hours on the road, the long, straight highway through flat, flat countryside began to wear on her. Her helmet felt hot and stuffy. And the only place they could find to eat was a burger shack in a tiny one-gas-station town. Maggie filled up the tank again, uncertain when she'd find another.

Hopefully Eagle Butte would provide an interesting diversion. And a decent place to sleep that night.

She was wrong.

The town barely poked up from the flat prairie and farmland around it. As they rode slowly through the town's main street, they passed an occasional hardware store, a small grocery, a church, a bunch of unmarked buildings, a "trading post," a gift shop. And not much else. Maggie detoured through some of the side streets, but most of the one-story frame houses looked weathered and in need of a paint job. Not many people seemed to be out and about. Maggie was beginning to wonder if they'd find a motel in such a small town.

Reagan yanked off her helmet as they puttered along. "Grams, can we stop already? I'm really thirsty and I gotta pee!"

Hmph. Bossy kid. But Maggie needed a break, too. She headed back for the gas station she'd seen that had a Dairy Queen attached. A couple of dark-haired kids were happily licking ice cream cones while a bored-looking teenage girl sat on the lone picnic table, tapping on her cell phone. She didn't even look up when Maggie pulled in with her passengers in the sidecar. But the kids—a boy and a girl—ran over and wanted to pet the dog. Reagan scrambled out of the sidecar and made a beeline for the restroom. Maggie spied a faucet and got water for Rocky, then went inside and ordered two double-dip ice cream cones.

"Are there any motels in town?" she asked the woman who handed her the cones.

"Could say that. Got two if you ain't too partic'ler."

"Two?" Maggie felt relieved. All they needed was one.

The woman pointed back the way they'd come. "Cheyenne River Motel back thataway, less'n a mile. Can't miss it." Though they obviously had. "Be on your right." Then she winked. "But like I said, if you ain't too partic'ler."

Reagan had reappeared and heard what the woman said. Pulling out her phone, she busied herself on it while they sat and ate their ice cream. Then she leaned close to her grandmother and hissed, "Take a look at the reviews, Grams. One person found *bugs* in the bed!" She shuddered. "No way!"

Maggie scrolled through several reviews. Not too flattering. Though even the one and two-star reviews said the staff was kind and helpful.

"Let's keep going, Grams. It's only two-thirty. Maybe there's a bigger town up ahead. We'll get where we're goin' tomorrow all the sooner!"

They'd already gone 250 miles. But maybe they could go a few more hours. She approached the woman again. "Are there any motels up ahead? Going west?"

The woman shrugged. "Mm, not much in the way of motels along 212. Might be somethin' in Belle Fourche though—a Super 8, I think. Near the Wyoming border."

Reagan checked the digital map. "Only 140 miles or so. What's that—three hours max? I'll run Rocky around, give him some exercise, and we'll be good to go." Her granddaughter had miraculously caught a second wind.

Spoiled. That's what they were. But Maggie had to admit that the "bugs in the bed" review had turned her off, too. A Super 8 sounded like the Ritz right now.

* * * *

It had been a long day—too long. Who knew South Dakota was such a wide state? Maggie flopped on the bed in the Super 8 after begging Reagan to order in. Her whole body ached. She didn't feel like going *any*where, even to eat.

Thank goodness they were going to stop tomorrow to spend a few days with her Baker cousins. She had always loved coming to Wyoming for family vacations when she was growing up—loved the wide-open country, the big sky, the smell of sagebrush. Her Uncle Brad had let her drive a tractor at age ten, showed her how to saddle a horse, and made her feel important by letting her open and close the gate to the branding chute when they branded the new crop of calves. Not to mention the assorted dogs and barn cats that were always underfoot.

Made her feel cheated though. Her three cousins had grown up in this paradise, first settled by Grandfather Baker way back when, and then it was taken over by her dad's older brother who'd stayed to farm. *Her* father, on the other hand, had decided to be a schoolteacher—which was why *she'd* grown up on the campus of a private Christian K-12 school in Portland, Oregon. No pets allowed.

Maggie cast an eye toward her granddaughter, who was on the phone ordering pasta-something from an Italian eatery. None of her grandkids had ever been to visit the Wyoming relatives, even though she and Coop had brought Mike and Stacy and Chris a few times when they were younger. Easy-going Mike had liked it okay. Stacy had been bored out of her mind. Chris, though, had been in hog heaven, just like Maggie had been as a kid, asking all kinds of questions like, "Why do they dehorn the calves?" and "What does 'artificial insemination' mean?" Ha. No wonder he wanted to become a vet.

Her eyelids started to drift closed. *Wonder what Reagan will think of my country cousins?* More to the point, what would her country cousins think of *their* cousin riding in on a motorcycle with a goggle-wearing dog and her citified granddaughter—tattoos, piercings, tri-colored hair, and all—in a sidecar?

Chapter 23

THEY SLEPT IN THE NEXT MORNING—well, except Rocky, who still had to go out at the usual time. Which meant Maggie didn't actually sleep in much either. Well, even the extra twenty minutes helped, though her muscles ached so badly, she could only roll out of bed, and had to haul herself up using a chair.

Walking Rocky helped some. And breakfast. She finally felt alive enough to call her cousin Charly for a repeat on directions to his place, and he said, "What? You're in Belle Fourche? Hey, you're not that far from Devil's Tower. If you come over on Route 24, you could stop there, show your granddaughter. After that, it's only another hour or hour-and-a-half to our place. Just catch I-90 into Gillette. I could meet up with you and you can follow me to the ranch."

"Uh, I've been avoiding the Interstates." Had she told him she was riding a motorcycle?

He chuckled. "Aw, it's nothin' out here. Two lanes goin' each way, big grassy median between. Honest. You'll be fine."

Reagan was excited about stopping to see the Devils Tower Monument. "They've got all these brochures about it." She waved a handful of brochures she'd picked up at the reception desk. "A real sacred place to a lot of Native American tribes. Listen . . ." She started reading various facts about some of the tribes that had peopled the Black Hills area—Lakota and Arapahoe, Cheyenne and Kiowa, Shoshone and Crow.

Given a choice, Maggie would have preferred to just get on to their destination. She'd been to the Devils Tower Monument a couple of times—once as a kid, and once when she and Coop had stopped with their three kids after a Baker reunion. But Reagan had never been and seemed eager to do some sightseeing. The

166

unusual geologic formation was definitely impressive, even in pictures. Maggie shrugged in resignation. Might as well.

What she hadn't figured on was the number of motorcycles thronging the road leading into the park and the attention her classic bike and sidecar attracted. Or maybe it was Reagan, who grinned and waved at their "fellow bikers" with teenage abandon. It was still fairly early in the day, so Maggie actually found a spot to park in the lot near the visitor center and closest to the hiking trails that circled the tower.

But she'd no sooner turned off the motor and removed her helmet than another biker sauntered over. "Hey, Granny. How ya doin'? Cool bike you got there." The guy was lean, shirtless, liberally tattooed, and chewed on a toothpick while he circled the bike. *Granny—hmph.* This biker assumed that was her "handle" without even asking. Just because she had gray hair. Talk about stereotyping.

The biker paused by the sidecar as Reagan removed her helmet, snapped the leash onto Rocky's collar, and started to get out. "Hey, little lady," he drawled, "need a hand?"

She ignored him and climbed out herself as the dog scrambled out after her. Then she faced him, hands on her hips, nose in the air. "I'm Cookie. You are—?"

His smirk widened as he looked from Reagan to Maggie and back again. "Okaaay. Granny and Cookie, eh? Nice to meetcha. I'm Ringo. That's my chopper over there." He jerked a thumb toward a souped-up, low-riding number with high handlebars. "Say, you two ever been to the Sturgis Motorcycle Rally? Not far from here, just back a ways over the state line in South Dakota. Comin' up in August. It's a great party!" He winked at Reagan. "You'd have a blast, Cookie."

"We're just passing through," Maggie said curtly. "Won't be around in August. "C'mon, Re—" She almost said 'Reagan,' but no way did she want this jerk to know her granddaughter's real name. "—Cookie," she finished. Taking Rocky's leash from Reagan, she headed for the visitor center. Reagan scurried after her.

"You should think about it, Granny!" the guy called after them. "You could enter your bike in the classics division! Probably win!"

"Keep walking," Maggie hissed at Reagan.

"Could show you a real good time, Cookie!" His voice sailed after them.

Out of the corner of her eye, Maggie saw Reagan flip him the finger without even a glance back. "Reagan!" she gasped. Her granddaughter just marched straight ahead, eyes narrowed, lips tight.

They had to leave Rocky outside while they went into the visitor center to use the restroom, where they also discovered no pets were allowed on the hiking trails. Maggie thought about offering to stay with the dog while Reagan went on the hike around the tower by herself, but after meeting "Ringo," she didn't like that idea either.

Hmph. Where were Buzz and Smoky and Hawk when you needed them?

Reagan shrugged when they saw the "No Pets on Hiking Trails" sign. "That's okay, Grams. We don't need to do the hike." Her eyes traveled up the long vertical ridges of the tower that stood a mere 150 yards from the visitor center. "What I'd *really* like to do is climb the tower. Lots of people do, you know."

Climb the tower? Maggie gaped at the huge rock formation, thrust up out of the ground hundreds of feet into the air—800 feet? 900? The girl had to be kidding! "Yeah, I know, but—" Maggie flipped open one of the brochures that said, "Climbing the Tower." "See? They ask people not to climb the tower the whole month of June out of respect for certain sacred ceremonies important to some of the tribes." There. Thank goodness for June.

Reagan giggled. "I know. But today is July first."

What? Maggie checked her phone. Well, darn it, the kid was right.

"Don't worry, Grams. I *am* gonna climb the tower one day. Just not today." Reagan took Rocky's leash and headed back toward the parking lot.

Hmph. Well, thank goodness for the month of June anyway.

* * * *

Cousin Charly was right. I-90 practically felt like a country road as they headed for Gillette. They met up with him at a Perkins Family

Restaurant just off I-90 in the middle of town—and her cousin burst out laughing when they pulled into the parking lot alongside his pickup and clambered off the motorcycle and sidecar. "Maggie Baker Cooper!" he bellowed. "What is *this*? You told me you were traveling with your grandkid and your dog. But you didn't say nothin' 'bout this contraption here!"

Maggie made a funny face. "Oops."

He took off his cowboy hat and scratched his head, which was mostly bald, still chuckling. "You are one crazy woman, you know that, cuz? C'mere." Parking the hat back on his head, he wrapped her in a big bear hug. "Been too long."

Smothered in his chest, Maggie suddenly teared up. It'd been months since she'd been hugged so warmly by a man. Not since Coop had died. For some reason, she felt safe. Loved.

Reagan cleared her throat.

"Hey. Where are my manners?" Charly released Maggie and held out his hand. "You must be Reagan. Welcome to Wyoming, young lady. Aw, forget the handshake. You're family!" And he gave her a big hug, too.

Maggie smiled. So much for worrying about how her cousins would receive her granddaughter. Well, Charly, anyway.

Charly glanced at his watch. "Hey, if you two can hold off for half an hour or so, Kitty's making a big lunch for us. You wanna just follow me in the pickup?" His shoulders started shaking again. "Just can't believe you came all this way in that thing. Hee hee hee." Then he raised an eyebrow at Reagan. "You wanna ride with me, young lady? Got more legroom than that thing, I promise you."

To Maggie's surprise, Reagan hopped into the cab of the battered pickup, which had once been red, but was now more rust than paint. Rocky had been busy lifting his leg on the tires of nearby cars, but she quickly got him back into the sidecar, put her helmet back on, and followed the pickup out of the restaurant parking lot.

The road led right out of town heading south, and the town quickly gave way to grassland as far as the eye could see. "Lots of running around room out here, Rocky," she said inside her helmet, which the dog couldn't hear.

Fifteen or twenty minutes down the road, the pickup turned off on a side road. In the distance, Maggie could see the cluster of buildings that made up the Grassy Butte Ranch. Grassy Butte wasn't the original Baker ranch Maggie used to visit as a kid—that was the Triple B, inherited by her oldest cousin, Ed, Charly's big brother. But Ed's wife had died of cancer a few years ago, and he'd retired to Casper, Wyoming. Ed's son Brad was running the home place now. Maggie's other Baker cousin, Deborah, Charly's sister, the youngest of her Uncle Barry's three kids, had also married a farmer and settled nearby. Hopefully she'd get to see all three families while they were here.

The side road was paved for a short distance, then gave way to gravel. Maggie was glad for her closed visor, but she also dropped back a hundred yards to keep from eating dust from the pickup.

She followed the pickup as it turned into the long driveway up to the main house, a modest one-story ranch surrounded by a lawn and trees and flowers—a mini oasis compared to the treeless landscape all around them.

As Maggie pulled up beside the pickup and turned off the motor, a big black Labrador loped around the corner of the house, gave a couple short barks, then skidded to a stop beside Rocky, who had hopped out of the sidecar. The two dogs circled each other warily, sniffing butts, as Charly's wife Kitty came out of the house wiping her hands on a dishtowel. "Oh my goodness! Is that you, Maggie Cooper?"

Maggie slid gingerly off the bike, took off her helmet, and gave her cousin-in-law a hug. "Oh, Maggie," Kitty said, her forehead wrinkled in concern, "we're so sorry to hear about your husband. You must miss him terribly. But now he's gone to glory, dear man."

Maggie just gave a weak smile. She wasn't ready to talk about Coop yet.

Reagan slammed the door of the pickup, introductions were made, and they were ushered into the house. "You must be famished!" Kitty gushed. "Why don't you wash up in there"—she pointed toward a bathroom—"and we can sit right down. We're having 'Pile On'— that's what the grandkids call it when we put out all the makings for taco salad, and you make your own. Hope that's all right."

Hands washed, they gathered around the kitchen table and Charly bowed his head. "For what we are about to receive, may the Lord make us truly grateful. And may we always be mindful of the needs of others, for Jesus' sake." A pause. Then, "And thank you for the safe arrival of cousin Maggie and her granddaughter. Amen."

Maggie smiled as she lifted her head. She hadn't heard that little prayer since, well, since the last time they were here. The memory felt warm, comforting.

Charly leaned conspiratorially toward Reagan as he reached for the bowl of chopped lettuce. "We call this an SOS meal. Stretch-or-Starve." He grinned. "Dig in, young lady."

Reagan laughed and started her "Pile On."

"So," Kitty said, "were you named after President Reagan, dear?"

The girl rolled her eyes. "Uhhh, hope not. He was before my time."

"Well," Kitty said sweetly, "you should feel honored. He was one of my favorite presidents."

"So!" Charly boomed, coming to the rescue. "Tell us about this trip of yours." Maggie shot him a grateful glance. She was definitely hoping they could avoid talking politics while they were here. She chattered about Coop fixing up the bike and planning this trip before he died, about Stacy and Chad's cruise in the Mediterranean, about Mike's oldest graduating from homeschool this spring. Then she got Charly talking about the lack of rain so far that summer in Wyoming, and whether the Bakers would get a hay crop this year or not.

"Chuck Jr. and his family are coming over for supper," Kitty said as they cleared the table after lunch. Chuck and Kitty's son lived in a newish two-story across the road, farming with his dad. "We'll eat kind of early—5:30 if that's all right. We usually go to prayer meeting Wednesday nights. Starts at 7:30—uh, if you want to go, that is."

"Oh," Maggie said. Not exactly her first choice on their first night here. "Will Chuck and his family be going, too?"

Kitty flitted a hand. "Oh, they go to that big new church in town. You know young people—they church hop, want all that contemporary stuff. But I thought it'd be nice if we all went together tonight since you're here."

Maggie presumed Kitty was referring to the small country chapel the Baker family had attended since Grandpa Baker's day. A bit stodgy, very traditional. But when in Rome . . . "Well, sure. I'll go with you." She didn't say "we," giving Reagan an out if needed.

"Great." Kitty beamed. "CJ—that's our grandson—is about your age, Reagan. He just graduated high school, going to state college in the fall. And Mitsy is thirteen. They were excited to hear you were coming. What year are you?"

"Uh, supposed to be a senior next year."

Maggie gave her granddaughter a sharp look. *Supposed* to be a senior? What did *that* mean?

Kitty sighed. "We'll sure miss CJ around here. He's been a big help to his dad and Charly, running this place. It's always a question, isn't it? Who's gonna take over the farm?"

* * * *

Charles Jr.—"Chuck" as they called him—reminded Maggie of Mike, her oldest, also in his early forties, easy-going, pleasant, not to mention good-looking in a tanned, Marlboro-cowboy kind of way.

"Yeah, I remember your kids," he told Maggie as they hung around the kitchen while his mom and his wife Paula set out two big pans of baked lasagna, garlic bread, and a humongous tossed salad that evening. "We were all just kids then." He turned to Reagan. "So, your mom is Stacy? If I remember right, she wasn't too keen on country life. Stayed in the house most of your folks' visit."

Reagan snorted. "Yeah, well, that sounds like my mom."

"What about you?" CJ asked. At seventeen, Charly's grandson was all legs and arms. "Do you like the farm?"

Reagan shrugged. "Don't really know. I just got here. But—" She shot a grin at Maggie. "I like getting away from the city. Riding the bike with Grams and Rocky is fun. And I've got an open mind. So, show me what's to like. Maybe I will."

CJ grinned. "Okay. I'll show you around tomorrow. You can ride fence with me. I've got some repairs to do in the east pasture. You can see our Angus herd. We've got a prize bull out there."

"A *bull*?" Reagan grimaced. "Uh, well, okay."

Maggie flashed her granddaughter a grin. *Good for you.*

Mitsy, the thirteen-year-old, had been shyly staring at Reagan. But with all this good-natured banter, she finally spoke up. "Are we cousins?"

Reagan shrugged. "I guess. Somehow."

"Third cousins," Maggie prompted. "Mitsy, your grandpa Charly is my first cousin. Our kids—your dad and my daughter, Reagan's mom—are second cousins, which makes you and Reagan third cousins. Make sense?"

Mitsy nodded and got braver. "So, do all the city kids dye their hair colors like that"—she pointed at Reagan's tri-colored forelock that fell over half her face—"and wear those little rings in their lips? I mean, doesn't it hurt?"

"Supper's on!" Kitty sang out, bringing out the last dish. "Come sit down everybody!"

Good save, Kitty, Maggie thought.

But Reagan didn't seem perturbed. "Nope, and—yeah, a little," she stage-whispered to the younger girl. "Tell you about it later."

Maggie noticed that Mitsy made a point to claim a chair at the table next to Reagan. She smiled to herself. Country mouse meets city mouse. So far, so good.

Chapter 24

Maggie had intended to sleep in—the first time in a week that she didn't have to share a room with Reagan. *Or* Rocky. Reagan had asked if the dog could stay with her in the tiny guest room just off the family room in the finished basement, and Rocky had seemed content to curl up on an old towel beside the narrow single bed. The two had been bonding a lot, scrunched together in the sidecar for hours at a time. Maggie felt a little jealous.

But light was sneaking through the blinds in the guest room on the main floor where Maggie had slept, beckoning her outside. Putting in her contacts and pulling on her jeans from yesterday— she really needed to wash some clothes!—she crept quietly out of her room, hoping she wouldn't wake anybody. But the intoxicating smell of fresh coffee drew her toward the unoccupied kitchen, where a little radio on the counter was quietly playing some country-western music beside the gurgling Mr. Coffee.

Well, somebody was already up and out.

Maggie poured herself a cup of coffee and pushed open the back door onto the deck. The black Lab got up and sniffed at her. She stroked his silky head. "Hey there, Pepper. Wanna go for a walk with me?" But satisfied with his smell-check, Pepper just laid back down again with a *whuff.* Huh. So much for a canine companion. She was tempted to go back inside and get Rocky but decided against it. No telling what kind of ruckus might ensue.

Besides, it was so wondrously quiet. And the sky was so big! Along the horizon, a pile of clouds, still tinged with pink and yellow from the sunrise, framed the immense blue dome overhead. One of the things she loved about Wyoming and these other western states. Big sky.

Coffee cup in hand, Maggie walked down the driveway to the gravel road, deciding to walk down to the main road and back. She didn't want company just yet. Just wanted to soak up being here—her family home in a way, where her dad grew up, even if she didn't. Well, not *here* at Grassy Butte, but on the home place, the Triple B. What if her dad had been the one who stayed to farm instead of Uncle Barry? How different her life might have been!

Like the prayer meeting last night. Everyone went, including CJ and Mitsy, so Reagan came, too. They drove back toward Gillette in two cars but turned off on a side road on the outskirts of town and pulled up to a modest brick church with a simple sign: Gillette Bible Church. The Baker family—Charly and Kitty, Chuck Jr. and his family, and Maggie and Reagan—made up a third of the people there. Kitty played the piano while the song leader led them in singing the first and last verses of "Blessed Assurance"—familiar words she'd often sung in childhood:

> *Blessed assurance, Jesus is mine,*
> *O what a foretaste of glory divine!*
> *Heir of salvation, purchase of God,*
> *Born of His Spirit, washed in His blood.*
> *This is my story! This is my song!*
> *Praising my Savior, all the day long.*

At the piano, Kitty swung into the next song, "The Solid Rock," and Maggie felt herself soaking in the words of these old hymns: "On Christ, the solid Rock, I stand! All other ground is sinking sand . . ."

Whatever paths her life had taken, these hymns, these truths, were part of the fabric of who she was.

Reagan had squirmed when the pastor boomed a welcome "to our visitors" and asked Charly to introduce his guests. Charly, bless him, kept it simple, just introducing them as "my cousin and her granddaughter." Then, after announcing that the usual Saturday morning Women's Mission Circle was canceled because of the July 4th holiday, the pastor said they were going to do something different that night. A basket of prayer requests was passed around the room. Everyone was instructed to take one and then divide into groups of three or four to pray for the requests. Charly muttered under his breath, "What's he doing? Imitating the big boys?" but Kitty poked him in the side. Chuck Jr. and Paula huddled with their two kids, leaving Charly and Kitty to pull their chairs close to Maggie and Reagan. The requests were local: "Pray for rain." . . . "Anna Teague's mother has the flu." . . . "Church needs SS superintendent." . . . "Wicker family moving to Fort Collins, pray for good turnout at farm equipment auction next Saturday." Reagan shook her head when it was her turn to pray and passed her prayer request about the Wicker family to Maggie.

Poor kid was totally out of her element.

But that was it. Forty-five minutes tops. Ha—a far cry from the two-hour worship service they'd had back at New Hope Friendship. Still, Maggie had murmured to Reagan afterward, it was a good reminder that prayer meetings and worship services were going on every week in churches like this one—not just the big mega-churches or the ones on TV or even Grace and Mercy back home.

Still thinking about the tiny prayer meeting last night, Maggie had reached the paved road and turned back toward the house when she heard a vehicle come up behind her. Her cousin Charly pulled the rusty pickup alongside her and leaned out the window, grinning. "Wanna ride?"

She climbed into the passenger side. "Where have *you* been so early in the morning?"

"Over to the Triple B. Got a call from my nephew Brad at five this morning, some of their cows were out in the road. A fence was down. He needed some help rounding them up." He glanced at her coffee mug. "You didn't drink all the coffee, did you? I need a big coffee fix about now."

Maggie laughed. "I think you're safe. Reagan hasn't started on coffee yet."

The pickup rattled into the farmyard and pulled up beside the motorcycle. But Charly just sat for a moment, looking at her.

She squirmed. "What?"

"Dunno. Just havin' a hard time figurin' out what you're doing, riding that bike clear across the country, just you and the girl. I mean, Maggie! It's a little bit crazy, don't you think? Like, how far you plannin' to go?"

Maggie turned her head and looked out the side window. He was right. It was a little bit crazy. Actually, a lot crazy. After a long moment she turned back to him and sighed. "You're not alone. My kids think I'm crazy, too. It's just . . ." And she told him about Coop fixing up the bike and planning this trip for them to take together once she retired. And then the heart attack. "Guess it's my way of honoring my husband—taking this trip that he planned. I—I even brought his ashes with me. Maybe—" A new thought suddenly occurred to her. Maybe she should bury his ashes in the cemetery here—where her dad and mom and the other Baker relatives were buried. But for now, she just said, "Could we go to the cemetery while we're here? I'd like to show Reagan where her great-grandparents are buried."

"Sure," Charly said, finally opening his door. "Just say when."

* * * *

But as it turned out, Reagan was somewhere with CJ a good part of the day "riding fence," which Maggie vaguely remembered her Uncle Barry used to do on horseback, back when she was a kid visiting during a summer. Once when she was thirteen, he'd even invited her to ride with him for a couple of hours to fix a barbed wire fence that had snapped. She'd felt so proud, like a real cowgirl—until she'd gotten tangled up in the loose wire and got a nasty cut on her calf. Still had the scar.

But today CJ had taken a pickup and they didn't get back until four. By then Kitty was bustling around preparing food for the family BBQ over at the Triple B, and Maggie was helping. Well, Maggie thought, there was always tomorrow.

Reagan was grinning, babbling about King Tut, the "enormous bull" out with the Angus herd, and bragging about all the help she'd given CJ repairing breaks in the barbed wire fence. She was also sweaty and sunburned being out all day wearing just a pair of shorts and a tank top. "You should've given that girl a hat!" Charly chided his grandson.

And I should've given her some SPF50 suntan lotion, Maggie chided herself.

By the time Reagan had taken a cool shower and rubbed Aloe Vera gel on her face and shoulders, it was time to go. Reagan rode with Chuck's family in their big ol' SUV, while Maggie rode with Charly and Kitty. "Reagan seems to be having a good time," Charly mused, a twinkle in his eye. "Takes more after her grandmother than her mother, I'd say."

Maggie snorted. True enough—though it was Chris who had inherited her love for "all creatures great and small."

The day had been fairly mild for mid-summer—high seventies earlier, now starting to cool off as they passed the Triple B sign and headed up the long dirt driveway to the ranch buildings. The Triple B had changed over the years as the original homestead had passed from Grandpa Baker to succeeding generations. The old farmhouse had been totally renovated at least two or three times and now boasted central air, a shaded deck, a stone patio, an above-ground swimming pool, and the latest farm equipment parked neatly among the calving barn, corrals, auto shop, storage sheds, and a small vineyard.

The house and farmyard were already swarming with various members of the Baker clan as they parked the cars and climbed out. After a flurry of greetings and introductions, Reagan sidled up to Maggie and hissed, "I'll never keep everybody straight!"

"Don't worry about it," Maggie whispered back. "I'll sort it out for you later. They're all my cousins—three generations, all descended from my Uncle Barry, who was my dad's older brother. This motley crew is Uncle Barry's kids, and their kids and grandkids." She wasn't sure she could keep the third cousins—Reagan's generation—sorted by who belonged to whom either. "All you've got to remember are the three ranches: this one—the Triple B—farmed by Brad Baker. Then Grassy Butte, where we're staying with my cousin Charly. And my cousin Deborah's farm, the uh . . . can't remember the name, or even if it has one. Just Grigg's Farm, I think. Cousin Deborah married one of the local Grigg boys way back when."

"So, what does the Triple B stand for, anyway?" Reagan asked as they wandered toward the patio, which had three charcoal grills lined up, smoking and smelling delicious.

"Ha! Good question!" Charly, who happened to overhear, butted in. "My dad used to grouse that it stood for Bustin' Baker's Butt!"

Maggie laughed. "Sounds just like Uncle Barry."

"Oh, Charly!" Kitty slapped her husband's arm. "Don't keep spreading that nonsense. Ask Brad—he owns it now. It's got to be on the deed or something. There he is—Brad! Brad!" She hustled them over to their nephew, Brad Baker, who was manning the grills, along with his son Shane who was home for the summer from college. "Brad! Cousin Maggie and her granddaughter want to know what the Triple B stands for."

Brad Baker was about her son Mike's age, Maggie thought, maybe a few years older. Like Charly's son Chuck, who was primed to take over Grassy Butte, Brad had taken over the Triple B when his dad, Ed Baker, retired. Tanned and fit in his mid-forties, he waved smoke away from his face and snorted. "Why, Bustin' Baker's Butt of course. True then, still true now—right, Uncle Charly?" The two grinned like conspirators.

"Oh! You men are impossible," Kitty fussed and hustled away.

Shane elbowed his dad. "Ah, c'mon, Dad. Tell 'em . . . never mind, I will. Just don't tell Aunt Kitty," he said to Maggie and Reagan. "It's too much fun yanking her chain." The young man waved his long-handled spatula. "Old Grandpa Baker had two boys, Barry and Curtis—"

"Curtis was my dad," Maggie side-whispered to Reagan.

"—so the old man called it Baker, Baker, and Baker—the Triple B." Shane struck a dramatic pose. "Boring, isn't it?"

Now Reagan laughed. "Yeah. I like Bustin' Baker's Butt better."

You would, Maggie thought, but she grinned.

So far, so good.

"Hey, Shane," Charly said, grabbing for the boy's spatula. "I can help your dad do this. Why don't you take Reagan, show her around? Don't you and your sis have some heifers you're gonna show at the county fair later this summer? I know CJ and Mitsy would like to see them, too."

Maggie watched as the young people wandered off. "Thanks, Charly. This is all new for Reagan, but I think she's having a good time. I'm glad she's here." She suddenly felt awkward without Reagan or Rocky to be her social crutch. She needed something to do. "So, Brad, what can I to do help?"

"Nothin'," Brad said. "Go mingle! You're the reason all these Bakers showed up tonight. I know my wife, Beth, wants to hear about Chicago—she's always wanted to take a trip back there, see the museums and stuff. She's probably in the kitchen with the other ladies."

Indeed. Like a script right out of *Leave It to Beaver*, all the women had ended up in the large kitchen, chatting and putting the finishing touches on potato salads and baked beans and veggie platters and bread baskets and condiments, while most of the men lounged on the deck, popping the tops off bottles of Sam Adams or Miller Lite or passing out cans of Coke and LaCroix from a row of picnic ice chests. Maggie tried to visit each cluster, mostly listening to chatter already going on, answering the occasional question about Coop, the kids, the grandkids, his job, her job . . .

She was relieved when the shout went out, "Supper's ready!" and the young people drifted back from various parts of the farmyard and house. Folding tables had been set up on the patio, and food came out from the kitchen amid the platters of hamburgers, ribs, and chicken from the grills.

"Dig in!" Brad said—no one said a blessing prayer—and there was general hubbub as people filled plates and found places to sit around the deck and patio. Maggie chose a deck chair next to her cousin Deborah—Charly's sister, a youthful-looking sixty— hoping to catch up on the Grigg family with a one-on-one . . . until she heard Brad's voice rise above the hubbub.

"Hey, Cousin Maggie! I just heard you and that granddaughter of yours rode in on a motorcycle! Is that true—or is Charly here pulling my leg?"

"It's true!" CJ piped up, grinning at Reagan. "It's a real classic BMW with a sidecar. Cousin Maggie's dog Rocky is riding with 'em, too."

So much for a quiet one-on-one with Cousin Deborah. Before Maggie knew it, half the Baker clan wanted to drop by Charly's place to see the bike, and then the idea got floated that Maggie and Reagan and Rocky should ride the bike in the upcoming Fourth of July Parade in Gillette that weekend as a special "Baker Family Entry." Mitsy and some of the other youngsters deliriously started making plans to decorate it.

Reagan was grinning—she obviously thought riding in the parade would be fun. Maggie protested the idea. She was a visitor in town, not part of the community. "And not sure when we're leaving—we've got a long way to go to get to the coast." But she finally got everybody to pipe down by promising to "think about it."

As much as she was glad to see all her "kin," Maggie was relieved when the barbecue broke up around eight-thirty. Ranchers' workdays always started early. Chuck's family had already left, though Reagan had still been talking to Shane and his sister, Annie, so she told CJ she'd "ride home with Grams." While Kitty was packing up their leftovers, Maggie asked Brad for a quickie tour of the house and the new renovations since she'd last been there. Reagan, Shane, and Annie tagged along.

Reagan seemed surprised to see Brad's office on the lower level of the house, well-equipped with a couple of computers, ink-jet printer, fax machine, file cabinets, bookcases. "Guess I thought all your farm work was, you know, outdoors with the cattle and crops and stuff."

Brad chuckled. "Farming's a business, young lady. That's why Shane here is going to college. Gotta have a head for business to farm these days."

Maggie saw Shane shrug slightly and roll his eyes. Was there a bit of disagreement between father and son about Shane's future "career"? And what about Annie? The nineteen-year-old had started college, too.

"Mr. Brad, what's that?" Reagan pointed toward a large steel vault standing in the corner of Brad's office. The vault was at least seven feet high, five feet wide, and two or three feet deep, with a keypad and large wheel on the front. "Looks like a big bank safe or somethin'."

"My gun safe," Brad said. "That's where I store 'em. Can't be too careful. Don't want anybody breakin' in here and stealin' my guns."

Guns? Maggie was flabbergasted. How many did he have in there? Looked like it could hold an arsenal!

"Would you like to see my collection?" Brad made a move toward the keypad.

"No, no. Uh, that's all right. I'm not really fond of guns." Maggie tried to smile pleasantly, but she felt like getting out of there.

"Really? You don't have any guns?" Brad looked genuinely surprised. "I mean, with all those murders and racial stuff goin' on in Chicago?"

Maggie flinched. What did *he* know about all the "racial stuff" going on in Chicago? Did he have any idea about the ongoing racism and discrimination that still plagued the city's black residents in spite of civil rights gains?

She should say something. Coop would say something. On behalf of Mother Jones and Sister Regina and all the good people at Grace and Mercy Community Church. *And* Pastor Vic and Coop at New Hope Friendship who'd made *relationships* across racial barriers the Jesus way . . .

"I just don't think guns are the answer to the problems we have in Chicago. Too many guns and too easy access to guns *is* a problem—"

"Exactly! If the good guys don't have guns, just the bad guys will have guns. Now *that's* a problem."

Maggie saw Reagan roll her eyes. Didn't blame her. Sounded like a quote straight from the NRA. But she felt out of her depth. This was *not* a conversation she wanted to have just as they were getting ready to leave the nice evening they'd had with all the cousins. She opened her mouth to say Charly and Kitty were probably waiting on them so they could get home, when she realized that Reagan had already stomped out of the office and was heading back up the stairs.

Chapter 25

THE FULL MOON ROSE HUGE AND ORANGE along the eastern horizon as they drove back to Grassy Butte. "Ohh, look at that," Kitty murmured from the front passenger seat. "One of my favorite moments—moonrise over the prairie when the moon is full."

"Yes, it's beautiful," Maggie agreed from the back seat. She glanced at Reagan who sat grumpily beside her, arms folded, staring out the open window in the wrong direction, but she decided against calling her attention to the moon. The girl was obviously upset. The huge gun safe? Well, yeah, it was unsettling.

She and Coop didn't believe in having a gun in the house. She understood that some people wanted a gun for "personal protection," but it seemed like there were too many tragedies, kids finding a gun lying around the house, playing with it, accidentally shooting themselves or a sibling. Or the risk of having it stolen and used illegally. Not to mention her conviction that violence wasn't the Jesus-way to deal with problems, or even crime.

Back at the house, Reagan disappeared into her tiny bedroom on the lower level, not even offering to take Rocky for his evening walk. Well, didn't matter. The dog had been tied outside on a long lead with Pepper for company while they were gone. He'd be fine.

"Reagan okay?" Charly asked Maggie while Kitty made some chamomile tea as a nightcap. "She was awfully quiet on the way home."

"Oh, she'll be okay." Maggie shrugged. "I think she was taken aback by the big gun safe in Brad's office. We've never seen anything like that."

Charly snorted. "Oh, yeah. Brad never does anything halfway."

"Is it, like, full of guns? I mean, that thing was *big*."

"Pretty much. He's got a little bit of everything in there."

"Um, like semi-automatic rifles and stuff like that?"

"Yeah, I think so. Considers himself a collector."

"Whew. Have to admit, I'm pretty much anti-gun myself." Maggie grimaced. "I suppose that makes me an oddity around here."

"Ha. You said it, not me." Charly chuckled. "Guns are pretty common out here. Everybody does some hunting. I've got several rifles locked in a cabinet out in the barn. I keep one unloaded in the pickup—sometimes I have to put down an injured animal or scare off a wild varmint bothering my herd."

Maggie nodded. "Well, sure, I can understand that. Hunting, farm work—but semi-automatics? Assault rifles? I just don't understand why anyone would have one of those. I mean, they're military weapons, right? Their only purpose is to, uh—" Maggie choked on the words. "—uh, to kill as many people as possible in a short period of time."

Charly shrugged. "Guess Brad would say he's just exercising his Second Amendment rights. You know, the right to bear arms, form a militia—"

"A militia?"

"Well, that's what it says. The right of citizens to arm themselves in case the government runs amok."

Maggie frowned. "Wouldn't taking up arms against our government be treason?"

Charly threw up his hands in surrender and laughed uncomfortably. "Okay, this conversation is getting too deep for me this late at night! Sorry to bum out, but I've got an early breakfast meeting in town." He gave his cousin a quick hug, pecked Kitty on the cheek, and headed for the master bedroom. "'Night!"

Kitty watched her husband go, then shrugged and poured his tea down the sink. "Charly's on the Fourth of July committee, and this is their last meeting to mop up details for Saturday. Most of them are farmers or ranchers, so they meet early. And—" Kitty eyed Maggie over her own cup of tea. "—Charly doesn't like to argue. If you want to argue guns, maybe you should talk to Brad."

"I didn't mean—" Maggie started, but Kitty turned her back and started washing up cups and leftover dishes from the potluck.

Maggie sighed, finished her tea, and headed for the guest room. Her spirit sagged. The last person she wanted to offend was Charly. But not sure she wanted to talk about guns with Brad, the "true believer," either!

What *did* she want?

* * * *

Charly's pickup was already gone when Maggie took Rocky for an early-morning walk off-leash, accompanied this time by Pepper. It was fun to see the two dogs gamboling about, investigating one interesting smell after another and then chasing a bit of brush down the road. When she got back, breakfast had been set out on the kitchen counter—granola and bagels, OJ and coffee—with a note: "Help yourself!" Soon Kitty bustled in with a basket full of leaf lettuce and zucchini and early green beans from the vegetable garden. Maggie was relieved that her cousin's wife seemed her usual friendly self.

With Kitty's assurance that the washing machine was free, Maggie took her dirty clothes to the lower level and tapped on Reagan's door. "Hey, kiddo. Need your laundry. Time to get road dirt off our clothes."

Reagan opened the door, her tri-colored hair tousled. "Oh. Sure." She started picking up clothes off the floor.

"You okay, hon? You seemed upset last night."

Reagan rolled her eyes. "Well, *yeah*. Standing that close to all those guns made me feel totally weird. Like we'd stepped into some kind of alternative universe or something."

Maggie smiled. "Yeah. I felt the same way. But you gotta give Brad credit that he keeps his guns locked up. Really locked up."

Reagan shrugged. "Yeah. Guess so." Maggie saw the girl's chin quiver a nanosecond before she turned her face away.

"Honey? What's wrong?"

Reagan didn't answer for a long moment as she snatched up her clothes. Then she turned and glared at Maggie. "It's just . . . last year this guy in my class brought a gun to school. He was mad about something, posted something on Facebook, said he was gonna kill all the bullies and stuck-up kids—"

Maggie sucked in a breath. "Oh, Reagan!"

"He waved the gun all around in the cafeteria while we were eating lunch! Turned out the gun wasn't loaded, but we were all so *scared*, Grams! You know, all those school shootings an' everything." Reagan brushed something from her eyes with the back of her hand. "I never *ever* want anything to do with guns. Or be around people who stockpile them like . . . like an arsenal."

"Oh sweetie." Maggie stepped into the room and gathered her granddaughter in a hug. "I'm so sorry. I had no idea."

"Yeah, well." Reagan shrugged off the hug. "Just kinda hit me that it's so different here. Made me feel . . . I dunno. Like I didn't belong. Never would."

Maggie's spirit sagged. She so wanted Reagan to love this part of her family, this part of her history, as much as she did. "I know. But, they're still family. I think they're trying to make us feel welcome, to feel at home. We just gotta do the best we can to bridge all those differences."

She added her granddaughter's dirty clothes to her own load. "Hang in there, hon. Just a couple more days." *Yeah, once I figure out how to get us over the mountains to the West Coast.* That prospect seemed as foreboding as finding a wormhole in space.

Maggie headed for the laundry room and started a load, then heard Kitty calling down the stairs. "Reagan? Maggie? Mitsy and some of the other cousins are here to decorate the bike for the parade! Can you come up?"

Sure enough, Shane's sister, Annie, had driven over from the Triple B with Deborah Griggs' granddaughters, Ginger and Sammi, nine and eleven, who'd begged to stay over with their "big cousins" and go to the Fourth of July parade on Saturday. The next thing Maggie knew, she was giving rides in the sidecar to the younger set all around the Grassy Butte farmyard and even into one of the near pastures, with Rocky and Pepper running alongside and barking.

Finally parking the bike in the driveway again, Maggie was glad to see that Reagan had joined Annie and the younger girls. With a bit of misgiving, Maggie agreed to let this female "pit crew" decorate the bike and sidecar for the parade—*if* they washed all the grit and dirt off the machine first.

"What's this?" Charly laughed, after pulling his pickup into the farmyard in the middle of water hoses and buckets of sudsy water.

"Parade entry," Kitty snickered, as she and Maggie watched from the safety of the deck.

"Ah-ha. Wasn't sure if you'd decided to stay, Maggie, but just in case I added another Baker entry into the parade. Uh, wasn't sure what to call it, so I just put down 'Bustin' Baker's Butt.'" He was grinning.

"You didn't!" Kitty punched him good on the arm.

"Ow! Okay, you're right. I didn't. Though I was tempted." Charly winked at Maggie. "Just called it 'Baker's Beemer.' That *is* what they call a BMW, isn't it?"

Maggie made a face. If she wasn't careful, that nickname might stick—but the bike really belonged to Coop, and he wasn't a Baker. Still, it would do for the parade.

After watching the fun for a few moments, Charly leaned toward Maggie. "Glad you're staying for the Fourth. And you're welcome to stay as long as you like. But I know you wanted to visit the cemetery. Want to go today?"

Maggie nodded. "Yes. Very much. I thought Reagan and I could ride over there on the bike, but I think it's been co-opted."

"No problem. You can take the pickup. Or I'd be glad to drive you."

She smiled up at him. "That'd be nice. I'd like the company. Do you mind if we stop in town to pick up some flowers first?"

* * * *

Leaving the BMW and sidecar sitting ignobly in the farmyard— the metallic-blue bike was now decorated like a "horse" with cardboard ears on the handlebars and fluttering brown crepe paper mane and tail, and the sidecar was a colorful mishmash of red, white, and blue crepe paper—Maggie and Reagan crowded into the front seat of Charly's pickup. They stopped at the Walmart Supercenter on the south end of town to pick up some silk flowers, and then headed south to one of Gillette's smaller rural cemeteries.

Maggie wasn't quite prepared for the flood of feelings that came over her when Charly pulled up to the simple chain-link fence surrounding the half-acre cemetery. The last time she'd been here was when she'd buried her parents.

Two caskets. Double funeral.

Reagan was already out of the pickup and wandering among the upright gravestones. She stopped beside two older markers. "Who's Margaret Quincy Baker?" she called out.

Carrying the silk flowers, Maggie joined her, reading the faded dates. *Born 1891. Died 1969.* "My dad's mother. My grandmother. I'm named after her."

"Margaret? That's your real name?" Reagan seemed surprised.

"Sure." What other "obvious" information had she failed to pass on to her grandkids? Maggie took a few steps farther down the row. "Here are my parents—your great-grandparents. Curtis and Nancy Baker. They died a few years before you were born."

Reagan studied the dates. "Wait—they both died the same *day?*"

Maggie nodded slowly. "A car accident. They were on their way to Chicago from Portland to visit us, had planned to stop here to visit the Baker clan. My dad was driving, but he had a heart attack and lost control of the car. Fortunately, it was just a one-car accident." *Just?* Still brutal. She'd never forget that terrible phone call.

Reagan's eyes widened. "Whoa. Grams! That's awful."

"Yes. It was." Irritation pricked at Maggie's spirit. Why didn't Reagan know about this? What was *wrong* with Stacy—didn't she ever talk about her grandparents to her girls?

But, she and Coop were just as much at fault. They had moved two thousand miles away from the West Coast to the Midwest, their kids only seeing the grandparents every other year or so. Both sets of grandparents had made a valiant effort to remember their grandchildren's birthdays with gifts and calls, but it was a long-distance relationship. Maggie couldn't really blame Stacy— or Mike or Chris either—for letting their grandparents fade into the past once they were gone. So easy to move on, live in today—especially since "the past" seemed light years from their life in the city.

But she was suddenly glad Reagan had come on this trip with her. The past was important, part of who she was, part of who Reagan was. Maybe it would mean something—later in the girl's life, if not now.

Charly had wandered over to another part of the cemetery and was pulling weeds around a couple of headstones in another row—probably his own parents' graves—giving her and Reagan a little privacy. Grateful, Maggie bent down in front of the double gravestone and emptied the metal cup stuck in the ground of its collection of dirt and bits of grass and seeds, then carefully inserted the bouquet of purple and pink silk flowers—her mother's favorite color combination.

She stood up. "You know what, Reagan? The way my parents died turned out to be a blessing."

"What?" Reagan looked at her as if she were crazy.

"Well, for one thing, they died suddenly, gone just like that. My mom often said she didn't want to suffer a long, lingering illness. And, even though my dad ended up living most of his adult life in Portland after his brother Barry inherited the farm, he often said he'd like to be buried 'back home' with the other Bakers. So, it turned out to be God's mercy that the accident occurred less than a hundred miles from here. My Uncle Barry made all the arrangements, even bought the cemetery space." They stood quietly for several minutes. Finally, Maggie started back toward the pickup.

"Grams, wait. What about Gramps? You brought his ashes all this way. Maybe you could bury them here."

Maggie hesitated. Had she said anything to her granddaughter about that? When she didn't answer, Reagan muttered, "Fine," and flounced away.

Back in the truck, Maggie watched as her granddaughter seemed to deliberately take her own sweet time revisiting some of the headstones and taking pictures with her cell phone. Finding a place to bury Coop's ashes was one reason Maggie had brought the brass urn along. Here might be as good a place as any. But, without knowing exactly why, it didn't feel right. This wasn't the place. Or the time.

She'd know it when she found it.

Chapter 26

*B*ENEATH HER, THE "BEEMER" CHUGGED *up the steep hill, motor grinding. Encroaching darkness was sucking up the terrain, the steep mountainsides fading from sight—uh oh, what was that? Wet splotches on her visor. Starting to snow—no, more like sleet and ice! Panic licked at her insides. She'd never make it over the Rockies! Couldn't even see the road. Suddenly the bike started to slide . . . slipping, sliding . . . she was losing control! The edge of the highway loomed dark and empty . . . closer and closer. They were going to go over!—*

Maggie sat up with a start, heart pounding.

Oh, thank God! Only a dream.

She reached for the bedside lamp. No way was she going to go back to sleep right away. The dream—nightmare was more like it—might pick up where it left off.

Sliding out of bed quietly so as not to wake Rocky, Maggie crept to the kitchen, rummaged in the cupboard for a mug, and filled it with milk. Hot milk and honey—that would be soothing. But as she waited for the milk to heat in the microwave, she heard slippers padding down the hallway and Kitty came into the kitchen, pulling a bathrobe around her. "Maggie? You okay?"

"Oh, Kitty," Maggie groaned, catching the microwave before it beeped *END* loudly. "I didn't mean to wake you."

Kitty yawned. "You didn't. I forgot to put the coffee pot on the timer, so it'd be ready when Charly gets up. Brad's coming over early this morning." Kitty put a paper filter into the automatic coffee pot, filled it with coffee grounds, and poured cold water into the well. "He's going to borrow our flatbed trailer, wants Charly to help him hitch it to his new pickup before the parade and all." She eyed Maggie curiously as she set the timer. "So, what got you up? It's only four!"

191

Maggie spooned honey into the mug of hot milk and took a sip. "Needed something to calm my nerves. Had a bad dream—"

"About?"

Maggie flushed. "Um, to be honest, I'm nervous about riding the bike over the Rockies. Had a dream—nightmare, really—that, uh, we didn't make it."

"Oh, hon. I don't blame you. I'd be scared to ride that thing on a flat road, much less over the mountains! And with passengers! Are you sure you want to keep going? I mean, you've had a good trip so far. You could just stay here a while, then go back to Chicago, couldn't you?"

She could. Maybe she should. And yet, she so wanted to honor Coop by finishing the trip he'd planned and figure out why it was so important to him.

"Well, think about it. You're welcome to stay here as long as you want." Kitty yawned again. "Sorry, going back to bed. Need my beauty sleep for the parade." She grinned at Maggie. "You're a good sport, agreeing to ride your bike in the parade. It'll be a big hit." Charly's wife headed back toward the hallway. "'Night."

Maggie finished her milk, turned off the kitchen light, and went back to bed, too. But she dozed fitfully, not wanting to resurrect the dream—and woke with daylight streaming through the blinds. Oh help, had she overslept? The parade started at ten!

But her watch said only 7:10. Still, she'd better find out when the family wanted to leave.

Pulling on clean jeans and a T-shirt, Maggie stuffed her feet into her sandals and hustled out to the kitchen, followed by Rocky. No one there. The coffee pot was half empty, though, so Charly must already be up and out. Taking a moment to pour some coffee into the mug she'd used a few hours ago, Maggie stepped outside.

Over there. A flashy red four-door pickup with a flatbed trailer attached sat near the open sliding door of one of Charly's big machine shops. Brad must still be here.

Sure enough, both men, uncle and nephew, had their heads under the hood of the pickup, talking and pointing. "Good morning!" Maggie chirped. "Something wrong with the motor?"

Charly stepped back, wiping his hands on a grimy cloth. "Nah. Everything's good. Brad here just wanted an engine check before taking this baby over the mountains."

Brad pulled his head out from under the hood. "Yep. Nice havin' a natural born mechanic in the family." He slapped Charly on the back. "Thanks, Unc. I'll grease her up and change the oil, be good to go tonight."

Charly tossed the rag and cocked an eyebrow at Maggie. "Say, Cuz, I hear you're not too excited about taking your little rig there over the mountains."

Maggie made a face. "Aw, Kitty told on me."

"Yeah. Been a little concerned about it myself. But, maybe you wouldn't have to. You tell her, Brad. It was your idea."

Brad shrugged. "Well, Uncle Charly says you're heading for Portland. Just happens I'm leaving for Spokane tonight—gonna pick up two tractor tires on Monday from a buddy of mine over there who got me a real good deal."

"Tractor tires? Like those monsters?" Maggie pointed at the gigantic rear wheels on Charly's John Deere parked alongside the shop.

"Yeah. Too big for the back of my pickup. That's why I'm borrowing Uncle Charly's flatbed." He jerked a thumb at the trailer, which Maggie guesstimated was about fourteen feet long. "But it's empty going that way. Could take your bike and the sidecar over the Rockies as far as Spokane."

"Spokane? But I'm going to Portland—sounds a bit out of the way."

Brad grinned. "There's no straight highway over the Rockies to Portland. You can either go north and take 90 via Spokane or drop down and take 84 through Boise. Couple hours faster to take 90. Only thing—I'm leaving tonight after the fireworks. That way I'll hit the mountains when it's gettin' daylight. But," he shrugged again, "maybe you weren't planning on leavin' that soon."

Maggie stared. *O Lord! An answer to prayer I didn't even pray.* She found her voice. "Oh, Brad. Yes! If you're sure. I'd appreciate it so much."

Brad shrugged again. "Sure. No problem. Good thing I got this baby!" He lowered the hood of the big pickup with a bang. "Plenty of room for your granddaughter and the dog, too." He glanced around the farmyard. "Say, Unc, you got a ramp we can use to get Cousin Maggie's bike up onto the trailer?"

* * * *

"What?" Reagan screeched when Maggie told her. "Twelve hours cooped up in a pickup with Mr. NRA? Grams! You gotta be kiddin' me!"

"It's a new pickup, Reagan. There's a second seat, plenty of room for you and Rocky."

"Still!" Reagan slapped her forehead. "Why can't we just ride the bike like we've been doing—you, me, and Rocky. You've been doin' great, Grams! We'll be fine!"

"Because." Maggie wasn't in the mood to argue. "I don't *want* to ride over the Rockies if I don't have to—and Brad just offered us a lift. It's settled. We're going." She started to leave the little bedroom Reagan was staying in, and then turned back. "He's leaving right after the fireworks at the fairgrounds tonight, so we better get packed now, before we leave for the parade."

Reagan glared at her, arms folded across her chest. "Don't feel like riding in the parade."

Maggie opened her mouth to say, *Stop acting like a child! . . .* but closed it again. Fine. She and Rocky could ride in the parade by themselves. People would love Rocky in the sidecar. She shrugged. "Up to you." But at the door she said over her shoulder, "Maybe Rocky can wear the cowboy hat CJ brought up to the house for you. Looks new."

* * * *

Charly had given Maggie a couple red-white-and-blue bandanas, suggesting—with a wink—she could wear one tied around her head, road-hog style. She tried it on in front of a mirror in the house, took one look and muttered, "He's gotta be kidding." But she tied the second bandana around Rocky's neck. Perfect. Especially with his doggy goggles. "Okay, boy," she sighed. "I will if you will."

Rocky was already in the sidecar when Reagan showed up, the new cowboy hat perched jauntily on her head. "Move over, dog," she said, squeezing into the sidecar.

"Nice hat," Maggie said mildly as if nothing was amiss. "You can wear it in the parade if you want, but you gotta wear the helmet till we get there."

Reagan rolled her eyes, but traded headgear.

On the paved road to downtown Gillette, cars honked and people leaned out of windows and waved at them as she followed Charly's pickup to First Street where the various entries were lining up in the staging area.

The Campbell County Fourth of July was obviously a big deal for the whole county. The American Legion was there *en masse* on horseback carrying American flags. Old cars and "funny cars" dotted the lineup. Maggie saw Brad's kids, Shane and Annie, riding two nice-looking horses—a bay and a chestnut, manes and tails braided—with a 4-H group. A stagecoach pulled by a four-horse team rattled by. Everywhere they looked, floats, marching bands tuning up, horses, and more horses.

"Wish we could just be spectators along the street, so we could see the whole parade," Reagan grumbled. "We're gonna miss a lot of it."

Maggie gave her a Look. *She* wasn't the one who'd wanted to ride the motorcycle in the parade. But here they were.

"Ready?" Charly said, coming by with a clipboard in his capacity as one of the parade organizers. "Just follow that library float there, keep about twenty feet behind. Be ready to stop if they do. Sometimes the line gets a little backed up." Then he chuckled. "You guys look great."

Maggie wasn't so sure about that. She felt pretty silly in the bandana, not to mention riding a BMW decorated like some cardboard mule.

Still, it was kind of fun riding slowly down Second Street. Reagan lost her pout and got into the spirit of things, waving and grinning and throwing wrapped candies at kids on the sidelines. *Huh. Where did she get those?* Rocky leaned out of the sidecar with his doggy grin, tongue lolling out, and seemed to enjoy all the hoots and laughter and shouts of, "Lookit the dog!" along the way.

By the time their segment of the parade got back to the staging area, the sun was high overhead and the temperature nudging ninety. Maggie mopped her face with the bandana and headed for the nearest vendor to get something cold to drink—and lost Reagan and Rocky somewhere in the crowd. After wandering around fruitlessly for half an hour, her irritation growing, she remembered both she and Reagan had the Find Friends app on their phones. *Smart move, Grandma,* she told herself, tracking them to Bicentennial Park at the mud volleyball game.

The afternoon was crowded with all kinds of crazy activities, including a "Firemen Water Fight" and a "Strongman/Strongwoman Competition." How Charly found them, she didn't know, but he showed up, hot dog in hand, and said Brad wanted to load the bike onto the flatbed that afternoon, so they'd be ready to go right after the fireworks. Would that be okay?

"Fine with me," Maggie said. She was glad for an excuse to go back to Grassy Butte, get Rocky calmed down after all the excitement, even get a nap before heading out for an all-nighter in the big red pickup.

* * * *

Maggie found as many Baker family members as possible for a quick goodbye. And both Charly and Kitty came back to the ranch to help Maggie strip the BMW of its "patriotic" decorations and get it loaded onto the flatbed. Maggie was nervous about riding the bike up the ramp onto the trailer but managed to do it on the second try with encouragement from Brad, Charly, and Kitty. Once the bike and sidecar were strapped down securely, the two men went back to town in Charly's pickup, but both women decided to skip the fireworks, opting for a quiet supper of leftovers on the deck.

"Nice clear night for the fireworks," Kitty said. "We might even be able to see them from here."

"My last evening in Big Sky country," Maggie murmured, watching as the sun sank into the far horizon and the waning moon—still almost full—rose into the darkening sky. "This is more beautiful than fireworks. We've got those a-plenty back in Chicago."

Kitty snickered. "Quieter, too."

"I've really enjoyed my time here, Kitty. You and Charly have made us feel right at home. Thanks so much for everything."

"What about Reagan? She's a real city-kid, I think."

"She is that. But, high time my city family got to know the Baker clan—and vice versa."

Kitty was quiet for several long moments. "Your youngest—Chris, right? You haven't said much about him. Is he married? Kids?"

Maggie sucked in a long breath. Hadn't she mentioned Chris? She felt guilty. Was she embarrassed? No, not embarrassed— defensive. Once she mentioned he was gay, he'd be labeled. Maggie and Coop's "gay son." And Chris was so much more than his sexual orientation. So much more.

She blew out the breath. "Nope. Not married. No kids. Um, not sure who all knows, but Chris is gay. He lives out in LA. Works as a vet assistant. Crazy about animals, always has been." She reached down and stroked the top of Rocky's head, stretched out beside her deck chair. "He gave me Rocky for a birthday present a few years back."

"That's nice," Kitty murmured. "About Rocky, I mean."

Right. Maggie waited a beat. "Unfortunately, there's been some estrangement since Chris came out—between Coop and Chris mostly. That's been hard." Why was she telling Kitty all this? She wasn't that close to her cousin-in-law. Still, she'd asked.

"I'm sorry." Kitty patted Maggie's hand, gathered up their supper dishes, and went into the house. The screen door banged behind her.

Sorry. Sorry about the estrangement between father and son? Or sorry that Chris was gay? Maggie felt frustrated. She wished the Baker clan could know the Chris that she knew.

Maggie closed her eyes, drinking in the quiet, broken only by the low moo of a cow somewhere in a far-off pasture . . .

"Maggie?"

She awoke with a start. Charly was shaking her arm. How long had she been asleep? The night was full dark now, broken only by the bright moon and the big yard lights of the farmyard.

"Brad says he's ready to go when you are."

Chapter 27

THE NIGHT WAS STARTLINGLY BEAUTIFUL. Perfectly clear, brilliant with stars, the waning moon still bright and nearly full. "No wonder you want to drive at night," Maggie murmured in the front passenger seat as they left the lights of Gillette behind. She glanced into the back seat of the big pickup. Reagan was already stretched out as far as the width of the cab would let her, cuddling with one of the pillows Kitty had sent along so they could get some sleep. Rocky was curled up on the floor of the back seat, surrounded by their various backpacks, duffle bags, and Coop's ashes.

Reagan had rolled her eyes at the rifle in its rack above the back window and gave her grandmother a dark look that said, *"You expect me to ride with that thing hanging over my head?"* Brad must've caught the look because he'd said mildly, "It's a thirty-aught-six hunting rifle. Don't worry, it's not loaded. Got the shells safely stowed in the glove compartment."

"You plan on doing some hunting tonight?" Reagan's tone had been flippant.

"Nope. Not unless we hit a deer and I have to put it down. Never can tell when I might need that gun."

Reagan's mouth had dropped. But she shut up and withdrew into the darkness of the back seat.

Maggie and Brad made small talk quietly in the front seat for a while. "Did your dad ever resent that his brother Barry got the farm?" Brad asked at one point.

"Don't think so. He liked being a history teacher—mom taught English. They were both big advocates of Christian schools. But me . . ." Maggie laughed self-consciously. "I always thought I'd been born into the wrong Baker family. I was the proverbial horse-crazy kid, loved animals period. But we lived on a school campus, no dogs allowed. My pets were limited to parakeets, hamsters, goldfish, and *imaginary* dogs. All my cousins, on the other hand, were surrounded by animals—dogs, cats, cows, horses. Cousin Deborah even had a Shetland pony! I was so jealous."

Brad chuckled.

"Did *you* have a pony?" she asked.

"Mm, no. I was more into motors. I was driving tractors and pickups at age ten."

"See? I thought most of you cousins didn't even know how lucky you were. Took it all for granted." She heaved an exaggerated sigh. But after a few moments she murmured, "But God had other plans for me."

Brad gave her a quick look but didn't say anything. Finally, he said, "Feel free to get some sleep, Maggie. I've got ear pods and music on my Bluetooth that'll help keep me awake."

Maggie wasn't sure she could fall asleep in the truck, especially since the edge had been taken off by her evening nap on Charly and Kitty's deck. But she scrunched the second pillow Kitty had sent with them, leaned the seat back, and closed her eyes . . .

* * * *

Her eyes snapped open as bright lights shone into the cab. Brad was pulling into a gas station—looked like a truck stop. She glanced at her watch. Almost two a.m. "Where—?"

"Billings, Montana. Take a pit stop if you'd like. Do you want to wake her up?" He jerked a thumb toward the back seat.

Maggie glanced into the back. Reagan had a blanket over her head as if she didn't want to be disturbed. Probably okay. Kids her age didn't need to "go" during the night like she did. Rocky, on the other hand, scrambled over the console between the two front seats and wanted out when the second Maggie opened her door. Snapping the leash on Rocky's collar, she threaded her way between huge semi-trucks, their diesel engines rumbling even when parked, dwarfing Brad's pickup and trailer. She tested the taut straps. The bike and sidecar seemed to be traveling okay on the flatbed. So far, so good.

She tied Rocky outside the door and went inside. The café was serving up eggs and hash browns and coffee to its mostly male clientele.

So, this was a trucker's world when the rest of the world was asleep.

They were back on the road in fifteen minutes. Brad offered her some mixed nuts he'd bought. "We're about halfway to Butte. I'll stop there, get some shuteye for an hour or so, and then we can get some breakfast before we go on. Sound okay?"

"Sure. Whatever's good for you. We just appreciate the ride." She'd worry about how to get some real sleep when they got to Spokane. Maggie zeroed in on their location on her phone GPS. "Looks like we traveled through the Crow Indian Reservation while I was asleep. What are the towns like there?"

"Dark." Brad chuckled. "Most all the gas stations are closed during the night in the little towns—and not just on the reservations. Out here—Wyoming, Montana, the Dakotas—you better fill up when you can if you do any night driving."

"Hm. I'll remember that." She hadn't been asking about gas stations, but she dropped it.

Mesmerized by the long straight stretches of dark highway, lit only by headlights and the moon overhead, Maggie dozed on and off for the next few hours, but was grateful when the sky began to lighten, and road signs noted several exits for Butte. She needed to stretch her legs.

Reagan yawned and sat up as they pulled into the next truck stop. "Come on, girl," Maggie said, climbing out of the cab while Brad topped off his gas tank. "We're going to let our chauffeur, here, get forty winks while we freshen up. *You* got your beauty sleep. Me, on the other hand . . ."

Maggie let her granddaughter go into the restroom first while she waited outside with Rocky, watching as Brad drove the pickup and flatbed away from the gas pumps, no doubt looking for a quieter spot for his snooze. When Reagan came out, she handed the girl the leash and headed inside toward the neon-lit sign that said LADIES. Glancing into a mirror over the row of sinks, Maggie winced. What a mess! Hair askew, makeup non-existent, eyes bleary. Ack! She looked ten years older, at least. Well, they still had time while Brad caught some shuteye. She'd take her time here to wash up, look a little more presentable.

Feeling a little guilty at how long she took, but feeling much better, Maggie hurried out prepared to apologize to Reagan—but the girl wasn't in sight. The dog was gone, too. Okay, so she was taking Rocky for a walk around the truck stop. She looked at her watch. Six-fifteen. Brad had been snoozing for forty minutes or so. She was definitely ready for a cup of hot coffee. Her stomach pinched. Should she and Reagan just go ahead and get some breakfast? Brad wouldn't mind.

Better find her granddaughter first.

"Reagan?" she called, going around to the side. Nobody. Just a few trucks, engines idling, whose drivers were also catching some shut-eye. Anxiety licked at her insides. "Reagan?" she called again, heading around another corner to the back. There—two figures over by a big semi. A man and a woman. The man had the female by the arm, who was pulling away—and a dog barking somewhere. *Where?!*

Maggie began to run. "Reagan? Reagan!" she yelled.

"See?" the female screeched. Reagan's voice! "I *told* you I'm with my *grandmother.*"

But before Maggie got to the pair, another person appeared out of the shadows. A man—with a rifle. "Back off, buddy. Get your hands off that kid."

Brad. Leveling the rifle at the man's midriff.

"Now wait a minute," the man by the truck said. "We was just talkin'. No harm done."

"I *said,* back off!" Brad growled. "Can't you see she's just a kid?"

The man loosened his hold on Reagan's arm, and she yanked it away. "How was I s'posed to know she wasn't one of them hookers who work this place?" he muttered angrily.

Maggie, panting heavily, reached for her granddaughter. But Reagan, her face a storm cloud of anger and barely concealed tears, pulled away. "I gotta get Rocky," she snapped. "That man tied him up back here." She headed around the back of the truck toward a big dumpster at the edge of the parking lot.

With a glance back at Brad, who had the guy pinned against the side of his truck, rifle pressed sideways across the trucker's chest, Maggie hustled after her granddaughter. How in the world did that snake get the dog away from Reagan? "Honey, wait. I'm so sorry I left you out here alone for so long. I didn't think—"

"Let's just *go*." Her voice trembled. "I wanna go." Reagan untied Rocky from the garbage bin and stalked off.

"Of course!" Maggie glanced wildly around for the red pickup and flatbed just as Brad jogged up to them.

"Pickup's over there," he said, jerking his thumb over his shoulder. "The creep's leaving. C'mon. We'll find some other place to get breakfast."

As the trio walked quickly back the way they'd just come, Maggie saw the big semi pull out and watched as the red lights outlining the back of the truck disappeared onto the highway. And just beyond the empty space was Brad's truck and the flatbed. *Oh God, thank You that he parked over here,* she breathed. That's why he heard Reagan and showed up in the nick of time. *Thank You, thank You, thank You, God!*

They drove for twenty or thirty minutes until Brad pointed at a road sign. "Pancake House at the next exit. We can get some coffee and breakfast there."

"Okay. Sounds good." Maggie cleared her throat. "I—I want to thank you, Brad. If it hadn't been for you and that, um, rifle of yours . . ."

Brad snorted. "Ha. Didn't have time to load it. But the creep didn't know that."

"Really?" For some reason, Maggie felt relieved. "Still, you got there just in time. Thanks."

"Yeah," squeaked a voice from the back seat, the first the girl had spoken since she'd climbed into the pickup and curled up in a ball in the corner. "Thanks, Cousin Brad. I—I was really scared."

"Thank Rocky, there. He's the one who woke me up with his barking. Knew somethin' wasn't right."

"Ohhh, Rocky . . ."

Maggie could tell by Reagan's muffled voice that the girl had buried her face in the dog's fur.

* * * *

The ride over the mountains that morning was stunning. Once they passed Missoula, craggy peaks soared all around them, like monster teeth poking holes into the blue canopy above. It'd been a long time since she'd driven over the Rockies, but Maggie had a feeling of *déjà vu* as they crested Lookout Pass on the border between Montana and Idaho. On their many trips driving east over the mountains, her dad had always teased, "This is the Continental Divide, Pumpkin. If you were a river, it's all downhill from here to the Atlantic Ocean."

Reagan was on her cell phone, trying to look up facts about the Rockies, though reception was spotty. "Whoa," she murmured at one point. "Some of these peaks are over 14,000 feet. That's like, yikes, almost three miles above sea level!"

Maggie had to admit that I-90 wound its way through them without any crazy switchbacks or major drop-offs, and the weather was warm, even in the mountains. Still, she was glad she was encased in the cab of a late-model pickup rather than sitting *al fresco* astride a motorcycle.

They'd passed from Mountain Time to Pacific Time at Lookout Pass, so it was half past noon—again—when Brad pulled into the farm equipment dealership on the outskirts of Spokane, Washington. "This is as far as I go, ladies," he said. "You going to be okay from here on, Cousin Maggie?"

"Sure," she said, a tad more confidently than she felt. "We'll get a motel and some more sleep, then take off tomorrow. But I can't thank you enough, Brad, for the ride this far. Let me help with your gas."

He waved her off. "Nah. Was coming this way anyway. C'mon, let's get your bike and sidecar off the trailer."

Reagan was assigned the task of locating a nearby motel while Maggie backed the bike off the trailer using Charly's ramp. And then it was time to say goodbye. Maggie was a little surprised at the bear hug Reagan gave Brad, and she saw him whisper in her ear.

As they re-packed the bike saddlebags and sidecar with their stuff, Maggie said casually, "So. What did Brad have to say when you said goodbye?" She knew she was being downright nosy. The girl had a perfect right not to tell her.

But Reagan shrugged. "He apologized, said he should have warned me about some of the truckers. Didn't think they'd bother me since I was with you."

With an old lady, Maggie thought wryly. The whole thing was her fault, really. She was the one who'd left her granddaughter alone with just the dog.

"And he told me I was welcome to come back and visit the Baker clan whenever I wanted."

Maggie smiled. "I hope you do, hon." She buckled on her helmet. *That* was worth the whole visit.

"Uh, Grams . . ."

"What?"

Reagan studied her feet. "I, um, didn't exactly tell the truth about Rocky. I, uh, I was the one who tied him to the dumpster. I was, like, *bored* just walking him around. An' I was really hungry. I wanted to go in and find you an' get somethin' to eat. But that's when, you know . . ." Her eyes welled up again.

"Oh, honey." Now Maggie did wrap her arms around the girl. "It's okay. It's okay. I understand." She held Reagan for a long moment until the girl stopped sniffling. "Guess we all own a piece of this mess," she murmured. "Good grief. Just like the proverbial 'filthy rags.'"

"*Filthy rags?*" Reagan screwed up her nose. "*What* are you talking about?"

"Sorry. Thinking out loud—it's a verse in the Bible. 'All our righteousness is like filthy rags.' We—uh, never mind. I'll explain later." If she could. They'd all had good intentions, made natural assumptions, had normal inclinations—but Reagan still got hurt. "Right now, let's get to that motel you found. I need a nap!"

Chapter 28

AFTER SLEEPING FOR THREE HOURS THAT AFTERNOON at the Super 8 Motel Reagan found near the airport, Maggie was still awake when her phone rang around 9:30. Michael.

"Hey, Mom. Everything okay? Haven't heard from you for days."

"Oh, sorry, hon. Haven't been on the road, so didn't think you'd worry. We stayed several days with my Baker cousins in Wyoming, you know."

"You still there?"

"Well, no. Got a last-minute offer yesterday to catch a ride with one of my cousins." It really was too complicated to explain the first-cousin-once-removed business. "Brad Baker was taking a trailer over the mountains to pick up some farm equipment, so he was able to load the bike. He drove straight through, so we're actually here in Spokane, catching up on some sleep before we go on."

"Spokane! Well, guess that's good. Glad you didn't have to drive over the mountains. Uh, how's Reagan doing?"

"She's fine. Not here right now though—went for a swim in the hotel pool." No sense telling him about the panic at the truck stop. "Have to admit I appreciate her company." Maggie chuckled. "The farm was a new experience for her. But it was good. All good. Makes me wish all my grandkids could spend some time there. Family history, you know."

"Well, maybe we can one of these days."

"Sure." Maggie knew it wasn't likely.

"The bike holding up?"

"So far."

"Look, Mom, promise me you'll get it checked out before you go much further. Don't want you breaking down out in the middle of nowhere. Seriously."

Maggie smiled. So very Mike. "Good idea, son. I promise. We should get to Portland tomorrow or next day—" An in-coming call flashed on her screen. Strange number, looked international. "Oh, I think this might be your sister calling. I better take it."

Mike laughed in her ear. "Oh yeah. Good luck, Mom. Call me when you get to Portland, okay?"

Maggie switched to the new call. "Hello? This is Maggie."

"Mom! Where's Reagan! I tried to—" The connection crackled. *"—but she didn't answer! What's happening? Where are you? Why—"*

"Stacy! Stacy, slow down, honey. Reagan's fine. We're both fine. Where are you calling from?"

"Naples!" Stacy was practically shouting, as if she thought she had to yell to be heard halfway around the world. *"Staying in a hotel tonight, getting pretty darn sick of that boat. Why didn't Reagan answer? I'm going to throttle that girl!"*

Rocky raised his head from where he was sprawled on the second queen bed in the hotel room, his doggie brows making question marks at the loud squawks coming from the phone. Maggie took a deep breath. "Stacy, I can hear you fine. You don't have to shout. Please."

"Oh. All right. But where's Reagan? I'm her mother! I need to know."

"Of course. She's *fine*, Stacy. Swimming in the motel pool as we speak. We've been on the ranch with the Baker cousins for several days, but tonight we're at a Super 8 in Spokane, Washington."

"Spokane! Why would you go to Spokane? You're crazy, you know that, Mom? Driving that old bike cross country like that. Why I ever let you go on this trip, I'll never know. Need to have my head examined. And taking my daughter, too! I've got a mind to fly home and stop this stupid trip once and for all. You . . ."

Maggie sighed and let Stacy blow off steam. Reagan came in, hair wet, wrapped in one of the hotel pool towels. She looked wide-eyed at her grandmother. *"My mom?"* she mouthed silently. Maggie nodded. Reagan made a face and tip-toed into the bathroom. *"I'm not here yet!"* Maggie nodded again.

There was a pause on the other end of the call. "Mom, you there?"

"Yes, honey. How do you like Naples?"

She listened while Stacy expounded for sixty seconds on the highs and lows of Italy's famous city before saying, "—Oh! This call is costing me a mint. Gotta go. Tell Reagan to answer the phone next time I call!" Her voice turned away from the phone. *"Yes! I'm coming!"* And back again. "'Bye. I'll call you from Greece or wherever our next stop is." And the call cut off.

Well.

Reagan poked her head out of the bathroom. "She gone?"

"Yes."

"She mad?"

"Anxious about you. She's your mother. It goes with the job description."

"But she's not on her way out here to snatch me back to Chicago, is she?"

Maggie smiled. "No. Pretty sure not."

Reagan threw herself onto the second bed alongside Rocky. "Whew. That's a relief."

"Reagan, you really do have to talk to your mom one of these days. She tried your phone first. Next time she calls, pick up."

The girl threw an arm over Rocky, who stretched and rumbled in his throat, as if asking for a good body scratch. Reagan complied. "Okay."

"Promise?"

"Okay, okay! Promise."

But Reagan seemed unusually quiet as they got ready for bed. Maggie let her be. Maybe thinking about what she'd say next time her mom called. But as Maggie finally clicked off the light, hoping to get a good eight hours sleep before their trip tomorrow, her granddaughter murmured, "Grams?"

Now she wanted to talk. "What, hon?"

"Do you think the guy at the truck stop only let me go 'cause Cousin Brad had that rifle?"

So, that was it. "I don't know . . . no, I think it was mainly because both Brad and I showed up and foiled his plans. Though I suppose he was pretty nervous about Brad's rifle."

Reagan was quiet for a long moment, then spoke into the darkness again. "Remember what I told you about what happened at school last year? We had a bunch of discussions afterwards in class—about gun control and crazy people with guns and all that. One of my classmates was really against gun control stuff, said his father told him, 'Armed men are citizens. Unarmed men are subjects.'"

Maggie sat up. "He said *what*? '*Armed* men are citizens? *Un*armed men are *subjects*'?" She snorted. "Hmph. Sounds like one of those NRA mantras."

"Yeah, that's what I thought, too. But the kid insisted it was a quote by John Adams—you know, one of the Founding Fathers."

Maggie laid back down. Really? She didn't know that. "Hm. Well, guess that was the prevailing view back then when the colonies were trying to divest from Mother England." But now? "So, what did your teacher say?"

"She was pretty cool. All she said was, 'You don't need a gun to be a responsible citizen or even to make a change for good.'"

Maggie smiled into the dark. Good answer.

* * * *

Munching a granola bar for her breakfast, Reagan spread out the map her Grandpa Coop had used to trace his proposed route across the country. "Huh. Don't think Gramps figured on going to Portland via Spokane, but . . ." She ran her finger from Spokane down toward the Washington/Oregon state line and then over to Portland. "Hey, Grams. If we head for the Columbia River, I don't think we have to go through the Cascade Mountains at all. I mean, we can connect with the river *before* we get to the mountains, and then the road follows the river all the way to the coast, which means it cuts through the Cascades practically at sea level."

Maggie blinked rapidly as she put her second contact in, then laughed. "Sounds good to me. Let's ride, girl!" At least her "saddle soreness" in her hips and thighs had subsided during their stay at the ranch. Maybe she was toughening up. And she was excited to see her "bestie" from childhood, Wendy Thurston, who was expecting them when they got to Portland.

They filled up with gas before heading southwest out of town on I-90/395. Not bad, Maggie thought. The highway had two lanes going each direction with a wide median of stubby brown grass between, and traffic was light. After about twenty minutes on the road, she felt a tug on her sleeve. Reagan had her visor up. "Cripes!" she shouted. "Is it this bleak all the way to the Columbia? No trees, no hills, no nothin'! Just flat country and brown grass!"

Maggie shouted back, "Pretty much!" Even she'd almost forgotten that the eastern parts of Washington and Oregon were high desert until they got to the Cascades. Good thing they'd filled up with gas because once again towns were few and far between.

An hour down the road, I-90 took off toward the Cascade Mountains and Seattle, but Maggie kept the bike's nose pointed south on Route 395. The sun was relentless—had to be at least 90 degrees. Maggie felt as if she was riding in a stupor with nothing to break up the landscape, and she was sweltering inside her helmet. Open the visor? Might be cooler, but then she'd be eating bugs. She noticed that Rocky had curled up in a ball between Reagan's feet on the floor of the sidecar, and even Reagan seemed to be dozing off. Didn't blame them. There was no scenery to speak of. Just miles of flat brown grass. And her wandering thoughts . . .

Why did she have so many mixed emotions about her visit to the Baker clan this time? Even the smell of sagebrush seemed to tap into a great well of nostalgia deep in her spirit for the girl she used to be—that horse-crazy kid with the imaginary dogs who wished *she* was the cousin who'd grown up in these wide-open spaces. If she had, if *her* dad had inherited the Triple B Ranch—if she was the cousin who'd settled here, married, farmed the land and raised cattle—yeah, it would have been a good life. This country needed its farmers and ranchers, after all! Good solid folks. Salt of the earth.

And yet, she was a different person now. A person who wouldn't fit very well on a Wyoming ranch. God had taken her and Coop on a totally different path, one filled with people of color, different races, different ethnicities, whose American journey had been one of pain and struggle, who had to fight for every drop of respect and equality. But these people, so different in many ways from her own background, had enfolded her and Coop into their lives, enlarging her heart and her mind and her spirit. Would she—

"Grams!" A tug on her sleeve. Reagan's visor was up again, and she was pointing at a weather-beaten gas station at an unmarked crossroad. "Pit stop!"

Pulling in, Maggie topped off her gas tank, and they refilled their water bottles. But there was no shade anywhere, so she told her granddaughter to hose Rocky down to avoid heat stroke—and the next thing she knew, Reagan had turned the water hose on her! It'd been a long time since she'd been in a water fight, but gosh! It felt good! Still, that girl had it coming. Grabbing the hose, she turned it on Reagan and doused her, too. Rocky thought it was great fun, barking and dancing in and out of the flying water.

Back on the road, their damp clothes dried all too soon in the hot wind. But their spirits perked up again when they crossed the Columbia River at the town of Kennewick, where the river temporarily headed east before making a wide, lazy horseshoe turn on its way west to the state line between Washington and Oregon.

They'd been on the road two and a half hours when they met up with the river again at the state line. Crossing the bridge into Oregon where the little town of Umatilla huddled, they stopped at the first fast food place they saw—a Subway—to get some lunch and hose down the dog again.

But after they'd eaten, Maggie headed back across the bridge to the Washington side. Reagan flipped her visor open and shouted, "Hey! Portland's back that way!"

Maggie grinned at her. "Don't worry. We're just going to go along the river on this side."

"Why?" Reagan looked annoyed.

"You'll see."

* * * *

For quite a few miles along the majestic river, the landscape was still treeless. Would she recognize the turnoff after so many years? It had definitely been in the forest among the Cascade foothills. But Coop had circled the name of the town she was heading for: *Carson.* She giggled inside her helmet, remembering clinging to

Coop on the back of his motorcycle in her bunched-up wedding dress as tin cans bounced along the road behind them. He'd taken their everyday clothes and camping stuff up to the honeymoon cabin a couple of days before their wedding. Could she find it again? Was it still there?

As foothills and pine forests finally began to rise on either side of the river, she suddenly saw the sign: Carson Hot Springs and Spa. And then another sign: Wind River Road. That was it! Turning off the main road, they drove slowly through the small resort town. Visors up now, Maggie noted signs for "Luxury Cabins," "B&Bs," and "Hot Springs Resort." If she couldn't find their honeymoon cabin somewhere north of town, hopefully they could find a place to spend the night in Carson.

"Where *are* we going?" Reagan complained as the town disappeared behind them. "Isn't it getting a little late?" By now the mid-afternoon sun was peeking through the pine trees crowding both sides of the road.

"Where your grandpa and I spent our honeymoon. Somewhere up here along Wind River."

Had there been a sign pointing to the cabin? Did it have a name? She had no idea. It had belonged to a Cooper family friend, but that was forty-three years ago! A couple of times she turned off on an unmarked gravel road, but it usually dead-ended or went on too long or was too far from the narrow, rushing river. The cabin had definitely been just a few hundred feet from the mountain river.

"Grams," Reagan said impatiently. "Do you have *any* idea where you're going?"

Maggie didn't answer. That small sign they just passed said *Stabler, 2 miles.* Stabler! The cabin had been near the town of Stabler! And near the river. It had to be close.

As they came around a bend, she could hear the Wind River on her left—and there, also on her left, an unmarked gravel road. She turned.

Barely a quarter mile off the main road, tucked in among fragrant pines she saw it—their "honeymoon cabin." Still standing, but now barely more than a weather-beaten shell. She eased the bike next to the low porch that ran along the front of the cabin, braked, and turned off the motor.

"This is *it*?" Reagan's disbelief hung in the air.

"This is it." Maggie smiled to herself. The place was nothing if not rustic, and it had been rustic even back then. A pump outside had qualified as "running water," no bathroom, just an outhouse, and two lumpy beds that she and Coop had pushed together to make a double.

Rocky scrambled out of the sidecar and ran through the pine trees toward the mountain river, where he waded in up to his belly and drank. Stretching her back and sore muscles from the day's ride, Maggie stepped up onto the porch and tried the door. Locked. Locked? Whatever for? The place was clearly abandoned. She peeked into a window. Too dim to really see inside, but it looked empty.

Reagan had followed Rocky down to the river—Maggie caught glimpses of the two of them through the trees. Leaning against one of the posts holding up the porch, she breathed in deeply. The rich smell of damp moss, pine needles, and rotting wood filled her senses.

This was it.

This was the place she would scatter Coop's ashes.

Here, where their life together had begun.

Going back to the bike, she dug into the nose of the sidecar, pulling out Reagan's backpack and a few other small duffels, until she came to the brass urn that contained Coop's ashes. Didn't remember it feeling this light, but she cradled it in her arm as she sat back down on the porch step and carefully unscrewed the top.

What?! The bag with Coop's ashes had filled up the urn, could hardly screw on the top—but now, the bag looked deflated. Some of the ashes were *gone*.

"Uh, Grams?"

Maggie's head jerked up. Reagan stood a few yards away, as if keeping a safe distance. The look on her face—she looked *guilty*.

Maggie stared at her granddaughter. And then, teeth clenched, she hissed, "Reagan Marilyn Young. *What have you done with Grandpa's ashes?!*"

Chapter 29

R EAGAN'S VOICE CROAKED. "Grams, uh, I can explain—"
"*Explain?!* Explain what?" Maggie's voice shook. "There
should be nothing to explain!"

Regan scuffed a shoe in the dirt. "I—just listen a minute, okay?"
Maggie pinched her mouth into a tight line and waited.

Her granddaughter sucked in a deep breath and blew it out.
"This trip—it's all about Gramps, right? I mean, it's his bike, it's the
trip *he* planned, and all the places we're visiting have something to
do with him, right?"

"Not necessarily!" Maggie snapped. "The Bakers—they're *my*
relatives."

"Yeah, but—" Reagan threw up her hands. "When you got
married, they became his relatives, too, right?"

"Get to the point." Maggie held up the urn. "Ashes."

"It's just . . . you brought Gramp's ashes on this trip to find a place
to bury them. Or scatter them. Whatever. And that church we visited
in Minneapolis—I mean, wow! I never knew that stuff about you and
Gramps back then. The story Pastor Odell told us about what Gramps
did during the riot, how he saved that kid and now the kid is the
pastor of that same church? I mean, it seemed *wrong* not to leave part
of Gramps there! Seems like that's where you and Gramps got the
bug under your skin—or God 'called' you, or however you wanna
say it—to, you know, always live in multi-cultural neighborhoods
and hang out at churches that have lots of different kinds of people.
Like your church now—Merciful Grace, or whatever it's called."

"Grace and Mercy."

"Yeah. Like that."

Huh. If Reagan thought she could sweet-talk her way out of
this, she had another think coming. "So, what? You took it upon

yourself to steal some of your grandfather's ashes without telling me? Is that why you asked to go back by New Hope on our way out of town? Running around to the back of the building?"

Reagan shrugged. "Yeah. I dunno, didn't think you'd miss a little of the ashes."

"A *little*!" Maggie tipped the urn toward her granddaughter. "They're half gone!"

"Oh." Reagan inched forward and peeked into the urn. "Well, not exactly gone. I still have some left in a baggie in my backpack, even after I sprinkled some back at the cemetery."

Maggie gaped. "You . . . *what?* After I told you I'd decided to *not* bury Coop's ashes there?"

The girl hunched her shoulders, looking miserable. "Well, yeah. 'Cause by then I had this idea to leave some of Gramps' ashes at all the places he'd circled on the map. And you'd still have some in the urn to bury . . . wherever."

Maggie was so angry, she practically spit out her next words. "But that's *my* decision, not yours!"

Reagan drew herself up. "Maybe. But they're *Gramps'* ashes. An' I think that's what *he'd* want. But if that's how you feel—" The girl marched over to the sidecar, rummaged in her backpack, and pulled out a quart-size baggie full of grey powder. "Here. Take the stupid ashes. Do whatever you want." She snatched the brass urn from Maggie's hands, stuffed the bag inside, and set it down with a *thump* on the porch. "C'mon, Rocky!" she yelled. Then muttered, "Gonna go walk the dog." A moment later, dog and girl had disappeared into the trees.

Maggie stared after them, trying to get a grip on the mixed-up feelings twisting her gut. Should she call them back? No, she was still too angry. And scared. And lonely. "Oh, Coop," she moaned. Sinking down onto the warped, weathered porch, she picked up the urn, cradled it in her arms—and began to weep.

* * * *

A cold nose poked itself under her arm and touched her cheek. Startled, Maggie raised her head up off her knees. "Oh, Rocky," she murmured. She hadn't heard Reagan and the dog come back. Had she dozed off?

She reached for the dog and tried to pull him close—but the dog backed away from her arm and gave a sharp bark. *Huh. Some Comfort Dog.* Maggie squinted at the tall evergreens overhead. Pale blue sky still peeked through the thick branches, but the little clearing was in total shade. The sun had definitely slid behind the foothills now. What time was it, anyway?

"Reagan?" She stood up and looked around but didn't see her granddaughter. "Reagan?"

Rocky gave several sharp barks and dashed to the edge of the clearing, and then stopped, looking back at Maggie. A sudden unease gripped her. Something was wrong. "Reagan?" she yelled. "Reagan!"

No answer. Just the sound of water rushing over rocks fifty yards away.

Rocky barked again, this time running several yards into the trees, and then turning back toward Maggie. She hurried after him. "Where's Reagan, Rocky?"

The dog dashed away, and Maggie followed as best she could, her anxiety growing. Had something happened to Reagan? She stumbled on a tree root but managed to not fall. It was hard watching her feet and keeping Rocky in sight at the same time. Every few yards, she yelled Reagan's name, but still no answer. Now anxiety blossomed into downright fear.

And then—*What was that?* Maggie stopped. She strained her ears. Just an animal in the underbrush? Wishful thinking? The dog had disappeared from sight, and Maggie hurried forward. Then she heard it again—a moan? She stopped again. "Reagan!" she shouted. But all she heard was Rocky giving several sharp barks. She headed in that direction, off the path, down toward the river. The ground was full of roots and slippery pine needles and rocks, and Maggie had to pick her way carefully. But the barks grew louder.

And then she saw her—Reagan struggling to sit up, dirt and wood chips smudged on her face and body, a bloody gash on her forehead. "Good dog, Rocky, good dog!" Maggie cried, kneeling down beside her granddaughter as the dog anxiously licked the girl's face. "Reagan! What happened?"

Awkwardly propped up by her arms, the girl didn't answer, blinking as if dazed. Maggie had to push Rocky away who was trying to crowd in between them. "Here, honey, can you scoot back? You can lean against this tree." For a moment, the girl didn't respond, but her eyes finally focused on Maggie's face. "G-Grams?" Reagan winced as she pushed herself back against the tree. "Oww . . . my ankle." She pointed to her right foot.

Maggie's heart sank. Reagan must've tripped on those gnarly roots, twisted her ankle, hit her head on something. One of those nasty rocks sticking up everywhere. *Jesus, we need some help here! How was she going to get her granddaughter back to the bike? O Lord, please, help Reagan to be all right!* What if her ankle was broken? What if she had a concussion? What if—?

She had to stop. No what ifs. *Think, Maggie!*

Should she go for help? No, she couldn't leave Reagan here alone. They had to get back to the cabin at least. She patted the pockets of her jeans—just her phone and the key to the bike. Not even a tissue. Both she and Reagan had taken off their jackets in the heat and stowed them on the bike. All she had was the T-shirt she was wearing. Well, it would have to do.

"Be right back, hon." Maggie hefted herself onto her feet, her knees protesting painfully. Picking her way carefully to the swiftly flowing river, Maggie pulled her T-shirt off and soaked it in the cold water. Returning to her granddaughter, she gently mopped the blood away from the gash on her forehead. Not too deep, but might need a stitch or two. A concussion though—that could be a problem. And what about that ankle!

"Honey, I'm going to look at your ankle, okay?" Back on her knees—why did they have to act up so bad right now?—Maggie gently wiggled off Reagan's right gym shoe and sock, stopping when the teenager cried out, but finally she examined the ankle. Swelling for sure. But it didn't look out of joint or at some odd angle—hopefully not broken.

Maggie was suddenly aware that the shadows were deepening. Should she call for help? Digging out her cell phone, she groaned.

No signal. She waved it around . . . still no signal. They really had to get back to the bike!

Rocky seemed anxious, whining from time to time, getting in the way.

She eyed Reagan's ankle again. No way was her granddaughter going to be able to walk on that right now. Maggie wasn't even sure she'd be able to get the shoe back on. Okay, her shirt had to go. Holding it by the hem, she ripped it up the side seam. Then, using her teeth, she got a tear going sideways, ripping a strip from the bottom about three inches wide. Then another one, and another. So much for *that* T-shirt. Rewetting the strips in the cold river and wringing them out for a makeshift cold pack, Maggie wrapped one around Reagan's head and tied it, hoping to hold the gash edges together so it could be stitched. Then she carefully wrapped the other two around the ankle, one after the other, over and under and around. Shoot! She needed a safety pin to hold the end and keep it tight—but those, like the medical kit, were back with the bike.

Think, Maggie!

Rocky had found the loose shoe and was chewing on it. "Rocky! Stop it!" Maggie pulled the shoe from his mouth—and then almost laughed. The shoelace! She could use the shoelace to tie on her makeshift ankle wrap. "Good dog, Rocky!"

Five minutes later, Maggie had helped her granddaughter to stand up and, with Reagan leaning on her heavily, they tried walking. Even with Maggie at her side, the girl had to touch the injured foot down in order to help her hop, and she was whimpering. But little by little they made progress.

Heading back the way she had come, Maggie was careful to keep the river in earshot, but Rocky seemed confident of the way and kept looking back to make sure they were following. How long it took to make it back to the tumbledown cabin with Reagan hobbling the whole way, Maggie had no idea. But there was hardly any daylight left by the time they got back to the bike. The urn with Coop's ashes still sat on the porch. Maggie didn't even remember setting it down after realizing Reagan was missing.

A breeze wafted through the little clearing, and Maggie was suddenly aware she was half-naked on top, minus a shirt, wearing only her bra. Digging quickly into one of the saddlebags that held her clothes, she found another T-shirt and pulled it on. Turning around she realized Reagan had hopped onto the porch and eased herself down.

"Wait, wait, kiddo. Can't sit. We gotta get you into the sidecar and back to town."

"Ohh, Grams, I can't! I'm so tired!" Reagan listed sideways and laid down, curled on her side, and closed her eyes.

Maggie shook her. "Reagan! Don't go to sleep. We have to get you to town."

"I'm *fine*, Grams," Reagan murmured, pushing her hand away, "just gotta rest here." A few moments later, the girl's steady breathing told Maggie her granddaughter had fallen asleep.

Well, this was a fine pickle! She couldn't pick Reagan up and stuff her into the sidecar by herself. But she shouldn't let her sleep too long—what if she had a concussion? If they waited much longer, any medical clinic would be closed—might be closed already! Would they even be able to find a place to spend the night? Carson Hot Springs was a popular touristy town and might be full up.

Should they spend the night here?

What a crazy thought! But suddenly Maggie's shoulders started to shake as she laughed silently. *Oh Coop, you're probably loving this.* She could just hear what he'd say: *"Of course you can spend the night! It's mid-summer, won't get too cold. Make a fire to keep the critters away, use your clothes for a pillow, wake up Reagan every couple of hours to make sure she's okay—you'll be fine!"*

Maggie picked up the urn and hugged it to her chest for a moment. Crickets chirped. The river rushed and gurgled. Pine boughs overhead seemed to sigh in the night breeze. Rocky laid down with a *whump* next to Reagan on the porch and rested his nose on his paws. And in her head, she heard Coop's familiar voice again: *"'I will lie down and sleep in peace, for you alone, O Lord, make me dwell in safety . . .'"*

Huh. Psalm 4. One of their favorite psalms—a Scripture she and Coop often read together when one of them was stressed or worried and couldn't sleep.

And she also had Rocky.

A slight smile creased Maggie's mouth. Truth be told, she wasn't ready to leave the little "honeymoon cabin" just yet. She'd hardly had time to think about the reason that had brought her here. Hadn't had time to thank God for bringing Coop into her life—or now, hadn't had time to scatter Coop's ashes.

But first things first.

Setting the urn back on the porch, she fished in the saddlebag for the emergency kit she'd packed and found the little tin of matches. And then in the deepening dusk, she began to gather dried pine needles for tinder, tiny sticks and twigs, and then larger and larger dead sticks and fallen branches scattered around the forest floor.

Chapter 30

MAGGIE WOKE TO THE TIMER ON HER PHONE, which she'd set for every two hours all night long. But this time sunshine tipped the tops of the trees above her head, and birds were in full-throated concert.

But a glance at the phone told her the battery was almost gone. Not good. They needed to get back to town.

She awkwardly pushed herself onto her feet and glanced at the still-sleeping form of her granddaughter. The dog was sacked out, too. But every muscle Maggie moved made her want to groan. She couldn't remember ever feeling this stiff and sore—at least not since the last time she'd been thrown from one of the horses at the Triple B years ago. Last night she'd made lumpy pillows out of their clothes and covered Reagan with one of their rain ponchos. But her hips ached from lying on the hard porch floor.

Still, somehow, she'd managed to get a few "Z's" between waking up her patient to be sure Reagan hadn't succumbed to a concussion and adding more dry wood to the campfire she'd built directly in front of the porch steps.

Hearing Maggie moving around, Rocky yawned and stretched and then trotted off into the bushes to do his business. Maggie decided that was a good idea and headed stiffly in the opposite direction with a packet of tissues.

When she got back, Reagan was stirring.

"Hey, kiddo. How are you feeling this morning?"

Reagan winced as she sat up. "Uh, okay, I guess." She wiggled her foot. "Ankle's still sore, but . . . not as bad as last night." She gingerly touched the bandage on her forehead. "Head still hurts though." She looked around her. "Did we really sleep here all night?"

Maggie snorted. "Well, yeah. You went out like a light. Didn't have much choice."

Reagan gave a lopsided grin. "Ha. Mom would be horrified." Scooting on her butt over to the porch steps, she leaned against a post. "Man, I'm starving though. We, uh, got anything to eat?"

Maggie snorted a short laugh. "Well, sure. Bacon and eggs coming right up." She fished in the bike saddlebags and pulled out a couple of granola bars and a bag of trail mix. "This'll have to do for now. We can get some breakfast once we get back into town."

Sitting down on the porch step beside Reagan, she munched on some of the trail mix for a few moments. Then, glancing sideways, she said, "Did some thinking last night. You were right."

"Huh? Right about what?"

Maggie chewed thoughtfully for another long moment. "About leaving some of Coop's ashes at each of our stops along the way on this trip."

The girl eyed her suspiciously from under her flopping bangs. "Really? You were pretty mad at me last night."

"I know." How could she explain the jumble of thoughts and memories and prayers that had filled her head and her heart as she lay in the dark? "But I had time to think during the night—and decided you were right."

"So, you want to scatter the rest of the ashes here?"

Maggie shook her head. "Some. Not all. We've still got a few more stops."

"Oh, Grams." Reagan leaned over and squeezed Maggie in a hug. "I love you. I—I'm sorry I took Gramps' ashes without asking you."

Maggie held her granddaughter for a long moment. "I forgive you, honey," she murmured into the girl's hair. Then she stood up and picked up the urn that was still sitting on the porch where they'd left it the night before. "But this time I want to do it myself."

Pulling out the plastic baggie of ashes Reagan had stuffed back into the urn, she walked down to the river, which joyously tumbled and splashed over embedded rocks, making the lovely mountain-stream song that had lulled her to sleep in Coop's arms so many years ago. They'd had no idea where life would take them in the future during those precious few days after their wedding—just like she had no idea where all this water would go or finally end up. Probably in the ocean.

But back then, they didn't really care. They were together. That was the important thing. Wherever life took them, wherever God led them, they would be together—and now that she knew where life had taken them, knew about all the ups and downs, knew the challenges they'd faced, it was still the most important thing.

They'd been on the journey together.

"Except, you're not here now, Coop," she murmured. "I feel kind of lost. Don't really know how to do life without you." How did one do life alone?

But as she stared at the rushing river, a Voice seemed to whisper in her spirit, *Just finish the journey you're on right now, Maggie, and I'll show you what's next—just like I did for you and Coop all these years. You won't be alone. I'll always be with you.*

Maggie took a deep breath and blew it out. Right. That was the glue that had kept them together all these years—knowing that God was with them, showing them the way, step by step. It had taken a lot of trust when they'd committed themselves to the Jesus People commune as newlyweds—and trust again when they'd left the security of it and landed in the "ghetto" at New Hope Friendship Christian Church. Trust again when they'd moved to Chicago and stayed with Grace and Mercy Community Church during those years of "white flight." Trust when she'd given up teaching to work at the Good Neighbor Medical Center, and when Chris had told them he was gay—

Chris.

Maggie's heart clenched.

Where was the trust when Chris came out? She and Coop hadn't been together on how to relate to Chris after that. Part of their journey didn't feel finished. And now Coop was gone.

Trust Me.

For some reason, an odd peace settled in Maggie's spirit. Trust. It's what you do when you don't know. And as Sister Regina at Grace and Mercy so often said, *"God hasn't brought me this far to leave me now!"*

Opening the baggie, Maggie tipped it over the water and shook the ashes into the fast-moving stream. "There you go, Coop," she murmured again. "This is where we started. Continue your journey, and guess I'll continue mine. I wish it could be together, but—"

"Grams?" Reagan's voice sailed through the trees. "Can we go now? I'm really hungry!"

* * * *

Somehow Maggie got her granddaughter and Rocky shoehorned into the sidecar, clothes stuffed into the saddlebags, and the bike back onto Wind River Road. As they came into Carson, she pulled into a Texaco gas station to fill up her tank and ask where she could find a medical clinic.

The gas station attendant gawked at Reagan, her head still wrapped in the bloody strip of Maggie's T-shirt. "What happened to her?"

"She tripped and fell out in the woods," Maggie said impatiently. "That's why we need a clinic."

The man shrugged. "Ain't got any here in Carson. Folks usually go to Hood River 'cross the bridge back that-a-way." He pointed east.

"Are you sure?" Maggie could hardly believe they had to backtrack to find a walk-in clinic.

The man shrugged. "It ain't far. Only 'bout thirty minutes."

"Grams!" Reagan whined. "Let's eat first, *please*. I'll be fine."

The attendant grinned. "Now good eats—that we got. Try the Blue Collar Café just down the road—can't miss it."

The Blue Collar Café was already crowded when Maggie and Reagan went inside. As people in the café turned and stared at them, Maggie suddenly realized what a sight they must be— rumpled and grimy from their night in the forest, smelling like wood smoke, Reagan banged up with a bloody bandage wrapped around her head and limping on a bare foot still too swollen to get her shoe back on.

"Can you tell us where to find the closest medical clinic?" she asked the hostess who met them with menus and a questioning look. Reagan rolled her eyes and limped over to the closest table. "And," Maggie added pleasantly, "do you have an outlet where I can plug in my cell phone while we eat breakfast?"

They got the same answer: no clinic in Carson, but a real nice one in Hood River.

Trying to ignore the not-so-subtle glances in their direction, they ordered three-egg cheese omelets with a side of pancakes for Reagan and biscuits and gravy for Maggie. Ohh, that coffee tasted so good. With all the tension and emotional stress of the past sixteen hours, Maggie hadn't realized how hungry she was—but no wonder. They hadn't eaten since yesterday noon.

But once they'd eaten, there was nothing to do but ride back along Route 14 till they could cross the Columbia over to Hood River, Oregon. "Why don't we just go on to Portland like we'd planned," Reagan grumbled. "I'll be fine—it's just a sprain."

Maggie didn't answer. She felt guilty enough that her granddaughter got injured on a trip she wasn't even supposed to be on. She was at least going to get her checked out.

Unfortunately, getting Reagan "checked out" took the better part of the day. While the medical technician took her for an X-ray of her foot, Maggie called Wendy Thurston, her childhood friend who was expecting them "sometime that day," and warned her they might be late. She had to leave Reagan alone in the clinic a few times to give an unhappy dog some attention and fresh water and to make sure he was in the shade. It was mid-afternoon by the time they were assured Reagan did not have a concussion, her head had been cleaned and patched with a couple of neat butterfly bandages, and she was given an ankle splint to support her ankle while her sprain healed.

"Ugh, I need a shower," Reagan muttered as she fit herself back into the sidecar and hauled Rocky in after her. Maggie couldn't agree more.

The trip along the Columbia on the Oregon side was supposed to take only an hour or so, but they hit rush hour traffic as they came into Portland city limits, adding another thirty minutes before finding the address that Wendy had given her on the southeast side of Portland.

Maggie drove down the one lane street of the neighborhood untouched by gentrification and pulled into the driveway of a modest one-story house. The same little pale-green house Wendy and her husband had lived in a few decades ago—before the divorce—when Maggie and Coop and the kids had visited. Reagan pulled off her helmet and looked around, noting that the only place to walk was along the street itself. "Don't they have sidewalks in Portland?"

Pulling off her own helmet, Maggie chuckled. "Not in most of the older neighborhoods." She'd grown up in a similar neighborhood, had almost forgotten her surprise when they'd moved to Minneapolis to find sidewalks everywhere, even in the poorest neighborhoods. Here, similar small houses with tiny front yards lined the street, some with wire fences or tired pickets, others without, most neat and tidy, a few with weedy lawns and junker cars.

But the little house in front of them was bursting with colorful hanging plants along the porch and wind chimes tinkling in the slight breeze. Wicker chairs with bright flowered cushions just begged for chatting on the low veranda.

The front door opened and a woman in a long peasant skirt and blouse came hurrying out, her long hair streaked with gray and pulled back with a leather barrette. "You're here!" she sang out giddily. "Is this really Stacy's little girl! Oh, my goodness, you didn't tell me you brought your *dog*, too! And look at this amazing rig you're riding!" Wendy Thurston gave Maggie a big bear hug as she slid off the bike—"Cricket, you are really crazy, you know that!"—then gave Rocky an enthusiastic scratch on the rump and wrapped Reagan in another bear hug, chattering all the while. "Can you believe how hot it is today? Not exactly Portland! But I've got cold lemonade all ready, soon as we get you guys inside. Come in! Come in! What can I carry?"

Reagan raised an eyebrow at her grandmother and mouthed, *"Cricket?"*

Maggie gave Reagan a wink and grinned. Yep, this was non-stop Wendy. Almost made her feel ten years old again.

Chapter 31

AFTER SENDING BOTH MIKE AND JIANG A QUICK text that they'd arrived in Portland safely, they ate supper on Wendy's front porch—a quinoa salad with feta cheese, red onion, Kalamata olives, and sweet peppers in a lemony dressing, plus ears of hot, buttery corn on the cob. "Ohhh, Pigeon, this is so good!" Maggie purred, taking a second helping without a shred of guilt. After the trauma of the previous night, she finally felt relaxed.

"Okay, you two," Reagan said, nibbling tentative bites of the quinoa. "What's with this 'Cricket' and 'Pigeon' business?"

Wendy laughed. "Private nicknames. We had all sorts of secrets known only to the two of us when we were kids. We even had a secret code. Can you still read it, Cricket?"

"Ahhh, I think so." Maggie waggled her eyebrows.

Wendy disappeared into the house and returned with paper and pencil. After jotting some strange characters on the page for several minutes, she handed it to Maggie. Maggie studied it for a few minutes and grinned. "Sure! Sounds like a plan."

"Wait. Let me see that." Reagan snatched the paper out of Maggie's hand. "What does it say? Like, what's that word?" She pointed at a word with several characters.

"Sorry, can't tell you." Maggie smirked at Wendy. "Then you might be able to figure out some of the letters." Years ago, they had thrown a few "tricks" into the code to foil anyone who might try to figure out their secret language letter by letter.

"Ha. Can't be that hard. You were ten." Reagan frowned over the code, jotting possibilities with the pencil.

As the evening cooled pleasantly, Maggie and Wendy left Reagan icing her ankle on the front porch while they walked the dog—an excuse to talk out of earshot of a sixteen-year-old. They'd both suffered major loss—one through divorce, the other through death. Maggie's heart ached for her friend at the feelings of rejection Wendy's divorce had dragged her through—different than her loss of Coop, but a loss of hopes and dreams and companionship, nonetheless. It felt good to share some of her own not-so-brave fears of life without Coop. "I know this sounds dumb, Pige, but I feel kind of lost, just not sure what's next or what my purpose is now."

"Not dumb. It takes time. Give yourself a year to get your feet back on the ground." They paused while Rocky did his business. "Though I'm curious," Wendy continued, "why this trip? I mean, Coop's been gone only a few months. You've hardly had time to cope before taking on this whole new thing!"

Maggie stooped to clean up Rocky's mess with a baggie. "I know. But I was going crazy, needed something to do. Couldn't bury myself in work—I'd just retired!" She filled in her friend about discovering Coop's maps, and then his birthday gift of the motorcycle jacket and helmet that arrived after his death. "Made me realize how important this trip was to him. Still not sure *why* it was so important to him, but it obviously was. So, I figured maybe this was the best way to honor him, to take 'The Trip' anyway— and hopefully I'd figure it out on the way." She made a face that said, *Haven't figured it out yet, but here I am!*

Wendy laughed softly and shook her head. "Can't believe you learned how to ride that thing *and* made it this far across the country!" She waved a hand back toward the little house. "With that beautiful child *and* this dog, of all things."

Maggie sighed. "Yeah, I know. It's the sort of thing *you* would do, Wendy, not me. You were always the crazy one. Look at you—you still look like a flower child, and you're making all that gorgeous jewelry and stuff. How's that going, anyway?"

Wendy shrugged. "Okay, I guess. I do a lot of craft fairs—mostly weekends. That, plus my social security, I get by. Sort of." They walked in silence for a few moments, and then Wendy chuckled. "We were quite a pair back then, weren't we? You—you were always so sensible! Always doing the right thing. You even tithed your allowance!" Laughing, she gave Maggie a playful push. "Me, my allowance was to *spend*, not budget.

And my head was in the clouds, dreaming about my future Prince Charming." She snorted. "Huh. And look how that turned out."

Maggie grimaced. "I know. Wish I could kiss that boo-boo and make it all better." She always felt a little guilty when Wendy's divorce came up. Her marriage to Coop had been so different, so life-giving. "But still, I used to wish I was more like you. You were so unfettered! So fun! Remember when you crawled out of a window during a sleepover at my house to go to the Seven-Eleven to buy snacks—and I didn't go, because I was afraid of getting in trouble? It was hard always being a 'good Christian girl'—" Maggie suddenly felt stricken. "Wait—I didn't mean you *weren't*. Good grief, we both 'rededicated our lives'—I don't know how many times!—at those mission conferences they held every year at Calvary Academy!" She pursed her lips thoughtfully as they walked on. "It just took me a long time to realize I could make mistakes, and God would still love me."

Wendy laughed again. "Don't worry, Cricket. I know what you mean." She looked at Maggie sideways. "Guess we needed each other back then. Yin and Yang. Mutt and Jeff. Frodo and Sam."

Maggie slipped an arm through Wendy's and squeezed. "Still do, Pigeon."

* * * *

The insistent ringing near her ear dragged Maggie out of a deep sleep. *Whaaa . . .?* Why was her alarm going off? She didn't have to get up for anything in particular—*Wait.* That wasn't her alarm. It was the phone.

Groping in the dark, she found her phone where she'd plugged it in to recharge and tapped the "On" button. The time glowed green: 3:06 a.m. *Grr, this better be important.* "Hello?"

A brief silence. Then—"Mom! Is that you? I can hardly hear you! Why do you sound so croaky?"

Stacy. Of course.

Because I was asleep! she wanted to yell. But she cleared her throat. "Uh, hi, Stacy. Is everything okay? Where are you?"

"We're fine. We're in Venice. Where are *you*? Are you back home in Chicago? I tried to call Reagan and she didn't answer! Is she still with you? Is she okay? That girl! Why doesn't she ever answer her phone?"

"Stacy! Calm down, honey. Yes, Reagan's with me. She's fine. She probably didn't answer because she's asleep."

"Asleep? Isn't she up yet?"

"Stacy, it's three in the morning here."

"Oh." A pause. "Where's here? Aren't you back home?"

"No, not yet. We're, uh, in Portland. Visiting my friend, Wendy. Remember Wendy? My best childhood girlfriend. We—"

"*Portland!* Oregon? Mom!" The voice suddenly faded, as if Stacy turned away, but Maggie could faintly hear her spout off to someone in the background. "They're in Portland. Can you believe it? She took Reagan on that bike all the way to the West Coast! Un-be-*lieve*-able!" The voice came back on. "I am *so* angry, Mom. This is . . . is so . . . so irresponsible! And dangerous! You have no right to do this with my daughter! I thought you'd go back home after you visited the Baker cousins. That was bad enough! Why in the world are you in *Portland?* I have half a mind to get on a plane and go home right now. You are ruining our cruise, you know— worrying about you and Reagan. We . . ."

Maggie let Stacy blow off steam for thirty seconds more, realizing this was not going to be an actual conversation. Finally, she broke in. "Stacy? Stacy! It's the middle of the night here. Why don't we call you back when Reagan can get on the phone, okay? Talk to you later, honey!" And she hung up.

Maggie flopped back on the futon in Wendy's "guestroom"— actually her jewelry-making studio with a fold-out futon. *Oh brother.* By this time, she was wide awake. She lay there staring into the darkness. *Was* she being irresponsible? A renegade tear slid out of her eye. *O God, I really thought taking this trip is what I was supposed to do. Did I hear you wrong? I wanted to do it for Coop.*

She must have eventually fallen asleep, because the next thing Maggie knew daylight was pouring through the window blind and she could smell—*coffee.* Wandering into Wendy's tiny kitchen, she saw her friend pulling mugs out of the cupboard. The kitchen clock said 7:05. She jerked a thumb toward the couch in the living room. "I see my young hitchhiker is still asleep. Uh, where's Rocky?"

Wendy handed her a steaming cup. "I took him out back and let him do his business. It's fenced in. But *you,* my dear friend, can clean up after him."

Maggie grinned. "Thanks. But, uh, about today. I need to take the BMW into a service center first thing, probably have to leave it. Promised Mike I'd have it given a once-over when we got to Portland. Do you mind?"

"Of course not. We can follow you in my car. Still want to go by Calvary Academy? Show your granddaughter where we grew up? And then, how about a hike up Multnomah Falls? We'll take a picnic. Going to be another hot one, though."

A little research on Google pulled up a motorcycle service center in southeast Portland that had great reviews—but when Maggie called Cycletune and said she was only in town a couple of days, the center said she'd have a better chance of getting her bike serviced that day if she could get it there by eight o'clock.

"Eight!" she screeched to Wendy. "That's, like, in forty-five minutes!" The next fifteen minutes were a scramble—good thing she'd taken a shower the night before. Wendy shooed her out the door with a toasted bagel and a travel cup of coffee and said she and the kid would be along within the hour.

Chapter 32

WITH THE HELP OF GOOGLE MAPS ON HER PHONE, Maggie found Cycletune without much trouble, still on the east side of the Willamette River that ran north and south through Portland. The metallic blue BMW generated a long whistle from the service guy who was sent out to log in her bike. The name "Gus" was stitched onto his uniform shirt. "Wow. Is that a 1981 BMW R-series? Man, I haven't seen one of those except at vintage bike shows. Class-y!"

Maggie was pleased. At least this place knew her bike. And "Gus" didn't make any comment about her being an "old lady" riding it. "Do you think you can service it today? I'm in town only a short time."

The guy scratched his head. "Well, we can do a diagnostic today. But I gotta tell you, lady, we don't carry parts for vintage bikes like this. If anything needs to be replaced, we'd have to order it from this company that specializes in vintage parts."

Maggie's heart sank. No telling how long that might be.

"Or," Gus continued, with a friendly wink, "wanna sell it? My boss might be interested. He's got a thing for vintage bikes. Probably give you top dollar, cash on the barrelhead. Or do a trade-in, if you'd like." He jerked a thumb over his shoulder and grinned. "I could ask him."

Maggie shook her head. "Thanks, but not interested."

Gus shrugged. "Okay. We'll give 'er a once-over and give ya a call if she needs anything more than a simple tune-up."

Maggie found a signpost to lean against as she waited for Wendy and Reagan to show up. *Hmph.* Sell the bike? Coop would roll over in his grave if she sold his bike willy-nilly to some stranger just to get "top dollar." The next moment she almost choked on a laugh. *Roll over in his grave—ha.* What do you say if you're carrying around your husband's *ashes* in an *urn*?

As she waited, her thoughts replayed Stacy's scolding again in her ears: *"Mom! This is so irresponsible! And dangerous!"* Her daughter was worried. In spite of Stacy's melodramatic reactions to everything, she had a point. This trip *was* crazy. And potentially dangerous. And she *was* responsible for her granddaughter's well-being, who could have broken her leg out there in the woods by their honeymoon cabin. Maybe she *should* sell the bike, buy a couple of plane tickets, and take Reagan home. Now. That would make everyone happy. And—she might as well admit it—she was tired. Every day on the road took a toll on her joints and muscles. They'd come all the way to Portland— wasn't that enough? She'd given Coop's Grand Trip idea a good ol' college try. Maybe—

A series of beeps from a car horn jerked her head up. Wendy had just pulled up across the street in her trusty old Nissan, and Reagan was waving at her from the front passenger seat. Gratefully pushing her troubling thoughts aside, Maggie scooted across the street and slid into the back seat with Rocky.

"So, where we goin' again?" Reagan sounded dubious already.

"Where we grew up!" Maggie and Wendy chimed together, laughing, as Wendy headed for the northeast corner of Portland. They drove past the Gresham area, past signs for Mt. Hood Community College, and finally turned in at a sign that said, "Calvary Academy."

As they drove up the tree-shaded drive of the school campus, Reagan said, "Why do you say you 'grew up' here? I mean, just because you went to school here."

"You'll see," Maggie said as Wendy parked the car and they all got out, snapping the leash on Rocky's collar. "Wow," she murmured, "a lot of new buildings since I was last here. Do they still have the dormitories?"

"Nope. Just a day school now," Wendy said.

"Dormitories?" Reagan made a face.

"Calvary used to also be a boarding school for missionary kids whose parents lived overseas," Maggie explained. "Wendy's mom was the dorm mother when my parents first came on staff here. All the girls loved her."

"Yep, staff families lived on campus back then," Wendy added. "That's why your grandma and I literally grew up here."

"So, Great-Grandma and Grandpa Baker—what did they do?"

"My dad was Superintendent of Schools over both elementary and high school back then and principal of the high school. Mom was the high school librarian. And that's where we lived." Maggie pointed at a stately building that looked as if it'd been transplanted from the Tudor era. "The Administration Building. First floor was offices, second and third floor were staff apartments. But none of the apartments had kitchens, so we all ate in the staff dining room."

Standing in front of this building, old sensations stirred in Maggie's memory. The slick feel of yellow oilcloth covering the tables in the staff dining room . . . the sound of dishes clattering as her dad brought breakfast upstairs on a large tray so they could eat together as a family . . . the rich wood and velvety upholstery in the reception room on the first floor right under their apartment . . . the smell of yellow forsythia blooming in early spring all over the campus . . .

Wendy was snickering. "Your grandma and I used to play prince and princess on the fire escape outside the windows of their apartment—you know, like Rapunzel being rescued from the tower and all that."

Reagan snorted. "Seriously?"

"Yep." Maggie grinned. "Actually, living on campus was a marvelous place to grow up—forty acres to run around on, and school only a hundred yards away. Just didn't realize at the time how sheltered from the world we were."

Wendy laughed. "Didn't you tell me once that after you met Coop, he said someone on the street could walk up to you and call you a name, and you wouldn't even realize you'd been insulted?"

Maggie flushed. "Yeah, well, the way kids trash-talk these days, I'm not sure that was such a bad thing—oh." She noticed Reagan was still limping on her injured ankle. "Sorry, kiddo." They slowed their pace as they moved on.

Even though school was out, the campus wasn't deserted. A bunch of little kids on a grassy lawn were playing relays supervised by adults with whistles, while another group sat in a circle singing kid-friendly gospel songs with hand motions. What was this, daycare? Except the kids looked older than pre-school— more like six, seven, even eight. But her heart sank a little. The two groups of kids were still mostly white, with a few Asian kids and a token brown face here and there. Not much different than when she grew up here in 99 percent Vanilla-Land—

"Excuse me!" a woman walking by with a clipboard called out. "I'm sorry, but we don't allow dogs on campus."

For some reason, the woman's rebuke made Maggie cringe. Fifty years later, and she still got reprimanded for not following the rules. As an animal-crazy kid, she had tried a whole menagerie of pets to bypass the "No Dogs or Cats" rule: hamsters, gerbils, goldfish, parakeets, white mice. Which was okay—until the white mouse had ten babies that got loose on the second floor of the "Ad Building," creating general panic. Really, she should laugh—but instead Stacy's scolding again echoed in her head: *You're being so irresponsible!*

Irresponsible . . . irresponsible . . .

She could almost hear her dad chiding her for some childish infraction. When you're a "good Christian girl," being "irresponsible" topped the list of naughtiness. Double trouble when you're the PK—Principal's Kid—and expected to be a role model for all the other students—

"Right, Maggie?"

Maggie blinked, realizing Wendy had been telling Clipboard Lady that they were former Academy students, showing Maggie's granddaughter where they'd grown up decades ago. "Uh, yes, that's right." She extended a hand. "Maggie Baker Cooper. My father used to be the superintendent here."

"Oh! Superintendent Baker's daughter and *great*-granddaughter?" The woman was suddenly chatty. "I've seen his picture in the high school hallway!"

Realizing attention had been diverted from Rocky, Maggie asked what was going on with the children, and was told the

Academy hosted day camps on campus for several age groups during the summer. "This week it's early elementary," Clipboard Lady beamed. "And next month we do sports camps before school starts. It's also a way to advertise the school to new families."

Before she could stop herself, Maggie blurted, "Do you also recruit students from the black churches around town? The diversity ratio doesn't seem that different than when Wendy and I went to school here."

"Oh, we have a satellite campus in the city that is *very* diverse," the lady beamed. "We realized there's a real need for Christian education in the inner city. We're very proud of that campus." The woman smiled sweetly and said, "Well, just be sure to clean up after your dog if he, you know . . ." and then hurried on.

Don't judge, Maggie, she told herself. *You don't know the whole story.* But, darn it, why did there have to be a separate school for the "inner city" kids?

"Cheese Louise," Reagan whistled. "Was it like this when you guys lived here?"

"Not hardly." Wendy rolled her eyes. "Back then staff kids had to work in the summer starting at age twelve for a couple hours a day. My first job was sweeping sidewalks—gosh, I hated that job. Then I graduated to wiping tables in the staff dining room, then re-shelving books in the school library. That didn't last long, though, 'cause I kept reading the books."

Maggie sighed. "Same here. But if we complained about anything, my dad would say with a straight face, 'You kids think *you* got it bad? Why, in *my* day we had to walk ten miles to school! Barefoot! In the snow! Uphill both ways!'"

"Uphill both—!" Reagan snorted. "Yeah, right." Sinking down onto a bench, she moaned, "Though right now, I feel as if *I* just walked ten miles. My ankle is killing me."

Maggie joined her on the bench, glad to get off her feet as well. "We don't have to keep going. We've seen most of the campus."

"Hmm, maybe a hike up Multnomah Falls today isn't a good idea after all." Wendy flopped down on the bench on the other side of Reagan. Rocky followed suit, crawling under the bench to get some shade.

235

"Well, we could at least drive out there and eat that picnic lunch you brought. Wouldn't have to hike—oh!" Maggie's cell phone was buzzing. She jumped up. "It's Cycletune. Gotta take this."

Stepping a few feet away, she listened as Gus explained what her BMW needed. "Definitely needs an oil change after 2000 miles, but we'd need a filter we don't have on hand for your model. Your choke cable is starting to fray, so we'd be smart to replace it, too. And I'd recommend replacing your brake pads. All of which we can order from that vintage warehouse I mentioned—but it'd be day after tomorrow before they'd arrive. Once we got the parts, these are easy fixes—could have it done by the end of the day on Friday if the parts come in by noon."

Friday! Two more days—three actually, since they couldn't really leave till Saturday morning. At least that would give her some time to think about whether to abort their trip and go home now, or whether to go on. One way or the other, she needed to be thinking about "what next."

"Uh, hang on," she said to the service guy, muting the phone and making a face at Wendy. "Can you put up with us for a few more days? Like, till Saturday morning?" *If* the parts came in on Friday.

"As long as you like!" Wendy waved her back to the phone. "No problem!"

Telling Gus to go ahead and order the necessary parts—she'd never hear the last of it from her eldest child if she didn't—Maggie returned to the bench beside Reagan. "Well. I'm ready to go on up to the Falls if you guys are—even just for a picnic and the view. It's really beautiful, Reagan. You'll like it."

Reagan shrugged. "Okay. But, what about, you know, Gramps' ashes?"

"Here?" Maggie said. "Oh, I don't think so. I mean, Coop didn't have anything to do with Calvary Academy. This is just my story before I ever met him."

She saw Wendy and Reagan eyeing each other. Had these two been discussing this while she was on the phone?

"Yeah, but Grams, like you said, this is where you grew up and became the person Gramps fell in love with. So, if we're leaving a little bit of Gramps at every place with some significance to your life journey—why not?"

"Well, because we'd have to go back to the house and then come all the way back here, and—what?"

Reagan was grinning.   "Just back to the car. I brought the urn."

Chapter 33

*U*PHILL BOTH WAYS . . ."

Her dad's old punch line invaded her brain the moment Maggie woke up on the futon Saturday morning. For some reason, it had been niggling at the back of her consciousness the last few days at Wendy's.

Huh. Even as a kid she'd known it was silly. *"Yeah, right, Dad. You walked to school barefoot, in the snow, uphill both ways. Ha ha ha."*

But after the visit to Calvary Academy, she kept thinking about her growing up years there. Most all of her memories were happy ones—a gaggle of friends that included her and Wendy, slumber parties, mostly good grades, parents who were strict, but also loving. Church on Sunday, Pioneer Girls—the Christian version of Girl Scouts—Bible classes along with Algebra and American History and Latin. Marred only by the normal angst of puberty, not getting chosen for the romantic lead in the school play, boys who didn't ask her out because (she surmised) she was the "Super's kid."

Took it all for granted back then. Her little Christian bubble.

The real world had been a bit of a shock when she graduated and went off to college—definitely an uphill learning curve! It was the late sixties, early seventies. The Vietnam War. The assassination of Dr. Martin Luther King. Race riots. War protests. Kids dropping out and turning on. Woodstock. She'd had to confront a lot of her own racial prejudices and assumptions and priorities, some of which had rattled her faith.

Still, somehow, she'd managed to hold on to the most important things about her spiritual upbringing. A love for Jesus and respect for the Word of God, which had remained a solid foundation for everything that had happened next.

238

Uphill both ways . . .

Huh. Wasn't such a far-off analogy of her life with Coop. Not "uphill" in a ridiculous sense, like her dad's silly joke. But a challenging uphill journey nonetheless, starting from those early days when she first met Coop staffing a booth at the Jesus People Music Festival in Oregon . . . to all the life-altering choices they'd made along the way, which eventually landed them in Chicago, committed to a life of "breaking down walls" with their racially diverse neighbors—*including* all the challenges over the years to stick with Grace and Mercy Community Church in spite of white flight and racial tensions.

Yep. Uphill all the way. Good, yes, but *definitely* uphill.

But now that Coop was suddenly gone, here she was revisiting many of those people and places along that uphill journey—and going backwards *also* felt like going uphill! Why was she doing this? What had Coop hoped to get out of this trip? What was the point? And without Coop, the way forward also looked like an uphill climb. What was her purpose now? What did God want her to *do?* Or *be?*

"Okay, Jesus," she muttered, staring up at one of Wendy's mobiles gently twirling from a ceiling hook overhead. "You've walked with Coop and me our whole life this far, and we've trusted you to show us the way, step by step. I *want* to trust that you're still walking with me, but it feels like my life has turned a big corner and, to be honest, I can't see the way ahead any more. Please, God, I need—"

A knock on the door interrupted her prayer. "Grams? You awake?" The door opened a crack, then wider as Rocky pushed past Maggie's granddaughter, jumped up on the futon, and bestowed sloppy dog kisses on Maggie's face, his tail spinning like a pinwheel.

"Omph! I am now—okay, okay, Rocky! Enough!" She pushed the dog off the bed. "Just kidding, I was already awake." She scooted into a sitting position and patted the faded quilt. "Come, sit. What's up?"

But Reagan's eyes were taking a tour around the little workroom, taking in the various displays of funky jewelry, the worktable strewn with bits of wire, piles of colored stones, gold and silver chains, and boxes of earring hooks, and lengths of batik in different designs draped artfully around the walls and over the single window. *"Cool!"* she breathed. "Wish I could do stuff like this. Think she would teach me?"

"Mm, sure, if we were staying all summer."

Reagan crawled onto the futon, leaning against the wall. "It's been fun staying here at Wendy's. She's pretty cool—I mean, I like her free spirit, not all caught up in getting a big house in the 'burbs. She's got her own style, dresses like she wants, doesn't pay any attention to fashion. And the places she hangs out—even though she's kinda old, like you. The sidewalk cafés and funky shops she took us to, where she knows all those hip people."

Kinda old, like you? Huh. Maggie felt slightly offended. But yeah, that was Wendy, still marching to her own drum. Though Reagan didn't see some of the messes Wendy's "free spirit" had gotten her into. "Did you like driving up to Mount Hood yesterday?"

"Yeah, that was amazing—though you and Wendy *do* act a little crazy when you're together." Twisting a lock of her colored bangs idly around one of her fingers, the girl added wistfully, "You guys are lucky, though. I've never had a best friend like you two had growing up."

Maggie patted Reagan's knee. "I'm sorry, hon. Yeah, Wendy's been a really special friend."

"*Anyway*," Reagan said, "I know we're picking up the bike today. Just kinda wondering about the rest of the trip, and, you know, what you're thinking about getting back home?"

Home. There it was. "Feeling a bit homesick?"

Reagan shrugged. "Not really. Well, maybe a little."

Good, Maggie thought. Reagan had talked with her mom *and* her dad by phone last night. Far as she knew, there'd been no yelling this time from the Mediterranean. Maybe they were both ready to think about going home.

"But, my folks and Reese aren't due back for another week or so, so no point going home yet. And don't we still have two places on the map to visit? It's just—well, Gramps' maps don't give any hint at what he was planning for a return trip."

"About that," Maggie said. "To be honest, kiddo, I don't think I can face another two thousand miles riding the motorcycle all the way back to Chicago. So, I've been thinking. Maybe we should sell the bike and—"

"Sell the bike?!" Reagan looked alarmed.

"—and fly home."

"Oh, Grams, we can't sell Gramps' bike!"

"Well, we probably could. A guy at Cycletune thought his boss might like to buy it. Said the guy had a thing for vintage bikes. It's either sell it and fly home or ride it all the way."

Her granddaughter hugged her knees, frowning in silence for a long minute. Then she said, "Well, you can't sell it now, anyway, 'cause we haven't finished the trip. And you gotta finish it."

Maggie nodded slowly. "That's what I've been thinking." Though she hadn't put it into words until just now. Just a reluctance in her gut to take Gus up on his offer. "On the other hand, your parents would be *very* happy if I put you on a plane now and sent you home. You could probably stay with your Uncle Mike and your cousins in Indy till your folks got back."

"What? No! I want to finish the trip with you! Just, you know, we haven't really talked about where we're going next or anything."

Well, *that* they could do. Maggie swung her feet off the bed and pulled on the loose caftan Wendy had loaned her. "Sure. Let's go check out the maps, see what we do next." Besides, she smelled fresh coffee.

Following Reagan and Rocky to the cozy kitchen, she saw Coop's maps already spread out on the kitchen table. "Hey. What's this?" She eyed Wendy, and then Reagan, as she poured herself a cup of coffee. "I sense a little conspiracy going on here."

"Well, since you're picking up your 'chariot' this morning," Wendy sniffed, winding her long hair into a ponytail scrunchie, "we thought it'd be nice to know where you're headed next. Or maybe, why?"

"Well, duh, it's not such a mystery." Maggie bent over the West Coast map and used her forefinger to follow the yellow marker south from Portland. "Coop circled this area . . ." She pointed to an area just above Grants Pass in southern Oregon, "where—"

"Wait a minute!" Wendy squealed. "Isn't that where Wolf Creek Bible Camp was, where we went to summer camp as kids? And then signed up as camp counselors during college summers?" Wendy started to laugh. "And then Coop applied to be a lifeguard after he met you at the Jesus People Music Fest!" She turned to Reagan, who was listening to this with a raised eyebrow. "Ooo, girl, your grandma definitely had the hots for James Cooper that summer."

Maggie did an exaggerated throat clearing. "As I was saying—"

"Really, Grams? You and Wendy used to be counselors at a summer camp, like the ones mom and dad always ship me and Reese off to?"

"Well, kinda. Except Wolf Creek was a Christian camp, and kids only came for a week. We worked on staff all summer, but with a different age group each week."

"A Christian camp? You mean, like, *church* all week long?"

"No! I mean, well, there was definitely a spiritual emphasis at the camp. We had chapel every day with a special speaker, usually a youth minister who was popular with kids. But we had lots of other activities, too—like swimming and archery and crafts and nature lore and a ropes course and campfires at night. The older kids could choose an adventure camp, where they did a couple nights backpacking into the forest or white-water rafting—stuff like that."

Wendy snickered. "Actually, staff had a lot of fun, too—not all of it sanctioned by the, um, camp administration."

"Tell me!" Reagan grinned.

Wendy's eyes sparkled mischievously. "Well, there was a middle-aged woman, unmarried, who was the camp cook. Yikes, what was her name? Sybil or Sylvia—something like that. Anyway, I got this idea to hook her up on a blind date with one of the single maintenance men—"

"—which turned out to be a disaster," Maggie finished, rolling her eyes. "Okay, you two, moving on . . ." She ignored the giggling twosome and ran her finger down the map to the next circled city. "Right after Coop and I got married, we lived at a Jesus People commune here in San Francisco—right in the city. Actually, Coop had been part of the commune for a couple years before we met—that's why he was working one of the booths at the Music Fest. That was one of the things I admired about Coop in those early days, his desire to be a 'radical Christian'—living simply, sharing our money, serving the poor. But after a while your grandfather felt God calling him to urban ministry and wanted to go to seminary. Which was pretty dicey since we didn't have much money. But at least we had a roof over our heads and food on the table while he was in school. We lived in the commune about five years—that's where both Mike and Stacy were born."

"My mother was born in a *commune*?" Reagan guffawed. "Ha! No wonder she never told me."

"That's because she doesn't remember it. She was just a toddler when we moved to Minneapolis."

Wendy was still hovering over the map. "Hm. Looks like that's the end of the trip Coop planned." She straightened up and gave Maggie a meaningful look. "So, then what? How are you two—oh, excuse me, Rocky—you *three* getting back home? Going to ride that BMW all the way back to Chicago?"

Maggie sighed. "Good question. But can't see doing that." She locked eyes with her friend for a long moment, realizing the day of reckoning was almost upon them. "Reagan and I were just talking about that. Probably fly home—except not sure what to do with the bike—"

"Wait—Grams, look." Reagan turned the map sideways and pointed to some pencil jottings along the edge. "I never saw this before, did you?"

Maggie and Wendy both leaned close to the map. The penciled notes read: *"SF to SB?"* and *"SB to CHI?"*

"What do you think *that* means?" Reagan said.

Maggie shook her head. "I have no idea. But it does look like Coop's handwriting."

"Well, look," Wendy said practically. "SF probably means San Francisco, and CHI—could be Chicago. So, what's SB?"

"Another stop?" Reagan added.

The three of them stood silently over the map, each considering possibilities. Maggie frowned. *Was SB a person? A place? A town?*

"There are question marks. Maybe he was thinking of visiting one of the state parks," Wendy said. "SB . . . hmm." She tapped on her cell phone for a few moments. "Suppose it could be San Bruno Mountain State Park, just south of San Francisco. Maybe Coop thought, as long as you're there in 'Frisco, do some sightseeing?"

Maggie shrugged. "I don't know." She felt a little impatient. She didn't have time for this. "Right now—" She started folding up the maps. "—Gus said I could pick up the bike any time after ten, so let's get some breakfast and pack up our stuff before we wear out our welcome at Hotel Wendy's. Whaddya say, kiddo?"

Chapter 34

A s WENDY PARKED HER CAR ACROSS THE STREET from Cycletune, Reagan suddenly shook Maggie's shoulder from the back seat and pointed out the window. "Grams! Look! Isn't that—you know! Those guys!"

Maggie stared. Three bikers were pulled up next to one of the open garage doors of the service center, smoking cigarettes and talking to one of the mechanics. It couldn't be! But—who else would be wearing those familiar bandanas?

Reagan was already scrambling out of the car. "Hey, Buzz!" she yelled. "Remember us?"

Three heads swiveled in their direction. "Hey, yourself!" the big guy in the ponytail called back. "If it isn't Cookie and Granny!" He jerked a thumb toward their BMW which was parked off to the side, ready to go. "We saw your blue rig with the sidecar, figured it had to be you."

Maggie was only two steps behind, grinning. "What are the Three Musketeers doing here?"

Smoky spit and chortled. "Same as you. Best bike shop to give the Harleys some TLC before headin' cross-country."

Wendy joined the reunion, looking a bit wary. "Who's this?" Buzz asked.

Before Maggie could answer, Reagan piped up. "This is 'Pigeon.' She calls my grandma 'Cricket.' They've been best friends since they were in diapers."

Smoky and Hawk guffawed. But Buzz extended a hand. "Pleased ta meetcha, Pigeon. I'm Buzz, these are my cousins, Hawk and Smoky." He eyed Maggie. "So, where you off to now? Heading back to Chicago?"

Maggie shook her head. "Not yet. Going down the coast, as far as San Francisco at least." She racked her brain for what Buzz had

245

said about the bike rally—in Hollister, wasn't it? "Uh, you guys still on your way to the rally?"

"Nah," Hawk said. "That was over the Fourth. Headin' back now." He was giving Rocky a good scratch on the rump, acting pleased that the dog remembered them.

"But it was one smokin' hot time!" Smoky said, slapping his bike for emphasis. "Ya shoulda come with us, Granny."

Wendy mouthed, *Granny?* giving her a sideways look and a snarky grin. Maggie ignored her.

"Hey, uh, if you ever think about sellin' your BMW, let me an' Smoky know." Hawk gestured at his brother. "We might be interested, right, Smoky?"

"Huh?" Smokey stamped out his cigarette. "Oh, yeah, yeah. Sure. We might."

Maggie smiled. "Sure. If I do, I'll let you know. Anyway, it's great running into you guys again. Really appreciate you looking out for us back there in Minneapolis." She held out her hand. "But, we should get going. Have to get down the road a ways still today."

Buzz took her hand, but instead of shaking it, he pulled Maggie aside. "Where ya goin', Granny?" he said, voice lowered. "Most anywhere you need to go from Portland is on I-5. You more comfortable on the interstate now?"

"Uh, sort of, I guess. Once we're out of the city." She really was *not* looking forward to feeling like a kiddie-car squeezed between giant semis in Portland traffic.

Buzz looked at her intently for a brief moment. *He does have kind eyes*, she thought. Then heard him say, "Tell you what. Why don't me and the boys ride with you till you're out of the city. How far you want to go today?"

"Mm, about three-and-a-half hours down the road—to Glendale, I think. But you don't have to go that far! If you'd be kind enough to escort us through town, we should be okay once we get out of the city." Maggie felt a huge surge of relief. She only planned to spend an hour or so at Wolf Creek showing Reagan around—if the Bible camp even still existed. After that, they could take Route 199 over to the coast and hopefully make Crescent City just over the border by nightfall. Then it was beautiful Highway 101 all the way to San Francisco. No more interstate.

So, it was settled. Smoky and Hawk did a little eye rolling about the plan, but Reagan kept grinning as she transferred their stuff from Wendy's car into the saddlebags and the sidecar. After getting the low-down from Gus on the work they'd done on the BMW, Maggie settled up with the office and gave Wendy a final goodbye hug. "Thanks for everything, Pigeon," she whispered in her friend's ear. "Pray for us, okay?"

"You're the one who's crazy now, you know that, right?" Wendy murmured, returning the hug fiercely. "I want a phone call or text every night till you get home, promise?"

Maggie's throat tightened. Would she ever see Wendy again? "I'll try," she croaked.

A moment later Reagan and Rocky had settled into the sidecar, and Maggie fell into line behind Buzz as he headed for the on-ramp onto I-5.

Like the last time they were escorted by the "Bandanas," Maggie felt more secure riding in Buzz's wake, with Hawk and Smoky buffeting their rear from the giant semis that wanted to ride on their tail. But thirty minutes later, they were well out of city traffic, and Maggie expected Buzz to give a wave and pull off at the next exit. But he kept going. Reagan tugged on her sleeve and gave a questioning look through her helmet visor, but Maggie shrugged. She had no way to communicate with Buzz, and she certainly wasn't going to zoom up beside him to yell questions or whatever.

At one point Smoky did just that, though, roaring past Maggie and riding alongside Buzz for several minutes, gesturing and pointing behind him. But Buzz just gave a "forward ho!" motion, and Smoky dropped back till he and Hawk were riding caboose again.

As they approached the exits for Salem an hour down the road, Buzz finally put on his blinker and rode up the first off-ramp. Unsure what was happening, Maggie followed, and the little "biker gang" pulled off on the shoulder of the ramp, killing their engines.

Buzz ambled back to her. "You good?" He pointed at the highway below. "Traffic's thinned out. But if you'd like, we could ride with you to Glendale."

"No, no. We'll be fine now." Maggie slid off the bike and gave Buzz a hug. "You're an angel, you know that, Buzz? Oh! Wait a sec." She rummaged in her backpack for her small notebook and a pen and scribbled something. Tearing out the page, she handed it to him. "My address and phone number in Chicago. If you ever come to Chi-Town and need a bed-and-breakfast, give me a call. Coopers' B&B." She laughed. "I'd love to see you again. Your cousins, too."

Buzz grinned. "I'll do that, Granny." He leaned over and rapped the top of Reagan's helmet. "Take it easy, Cookie!" Remounting his bike, he motioned to his two sidekicks, and with beeps on their horns and some unnecessary revving of their engines, the trio crossed over the highway on the overpass, back down the opposite on-ramp, and soon disappeared heading north toward Portland.

"What are you doing, Lord?" Maggie murmured to herself as she got back on the bike and started it up. "Who would've thought your guardian angels wore bandanas and rode Harleys?"

* * * *

Once out of the city, traveling the interstate wasn't so bad. The day was overcast and mild—ah, Oregon! Perfect for highway travel. They stopped for a quick lunch and potty break in Eugene and got back on the road, which was now just two lanes each way, but surrounded by low hills covered with stately evergreens and thick underbrush. So beautiful—though Maggie couldn't imagine trying to hike through that dense forest.

They made it to the exit that would take them to the camp by mid-afternoon. Pushing back her visor and using the map on her cell phone, Reagan called out directions, using arm thrusts and finger-pointing for extra emphasis to guide Maggie along a winding two-lane road. They finally saw a large wooden arrow that said: WOLF CREEK BIBLE CAMP, pointing to a narrow lane that gave them occasional glimpses of a silvery creek playing hide-and-seek among the trees.

Saturday . . . would they be interrupting a camp in session? Maggie was suddenly aware of the bike's rumbling engine, sounding loud and aggressive among the stillness of the forest. But the campground seemed quite deserted as they drove under the camp sign at the entrance and pulled up to a large, rustic-looking log building with a door on one side that said, "Camp Office." She should stop in, make sure it was okay to wander around.

Reagan and Rocky were climbing out of the sidecar when the office door opened, and a middle-aged woman stepped out. "Hello! Uh, we aren't expecting campers until tomorrow—oh, I'm sorry. But dogs aren't allowed on the campground."

Maggie hustled up onto the low porch and held out her hand. "Oh, don't worry. I'm not bringing a camper. I'm Maggie Cooper—I used to be a camp counselor here years ago, when I was in college. And I was a camper before that. We're just passing through, and I wanted to show my granddaughter where I used to go to camp."

"Oh!" The woman looked flustered. "Well, I—"

"Who is it, Annie?" a masculine voice boomed through the open door. Half a second later, a middle-aged man in his fifties stepped out. "Well, this is a surprise!" He beamed a friendly smile. "We don't have many bikers stop into camp—especially not the feminine kind." He thrust out a work-worn hand. "I'm Cutler Davis, camp director. This is my wife, Annie. You are . . .?"

Maggie introduced herself again, including Reagan and Rocky this time. "I'm sorry about the dog. We'll keep him on the leash and clean up if he poops. I'd just like to show my granddaughter around a bit, and then we'll be off. We've been revisiting a lot of places from our family's past."

The man chortled. "No worries. We don't allow dogs as a rule, but there's no one here right now except Annie and me and our maintenance crew. Junior high campers just cleared out this morning and high schoolers don't arrive till Sunday afternoon." He winked at his wife. "Our twenty-four-hour reprieve until the next boisterous bunch takes over the peace and quiet. But, feel free to look around! I'm sure there are plenty of changes since you were here." With a wave, the camp director and his wife disappeared back into the office.

A lot of changes was right. Maggie hardly recognized the place. Backing up to get a good look at the large log building that housed the office, she saw a sign over the main double doors that said, "Wolf Creek Lodge." Stepping just inside the doors, her eyes swept over the nice size meeting room with comfy couches, overstuffed chairs, and a huge stone fireplace at the far end. A staircase on one side led to the second story—probably bedrooms for small groups having retreats. Nice.

A row of framed photographs lined one wall. She moved closer. Different groups of campers and staff from the past several years. Mostly white, though there were a few darker faces among them, even occasional staff. Change . . . slow.

Reagan was waiting outside with the dog. Next to the lodge, the ancient dining hall with peeling paint had been replaced with another "modern rustic" log building. Further on, a large A-frame stone-and-log chapel had replaced the old clapboard building, and the camp now boasted two large, two-story dormitories, as well as a string of cabins tucked among the trees.

Floods of memories washed over her as Maggie wandered around the campground, Reagan following her with Rocky on the leash. Going to camp as a kid had always been a summer highlight! She was sorry Reagan didn't like her summer camp. Maybe it was too long—a whole month, for goodness' sake! And as far as she knew, neither of her granddaughters' camps were Christian camps. Which didn't make them bad camps. But a lot of meaningful spiritual growth had happened at Wolf Creek for her—especially the early morning "quiet time" campers were encouraged to have with their Bibles and a notebook before breakfast. She'd felt very close to the Creator hunkered under a tree, listening to an orchestra of bird songs, a breeze rustling the pine boughs overhead, reading the Psalms or one of the Gospels, writing her prayers. Those morning "quiet times" had become a regular habit—more or less—throughout her life.

Except, ever since Coop's sudden death, her communication with God had been mostly "gut prayers."

She missed those "be still and know that I am God" times—though time alone had been hard to find bunking with Reagan and Rocky every night on this trip. Still . . .

Rocky pulled on the leash and wanted to sniff the ashes as they came to the campfire ring in the woods. Maggie chuckled. "Probably some old marshmallows or burned hot dogs in there." She rested on a log for a minute. *Evening campfires.* She'd made a number of promises to God around that campfire ring as a speaker or counselor encouraged the campers to take their "walk with God" seriously. Had she kept them? One thing for sure: she hadn't completely understood what following Jesus might look like in the years to come.

Still, those promises had been stepping stones.

The path through the woods suddenly opened up on the shore of a small lake, bordered by a strip of sandy beach with several upside-down canoes pulled up on it, a long dock, and a square floating dock just beyond. Maggie stopped, suddenly overcome. "I was baptized in that lake when I was sixteen," she murmured.

"Huh? At camp? Don't people, like, do that in church?"

"Sure, sometimes. If they've got a baptismal. But if there's a lake or river nearby, a lot of people choose to do it there. Like Jesus did."

"But . . ." Reagan seemed genuinely puzzled. "Why did you do it here? Away from home. Did your parents come?"

Maggie shook her head. "That was the point—for me, at least. I decided that summer *I* wanted to follow Jesus—not because my parents did or expected me to. But, me, Maggie Baker, making my own decision to follow Jesus. To be a Christian. So . . ." She smiled. "I got dunked. In the name of the Father, Son, and Holy Spirit. Along with some other teenagers. It was—" Her eyes threatened to water. "—wonderful."

"Oh." Reagan drew some squiggles in the sand with a stick. A loon called out somewhere from the shoreline. A fish jumped and sent ripples out in perfect rings.

After several long moments, the girl broke the stillness. "Hey, Grams! I've got my swimming suit in my backpack. Can we go swimming?"

"Hmm, don't think so." Maggie pointed at a sign: *No Swimming Unless Lifeguard on Duty.* Good thing she had an excuse. She'd seen Reagan's itty-bitty two-piece at one of their motel pools. Camp Director Davis would probably not approve.

"But speaking of lifeguards . . ." She grinned at her granddaughter. "The last summer I was a camp counselor here, a certain James Cooper showed up as the Waterfront Director. That was the summer *after* we met at the Jesus People Music Fest. A sly one, your grandfather." She beckoned with her hand. "Come here, I want to show you something."

Maggie made her way into the brush along the shoreline, which no longer showed any signs of a path. Rocky pulled at the leash, obviously wishing he could go exploring. "Grams!" Reagan complained. "Where are you going? There's nothing here!"

But Maggie just picked her way along the very edge of the shore, mostly rocks now. Going around a little bend, she suddenly stopped. "This is it. This is The Rock."

Reagan squinted at the large bolder, about the size of a Volkswagen Bug, that jutted halfway into the water. "Uh huh. So?"

Maggie couldn't stop grinning. "Coop used to leave me little notes that said, 'Meet me at the Rock 6:00.' Or something like that. It was our little rendezvous that summer—before the big bell rang waking the campers up, or sometimes after campers were asleep."

Now Reagan giggled. "Ooo, naughty you."

"That's not all." Maggie held out her left hand. "This is where he gave me this." She wiggled her ring finger.

Reagan's mouth dropped. "Oh my gosh, Grams! He proposed to you *here?*" She suddenly handed off Rocky's leash to Maggie. "You wait right here!" And the girl scrambled back along the shoreline and out of sight.

Maggie had a good idea where she was going.

Could she climb up on the Rock? She and Coop used to sit together on the old bolder, either listening to the birds waking up the day, or—if it wasn't a cloudy night—pointing out constellations among the pin-prick stars. She tried to find a handhold, but realized Coop was the one who usually pulled her up onto the rock. She obviously wasn't twenty-one anymore.

At least ten minutes passed before Reagan returned. But it was just as Maggie figured—her granddaughter had the brass urn of Coop's ashes tucked under an arm.

* * * *

Maggie was glad Reagan hadn't been very talkative during their tour of Wolf Creek Bible Camp. For some reason, walking around the camp had been more emotional for her than even walking around Calvary Academy—not just because this was where she'd made her own decision to be a Christian, but where she truly fell in love with James Cooper. He was fun, funny, so darn good-looking. But in this setting, she'd also seen how he'd related with kids, and he had this serious side, this passion to follow God wherever that led.

He also had that Harley, which he'd adorned with her initials— MB. Though sometimes, annoyed by how much time he spent keeping that Harley running, she'd wondered which he loved more—her or the Harley.

Which was dumb. He'd been willing to give up the Harley when baby Mike came along, and a motorcycle wasn't practical anymore. But, she mused now, feeling the engine of the restored BMW humming between her legs as they headed down I-5 again, guess you could take a bike away from the guy, but you couldn't take a passion for bikes out of that guy!

It'd been tempting to dump all the rest of Coop's ashes around The Rock, but she'd decided against it. They still had at least one more stop on the map that was significant in their journey together—the Jesus People commune in San Francisco. And if she and Reagan had figured it right, they could make it to Crescent City on the coast just over the California border still this evening, where they could spend the night. And even though it'd be a long day, they could make San Francisco tomorrow.

As Maggie turned off I-5 at Grants Pass, following the signs to Route 199 which would take them over to the Pacific Coast, Regan pumped her fist in the air and yelled, "Watch out, California! Here we come!"

Chapter 35

IT WASN'T EASY FINDING A ROOM in the lovely seaside town of Crescent City without a reservation, but by heading out of town on Highway 101, they found a motel right near the beach with a vacancy. Reagan was bug-eyed at the ocean just yards away out the sliding door of their room. "I've never seen the ocean!" she screeched. "Can we stay here a few days, Grams? Please? Please?"

That wasn't going to happen—but Maggie didn't blame her granddaughter for falling in love with the foamy waves rolling in along the long stretch of sandy beach. Supper was forgotten as they walked barefoot in the damp sand, letting the tide wash over their feet, laughing as Rocky chased the flocks of seagulls landing and taking off, soaring just out of reach. They found a sand dollar in the damp sand as the edge of the water sucked back into the incoming waves before rushing in again.

As the evening grew chilly, Maggie drove into town, picked up some Mexican takeout and brought it back in time to sit on the beach with Reagan and the dog, licking their fingers and watching in respectful silence as the sun finally disappeared into brilliant obscurity.

Maggie hugged her knees as twilight deepened and stars began to wink into existence. *Why* did she and Coop ever move away from the Pacific Coast to the flat plains of the Midwest? Why trade all this beauty for urban sprawl and flat cornfields?

But, she knew why. That deep desire to do something significant, to help change the world, to love God with everything and love their neighbor, too—the "neighbor" who was different, the one unlike themselves, the unfortunate-man-on-the-street in Jesus' Good Samaritan parable. They'd met this "neighbor" in Coop's

254

first pastoral assignment in Minneapolis—and after that, there was no turning back.

Had they changed the world? Probably not.

But *they* had changed.

* * * *

Maggie woke before sunrise and took Rocky for a walk along the deserted beach, now shrouded in morning fog, before waking Reagan. Well, *she* walked, but Rocky tore this way and that across the sand, chasing seagulls, stopping to sniff driftwood and shells, then taking off again. She really needed to give him more exercise on their travel days.

Finding a knotty log to sit on, Maggie soaked in the quiet—a quiet consisting of the constant roll of incoming tide, the occasional screech of a seagull. She smiled at the irony. Stillness . . . constant motion. Quiet . . . constant roar.

Today was Sunday. Sitting on the beach seemed a nice way to commune with God and creation for a change. She tried to empty her mind, to just *be*—but a jumble of thoughts about the last several days filled the empty spaces. She had such mixed feelings about growing up on the campus of Calvary Academy and even her summers at Wolf Creek Bible Camp. She had been thoroughly cradled there, safe in the bosom of conservative Christianity. But a lot had changed in her life journey with Coop since then. Life in the Jesus People commune, the inner-city church in Minneapolis, and urban life in the Windy City had immersed her in cultures not her own, challenged many of her assumptions, stretched her mind, changed her politics, fed her spirit, and turned her worship upside down—or maybe right-side up.

But one thing had never changed—her foundation. In that cradle she had decided to follow Jesus, no turning back, no turning back . . .

The motel provided a light breakfast of cereal, oatmeal, fruit, and coffee, after which it took some persuasion to tear Reagan away from the beach, but they were back on the road by eight o'clock. Scenic Highway 101 along the coast promised to take them to the Bay area by late afternoon, depending on how often they stopped to soak up glimpses of the Pacific before heading inland among the rolling evergreen-covered hills.

But as the hours passed and the bike ate up the miles, Maggie realized she'd been avoiding an uncomfortable reality: She had no idea what she would find even if she located the few blocks in the Tenderloin district that used to house the Jesus People commune where she and Coop had lived those first few years of their marriage. She'd tried to do a Google search for "Jesus People" in San Francisco, but nothing came up.

What was she getting Reagan and herself into?

But there was no turning back—a notion that took on sober reality later that day as 101 funneled them over the legendary Golden Gate Bridge with its reddish suspension cables connecting the two tall towers and deposited them directly into the streets of San Francisco. After several blocks, Maggie pulled into the parking lot of a diner so they could get a snack, use the bathroom, and try to figure out where to go.

Sipping her chocolate milkshake at one of the two sidewalk tables outside the diner with Rocky panting at her feet, Maggie stared at the map app on her phone. The commune had been in the Tenderloin district on the east side of the city, just south of Chinatown. Should be just west of Union Square and the upscale Financial District. She zoomed in so she could read the names of the cross streets: *Geary Street . . . O'Farrell . . . Ellis . . . Eddy . . .* She stopped. Ellis! That was the name of the street! If they just followed 101 going through the city, it would take them right there!

By the time Reagan returned with her milkshake, Maggie was ready to go again. But, darn! She'd forgotten about the one-way streets. Ellis had several one-way blocks—going the wrong way—mixed in with two-way. Never made any sense to Maggie. But between slurps of her milkshake, Reagan guided her this way and that till they ended up on Ellis on a block that looked vaguely familiar.

Maggie pulled the bike into a parking space next to a building undergoing some kind of renovation. But across the street—there it was. The three-story building that used to be the Jesus People commune back in the seventies, tucked between a fenced off vacant lot on one side and two SRO "hotels" on the other. A large sign now said: *Bay Area Women's Place*. But some things still hadn't changed. Here and there along the sidewalk, homeless folks stood in doorways or sat on large pieces of cardboard with their backs against the buildings, their belongings stuffed in shopping carts or just piled beside them.

Reagan was bug-eyed. "Grams. You gotta be kidding. This is *it*?"

Maggie's heart was thumping faster than usual under her T-shirt, but she managed to say calmly, "This is it. I want to go in." She slid off the BMW, feeling butt-sore from the long day's ride, and then realized they had a major problem. No way could they leave the bike with all their stuff strapped to it, but she wasn't about to take it all into this "Women's Place" until she knew what-was-what.

"You go," Reagan said hurriedly. "Rocky and I'll stay with the bike. Just don't, like, take a long time, okay?"

Leaving her helmet with the bike, Maggie crossed the street and pulled open the door under the *Women's Place* sign. A bell tinkled and a pleasant-faced young woman with a cap of curly brown hair looked up from a desk in the small reception area. A hand-lettered sign taped to the front of the desk said, "Welcome! God Loves You and So Do We!" She smiled. "Can I help you?"

"Uh, yes—but is there a manager or someone in charge I could speak to?"

"Oh. Well, sure. I'll see if they're done." She stepped over to a set of double doors, pulled one open and peeked inside the large room just beyond. "Oh, good. They've just finished the afternoon prayer circle." The young woman craned her neck. "Julie? Julie, could you come here a minute?"

Soon a vivacious woman swept into the reception area, her short ash-blonde hair touched with grey, glasses with red frames perched on her nose. "Ah! We have a visitor!" She pumped Maggie's hand. "Welcome to the Bay Area Women's Place! My name is Julie Barnes. How can we help you? Sit, sit!" She swept her hand toward two simple armchairs in a corner of the small foyer. "Would you like some water? Or coffee?"

"No, no thank you. I'm fine." Maggie hardly knew where to start. "This may sound strange, but my husband and I used to live here when it was a Jesus People commune back in the seventies. And I wanted to stop by, see what has happened to it since. But—" She pointed out the large storefront-type windows on either side of the front door, her voice rushing. "That's my bike and my granddaughter and my dog across the street there. I really want to talk with you, but I can't leave them out there, and I don't want to leave the bike on the street, and . . ." She gulped for a breath. "Do you have someplace I could safely park the bike?"

The young receptionist's eyes had grown large, and she shot a slightly frantic look toward the woman named Julie. But Julie threw back her head and laughed. "Well, now! This is definitely a story I want to hear! So, hmm. What can we do with that bike?" She frowned as if thinking, then pulled out her cell phone. "Excuse me just a minute."

The woman stepped into the other room, spoke on the phone a few minutes, then was back. "Ha! Thank God for good friends— and a pastor who owes me a favor." She laughed. "There's a small church about two blocks from here with some parking spaces behind their building. Pastor Tim said you're welcome to park there since it's Sunday evening, and it won't be needed for a few days." She glanced out the window and took in the bike, girl, dog, gear. "Hmm. Probably should bring your stuff in here though." She turned and called into the large room. "Birgitta! Susie! Tina! We need some helping hands here!"

A moment later, three females of assorted ages moseyed into the reception area, whom Julie quickly introduced. Birgitta was a large woman on the mannish side, grey eyes guarded beneath nondescript wisps of thinning hair. Susie had bottle-blonde hair pulled back in a messy ponytail with too much makeup that did little to cover her leathery skin, but her smile was genuine, showing off a missing tooth. Tina, on the other hand, couldn't have been much older than Reagan—maybe eighteen? nineteen?—sporting spikey black hair, a nose ring, and visible tattoos on her bare arms. Julie started to explain that "this lady needs help bringing her stuff in," when Tina glanced out the window and screeched, "But there's a dog! I'm scared of dogs!"

Maggie tried to jump in and say that Rocky was gentle as a lamb, but Julie just said, "Oh, okay, sweetie. Why don't you cover the phone for Cindy, and she can help us."

Maggie hurried across the street to assure Reagan that everything was okay as the four women trooped behind her. But the girl watched wide-eyed as Julie and the others unloaded their saddlebags, backpacks, and duffle bags and marched it all back across the street, disappearing into the Women's Place.

Retrieving the urn of ashes from the toe of the sidecar, Reagan said, "Uh, what's happening? What about Rocky? Is he supposed to come, too?"

Maggie shrugged uncertainly. "I'm not sure. I—"

But at that moment Julie was back with a smile for Reagan. "Honey, just take the dog inside and wait for us in my office—Cindy will show you where. We'll be back in a few minutes." She turned to Maggie. "Pastor Tim said he'd wait for us outside the church and show you where to park." She eyed the sidecar dubiously. "Think I can fit in that thing?"

* * * *

Reagan and Rocky were waiting for them in a small office behind the reception area that said, "Julie Barnes, Administrator," on the door, chatting away with Birgitta and Cindy, who were making a fuss over Rocky. Tina stood safely outside the open door by Cindy's desk, peeking in.

Julie clapped her hands. "All right, ladies, give us some room here. Cindy, would you bring some water for our guests—and some water for our four-footed friend here, too."

The room cleared out, broken only by Cindy a few moments later with two bottles of water and a bowl of water for Rocky. But finally, Julie closed the door. "Now then—" And she laughed. "Where were we? Oh, yes. You and your husband lived here back in the seventies—in this very building? I admit I'm curious. You arrived here today on a motorcycle with this lovely grandchild *and* a dog *and* some serious luggage. Not the usual way our guests arrive—or our volunteers either. Please, fill me in!"

Her laugh was infectious, and Maggie had to laugh, too. The whole situation must seem bizarre—actually, it *was* bizarre. But there was nothing to do but launch into her story, beginning with Coop's death and the motorcycle he'd been restoring and finding the maps and the trip he'd wanted to take . . .

* * * *

When she was finished, Julie just sat quietly for a few moments, cleaning her red-framed glasses. When she put them on again, she reached out and laid her hand on Maggie's. "Maggie, God brought you here. You know that, don't you?"

Maggie was startled. "Well, I—"

Julie held up a hand. "You don't have to answer. In fact, you might not have one. But I think God is going to show you why He brought you all the way cross-country to land here at the Bay Area Women's Place today. The Holy Spirit is giving me a sense that this trip you're on, including your visit here, is not an accident."

"I know," Maggie gulped. "I keep asking God what the purpose of this trip is, and I've been reflecting about a lot of stuff along the way. Still, not sure I understand it all yet."

"No worries, my friend. God will show you in His own time."

God will show you in His own time. Hadn't Jiang prayed that over her just before she left?

Julie leaned back, looking a little sheepish. "But, selfishly, I have to admit that you couldn't have come at a better time. We just lost two of our volunteers—sisters—who had to go home to attend an aunt's funeral. Any chance you two could stay for a couple of days? Tomorrow is our food pantry, and we really need the help. And Tuesday is Nail Day—which blesses the socks off our ladies from the street. And blesses us, too. What do you think?"

"Food pantry! Well, that brings back a few memories." Maggie chuckled, recalling the Jesus People efforts to feed the hungry back in the day at this very address. Going out at night with sandwiches and hot coffee, inviting street people to join them once a week on

Chili Night. But, stay a couple days? Maggie glanced at Reagan, a question in her eyes. She had only thought to stop in, look around like they did at Wolf Creek Bible Camp, and then go on. But this was the end of the line as far as Coop's maps went, unless those initials on the side meant something. So far, they didn't have a "next stop," except to decide when—and how—to go home.

She got no help from Reagan, who had slipped off her chair to sit cross-legged on the floor next to Rocky and was leaning against the wall with her eyes closed. Maggie turned back to Julie. "Well, let me talk with my granddaughter. It's a gracious invitation. But we do have a problem. We just rode into the city this afternoon and don't have a place to stay yet—unless you can recommend something not too expensive close by. And, uh, there's the dog."

"Oh! No worries there! Like I said, two of our volunteers had to go home suddenly, so we have an empty room upstairs—on third floor, though, I'm afraid. And bunk beds, if you don't mind. That's where our volunteers stay—second floor is mostly classrooms and my studio apartment. As for the dog, hmm, he seems very well behaved. I'll check with the other volunteers who live here, see if it's okay with them." She laughed again. "I might be breaking the rules, but we don't actually have a rule about dogs, so—" She winked. "—let's give it a go."

"But Tina—she seems afraid of dogs."

"Oh, Tina's not a volunteer. She's one of our guests, and all our guests will be leaving soon."

Maggie felt confused. "Leaving? Isn't this a women's shelter?"

Julie shook her head. "Not all of our guests are homeless. For those who are, there are a couple of overnight shelters nearby, as well as the SRO hotels. At most of the shelters, everybody has to be out by 7:00 a.m., so we offer a safe place where women can hang out during the day, sit, get coffee, play cards, nap, whatever. We serve lunch most days—except Monday, because of the food pantry. They can also get help applying for Medicaid or Social Security or an ID, things like that. Twice a month an attorney stops in to offer *pro bono* legal aid. And our volunteers also teach various classes—ESL, arts and crafts, yoga, a Bible study. Even a poetry writing workshop!" Julie grinned. "You'd be surprised what these women write."

Rocky whined, and Maggie realized she'd need to take him for a walk real soon. Another problem. Where would she walk the dog?

"And I'll be honest, Maggie—a number of our guests are sex workers or live with a drug or alcohol addiction, which needs another whole level of intervention. Sometimes a teenage runaway shows up here, or—like Tina—a foster kid who got kicked out of the system at eighteen. She's been couch surfing with friends but spends most of her time here."

Julie smiled, but Maggie caught a weariness in the smile this time. "We can't solve all their problems, but as far as we're concerned, all of these women need the same thing—respect for them as a human being, to know they are loved by Jesus, people who care and will listen, a place they know they're welcome. As for today—" Julie pushed up her red frames, which had slipped down her nose. "—we had just finished our Sunday afternoon Prayer Circle when you showed up, and it's just popcorn and munchies now."

Reagan's head jerked up. "Did you say popcorn? Any chance there's some left? I'd love some popcorn!"

Chapter 36

To Maggie's surprise, it was Birgitta who volunteered to help walk the dog. They left Reagan in the big room munching a fresh batch of popcorn with Cindy and Tina, as Birgitta unlocked a side door and accompanied Maggie and Rocky into the vacant lot next to the Women's Place building. Except it wasn't vacant. The fenced-in lot—a six-foot chain-link fence with a locked gate at the back side—had been turned into an urban garden.

"This is amazing," Maggie breathed, gaping at the rows of large cedar boxes growing a jungle of sweet potato vines, bush beans, squash, and lettuce, as well as big pots with tomato plants, cucumbers, sweet peppers, and who knew what all.

"Yep. We'll be harvesting some of this tomorrow morning for the food pantry," Birgitta said, eyeing Rocky who was marking several boxes with a lifted leg. "Uh, say, d'ya mind if we take the dog out back in the alley to do his business? Letting him pee in the garden is okay if he's gotta go right away or if I'm not around. Probably not a good idea to walk him by yourself in the neighborhood, though, 'specially at night. But everybody knows me around here. We'll be fine."

"Oh, sure, sure." Maggie clipped on Rocky's leash and followed Birgitta out through the back gate. Had to admit she felt more secure with the big woman for company. *But what if Rocky has to go and she isn't around?* Didn't Julie say the guests were going to leave soon?

They moseyed down the alley, letting Rocky set the pace, who had to stop and sniff at every garbage can, old shoe, and building corner. "Nice dog," Birgitta murmured. "I like dogs. Never had one of my own, but I got to be a Paws Prison Partner when I was inside. Best thing ever happened to me. Once I get my own place, I'm gonna get a Rottweiler!" She guffawed. "Nah, just kidding.

Maybe a Golden. They're sweet. Smart, too. We trained a couple of 'em to help people with disabilities."

"Paws Prison Partner? Uh, you were . . .?"

Birgitta shrugged. "Yeah. Ex con. Did my time, and this here place was a godsend when I first got out. So, I decided to give back, become a volunteer."

"Oh! You're a volunteer!" Maggie felt stupid. She'd assumed the woman was a guest. For that matter, there'd been quite a few people hanging around the big room, and she had no idea who were volunteers and who were guests.

Once Rocky did his business and Maggie had bagged and tossed it, they headed back to the Women's Place, through the chain-link garden gate and into the side door. In the big room, Reagan was laughing and talking with Tina, still munching popcorn, leg draped over the end of an overstuffed sofa that had seen better days. Rocky immediately scrambled over to them, tail wagging, nose pushing between them to get some petting. But Tina screeched and pulled her legs up into a fetal position, pressing as close as she could to the back of the couch.

"Oh, so sorry," Maggie said, hurrying over to pull Rocky away.

But Reagan held up a hand. "No, Grams, it's okay." She sat up and said sternly, "Rocky, sit!" The dog sat, cocking his head in that comical way of his, ears flopping in two different directions, as if saying, *What? What?* "See?" Reagan said to Tina. "He was just excited. But he's very friendly. He likes you! Let him sniff your hand."

It took a long thirty seconds, but Tina gingerly stretched out her arm, fingers clenched safely into a fist, and let Rocky sniff. Then he licked her hand and she squealed. Reagan laughed.

Maggie hated to interrupt, but she signaled to Reagan that she needed to see her. Snapping the leash back onto Rocky's collar, she led the way to an empty corner of the room. "What do you think, Reagan? Julie invited us to stay and help out for a couple of days. She lost a couple of volunteers and—"

"Yeah, I know."

"Oh. Well, what do you think?" Maggie herself was feeling conflicted. Once the concept of *Home* was on the radar, the tug was getting pretty strong. "Or, we could also just get a hotel tonight and work on getting ourselves back home."

"Huh. That's gonna take a couple days anyway," Reagan said.

"Gotta decide what to do with the bike. And what about Rocky?"

True. What about Rocky? If they flew, she'd need to buy a dog crate and fly him home, too.

"Anyway, yeah, I wanna stay. Helping with the food pantry and Nail Day sounds fun." Reagan broke into a grin. "Besides, I like Tina! She's comin' to help with the food pantry and stuff—it'll be a blast! Cindy's not much older'n me, either. She's gonna be a junior at some Christian college here in California—Westmont or something. This is the second summer she's volunteered at the Women's Place."

Maggie smiled. "Okay, I get it. You'd like to stay." Well, she *had* given her granddaughter a choice. "But we'll need to work on plans for getting home while we're here, too, got it? And—"

But before she could ask her granddaughter to help take their luggage up to third floor, Reagan gave her a quick thumbs up and scooted back across the room, flopping down beside Tina on the old sofa. Seconds later their heads were together—Tina's spiky black hair, Reagan's short chestnut cut with the colorful streaked bangs, and their twin nose rings—whispering about something.

Oh well. It'd been a while since Reagan had someone her own age to hang around with. She could manage the luggage if she took it slow.

But she didn't have to. When Maggie peeked into Julie Barnes' office, it was empty. No Julie. No luggage.

"Oh!" Cindy said from the reception desk. "Julie and Birgitta just took all your stuff up to third floor. Except this." Cindy reached under her desk and produced the urn with Coop's ashes. "They thought you'd want to take care of this yourself." She handed it carefully to Maggie. "Oh, yeah, Julie said to tell you supper's at six-thirty."

* * * *

Maggie woke the next morning feeling stiff and sore. The bottom bunk wasn't exactly the comfiest bed after six hours on the bike yesterday. Both she and Reagan had gone to bed before ten after a simple supper of tasty bean soup, hot cornbread, raw veggies, and brownies-from-a-mix, served to the volunteers from the kitchen counter at the far end of the main room. Before they ate, Julie had introduced them to the other volunteers—Sandy, Hannah, Olga, Kenyata, and Iris, as well as Birgitta and Cindy. About ten in all, if she included Julie and the two she and Reagan were replacing. Mostly twenty-somethings or early thirties, except for Birgitta and Julie, who might be in their forties.

Everybody had had a job after supper—washing dishes, stacking chairs, taking out garbage, sweeping the main room. Maggie and Reagan had plugged in where they could, then before people scattered Julie had called a quick meeting to assign jobs for the next morning, getting ready for the afternoon food pantry.

Maggie squinted at her watch. Almost seven! Why'd she sleep so late? Breakfast was supposed to be at seven-thirty, and she'd wanted to get a shower, even some quiet time if she could. But Rocky was already standing nose-to-door, needing to go out. She guessed it'd be okay to just take him out into the garden for now. Maybe she and Birgitta could walk him later.

When she and the dog got downstairs, Birgitta, Cindy, and a few of the other volunteers were already out in the urban garden, harvesting vegetables. "Here!" Birgitta called to her, tossing her a closed jackknife. "Cut some of the leaf lettuce in those boxes next to the fence and put it in that big basket over there."

Oh well. So much for a shower. Rocky wandered around the garden, sniffing the boxes, getting pats on the head and scratches on his rump while Maggie cut the sweet green leaves of leaf lettuce in the grow-boxes toward the front of the garden. On the other side of the chain-link fence, Maggie caught glimpses of street people, still curled up on large pieces of flattened cardboard, their belongings stuffed in a wire cart, or sitting in a doorway, smoking a cigarette. She felt caught in a time-warp, harvesting fresh vegetables here in this reformed vacant lot, while people—probably hungry people—slept on the sidewalk on the other side of the fence.

Birgitta must've noticed her discomfort, because she wandered over to the lettuce boxes and said quietly, "I know. I never get used to it either. But in a few hours, anybody can come into the food pantry when it opens and get some of these vegetables."

Maggie nodded and finished the job in silence.

A bell rang somewhere inside, and the "pickers" all trooped in with their harvest. Maggie was glad to see Reagan had made it downstairs on her own. "Super!" Julie beamed, as the food was spread out on the tables near the kitchen. "We'll get it washed and bagged right after breakfast. Pastor Tim said he'd get here with donations from Trader Joe's and Whole Foods about ten. We'll need all hands on deck to unload his van and set up, including the staples the county food bank brought on Saturday."

Breakfast was get-your-own—cold cereal, hard-boiled eggs, toast—and Julie never did seem to sit down, but bustled here and there with her clipboard, assigning jobs and checking off duties. Maggie was assigned to wash and bag the freshly picked vegetables with Kenyata, a lovely black girl with braided hair and an accent, while Reagan ended up with Cindy and two other volunteers bringing cans and boxes of non-perishables from a storeroom. When the church van arrived, everyone formed a line to unload the donations of food just past their sell-by date—bread and baked goods, eggs, dairy, an assortment of slightly damaged fruits and wilted vegetables, even some packages of partially thawed meat.

Maggie noticed that sometime during the morning Tina showed up to help and managed to get teamed up with Reagan loading paper shopping bags with cereal, rice, and other staples. *Interesting.* Especially after what Reagan said about not having a best buddy like she and Wendy. Yet those two were bonding in less than 24 hours. Made Maggie feel a little nervous. Who knew what kind of influence Tina—a kid who'd been bounced around in the foster-care system most of her young life and was now more or less out on her own—would be on Reagan.

She really did need to get her granddaughter home soon.

But the day was so busy, Maggie did not have much time to think about anything, much less plans for getting home. Lunch was a quick affair of sandwiches, chips, and carrot sticks, and as the hands of the wall clock inched toward one, Julie gathered all the volunteers into a circle and offered a prayer: "Lord, we commit today's food pantry into Your care. Give us kind words and loving actions so that each person who enters today will leave, not only with food for their stomachs, but with nourishment for their hearts. Thank You that we can be Your hands and feet today, serving those society often ignores." Her prayer was followed with hands stretched toward the center, like a football huddle, and a loud, "Amen!"—which got a giggle from Tina and Reagan.

People had been lining up outside since noon, and when the front door opened, the initial crush was a bit nerve-racking with not a few loud arguments about, "I was here first!" and "Quit pushing!" But Birgitta, bless her, functioned quite effectively as a sergeant-at-arms, lining people up, quelling disturbances, barking orders, and in general keeping order as a steady stream of folks from the Tenderloin passed by the tables of food. Julie seemed to be everywhere at once, welcoming people, giving hugs, calling people by name, looking as delighted to see the old man shuffling into the big room in his ill-fitting clothes as the young mom with a baby strapped to her back African-style and two other little ones clinging to her skirt. And, one after another, tiny Chinese women pulling "grandma carts" behind them, chattering loudly in Cantonese.

Maggie and most of the other volunteers had been assigned to walk each visitor along the tables, taking only the allotted amounts posted—two bread items, one dairy, one pre-packed bag of staples, one bag of garden vegetables, etc. A few people grumbled about not being able to take two items from *this* table if they didn't want anything from *that* table, but most people murmured, "Thank you so much," or "God bless you folks," as she showed them out the door—and then it was back to take the next person through the line.

The doors closed at 3:00 p.m. and then it was an hour of hard work putting everything away, wiping down tables, and trying to decide which of the leftover perishable food should be saved to help make lunch tomorrow and what had to be tossed.

"Ice cream!" Julie called out gaily as everyone collapsed on the various chairs and couches around the room. "Pastor Tim left a couple half-gallons in the freezer for all you hard-working folks. Who wants to dish up?"

No one moved at first—then Tina and Reagan leaped up. "First dibs!" Tina giggled as they disappeared into the kitchen.

Maggie slipped off her shoes and rubbed her aching feet. She should've known a sixty-five-year-old couldn't really replace one of the younger volunteers. But she gratefully accepted a dish of chocolate ice-cream as the girls passed them out and smiled as Julie pulled up a chair close to her. "Have to hand it to you, Julie. Your food pantry is way more organized than our attempts to feed hungry people when this was a Jesus People commune—at least when my husband and I were here."

"Speaking of which," Julie said, licking chocolate ice cream off her spoon before loading it up again, "I'm wondering if you'd be willing to share with the volunteers about the time you lived here. Tell us about the Jesus People and the commune. They should know the history of this place."

The history of this place. What could she say looking back after forty-plus years? They'd been so young, so idealistic back then . . .

Chapter 37

Maggie barely tasted supper that night—a do-it-yourself spread on the counter cheerily dubbed a "taco salad bar." She'd hid out in their third-floor bunkroom before supper trying to decide what she could share about the five years she and Coop had lived in this very building as part of the Jesus People commune.

Remembering was hard. The early seventies were a painful time in the country. The tumult of the sixties spilled over into the seventies as women, blacks, gays, and other marginalized people continued their fight for equality. The Vietnam War was in full swing, and protests against the war were loud and angry. College students like her had been left reeling by the Kent State shooting of four students by the National Guard.

James Cooper's way of "protesting" had been to join the loosely connected "Jesus movement"—sometimes called "Jesus Freaks" by their detractors—who turned their backs on capitalistic, middle-class Christianity, calling other young people to live by the radical message of Jesus: sell all your possessions, give to the poor, follow Jesus. Some wanted to "get back to the land," but some Jesus-People types formed their communities in the city, bringing their blend of countercultural lifestyle and commitment to Jesus "to the streets."

Including San Francisco.

In the midst of all this, she'd met Coop at the Jesus People Music Fest in Oregon. They fell in love, got married as soon as she graduated from college. They'd moved to San Francisco right after the wedding, right here to the fledgling commune in the Tenderloin district. With the war still raging, she'd been afraid for Coop, but his draft number in the lottery didn't come up until 1974—two years after they got married—but by that time he was in seminary, so he got a deferment.

When Julie quieted the chatter around the supper tables and asked her to share, Maggie tried to put all these thoughts into words for the volunteers. But the harder part to explain was: what had it all meant to her?

She had no idea what background or experiences each of the volunteers brought to their stint at the Women's Place. But it did say something about them. All she could do was share her own journey and hope it intersected with them in some way. "In many ways," she confessed, "my life with Coop meant leaving the safety net of how I was raised and putting my faith to the test in a whole new context. Coop and I initially thought this Jesus commune was going to be our whole life. Life in Christian community with others rather than a typical individualistic life as American consumers."

Maggie glanced at her granddaughter to see how she was taking this. Tina had stayed for supper, and the two girls were sitting together. Reagan seemed to be inspecting her fingernails, but Tina's eyes were locked on Maggie.

"Well," she went on, focusing on Julie in order to get her bearings back, "as you can probably guess, living together with a group of people had its, um, challenges—" She heard snickers. "—but working through personality conflicts and differences of opinions 'the Jesus way' was something I'd actually never been taught before."

"Whaddya mean, 'the Jesus way'?" Tina piped up.

"I'm guessing you mean using what Jesus said in Matthew 18 as your guide," Julie said. "That's what we try to do here."

Maggie breathed. Julie understood. "Exactly. I'd been really good at stuffing negative feelings as a kid, because I was expected to be 'a good Christian girl' who didn't *have* negative feelings or get angry. But in the community, we were encouraged to go to the other person and work out the conflict, confessing any sin involved, forgiving one another." She looked around the table. Even Reagan seemed to be listening. "It was life-changing for me."

She didn't carry on too long. Mentioned that some people came to visit the commune—even reporters—because they thought it was "cool" that this motley crew of young people were pooling their money and living in a "commune." Which had troubled her. The main thing should be Jesus. That's what—Who—people should be curious about. Jesus was the reason they were doing this. Everything else was secondary—or should be. Had communal living become "a thing" that outshone Jesus?

Coop was feeling the same way, she said. He wanted to take the message of Jesus to the hurting people on the street, but felt he needed Bible training. The leaders of the commune agreed he should go to seminary, which he did for three years. And then he got the invitation to be an associate pastor at New Hope Friendship Christian Church in Minneapolis, which meant leaving the commune—a big transition since they now had two little ones.

"We visited that church on this trip," Reagan said suddenly. "Some of the people my grandma knew back then were still there. In fact, the pastor told her some stuff she didn't even know, about how Gramps—my grandfather—pulled him out of a riot and saved his life. And now he's the preacher."

"Whoa!" Tina sputtered, wide-eyed.

"Okay, that's a story for another time." Maggie laughed self-consciously and stood up. "I think I'm on dishes, right?"

Gathering up her own dishes and several others, she headed for the kitchen. Birgitta and Olga helped clear the table and joined her. But when she peeked back out into the main room several minutes later, she saw Tina and Cindy and a few of the other volunteers clustered around Julie who had her Bible open. Reagan, too, though she stood a little offside. From the few words Maggie caught, it sounded like Julie was reading the passage in Matthew 18.

* * * *

Dishes done, Maggie slipped away to their room on the third floor after asking Birgitta if she'd mind taking the dog out. *Whew.* She couldn't climb these every day. Flopping on the bottom bunk, she realized she was really tired. And they'd agreed to stay another day—though Nail Day didn't sound as exhausting.

"What do you think, Coop?" she murmured. "Do you think my sharing at supper went okay?" She hadn't planned on mentioning the business about following Matthew 18 to reconcile relationships—it just came out. And it had certainly been something she and Coop had taken from their time here at the commune and tried to practice throughout their life together. But as she lay on the bunk, letting her weariness sink into the mattress, another heaviness came and seemed to sit on her chest.

So, what had happened to all that business about *reconciling* when Chris came out to them at Coop's retirement? When he told them to stop trying to line him up with a girlfriend, because he was *gay*. They'd both felt like they'd been blindsided by a Mack truck. But why hadn't Coop been willing to talk? He'd just walked out of the room, said he had "nothing to say" to his son. And afterwards—why hadn't he made an effort to reconnect? Had he been waiting for Chris to make the first move? To change?

"Oh, Coop," she moaned, tears welling up. "That wasn't like you! He's our *son*! Why? *Why?*"

Huge gulping sobs followed, and Maggie cried for a long time into the pillow . . . but struggled to sit up when the door suddenly opened, and a dog's slobbery kisses on her face threatened to lick up all the salty tears. "Oof! Rocky! Okay, buddy, down!" She sat up, reached for a tissue, and blew her nose.

"Grams! Are you okay? What's the matter?" Reagan plopped down on the bunk beside her and rubbed her back.

"I—I'm okay, hon. Just thinking about Chris. Missing him." More nose blowing.

"Uncle Chris!" Reagan bounced off the bed. "That's why I came to find you! 'Cause—get this, Grams—Cindy and I were talking downstairs after Tina left, and she said she was going back to Santa Barbara in a few weeks, 'cause that's where she goes to college. An' it hit me: Santa Barbara! *SB!* Maybe that's what SB stands for on Gramps' map. *SF to SB*—San Francisco to Santa Barbara."

Maggie frowned. "I suppose it could," she said slowly. "But I don't know why Coop would want to go to Santa Barbara. We don't know anyone there."

Reagan crawled back onto the bunk beside Maggie. "Could be Uncle Chris! Maybe Gramps was thinking about going to see Uncle Chris."

Maggie stared at Reagan a moment, then shook her head. "No, don't think so. Chris never said anything about living in Santa Barbara. I think he said LA." Or did he say southern California and she just assumed it was LA?

Reagan shrugged. "Do you have his address?"

"No. He never gave it to us. Just his phone number." Though Chris never answered his phone. She always had to leave him a message and then he called back.

"Lemme see. Where's your contact list?"

Maggie called up the list, then handed over her cell phone. "Don't call him, Reagan," she warned. "That's up to me."

"I won't! I just wanna see." Reagan scrolled through the list. "Hmm. His cell still has a 312 area code—that's Chicago. But what's this other number? 805 area code."

"That's his work number. He gave it to me after he qualified as a vet tech. Said it's *just* for emergency."

"Fine." Reagan handed the phone back. But then she got out her own cell phone and played around on it. A moment later she grinned, turned her phone around, and showed it to Maggie. The screen said: "Santa Barbara area codes: 805 and 820."

* * * *

Maggie could hardly sleep that night. Chris worked in Santa Barbara? A work number wouldn't be a cell phone, so it had to be a landline. That was more information than she'd had about his whereabouts the past few years.

SF to SB . . .

Had Coop actually been thinking about going to see Chris? If so, how did he know their son worked in Santa Barbara? She supposed he could've figured it out by the area code, just like Reagan had. Though she was pretty sure Chris had given the work number to her, not his dad. Had she shared it with Coop? She couldn't remember.

She must've fallen asleep eventually because Maggie woke with a start when the bell rang for breakfast the next morning. Good grief, she'd overslept. The upper bunk was empty, and both

Reagan and Rocky were gone. Bless her, the girl had taken the dog out.

But no way could she make it to breakfast on time, and she desperately needed a shower after missing one yesterday. Hopefully the Scripture passage on forgiveness applied to older ladies unused to the schedule at the Bay Area Women's Place.

By the time she got downstairs, most of the volunteers had finished breakfast, though boxes of cereal, bowls, and milk were still on the pass-through counter. Rocky bounded over to her, tail whipping, and she gave him a good scratch on the noggin. *Somebody's glad to see me.* But just then Reagan came out of the kitchen, all grins, and said, "Julie told me to let you sleep in—but here you are anyway."

Maggie nodded ruefully at the wall clock that said ten after eight. "This is me sleeping in. But thanks, guess I needed those extra winks. What's going on?"

"It's Nail Day!" Reagan's eyes danced. "We're supposed to set up soon, because the ladies start coming around ten. Except, Kenyata and I got assigned to making sandwiches for lunch— for everybody. Oh, hey." Her granddaughter leaned close and whispered confidentially, "Since I'm in the kitchen, how 'bout I scramble you a couple eggs? Julie said it was okay."

Scrambled eggs. That sounded wonderful.

Not having an assignment—Maggie hadn't seen Julie yet— she pitched in after her scrambles and toast and helped Kenyata and Reagan make several dozen sandwiches for the lunch crowd, trying not to think about Chris. Not yet, anyway. Baloney-and-cheese sandwiches and PB-and-J on bread left over from the food pantry were stacked on platters, covered with plastic wrap, and set inside the large refrigerator alongside quarts of donated deli potato salad. They also set out commercial-size cans of tomato soup to be heated up a half-hour before lunch.

They'd just turned the big coffee pot on and set out day-old doughnuts when Julie poked her head into the kitchen. "Prayer time! Doors open in half an hour."

Maggie hid a small smile as she, Reagan, and Kenyata joined the group of volunteers in the large room, forming a circle, holding hands. Reagan had been worried about a Christian summer camp feeling like "church every day," but she didn't seem to mind Julie's prayer meetings before the Women's Place events. At least Maggie hadn't heard any complaints. Maybe because the prayers felt like friends talking to their Friend about their friends.

". . . and Jesus, help us to remember many of these women are lonely," Julie was praying. "Nail Day isn't just about pretty nails, but about making these sisters of ours feel beautiful and loved, inside and out. Help us to be Your hands touching their hands, help us to listen more than talk, and let each woman leave here knowing how much You love them. After all—"

Maggie expected an "Amen," but was startled as the other volunteers gleefully joined in unison: "—we've got love! We've got Jesus! We've got coffee!" The group broke up with hugs and laughter.

We've got love! We've got Jesus! We've got coffee!

Maggie chuckled to herself as she headed for a chair at one of the nail tables. Guess that summed it up.

Chapter 38

As the volunteers chose their tables, Julie gave some last-minute instructions about washing their hands and replacing the bowls of warm soapy water between clients. Three tables with two or three "stations" at each had been stocked with nail polish remover, an assortment of nail polish colors, nail files, emery boards, cuticle sticks, hand cream, rolls of paper towels, boxes of tissues, and a large container of hand sanitizer. No nail clippers, Maggie had been told, because of the possibility of nicks and the risk of spreading HIM, Hepatitis C, and potential for infection.

Another table off to the side had art supplies—markers, adult coloring pages printed off the Internet, blank paper, card stock, scissors, tape, and glue. A boom box on the kitchen pass-through counter next to the coffee played a CD of relaxing "nature music" with bird calls and rippling water.

At least twenty women crowded through the front door when ten o'clock rolled around. Maggie recognized a few faces from the day before, but many were new. And Tina, of course. The girl seemed to show up anytime the doors were open. Julie and Birgitta managed to seat the first set of women—two or three to a table—while the rest were encouraged to help themselves to coffee and doughnuts, read magazines, or work on some art projects.

A sense of peace filled the room in spite of the excited chatter.

Maggie's first "customer" was a woman, maybe in her late forties—hard to tell exactly—with reddish hair, rough hands, and a hoarse voice. "Wouldn't know it, wouldja, from this voice now," the woman snorted as Maggie guided her hands into the warm soapy water. "But I useta sing with a band. I was good, too. But, I smoked too much. Now I'm hoarse alla time. Can't get any gigs. By the way, name's Rosie."

"Hi Rosie. I'm Maggie." Maggie lifted one hand at a time out of the warm soapy water and scrubbed the nails. She felt like a total amateur since she didn't wear nail polish herself. "Can't a doctor help that hoarse voice?"

Rosie snorted again. "Maybe. But I gotta stop smokin' first." She shook her head. "Ain't gonna happen. Only thing 'at's keepin' me off drugs."

Maggie just nodded. What could she say to that?

"Hey," Rosie said, as Maggie used the emery board to trim her nails, "word's out on the street that some grey-haired broad an' a kid rode in here on a motorcycle. 'At you?"

Maggie froze. Word was out *on the street* about her motorcycle? Worry crowded into her thoughts. She'd just assumed her bike and sidecar were safe behind Pastor Tim's church. But if people were talking, she'd better get over there this afternoon and check on it. For the moment, she just gave a non-committal, "Mm-hmm," and resumed filing.

Rosie chose baby blue for her nail color, which actually went nicely with her coppery skin, which looked more like she'd spent lots of time in the sun than any particular ethnicity. As Rosie stood up, holding her ten digits in the air to keep them from smudging before they dried, Maggie looked up at her and smiled. "I enjoyed meeting you, Rosie. Wish I could've heard you sing—I bet you were good."

"Thanks," Rosie rasped. "I was."

At another table, Tina was getting her nails done by—who else—Reagan. Slipping into the kitchen to wash her hands and replenish her "finger bowl" of warm soapy water, Maggie was tempted to grab a cup of coffee and a doughnut. But another woman had already taken Rosie's seat on the other side of the table and was waiting for her.

Several more women showed up throughout the morning, so that by the time Julie called time for lunch, Maggie had done nails for four different women—most of their hands cigarette stained or badly in need of scrubbing and trimming. Monica, an older Latina woman, practically purred as Maggie scrubbed her nails and massaged her hands with hand cream before applying the

Very Red nail polish. "Nail Day my *favorito* time of the week," she murmured, eyes closed. "*Gracias, Senora* Maggie."

Maggie was trying to clear the table for lunch when Reagan scurried over to her and whispered, "Grams! My lady—over there, see?" She tipped her chin to an African American woman in big bangle earrings and short natural hair who was blowing on her freshly painted nails. "She asked me if there were any black people in the Bible—kinda implying there aren't." Reagan's eyes were pleading. "Are there? Can you, like, talk to her? I don't know what to say!"

"Uh, well, sure." Interesting. Maggie's mind sorted through the possibilities: Moses's wife . . . Simon the Cyrene who carried Jesus' cross . . . the Ethiopian eunuch who was baptized by Philip . . .

Julie must've overheard because she joined Maggie and Reagan, peering over the top of her red glasses. "Great question. I think that's something everyone might like to know. We can have a story time during lunch. Maggie, would you do the honors? You have a gift for story-telling."

Maggie gaped at her. A gift for story-telling? What was Julie talking about? But, okay. Why not? Hadn't Peter the Apostle urged believers to "always be prepared to give an answer to everyone" who asked a reason for the hope they lived by?

While everyone was munching on sandwiches and potato salad, Julie quieted the chit-chat and said an interesting question came up about whether there were black people in the Bible. "Maggie, why don't you tell the story about the Ethiopian official?"

Maggie was surprised at all the eyes turned her way. She'd expected disinterest or boredom. Just think of this as Sunday school, she told herself—all the Bible stories she'd told over the years, from the kindergarten kids at New Hope Friendship to the seniors at Grace and Mercy. Even though she hadn't gone to seminary, she'd had Bible classes each and every year at Calvary Academy, plus family Bible reading since she was just a rug rat. She knew this story.

She started with a little background. Jesus the Messiah had been crucified, buried, resurrected, and had returned to heaven, leaving his disciples astonished and wondering, *What now?* Then God sent the Holy Spirit, and the disciples were on fire to tell everybody about the saving power of Jesus to forgive their sins and begin a new life living in the Kingdom of God now. Unfortunately, she said, the religious leaders of that day called this heresy and began to persecute these Christ followers.

"Mm-hmm," someone muttered. "Same today. My mama was a teacher. They wouldn't let her talk about Jesus in school. Got fired when she wouldn't stop."

Maggie eyed Julie, who nodded at her to go on.

"One of the disciples—Philip—was nudged by the Holy Spirit to walk out into the desert on a certain road that led south from Jerusalem. On the way he noticed a fancy chariot traveling slowly along the road with a man reading a scroll—a black man dressed in fine clothes."

"Did the chariot have a driver?" Kenyata asked.

"Maybe. Or maybe the man was letting the horse plod along on its own. The Bible doesn't say. Anyway, Philip caught up to the chariot—that's why I think it was going slow—introduced himself and asked what the man was reading. Turns out he was reading from the Book of Isaiah, the same one we have in our Bibles today. The man was an important official in the court of the queen of Ethiopia—"

"Prodigious!" Tina piped up. "The *queen*?"

"That's right. And he'd come all the way to Jerusalem to worship God at the temple and was now heading home. Philip asked him if he understood what he was reading. Turns out it was a prophetic passage that talked about the coming Messiah 'being led like a sheep to slaughter' without defending himself. 'Please tell me,' the man begged. 'Who is it talking about?' So, Philip climbed into the chariot and used the opportunity to tell his new friend the good news about Jesus."

The woman with the large earrings frowned. "You sure that man was black?"

Maggie nodded. "All the Bible scholars think so, because he came from Ethiopia in Africa. But here's the best part." She grinned at Tina. "They came to some water—maybe a little stream or a watering hole. We don't really know. But the man from Ethiopia said, 'Look! There's some water. What's to stop me from being baptized?'"

"Baptized? What's baptized?" Tina said.

For some reason Maggie felt a stir of excitement. How easy to share the Gospel when people were interested and asking questions. "It's something people do to show when they've made a decision to follow Jesus. It's like washing away your old life and starting a new life as a Christian." Okay, that was a pretty simple explanation, but it was enough for now.

"So, the man just up and did it right then?" Tina persisted.

Maggie nodded. "Right then."

"Okay." Tina stood up. "I wanna get baptized. Right now."

Maggie blinked. Around her, faces looked startled and eyes popped. She heard a few giggles. Reagan was staring at her new friend, her jaw dropping.

"Wait everybody." Julie spoke up, her voice authoritative. "Tina just said something important." She walked over to the girl and laid a hand on her shoulder. "Why do you want to get baptized, Tina?"

Tina shrugged. "Like that story. The guy wanted to follow Jesus, so he decided to get baptized right then. With the guy who told him about Jesus. Why wait? An' you guys here talkin' about Jesus all the time. He's the Son of God, right? An' last night Miz Maggie shared her story about how she and her man wanted to follow Jesus their whole life. She didn't say anything 'bout getting' baptized, but I bet she did, right, Miz Maggie?"

Maggie's heart was pounding. "Right." Her voice came out ragged. She cleared her throat and tried again. "Right. When I was sixteen."

"See? An' I'm eighteen already, state says I'm on my own, so I can decide to get baptized if I want to. An' I want to. I want to be like you guys here, an' like Miz Maggie. You know, be a Christian and follow Jesus." She crossed her arms defiantly, daring anyone to argue with her.

Olga, bless her, said the obvious. "But we don't have any water. I mean, no lake or river—not unless we go over to the bay."

Julie smiled. "Water's not a problem. People can also be baptized by pouring." She looked around the room. "Does anyone have any objection to Tina getting baptized today? Right now?"

Maggie's thoughts were tumbling. At Grace and Mercy, anyone who wanted to get baptized went through a baptism class, so they fully understood the choice they were making. A slew of Bible verses, instruction on who Jesus was, how to live as a Christian— all that stuff. But, hadn't she just told a story straight from the Bible where this important black official from Ethiopia heard about Jesus, believed, and wanted to declare his belief on the spot by getting baptized?

Why not Tina? Learning to know God and how to live as a Christian was a lifetime journey. She, of all people, should know that. Baptism was just the start.

"I'm good with it," she said. "Pretty sure God is too!"

Kenyata was sent for a pitcher of tepid water. Birgitta rustled up several large towels. When they returned, Julie asked Tina to kneel on the floor and motioned everyone to gather around her. Tina knelt, but then she looked around and said, "Wait! Reagan? Will you come hold my hand?" Reagan, who seemed to be in shock over this turn of events, nonetheless moved close to Tina and gripped her hand.

Julie took the pitcher and said, "Tina, on your confession of faith, that you believe in Jesus as your Lord and Savior and desire to follow him—" She started to pour the water over Tina's head, who gasped and gripped Reagan's hand all the harder. "—I now baptize you in the name of the Father, of the Son, and of the Holy Spirit." Julie poured all the water over Tina's head, thoroughly soaking the young woman and much of the floor. "Amen."

All the volunteers and most of the Nail Day ladies began to clap and shout. "Hallelujah!" "Way to go, girl!" "Love you, Tina!" Several hands reached out and helped Tina to her feet, while Birgitta swathed her in a big towel and used another to mop up the floor. Tina began to laugh and cry at the same time. "Wow. So, I'm a Christian now?"

Julie gave her a big wet hug and tapped her on her chest. "It's what's inside your heart that makes you a Christian, Tina. The baptism was just a shout-out to the rest of the world."

More laughter and hugs from the volunteers and Nail Day ladies. Finally, Maggie waded in and wrapped her arms around the young woman. "I'll never forget you, Tina," she whispered in the girl's ear. Right now, this two-thousand-mile ride to San Francisco, this moment, this baptism, was worth the whole trip.

As Tina was led away to find some dry clothes for her, Maggie scanned the room for Reagan. But Reagan had disappeared.

Chapter 39

Birgitta was gathering up the towels she'd used to mop up the floor. "Birgitta!" Maggie stage-whispered. "Do you know where Reagan went?"

Birgitta shrugged as she glanced around. "Don't see the dog either. Maybe she took him out to the garden."

"I'll check." Maggie made a bee-line for the side door, ready to feel relieved—but the fenced-in garden was vacant.

A check of the second- and third-floor rooms also came up empty.

Okay, now she was worried.

"She's got the dog. And it's the middle of the day. She'll probably be okay," Birgitta said. "But c'mon. I'll help you look."

Maggie hustled to keep up with Birgitta's long strides as they headed up the street. Why would Reagan take off without saying anything? Even if she thought Rocky needed a walk, she usually said something. Was she upset about Tina's baptism? It did take everyone by surprise, but why should it make her upset?

They walked around the block, then through the alley. Maggie wanted to ask people they met if they'd seen a teenage girl and a dog, but Birgitta shook her head. "Best not to let folks on the street think she's missing," she murmured, "not yet, anyway."

Maggie's heart hammered out a string of prayers, mostly, *"Please, God, help us find Reagan and Rocky!"* At Maggie's request, Birgitta walked her by Pastor Tim's small brick church where she'd parked the bike and sidecar on the off-chance Reagan had decided to check on it—though it wasn't likely the girl knew where it'd been parked. Still, wouldn't hurt to check on it anyway.

At first, all she saw were two dumpsters and an old van parked behind the church. Where was the bike?! Then, she noticed an odd-sized lump under a big brown tarp between the van and the dumpsters. Had to be her bike and the sidecar. Pastor Tim, bless him, had covered it with the tarp and strapped it down with bungee cords.

Birgitta snorted. "Ha. Doesn't even look like a bike with that sidecar all lumped out to the side under that tarp. That Tim—he's smart."

"Thank you, God," Maggie breathed. But she was anxious to move on. "Now we just need to find—wait." She slapped her head. "Reagan's always got her phone! Why didn't I just call her?" Grabbing her own phone, she mumbled, "Not only that, we have that 'Find Friends' app thing." A moment later she looked up at Birgitta, puzzled. "The app says her phone is back at the Women's Place."

Birgitta shrugged. "Either she forgot her phone, or she got back while we've been out looking."

"That girl!" Maggie growled, hitting the Call button.

The phone picked up on the first ring. "Yeah?" Not Reagan's usual perky voice, but it was Reagan all right.

"Reagan! Where—"

"I'm at the Women's Place." Her voice was low, almost mumbling. "I know. Shoulda told you I was gonna go for a walk. Sorry. But I took Rocky." Her tone got defensive. "We were fine. And I'm back now."

Maggie opened her mouth to give her granddaughter a piece of her mind—and then closed it. Taking a breath to calm down, she said, "Okay. Glad you're all right. We'll be back in ten minutes or so." Rolling her eyes at Birgitta, she put her phone away, suddenly realizing her knees hurt from navigating San Francisco's hilly streets. Might be longer than ten minutes. Besides, she needed time to pull herself together.

Most of the women who'd come for Nail Day had left by the time Birgitta and Maggie got back to the Women's Place, though a few were still hanging around, relaxing on the various couches, chatting, flipping through magazines, scrolling through their phones. She didn't see Reagan or Rocky. Might be up in the bunk room. Julie and Tina didn't seem to be around either. Maybe Julie had taken the girl to wherever she was staying to get her own dry clothes. The other volunteers were still cleaning up from Nail Day and lunch. "Oh, good grief," Maggie muttered, feeling a stab of guilt. She'd taken off and taken Birgitta with her, leaving all the cleanup to the other volunteers. Grabbing a broom, she started sweeping.

Birgitta gave her a look and took the broom away. "Don't be silly, Maggie. Go find your granddaughter. I'm guessing Tina's impromptu baptism kinda blew her away, and she needed some space. Go easy on her."

By the time Maggie climbed to the third floor, she'd decided Birgitta was right. She opened the door and peeked in. Reagan and Rocky were both sprawled on the lower bunk with Rocky taking up most of the room. "Hey. Just making sure you're okay. I got worried."

Reagan sat up and pushed the dog off the bed. "Yeah. Sorry 'bout that. I just, you know, needed some time by myself." She shook her head. "I mean, that baptism business was, like, kinda weird."

"You want to talk about it?"

Reagan shrugged. "Not really. Maybe later." She got off the bed. "You wanna lie down? You look pretty tired, Grams. Rocky and I can go downstairs."

Maggie nodded. She was tired. And she did need to lie down, get off her feet. "But maybe a little later we can talk about tomorrow—you know, going home and everything."

Reagan paused at the door. "Have you, um, thought about going to see Chris?"

"Let's talk later." She crawled onto the bunk as the girl closed the door.

Maggie shut her eyes, hoping she could catch a nap for half an hour or so. But her mind wouldn't sleep. *Chris.* Why was she hesitating to go see her youngest? If he was really in Santa Barbara, it couldn't be that far—a few hundred miles? Couldn't be more than a day, even on the bike. And it had been four years. *Four years!* Yes, yes, she would dearly love to see him, to get one of his wraparound hugs, to hear his laugh.

But, would he want to see her? He hadn't returned her call when she'd wanted to tell him about the trip. What if she called now, and he said no? She couldn't bear it.

She hesitated. Was she afraid of what she'd find? She heard a lot of talk on Christian radio and in some churches about "the gay lifestyle" as immoral and debased. But from the gay people she'd met at the Good Neighbor Clinic, most were ordinary people on the spectrum of other ordinary people that came to the clinic. Everything from stodgy professors to free-wheeling singles. Couples with children who had sniffles to loose-living moderns making serial hook-ups—just like their straight counterparts. Not just one "lifestyle," any more than the rest of society.

But, where did Chris fall on that spectrum? They simply hadn't talked much about his admission that he was gay, not after Coop had squashed the conversation. There was a lot she still didn't understand about what made someone gay. She'd tried to read a variety of books, but she still had a lot of questions. The only thing she knew for sure was . . . she loved her son. And she wanted to see him.

And if Reagan's guess was right about the initials on the side of the map, Coop had wanted to see him, too.

Maggie's eyes flew open. Swinging her legs over the side of the bunk bed, she got up and rummaged through the duffle bags stashed in a corner of the little room. She found the two maps and spread out the one for the West Coast part of their trip. There, along the edge near the map of California, the penciled initials.

SF to SB. SB to CHI.

San Francisco to Santa Barbara, where Chris probably lived. At least his work number had a Santa Barbara area code.

Santa Barbara to CHI—definitely Chicago. Nothing in between. Which meant Coop had had the same idea she had, to fly home.

But if he planned for them to fly home from Santa Barbara, what about the bike? The classic BMW he'd worked so hard on restoring? It was one thing for *her* to consider selling it on eBay. But not Coop. He loved that bike. He'd poured himself into it.

And suddenly she knew.

* * * *

Reagan was wide-eyed when Maggie told her. "Grams! You think Gramps was thinking of giving the bike to *Chris?* As, like, a peace offering?"

Maggie nodded. "I do. That last weekend Chris was home for his dad's retirement, he was *ga-ga* over the bike. The two of them spent a couple of hours out in the garage with Coop telling Chris all the things he was doing to restore it. He'd been so tickled at Chris's excitement over his pet project. The other kids—well, you know what your mother thought. Even Mike was so-so about it. More like, well, if that's what dad wants to do, fine. But not Chris. The two of them were bonding over this, until—well, you know the rest."

"Not really. No one ever told me exactly what happened."

"Oh." Maggie told her briefly about the match-making Coop had been up to at his retirement party in the back yard, and the bomb Chris had exploded to the two of them afterward. And Coop's reaction that had sent Chris away hurt, feeling rejected by his own father.

Reagan shook her head, frowning. "I don't get it. Just doesn't sound like Gramps. He was always so big-hearted, loved everybody! I mean, look at that story the preacher told, back when he was a kid in Minneapolis. Gramps didn't judge him, just gave him safety during that scary riot—and look what happened! He's a preacher now!" The girl slumped to the floor, chin in her hands. "Wish I could talk to Gramps right now. I just don't get it."

"I know. Wish I could, too."

They were both silent for a long moment, and then Reagan lifted her head. "So, are we going to go see Uncle Chris?"

Maggie sighed. "Except we still don't know where he lives."

"But we *do* know where he works." Reagan scrambled to her feet. "At least we can find out. Gimme your phone." She held out a hand.

"No! That number's only for emergency, remember?"

"I'm not going to call *him* at work. Trust me, Grams. I just wanna find out the address. Your phone?"

Reluctantly, Maggie punched in her entry code and handed over her cell phone. Reagan found her contact list, found Chris's info, and tapped the work number and the Speaker button.

"All Creatures Animal Clinic," said the voice on Speaker.

"Uh, yeah, we just moved to Santa Barbara, and our cat is gonna need her shots pretty soon, so we need to find a vet near us." Reagan winked at Maggie. "Can you tell us where you're located?"

"Sure." The voice on the speaker spelled out the address and Reagan gestured wildly at Maggie to write it down. "Uh, could you say that once more? Wanna be sure we got it . . . okay, thanks. Sounds good!" Reagan pressed the red "Off" button and looked at Maggie, her eyes dancing. "Okay. We know where he works. What are we gonna do?"

* * * *

Julie Barnes leaned against the doorjamb of her office door, looking on as Maggie and Reagan stacked their duffle bags and backpacks in the foyer the next morning. "Are you sure you two wouldn't like to stay for the rest of the week? Our two volunteers don't get back until next Sunday. And you've both been a wonderful help."

Maggie glanced out the front window, where Birgitta was leaning casually against the blue BMW that Maggie had brought over and parked in front of the Women's Place. No worries there. People on the street seemed to respect Birgitta. "Wish we could, Julie, but we've got one more stop to make, then we need to get home." She smiled a bit ruefully. "Besides, don't think I could do those stairs to the third floor one more day, much less four. My knees aren't what they used to be."

Reagan peered impatiently out the door, then turned anxious eyes on Julie. "Are you sure Tina is coming this morning? I don't want to leave without saying goodbye!"

"She'll be here—there! What did I tell you?" Julie pointed out the front window. A breathless Tina was darting across the street between cars. "If she doesn't kill herself first," the director murmured.

The dark-haired girl burst through the front door. "You're still here!" Tina grabbed Reagan in a bear hug. "Please don't go! I want you to stay! *I'm* gonna stay—did Miz Julie tell you?" But without waiting for a reply, she dragged Reagan into the next room where they were joined by Cindy. Peeking into the large room a moment later, Maggie saw the three young women huddled on one of the lumpy couches talking like a hen party.

Maggie gave Julie a questioning look. "What does she mean, stay?"

Julie motioned Maggie into Cindy's desk chair while she leaned against the door frame leading into the next room. "Tina badly wants to be a volunteer here. Wants to live with the other volunteers." She waggled her eyebrows. "*Might* have something to do with why she wanted to get baptized yesterday—but, we'll let the Holy Spirit figure that one out. I'm not going to question her motive. But as you know, we're not a shelter. Our volunteers pay their own way here—I mean, they raise support for their room and board or get short-term mission scholarships from their church, that kind of thing. I'm the only full-time staff here, and Birgitta is paid half-time by our board. But . . ."

Julie paused, glancing into the next room. Her eyes were tender behind those bold red glasses frames. "Tina's still young, she doesn't really have a place to live, she can't keep couch-surfing much longer. And she does love it here. She's here every day, always helping out." She turned back to Maggie. "I told her we might be able to get her a scholarship to be a volunteer. Pastor Tim once told me his little church might be able to squeeze out some money from their benevolence fund. She's eighteen—that's our bottom age limit for volunteers." Julie broke into a smile. "Who knows what the Holy Spirit wants to do in that young woman's life? She certainly could use a break—physically, emotionally, spiritually."

"Well, let me know if Pastor Tim's fund doesn't cover it," Maggie blurted. "I might be able to help out with her support." If she wasn't broke by the time she got home. She'd dipped into her retirement big time for this trip.

"Thanks, Maggie. I'll let you know. But . . ." Julie smiled warmly. "I was right, you know. God brought you here for a reason. I think you and your granddaughter have had a big impact on Tina."

Maggie nodded slowly. "You're right. I do think God brought us here for a reason. But Tina might only be one small part of it. You and Birgitta and everything you're doing here at the Women's Place have had a big impact on *me*—and Reagan too, I think." She laughed self-consciously. "Still figuring it out, though. Might have to write you a letter."

Julie laughed. "You do that!—oh, here they are."

The three young women bustled into the foyer. "They want to help us scatter Gramps' ashes, Grams!" Reagan said breathlessly. "Can they?"

Maggie shrugged helplessly. "Can't exactly say no, can I, when you ask me in front of everybody, young lady." But her smile gave her away. "Okay. Let's do this. But this is a solemn occasion, not a circus. Got it?"

All three of the young people nodded obediently.

Maggie picked up the urn with Coop's ashes and led the little group to the side door and out into the urban garden. Julie followed. Opening the lid, Maggie gave each girl a small handful of ashes, then offered some to Julie and took some herself. "Just choose one of the grow boxes where you want to sprinkle the ashes."

The girls fanned out, each choosing a box. Maggie glanced around. "Where do you want to rest, Coop?" she murmured.

There. The box with the tall trellis of green beans. Coop had always loved green beans. She opened her hand and let the ashes fall among the dirt. Coop would love to know they'd scattered some of his ashes in this vacant-lot garden, next to the place where their life together had begun.

But once they left the Women's Place, she'd be taking the remainder of Coop's ashes to a place they'd never been. But a place, she believed, Coop had wanted to go.

Chapter 40

B<small>Y LEAVING THE</small> W<small>OMAN'S</small> P<small>LACE BY</small> 8:00, Maggie figured they could get off Highway 101 and go right along the coast on Highway 1 all the way to Santa Barbara, even though it took a little longer with stops along the way. But it was great traveling weather—partly cloudy, mid-sixties, going up to mid-seventies by early afternoon, and supposed to cool off again by evening.

"That's the Pacific Coast for you," she teased Reagan. "Here it is mid-July, and we aren't baking in the sun or sweltering in our helmets." But it wasn't long before Reagan stashed her leather jacket exposing her bare arms and fish tattoo in a skimpy tank top. Working on her tan, no doubt.

Maggie felt pretty comfortable navigating the two-lane highway, as traffic was moderate—though she pulled off from time to time to let any traffic that built up behind her go by. It was tempting to stop and soak up the beauty of the ocean at places like Big Sur, but she pushed on. As it was, with several rest stops along the way to fill the gas tank and exercise Rocky, it was close to five o'clock by the time they got to Santa Barbara.

They pulled into the first gas station within city limits to get their bearings and check directions to the All Creatures Animal Clinic. "Are you sure they close at six?" Maggie asked her granddaughter, who was checking the web site again on her phone.

"*Yes*, Grams." Reagan typed in the address. "Okay, should only take us ten minutes to get there. We gotta take 101, then go north a few blocks, close to the Los Padres National Forest—huh! Santa Barbara's not all that big." Reagan looked up from her phone map and took in their surroundings. "Pretty nice, though—all those palm trees along the streets, and being so close to the ocean. Everything looks kinda Spanish."

But Maggie wasn't thinking about palm trees or Spanish architecture. She was exhausted by the long day. "Let's get to the clinic. Don't want to miss him when they close." She didn't let herself think that it might be Chris's day off or something. They were here. She was *this close* to seeing her son again.

With Reagan giving directions, they followed 101 toward downtown but turned north and followed the streets to the address. There. Up ahead. A large sign: *All Creatures Animal Clinic.* As Maggie pulled over to the side of the street, Reagan suddenly burst out laughing and pointed. A movie-style marquee below the clinic sign read: "Free Belly Rubs with Exam! Sorry, Pets Only."

Maggie chuckled, too. Five bucks said that was Chris's doing. He was always the jokester.

"There's a parking lot," Reagan pointed out.

"I know. But . . ." She turned off the motor. This was close enough.

Maggie winced as she slid off the bike, her legs and arms aching. Even Reagan looked a little wobbly as they stretched their legs, letting Rocky pee against a palm tree. Then, leaning against the bike, they waited. From their vantage point about fifty yards away, they watched clients come out—one with a cat carrier, another with an elderly yellow lab—and drive out of the parking lot. A mother and young daughter came out minus their pet—must've had to leave it overnight.

Five minutes to six. The parking lot emptied except for a few cars. Staff? Maggie didn't recognize any of the cars, vaguely remembering Chris told her he'd had to trade in his old one.

Six o'clock. Chris didn't come out. "I'm going to the door," Maggie said abruptly. Reagan and Rocky were right at her heels.

The glass door was locked. But Maggie could see someone still at the reception desk. She knocked and gestured. The woman at the desk shook her head and pointed at the wall clock. Maggie looked down at Rocky, visible to anyone inside. *She must think I'm here about my dog.* She knocked again, then pointed to Rocky and shook her head vigorously, then pointed to herself and nodded.

The woman, forty-ish, blonde hair, dark roots, came to the door but didn't open it.

"I'm looking for Chris Cooper!" Maggie said loudly through the door.

At this the woman unlocked the door and opened it a couple inches. She was wearing a blue smock that said, *Vet Tech*. "You're looking for Chris?"

Maggie's heart thumped. The woman didn't say, *Who?* "Yes. Is he here?"

"Well, yes. Somewhere in the back." She frowned at Rocky. "Is that Bella? Where did you find her?"

Maggie shook her head. "No, no. This is my dog, Rocky. Uh, about Chris . . ."

"Huh, sure looks like Bella." She looked back at Maggie. "Who should I say—?"

"Just tell him someone's here to see him."

After a moment's hesitation, the receptionist locked the door again and disappeared.

"He's here, he's here," she whispered aloud. Rocky whined and scratched at the glass door. Did he smell Chris? Did he remember that Chris was the one who rescued him as a pup and brought him to her? Or did he just smell other dogs?

A minute crawled by. Another. Maggie turned her back to the door. Somewhere inside a phone rang. A fly buzzed around her head. She could almost hear the *tick tick* of the count-down numbers on the Do Not Walk sign down at the corner.

The waiting was killing her.

Then behind her she heard the door open. And a voice—Chris's voice—said, "Wha—? *Mom?*"

Maggie whirled. There he stood, eyes wide, glancing from her to Reagan to the dog trying to jump up on him. He'd grown a beard—short, trim—and he was wearing a blue smock. His mouth was laughing. "What *is* this? Mom? And is this—? Can't be! Is this little Reagan? When did you get all grown up, girl? And . . . okay, okay! Down boy!" He couldn't ignore Rocky, who alternately pawed his leg and kept trying to jump up on him. Chris squatted down and scratched Rocky's noggin, getting some slobbery face kisses in return. "Boy, oh, boy, you sure do look like Bella."

He stood up, staring first at Maggie, then at Reagan, and wagging his head. "I can't believe this. *What* are you two doing here?" But before she could stammer an answer, Maggie felt Chris's arms around her, pulling her tightly against his chest, his beard scratching her cheek. "Oh, Mom. I am *so* glad to see you," he whispered into her ear.

Maggie couldn't answer because the floodgates behind her eyes broke through. All she could do was hold him tight and hug him back.

* * * *

As it turned out, Chris had to feed and water all the "overnighters" before he could leave work. He invited them inside to wait in the reception room and introduced them to the receptionist—"Margo, this is my mom, and my niece, *and* Bella's litter mate"—before disappearing into the back rooms.

"Hmm," Margo said, peering over her reading glasses. "Told you that dog looked like Bella." But she offered them some Starlight peppermints sitting in a bowl.

Maggie used up a whole packet of tissues mopping her eyes and blowing her nose. When Chris finally came out, he said, "Do you have a car? You can follow me back to my—what?" Reagan was laughing. "What?"

"Uh, no car. We have the bike," Maggie said. They had stepped outside now, and she pointed to the BMW parked on the street. "But we can still follow you to your apartment or wherever."

Chris stood stock still, staring at the blue motorcycle and sidecar, loaded to the gills with their backpacks and duffle bags. "Un-be-liev-able," he said finally. "Is that Dad's bike? It *is* Dad's bike, isn't it! And you—" He suddenly bent over, hands on his knees and started laughing. "You . . . you learned how to ride that old bike? And you rode it clear from Chicago—*here?*" His laughter had become gasps, but he finally straightened and walked back and forth, running his hands through his hair. "*And* you brought

Reagan *and* Rocky in that . . . that sidecar thing?" He kept pacing and laughing and shaking his head. "No one is going to believe this. My *mother* . . ."

Maggie hardly knew what to say. It *was* funny. It *was* unbelievable. She glanced at Reagan who had a big grin on her face, obviously enjoying the whole show. "I tried to call and tell you I'd decided to get my license and learn to ride, maybe take the trip your dad had planned."

"I know. I mean, I know you tried to call a couple weeks ago. I tried to call back once, but for some reason the call didn't go through. Then things got busy at work and—I'm so sorry, Mom. I should've tried again. But I had no idea it was about *this*." His shoulders shook again. But after another minute or two, Chris finally got hold of himself. "Okay." He blew out a big breath. "That's my VW beetle over there. Need to go by my place first, gotta clean up after my twelve-hour shift. Then I'm taking you two to dinner. And I want the whole story. First to last." Still grinning, he eyed Rocky. "Hey, fella, you wanna ride with me?"

* * * *

Chris's "place" turned out to be a single-wide trailer in a mobile home park on the outskirts west of town near the ocean. "Not the fanciest place, but I like it. Quiet neighbors. Dog friendly. Come on, meet Bella."

The trailer had a deck-like porch running the length of the trailer with a few comfy porch chairs and baskets of hanging flowers. He opened the front door and was nearly bowled over by a Rocky-lookalike, who then saw Rocky. The two dogs did the *sniff-sniff* thing, head to tail, and walked in circles, and then they started racing each other from one end of the porch to the other. "They'll be fine," Chris said. "Come on in."

Chris disappeared into a back bedroom and they heard a shower running. A calico cat was stretched out on the back of the sofa and purred when Maggie petted it. Reagan flopped on the sofa, and the cat took up residence on her lap while Maggie poked around. There was actually a second bedroom at the other end of the long trailer. The place was neat, casual comfy, but everything had its place. Even the small kitchen was tidy, just a dish or two in the sink. So, this was where he lived. And she'd seen where he worked. It meant so much to be able to visualize him at home, at work. Why had she ever hesitated to come see him?

Chris came out in a change of clothes, hair slicked back, though a stray lock fell over his forehead—just like Coop's used to do. "Oh, that's Patches." He grinned at the cat pinning Reagan to the sofa. "Somebody brought her into the clinic last year, never picked her up. All the vet techs end up with pets this way." He opened the front door and let both dogs in. Calico took one look at Rocky and dashed for the back bedroom. Chris shrugged. "No worries. They'll figure it out. Uh, you guys are welcome to stay with me tonight—unless you'd rather get a motel. There are a couple near—"

"No, no, here's fine. I see you have a spare bedroom back there."

"Yep. Clean sheets and everything. Don't have many guests, though. You're the first family to visit."

Maggie winced at the subtle barb. But Chris went on, "That is, if Reagan doesn't mind sleeping on the couch with the cat. Uh, shall we go?"

"If you can give me five minutes and a washcloth. My turn to clean up," Maggie said. She needed a moment to collect herself. "Nine hours on the road, you know."

Chris looked stricken. "Oh, Mom! I'm sorry. Of course! Uh, bathroom's back there. I'll get you a washcloth and towel."

The bathroom was also clean. Why was she surprised? All her kids had had to do chores, including cleaning the toilet and tub. But a single guy . . . Maggie smiled at herself in the bathroom mirror. Guess she'd raised him right. But the smile faded when she took a second look. She'd forgotten about "helmet hair." *Ack.* She looked terrible. But a hot washcloth on her face, a touch of mascara, and a comb-through of her hair made Maggie feel half-way presentable. It would have to do.

Chris took them to a modest Mexican restaurant in Santa Barbara with a cheerful decor and fended off questions about himself. "First, you gotta tell me about the trip. I'm dying here till I know how you pulled this off. I mean, my sister let *you*"—he nodded at Reagan—"come on this crazy trip with your grandmother?!"

Reagan happily supplied that part of the story, causing Chris to alternately shake his head and burst out laughing. Their travel story spilled out in pieces as they talked through an appetizer of nachos, followed by chicken fajitas, a giant burrito, and enchilada entrees. Maggie watched her son as they talked. He listened intently, shaking his head at the encounters with the three bandana bikers, and frowning deeply when they got to what happened at the truck stop. But he didn't interrupt and seemed deeply interested in their past few days at the Bay Area Women's Place.

"Well, that's the rough overview anyway." Maggie finally put down her fork and wiped her mouth with a paper napkin. "It's hard to tell everything that happened all at once." She touched his hand. "How about you? How are you doing?"

He grinned—that boyish grin she loved so much. "Good. Really good. I love my job at the animal clinic. The vets are great to work with. They give the vet techs a lot of opportunity to help with surgeries and do actual medical stuff." He shrugged. "I might go back to school one of these days and get my veterinary license."

Maggie smiled. "That would be great—but only if you really want to."

"Well, to be honest, vet techs don't make that much. I get by, but it's kinda slim."

"Why Santa Barbara?" Reagan stuck in. "I mean, why not Los Angeles? Big city, lots of stuff going on. More like Chicago."

"Exactly. Too big. I like Santa Barbara. Big enough—population around 90,000 or so. A number of colleges and universities here— even a University of California satellite campus. Only a couple hours to LA if I really need to go there. But mainly I like living so close to the national forest area—*and* the ocean. Bella and I often go hiking or fishing on weekends. There's a big lake and recreation area only thirty minutes north of here."

"Friends?" The moment she said it, Maggie was afraid she'd gone too far. What was she asking?

Chris looked at her for a long moment, then he nodded. "Some. I do stuff with the other vet techs sometimes. There're six of us—four around my age, plus Margo who's older, married, got teenagers. And I've made a couple of friends at church. Well, more than a couple."

Maggie's heart skipped a beat. "Church?"

Chris looked away for a moment, then toyed with his glass of water. "Yes, church, Mom. I'm a Christian, remember? I got baptized by Pastor Hickman at Grace and Mercy when I was, what? Fourteen or fifteen? Nothing's changed—not on my end, anyway. God is still important to me. Took a while to find a church where I felt truly welcome, but I did. They preach Jesus, they live Jesus."

"So, like, it's cool with them that you're gay?" Reagan asked. Maggie wanted to stuff a sock in her mouth.

Chris smiled ruefully. "Let's just say they're not judgmental. There's even an affinity group for LGBTQ folks—a support group where we can share stuff, pray for each other, do stuff together from time to time. And some of the straight couples at the church have 'adopted' some of us—you know, Sunday dinner, outings with the family, that kind of thing." He locked eyes with Maggie. "Having a family is important to me."

Maggie felt like she'd been sucker punched. Her eyes teared up. "Oh, Chris . . ."

The waiter came by just then with the bill. Maggie started to reach for it, but Chris took it, fished for his wallet, and pulled out a credit card. "My treat." He stood up from the table. "Only take me a minute to take care of this. If you guys are done, we can drive around a bit, I'll show you the town."

Maggie and Reagan watched him go up to the cash register. "Cheese Louise," Reagan muttered under her breath.

Chapter 41

Squeezing everyone into his Volkswagen, Chris drove them first by the historic Santa Barbara Mission, its classic Spanish architecture lit up with spotlights as twilight settled over the city. "It's beautiful inside if you want a tour during the day," Chris said. "It has a museum maintained by Franciscan friars, but it's also used as a Catholic church." He didn't ask how long they were going to stay.

Maggie didn't really want to be driving around, she wanted to talk to Chris. But she held her tongue as he drove to one of the parks right on the beach. The sun had already set, but the sky was still streaked with long fingers of orange and yellow clouds. They got out of the car and walked on the damp sand as the twilight deepened and the colors disappeared. Soon, only the white foamy tips of the waves sweeping in were visible. Behind them, the city came alive as lights lit up the white stucco buildings and their red-tile roofs.

"It's beautiful here," she murmured. "I can see why you like Santa Barbara so much. But—" She put a hand on Chris's arm. "Could we go back to your place? I'd like to talk to you about something."

Chris shrugged. "Okay." He sounded wary. "Need to walk Bella anyway."

Back at Chris's single-wide, Maggie put Rocky on the leash and joined Chris and Bella as they walked the road throughout the darkened trailer park, lit only by lights behind window curtains of the trailers they passed. They were silent at first, letting the dogs sniff and pee here and there. Finally, Chris said, "How are you getting home, Mom? It's a long ride back to Chicago. Even if you go on a diagonal, there are a couple long stretches through deserts from here."

Maggie drew in a breath and blew it out. "That's what I wanted to talk to you about, honey." How to say this exactly? She felt as if she were standing on a cliff, but the only way was forward, like Moses at the Red Sea. Would she fall off and crash to the bottom? Or take a leap of faith and soar like a hang glider?

She wouldn't know unless she stepped off.

"First, I'm really sorry I didn't let you know about this trip ahead of time, Chris. I meant to, which is why I tried to call, but when I didn't hear from you—though I realize now I was probably on the road without good cell phone access when you tried to call back—I wasn't sure you'd want to hear about it, since it has everything to do with your dad, and, well, things have been so strained."

Even in the deepening twilight, Maggie saw Chris give a helpless shrug and shake his head. But she couldn't stop now.

"I decided to take this trip on the bike as a way to honor your dad's memory. He had worked so hard on restoring the BMW and planned this amazing trip for the two of us, revisiting places where we'd lived and worked during our life together. But to be honest, I kept wondering what it was all for? God has been showing me things, reminding me of things I needed to learn at each place. The maps led us to San Francisco where our marriage began, but then what? There was no map for getting back home. And that's when I discovered—"

"Bella, no!" Chris snapped and pulled Bella away from a greasy McDonald's bag that had fallen out of someone's garbage can. They walked on, the road circling back to where they'd started. After a moment he said tightly, "What do you mean, discovered?"

"Discovered what Coop wanted to do. I found notes on the side of the map that said 'SF to SB' and then 'SB to CHI.' At first, I didn't know what SB stood for, but then we figured out it meant Santa Barbara— where you happen to live." Maggie stopped and turned to face her son. "Chris, your dad wanted to come to see you. And there were no plans for getting home except 'SB to CHI'—Santa Barbara to Chicago. That's when I realized Coop didn't intend to ride the bike back to Chicago. He probably meant for us to fly or take the train or whatever, because he wanted to leave the motorcycle here—with you."

Chris snorted. "With me? Huh. I doubt it."

"No. Believe it, Chris. Your dad wanted to come to Santa Barbara to give you the motorcycle. As a peace offering."

"A peace offering!" Chris's laugh was bitter. "Why didn't he tell me himself, instead of leaving cryptic notes on the side of a map?"

They had arrived back at Chris's trailer. Both dogs noisily lapped water from Bella's water bowl, then they flopped on the floor of the porch, panting happily.

Maggie sank down on the top step to the porch and patted the step beside her. Chris sat down.

"Because he died, son. Died before he could do it in person."

Chris sat with his arms resting on his knees, hands clasped, staring at the ground for several long minutes. Then he stood up abruptly and started for the front door. "I'm sorry, Mom. I don't want it."

* * * *

"I don't want it." Well, what had she expected him to say? He was hurting.

Every time she woke during the night, she breathed a prayer. "We need healing as a family, Lord. I don't understand why Coop reacted like he did—and since he's gone, I might never know. Chris and I need healing, too. There's so much I don't understand. I feel caught in the middle. But I honestly believe Coop was reaching out, that he wanted to reconcile with our son . . ."

Chris had to go to work the next day. "If I'd known you were coming, I might've been able to trade with someone, take the day off. But—"

"That's okay, Chris." They hadn't spoken much since the night before. She needed some space. Maybe he did, too. "I need to work on finding a flight for Reagan and me. Stacy and Chad will be back from their cruise next week, and I want to get this girl home before her parents get there."

Reagan came flying out of the bathroom, tousled hair wet from her shower. "Uncle Chris! Can I come to work with you? *Please?*"

He scratched his beard. "Don't you want to go to the beach? Or wander around the shops or something? Grandma could ride you into town."

"No, no! I can do that some other time. But this is my only chance to hang around an animal clinic. Please? I promise I won't get in the way. I'll even clean up poops or whatever if you want."

Chris chuckled. "Hmm. This is highly irregular. But if I just show up with you, guess there's not much they can do." He grinned. "Okay—unless your grandma doesn't want to end up by herself all day."

Maggie couldn't think of anything more wonderful than to have a whole day to herself. "No, no, go! I'll be fine. Besides, I'll have Rocky and Bella and Patches."

After grabbing a banana and a bagel each, they were gone.

O Lord, what a gift. She needed time to think. And pray.

* * * *

By the time Chris and Reagan arrived home around six-thirty—one of the other vet techs was on duty settling the "overnights"—Maggie had found a flight on American Airlines the next day from Santa Barbara to Chicago via Phoenix that would get them in at nine o'clock in the evening. She'd gone ahead and purchased the tickets, with twenty-four hours to cancel if needed. She had also picked up some steaks in town and had them marinating in the refrigerator.

Chris held up a grocery bag. "More steaks. Guess great minds think alike, Mom." But he shrugged. "No worries. I'll just toss these in the freezer." Grabbing a bag of charcoal briquettes, he went outside to fire up the little Weber grill.

During supper on the front porch a while later, Reagan babbled on constantly about her day at the animal clinic. She got to hold cats that didn't want to get their rabies shots, calmed a Golden Retriever that was recovering from surgery, even answered the phone when the person on desk duty was needed in one of the exam rooms.

"It was so cool, Grams," she gushed. "Maybe I'll go to college and become a vet tech—or even a vet! Whaddya think? Two vets in one family."

Maggie gave her a thumbs up. At least it got Reagan talking about going to college, which would make her parents happy.

Well, maybe. Stacy might complain that a veterinarian didn't have the social status of an M.D., but that would blow over.

Chris took the garbage out while Maggie and Reagan carried the dishes in and did the washing up. But he seemed to be taking a long time. Maggie glanced out the window and saw him standing beside the BMW, giving it a once-over. Was he reconsidering? Even if he didn't want it, she had to leave it here for him to sell or whatever. No way could she ride it all the way back to Chicago. She was done.

Dishes finished, Reagan flopped on the couch and grabbed the TV remote. Taking advantage of the moment, Maggie dried her hands on a dishtowel and let herself quietly out the front door. She joined Chris beside the bike but decided to wait before breaking into his thoughts.

They stood in silence for several minutes. Not looking at her, Chris finally said, "I've been thinking about what you said last night—about Dad wanting to give me the bike. As a peace offering. An attempt to reconcile. Whatever." Another silence. "If it's true, it's a nice gesture. But to be honest, Mom—" He practically spit out the words. "—I wish he would've *talked* to me. Told me in his own words he's sorry for dropping out of my life in two minutes flat. He had *no idea* how that devastated me." Chris's voice suddenly wavered, and he turned his face away. The back of his hand brushed across his eyes.

Maggie's own throat choked up. "I know, son. I wish that could've happened, too." Tentatively she laid a hand on his arm. "But I truly believe that if he hadn't died of a heart attack, if the two of us could've taken this trip together, he was coming here to talk with you. To make things right—as best he could."

Still not meeting her eyes, Chris snorted a hollow laugh. "Pretty thin evidence, don't you think? Those initials on the side of that map? Huh."

"No, I don't. Actually, those initials practically shout his intentions to me. *San Francisco to Santa Barbara . . . Santa Barbara to Chicago.* Shorthand, yes. But those were his very last words to me. And to you."

Chris shook his head slowly, then his shoulders shook. He was crying.

Maggie moved close and put her arms around him. "Oh, Chris . . ." After a moment he turned and put his arms around her, holding her tight, and they cried together.

When the tears seemed spent, Maggie said softly, "Chris, come sit down on the porch with me. What would you like to tell your dad? Tell me. I want to listen to you."

He followed her onto the porch and they dragged two chairs to the far end, away from the front door. They sat quietly as the sun sank behind the palm trees toward the ocean. She waited.

His voice was hoarse when he finally spoke. "I didn't choose to be gay, you know. Just knew I was different in middle school when all my buddies couldn't stop talking about girls. And I . . . just wasn't interested." He leaned forward, arms on his knees. "Didn't have a name for it until high school—but there was no way I was going to tell anybody. All the ugly 'fag' jokes, all the shame and blame I heard from youth leaders talking about 'the gay agenda,' how horrible gay people were." His voice cracked. "You have no idea how that felt! They were talking about *me*! But, I was the same Chris I'd always been. Grew up loving Jesus. Got baptized . . ."

He ran a hand through his hair and shook his head. "Oh, believe me, I tried to 'pray the gay away.' I prayed *every night*. I just wanted to be normal, to *be* the person everyone thought I was. I pleaded with God. I cried into my pillow. But, I was still gay." He took a shuddering breath and didn't speak for a long moment.

Maggie swallowed. *Oh, Chris,* her heart cried. *I didn't know . . . I didn't know.*

Again, a long silence. Then, "At the university it was a real struggle, because the only people who really accepted me were other LGBT people. I tried to join one of the Christian campus groups. But when I told one of the leaders I was gay, our relationship changed. I wasn't just Chris anymore, I was 'Chris the gay guy,' their project." Chris shook his head. "I wasn't sleeping around like some of the other gays on campus—and, a *lot* of the straight guys, too—because I still believed in a 'Christian ethic' when it came to sex. I just didn't seem to fit in anywhere."

He looked at her and allowed a wry smile. "How're you doing, Mom? It's a lot to dump on you all at once, I know."

Maggie swallowed. She had a lot of questions. "I think your dad blamed himself, thought maybe it was his fault. You know, the 'cold and distant father' theory. I told him he was anything but! He was a good dad, always doing stuff with you kids." She picked at a piece of lint on her slacks. "But to be honest, I struggled, too. We read a book that blames the 'smothering mother' for turning their sons gay. We—"

"Oh, good grief, Mom. You guys were good parents. No family's perfect, but we were pretty darn normal. Fact is, I had a great childhood—until it wasn't. But it didn't have anything to do with you."

Relief flooded through Maggie's body. If only Coop could hear that from Chris. "Still, I'm so sorry, Chris. Wish we'd known you struggled with your sexual orientation for so long. We—we didn't know."

"You know what, Mom? I mostly struggle with other people's presumptions about me and my supposed 'lifestyle,' not with *being* gay. Not anymore. 'Cause one day while reading the Psalms—I think it was Psalm 139—I had a revelation: *I am God's creation.* God knows me, inside and out. God loves me just the way I am. I don't need to choose between my faith and my sexuality. Just be me. Just be faithful. Obey the two commandments Jesus said were the greatest: Love God. Love other people. Trying to do that the way Jesus would. And trust God's grace when I fall short."

Maggie let that sink in. The familiar words in Romans 8 surged into her mind: *"Nothing can separate us from the love of God . . ."*

"Not that I don't have questions," he added. "Don't really want to be alone the rest of my life. I'm thirty-three. I like kids. I'd love to have a family. If I didn't *choose* to be gay, if this is just who I am, why not?"

Maggie winced. That was the rub. The thing that set off fireworks. She knew what so many Christians and churches were saying: *If you're gay, just be celibate. Forever.* No life companion. No family. Just be alone.

She'd never thought about that from Chris's point of view.

Reaching out, Maggie took Chris's hand. "I don't know, son. I—I don't have answers, not yet anyway. Right now, I only know one thing: *we* are family. You are our son. I love you so much. We—your dad and me—we were wrong to let this come between us. Please forgive—"

She had to let go and fish for a tissue as the tears threatened to flood again.

Just then the front door opened, and Reagan poked her head outside. "Hey! Dogs need to come out. They're bugging me to death!—oh. Sorry. Didn't mean to interrupt something." But by then, the dogs had pushed past her legs and were clamoring for attention from the porch sitters. The door banged as the girl disappeared back inside.

Jostled by Bella's and Rocky's nose-pushing and tail-wagging, Chris started to laugh. And then Maggie, still blowing her nose, couldn't help laughing either.

"Leave it to the dogs," Chris snorted. "Dogs know just the right time to let you know you're the most important person in the world." He held out a hand to his mother. "Come on, let's take them for their nighttime walk."

But as he pulled her up from her chair, he kissed her on the cheek and murmured, "I forgive you, Mom. As for Dad, that might take a little longer. But tell you what, I'll keep the bike and think about it."

Chapter 42

MAGGIE OPENED HER EYES TO SUNLIGHT STREAMING into the spare bedroom of Chris's trailer. Had she overslept? But she heard noises from the kitchen and smelled—coffee.

"Good morning." Chris grinned at her as she came out of the bedroom, wearing the short kimono she'd brought along as a robe. "So, that's what you look like just getting out of bed."

"Oh, stop it." Maggie knew it was high time for a haircut after a couple weeks of helmet hair. "Just give me some coffee."

He handed her a mug. "Sorry I have to go to work again, but I'm taking a couple hours off at noon to get you and Reagan to the airport. But . . ." He eyed her, a tease in his grin. "I have a proposition to make."

She shook her head. "No proposition until I've had coffee."

He laughed. "Can't wait that long. Proposition: Instead of buying a big dog kennel and shipping Rocky back to Chicago in the belly of your airplane today, what if you leave Rocky with me? And—"

Maggie spluttered her coffee. "No! Are you kidding?"

"Now, hold on a minute. Let me finish." Chris mopped up the coffee splatters with a paper towel. "I have a vacation coming up in August. What if you leave Rocky with me and Bella, and I'll *bring* him to you. It's—well, last night God and I had a long talk, and He told me it's high time I came home for a visit. I mean, look how much Reagan has grown! I gotta see my other nieces and nephews before they forget who I am."

Maggie thought her heart might stop beating. "Oh, Chris. That would be wonderful! Except—" She hated to throw water on his great idea. "Do you even know how to ride that thing? And it might take all your time just coming and going." Not to mention *two* dogs in the sidecar. She couldn't imagine it.

Chris burst out laughing. "Oh, no. I don't mean ride that bike all the way to Chicago! I'll leave that up to my crazy mother and her sidekick. Me, I'll drive the car, thank you very much." He eyed Bella and Rocky who were gulping their morning kibble. "Right, dogs?"

So, it was settled. Rocky would stay with Chris and Bella for a few weeks until his vacation the first part of August, then Chris would drive to Chicago with the dogs to see the family. All of them. Mike and Susan and the kids, and Stacy and Chad and the girls.

"It's a good time to visit, Chris," Maggie said. "Alex will be starting public high school this fall after, you know, eight years of homeschool. And Reagan will be starting her senior year and making decisions about college. I think an 'outside ear' would be good—not just her mom and dad and grandma."

"Wait—what?" mumbled a voice from the living room sofa. "Uncle Chris is coming to Chicago to visit?" Reagan appeared, still half asleep and rumpled in her T-shirt and shorts, but she high-fived her uncle. "Alriiight, Uncle Chris! You can, like, talk to my parents about which college would be the best to pursue vet medicine and stuff."

Chris rolled his eyes. "Maybe." He gave them both a hug. "Gotta go. See you in a couple of hours."

They heard the VW start up a minute or two later, then fade away.

A last-minute load of laundry—she really didn't want to send Reagan home with dirty clothes—packing their duffle bags and backpacks and spending some *gonna-miss-you-boy* time with Rocky, and they were ready to go. But first, Maggie had something she needed to do. Better to do it before Chris got back.

Taking the urn with what was left of Coop's ashes, Maggie walked around Chris's trailer, scattering a few precious ashes along the porch, then the side, around back, and around to the porch again. Then she walked over to the BMW. "You did good, Coop," she murmured. "This classic got us here, thanks to all the work you did restoring it, all the good maintenance. Now it's home, just where you intended." She took a small handful of the ashes—there wasn't that much left—and dusted the inside of the sidecar, the pedals, the handlebars, and saddlebags. "There. Now you and your son will be riding together. Like you would be if you had lived."

* * * *

A few hours later, after boarding their plane, Maggie leaned sideways from her aisle seat and tried to see if Reagan was settled. They hadn't been able to get seats together because of their last-minute tickets, but Maggie had lucked out with an aisle seat. Reagan, however, was stuck in a middle seat several rows ahead.

The plane backed out of its gate, then slowly taxied toward the runway ready for takeoff. It was hard leaving Rocky behind. On the other hand, she knew he was happier at the moment riding with his head out the window of Chris's VW, ears flapping, tongue lolling, than cooped up in an animal kennel in the baggage hold of this airplane.

And Rocky had provided a good excuse for Chris to drive all the way back to Chicago for a family visit. "Bless you, Rocky," she murmured.

The two planes in front of them took off, then it was their turn. As inertia pushed her against the back of her seat and the plane lifted its nose into the air, Maggie chuckled to herself. She was on her way home, still "going uphill."

The plane finally leveled high above the ground, though the seat belt sign stayed on. She leaned back and closed her eyes. She was glad she'd revisited the people and places that made up her life, that God had used to shape the person she was now. It was all important. She'd taken so much for granted, especially growing up on the campus of Calvary Academy—but looking back had helped clarify the way forward.

Not that she knew exactly what she was going to do, but even though her heart had a hole in it with Coop gone, she didn't feel lost and useless any more. At each stop along the way, she'd been reminded of the building blocks God had used to form their marriage into the "new thing" the Cooper family had become.

A bedrock of mutual faith had laid the foundation. But God had pushed them outside their comfort zones, had pruned away old cultural presumptions and assumptions, had shown them the beauty and mystery of other parts of the Body of Christ, had shown them God works in different ways with different people, and had expanded their understanding of God's mercy and grace.

And some of those lessons had to be learned all over again. Reconnecting with Chris was a big part of it. The painful wound in their family had been lanced, and she had faith that it was starting to heal. He was coming home for a visit, wasn't he?

God's mercy and grace.

Jiang, bless his heart, was going to pick them up tonight when—

"Grams? You asleep?"

Maggie jumped. Her eyes flew open. Reagan stood in the aisle beside her seat, holding a can of Coke in her hand. "No, no. Just thinking." Had the drink cart come by already? "Everything okay?"

"Yeah." Reagan looked this way and that, then lowered her voice. "Wish we had seats together. I wanna talk to you."

Maggie glanced at her seatmates, a young couple who were cuddled up with each other, eyes closed, zoned out, leaning against the window. "I know," she whispered. "Can't do anything about it, though. The plane is full. Maybe on the next leg from Phoenix?"

"Excuse me," said a female voice. The woman in the aisle seat across from Maggie leaned toward them. "Would you like to sit here? Across from your grandmother?"

"Oh, uh . . ." Reagan looked flustered. "Not sure you'd want to switch. I'm in a middle seat."

The woman unbuckled her seatbelt, holding on to the magazine she'd been reading, and stood up. "No problem. We'll be landing in Phoenix soon. Which row?"

Reagan led her up the aisle and was back in half a minute. "Wow. Some people are pretty nice." She buckled herself into the other aisle seat and leaned toward Maggie, her dyed bangs flopping over one eye. "Just been thinking about the trip. I told you I really liked your friend Wendy, kinda wanted to be like her. She has this free spirit, just doin' her own thing."

"She is that." Maggie smiled. "A free spirit."

"Yeah, but kinda realized something. You and Wendy both grew up at that Christian school, went to that Christian summer camp. But your lives turned out so different. All the places we visited—especially that church in Minneapolis, Friendship Something-or-Other. And the Women's Place in 'Frisco that used to be a Jesus People commune. I mean, you said you and Gramps decided to follow Jesus, an' look where it took you!" She grinned at Maggie. "Never thought of you and Gramps as free spirits—can't imagine you with a tattoo." The girl snickered. "But you and Gramps—you're *radical*. Think I wanna be more like you."

Maggie felt a flush rise to her cheeks. *Could anything be sweeter than that, Coop?*

"Oh, I dunno," she teased. "Riding that BMW bike your grandfather restored all the way to the West Coast and down to Santa Barbara—with a teenager and a dog in the sidecar no less. Wasn't that kind of 'free-spirit-y'?"

Reagan snorted. "Nah. Grams, that was just plain *crazy*."

* * * *

Maggie stood in front of the kitchen calendar a week later, counting the days until Chris's vacation. Still ten days off, including a couple of days for the drive. But his upcoming visit confirmed a decision she'd made. Definitely needed to keep one of the extra bedrooms as a guest room. As for the other two . . .

She'd already told Jiang she was going to stay in the house, and he was welcome to rent the room for the coming school year. And if he knew someone at the seminary who needed to rent a room, she wanted to use this big house as a home-away-from-home for whoever needed it. He'd already found someone—a young woman from Haiti who was just starting her first year. He'd met her at the International Students Meet-and-Greet last spring when she came for a school visit.

Another woman in the house. That would be nice. Maggie was looking forward to meeting Fabienne. Jiang was bringing her for supper tonight.

But poor Jiang. He had seemed so disappointed that she'd left the BMW in California. "But you just learned to ride!" he had protested. "And you took that long trip—very brave, very strong woman. So proud of you, Mrs. C."

Should she have given the bike to Jiang? He was the one who taught her to ride. And he'd owned a motorcycle in China. Might never be able to afford one here in the States. Had she been too quick to—

No. The bike was meant to go to Chris. She had no doubts about that.

The house phone rang, snapping Maggie out of her reverie. She glanced at the Caller ID: *Stacy Young.* Of course. She and Reagan had picked up Stacy and Chad at the airport last night, and Reese was due home from her summer camp this weekend. They really hadn't had any time to talk or debrief about either trip, or the fact that Reagan had run away, or that Maggie had taken her on a 3,000-mile trip—by motorcycle—without their permission.

Maggie took a deep breath, picked up the phone, and said cheerily, "Hi, Stacy!"

"*Mom!* What's all this stuff Reagan is talking about? She announced this morning that she wants to be baptized—in Lake Michigan, of all things! And—and she's saying she wants to go back to San Francisco next summer after she graduates from high school and be an intern or something at some 'Women's Place' and paint fingernails and grow vegetables and give away free food! What is she talking about? Did you put her up to this? We're gone for one measly month, and my daughter is a completely different person! After spending that month with my mother, of all people!"

Stacy gulped and there was a brief pause—long enough for Maggie to say, "Oh. Has she said anything yet about going to college to be a veterinarian?" Maggie stifled a laugh that threatened to come out. *Oh, Maggie, you are so bad.*

"What? College? A veterinarian?"

Maggie let Stacy fuss for another moment or two, then broke in. "Tell you what, honey. Let's get together for Sunday supper and catch up with each other. So much to talk about! Okay? See you at six? Better yet, five. Love you!"

Hanging up the phone, Maggie picked up the brass urn that had once been full of Coop's ashes and unscrewed the top. Good. A little bit left. Going through the sunroom and out the back door, Maggie headed for the fence where a flowerbed should be. Still time to plant some zinnias or mums or other fall flowers.

She was still chuckling over Stacy's phone call. Reagan wanted to get baptized? How wonderful!

Tipping the urn, she sprinkled the last of Coop's ashes along the empty flowerbed. "Guess what, Coop?" she murmured, her heart full. "We're home again."

Acknowledgments

Whew! Writing this novel has been a journey, too. Took me three years to write, and I was often discouraged—but God helped me persevere! I'm so grateful for God's faithfulness.

It all began with a few people encouraging me to write a "memoir," because, well, Dave and I have some stories to tell about the experiences God had led us through and the people He has used during our fifty-two years of marriage to teach us about the wideness of God's grace, mercy, and love that we might never have learned otherwise. But . . . instead of a memoir, I decided to write what might be called an "autobiographical novel."

Yes, there are parts of this novel that reflect some of our own experiences. At the same time, this is a work of fiction! (I cannot ride a motorcycle—except on the passenger seat, ha ha.) And, as always happens, when I create a character and put that character into a story situation, things start to happen I never saw coming. So keep in mind: This is a novel.

I couldn't have done it without the faithful prayers of my Yada Yada Prayer Team who've prayed me through many a book. **Dawn, Heather, Janalee, Jodee, Julia, Karen, Keri, Khara, Kyella, Linda, Mia, Nancy, Pam, Sandra B, Sandra T, Sherri, Sue, Theda,** and **Tish** . . . thank you from my heart, praying sisters.

There are also some special people who inspired parts of this story—like **Julia Pferdehirt**, who is on staff with Because Justice Matters (a YWAM ministry in the Tenderloin district of San Francisco). Julia, I love your heart and the way you give 110 percent of yourself and the love of God to desperate women just trying to survive—including sex workers in those "gentlemen's clubs," who also need to know how much Jesus loves them. "Thank you" doesn't quite cut it.

To **Faith Community Church** on Chicago's West Side and our former pastor—**Rev. Ed Turner** and his wife **Tran**, now with Jesus—who started us on our journey "out of the box" and into the real world back in the Sixties and Seventies. It all began with this little storefront church who loved on us and folded us into your lives in the midst of the civil rights movement, opening our eyes to the inequities and discrimination in our own society. You planted seeds that God has watered and borne fruit in our lives. We are so grateful.

To my childhood friend, **Heather**—growing up with you could fill another whole book! Love you still.

To **my ranching cousins**, whom I love to visit "out west" . . . thank you for being my family. You are so important to me, even though our life experiences are different in so many ways. And bottom line, we share our faith and love for Jesus which will always keep us "one."

And then there are my motorcycle friends who have (hopefully) kept me from sounding as ignorant as I really am about taking a cross-country road trip by motorcycle. **Ceri Ann Lewis**, you rock! **Ronn Frantz**, your thoughts were invaluable. **Bill Denney** and **Isso Rosado**—thanks for the rides on your amazing machines. And you bikers in my own family—**Brian Thiessen Love, David Thiessen**, and **Marge Thiessen**—thanks for the inspiration!

Also, thanks to the basic rider coarse instructor at the **Harley Davidson** store in Glenview, Illinois, who welcomed me to sit in her class and observe the new riders practice their skills for a few days, while I became an "armchair biker." Who knows, if I were a decade younger, I would be tempted to get my license!

Dave, there are no words for the support and encouragement you give me all day, every day. I love you for this—and a whole lot more.

Last but not least, thanks to you **readers**, who have joined me for yet another journey. Would love to hear your thoughts! Send them to: neta@daveneta.com. And leaving a review on amazon.com will help pass the word about this book immensely! Hugs to all.